SMOKE

SMOKE

SUE FARWICK

TRIBUS PRESS | CEDARBURG, WISCONSIN USA

Published by Tribus Press LLC
Cedarburg, Wisconsin USA
www.tribuspress.com

Cover illustration by Madeline Friend

ISBN 979-8-9884459-6-8

For discounts for schools, bookstores, libraries, and nonprofit groups, bulk sales, media inquiries, or questions please contact:

Email: tribuspress@tribuspress.com
Phone: 262-421-5158

FOR SOMEONE WHOSE PAINTINGS INSPIRED
THIS STORY

I would like to thank my family for their continued help and
encouragement and my good friend Jo who assisted with the editing of this
book. I would also like to thank Madeline Friend, who captured the spirit of
the story with her wonderful artwork.

1

EXCERPT FROM MARIANNE'S JOURNAL

MORNING ARRIVED SO QUICKLY THAT IT CAUGHT US BY SURPRISE. The sun chased away the night while we were still clinging to each other, leaving us with little time to say our goodbyes.

Maybe I should have come to a place like Bartlett Hall sooner. But it's pointless to dwell on the past. There is no room for 'what ifs' in my life now. Or at least, I try to push them back, but it isn't always easy. They crowd and clamor to be let out, especially when I'm alone.

Of course, I'm seldom alone these days. There is always someone looking in—"Just to see if you need anything, dear," or "Would you like to talk for a while?" But occasionally, during the day, I have moments of solitude when I can sit, gaze out of the window, and feel that I'm still a part of the world outside.

On days like this, I like to watch the seagulls. Bartlett Hall is near the coast, so they are my constant companions. But despite my present contentment, I can't help asking myself the question that creeps into my thoughts with increasing regularity. Will I ever go home again? They tell me, "Soon," but in a week? A month? A year? The days seem to blend into one another, so much so that I can hardly recall how long I've been here.

There are times, like today, when everything is so clear that I can remember places, people, and events right down to the last detail—the smell of roses in the rain, the sound of someone playing a piano or singing a song filled with so much emotion that you could feel your heart burst, just from the joy of hearing it.

And then there are those days when things just won't come into focus. My thoughts seem caught up in a cloud of smoke that swirls and flows, leaving my mind grasping ineffectually at the fleeting glimpses of once-familiar faces and forms.

Everyone has been extraordinarily kind to me, but I know that my life will never be the same. Despite everything they've done to help, and God knows their efforts have been tireless, the nightmares still haunt me. Although, at times, I can tell by the look on their faces that they think they've discovered the truth behind the events that brought me here to Bartlett Hall, some things lie buried too deep in their hearts and minds. None of them will ever understand the reality of what happened at Paradise House.

Not that I've tried to deceive anyone. I've been very open and honest about everything,

For the present, my world is here in this room. They've spared no effort to make it seem like home. I have everything I need. My wants are simple. And I have no desire for company. It seems strange to think that not so long ago I was accustomed to spending much of my time surrounded by fashionable and vibrant people.

Sometimes I sit and sketch or write in this journal that Dr. Philips has encouraged me to keep. My drawings, though by no means masterful, are, I hope, recognizable. They represent the images that no camera could ever capture—fleeting moments from my past and the demons that torment me so relentlessly now. Dr. Philips says the pictures help him visualize my thoughts. Well, that may be true, though I somehow doubt that he could ever really see the true nature of the things that haunt me still. Goodness knows, if I could reach in, pluck out those phantoms from my mind's eye, and lay them down for all to see, I would gladly do it.

The thick fog that rolls inland from the sea—as it does every night—has cleared now. How I welcome it, and yet it terrifies me, for one never knows for sure whether it is indeed the heavy ocean mist that clouds one's view or something more sinister. What, or who, is hidden within its swirling shroud?

One day I might be permitted to return to the life I once knew. For now, I must occupy myself with the new task that they've set for me. I must fill up these empty pages with an account of what occurred at Paradise House. And before that, back to a time when my life was uncomplicated and free of the terrors that threaten to revisit me, should I ever let down my guard.

I have been asked so many times to explain why the events of the past year happened. To loved ones, most especially, do I feel an obligation to try to put into words the processes that led us all down such a precarious path. My friends also deserve some explanation, for they too have been affected— albeit to a lesser degree. They had to watch helplessly as I made my way along that predestined course to meet my fate. Alas, for some, the answers will come too late.

I've tried so many times to convince myself that it wasn't my fault. Sometimes, I almost succeed. In these futile attempts to absolve myself of any guilt, I reason that, after all, I wasn't the only one involved. There was a whole cast of players, all coming inexorably together like performers in some epic Shakespearean tragedy.

Damn! If only I could clear my head of all these memories.

Sometimes, in my blackest moods, I feel that I would give anything to just relinquish my hold on life. Save for one person, I would willingly leave it all. And they know it—those people who watch me constantly, scrutinizing my every move. They do not let one gesture or sigh go unnoticed. They are determined, at all costs, to solve the mystery. But to what end? Who would it benefit now?

But, if it pleases them, I will endeavor to tell my story one final time— no matter how painful. To tell how love, hate, jealousy, and all the frailty of such human emotions stepped upon the stage that was my life. Maybe then, when there is true acceptance of my story, I will know some measure of peace. But I wonder—in that moment of release from mental anguish, will sleep or death be the first to reach me?

2

THE SLEEPING DRAGON

MARIANNE CLAY WAS UNAWARE OF THE STRANGE PHENOMENON that dwelt within her. It must have taken root when she was still a child and lain dormant for those first fledgling years. Then one day it stirred and stretched like a sleeping dragon and began to gain strength. Each time it got stronger, it sent a fleeting message. But then, she was too busy with the business of growing up to realize that this hidden element, as ephemeral as a whisper and as unsubstantial as smoke, was evolving into an all-consuming inferno.

Just where and when did the journey begin? Although maybe not strictly accurate, Marianne felt compelled to say that it all began on the day that she first met Vincent.

She discounted the years that had been spent living in London with her mother and father, older sister Clare, and younger brother Matthew.

Marianne's father, always a very private person, had become more introverted and increasingly morose with the passing years. He had a quick temper and little time for small talk. His alcohol consumption increased as he got older, but no one would have dared to suggest that he seek help for his addiction. He never actually struck any of the children. A single glare would suffice to assure their obedience. They were all afraid of him, and Marianne was certain that on more than one occasion he had hit her mother. Ron Clay was a man who worked hard to support his family but seemed to find little pleasure in them.

Marianne's mother, a typical housewife of the 1950s, devoted her life to the care of her family and home. She was subservient to her husband in all things. When they first discussed the idea of getting married, she had even agreed to become a Catholic, a move that had been prompted, in large part, by Ronald Clay's mother.

"Is she a good Catholic girl?" she had asked her son when he announced their engagement.

"She's good, but she's not a Catholic."

"Then you must see about getting her instruction, Ron."

Naturally, the young Mrs. Clay had not objected to their children being raised in the Catholic faith and Clare, Marianne, and Mathew had all been christened at St. Simeon's Church.

Rosemary Clay died shortly after Matthew's twelfth birthday. Marianne never thought of her as a particularly happy person, and she sometimes imagined that her mother had died of a broken heart. She had married Ron Clay for love but had found little of it during their time together.

Clare eventually married, while Matthew, who seemed to bear the brunt of his father's ill humor, remained single. He moved out of the family home as soon as he was old enough and, with the help of a good friend, had worked to put himself through night school.

Marianne stayed at the house with her father, partly out of a sense of duty, but it was also convenient from a financial aspect. Up to that point, she had never made full use of her photographic skills. Well-paying jobs in that field were few and far between, and she chafed at the thought of spending her time developing other people's pictures. She had submitted several of her photographs to magazines with little success and had even done a short spell of work for a local newspaper, but she did not find this satisfying and longed for a greater sense of independence.

Eventually, feeling that her presence at home was no longer required, and becoming increasingly frustrated by her father's constant bouts of drinking, she applied for a job as a photographer's assistant in Swannington and moved to a bedsit in the neighboring town of Birchford.

Marianne got on well with Lucy Rowe, the young woman who owned the house where she lodged. They were of a similar age and both were fully immersed in their work. Although they were on friendly terms, they rarely spent time chatting. Marianne knew nothing of Lucy's past and she, in turn, had said very little about her family life.

Marianne felt there was a special bond between them; something that she couldn't exactly put her finger on, but there was definitely a shared intimacy that linked them. Had it been fate that had thrown the two of them together? Marianne didn't really believe in such things but it was an ideal arrangement and it continued comfortably, with only one exception, for several years.

It hadn't taken them long to settle into a routine. After the first six months, Marianne had come to look on the house on Dover Street as her home. She paid Lucy regularly every month for her rent, usually on the first Monday of the month.

It was on one such evening when Marianne was just returning from work, as she let herself in, that she thought she glimpsed Lucy going up the stairs.

Marianne called after her, "Lucy! Wait a bit. I'll give you my rent check." By the time she reached the landing, Lucy was already disappearing into the room that she used as a studio for her art projects. Marianne opened her purse and took out the check, but when she tapped on the door and peered in, the room was empty.

She must have been mistaken. Lucy had probably gone into her own bedroom. Marianne didn't want to bother her and waited until later that evening to speak to her.

"I was going to give it to you when I saw you going upstairs, earlier," Marianne told the other woman later that night when they met in the kitchen, both with the idea of making a bedtime drink.

Lucy appeared puzzled. "When was this? I've been out all evening."

"It must have been when you came home to change," Marianne replied.

"But I went straight from work to a friend's house. I only just got in a little while ago." They looked at each other in bewilderment.

"I thought you went into the studio but there was no one in there when I looked. Perhaps we should go and check to make sure nothing's missing," Marianne suggested.

The two women hurried upstairs but when they looked about the studio, Lucy shrugged and said, "I don't see anything out of place. There's not much in here for anyone to take. I think you must be mistaken."

Marianne felt rather foolish and said, "I'm sorry. I could have sworn I saw someone but it's been rather a hectic day. Probably just my imagination."

"No harm done. We could both use a good night's sleep, it seems," Lucy said, but she still appeared rather unsettled. And, although Marianne tried to tell herself that it had been a mere trick of the light, she was certain that she'd seen someone go into the studio; a woman who bore a striking resemblance to Lucy.

She couldn't help wondering, too, who her landlady had been visiting that evening. Neither woman seemed particularly interested in serious romantic relationships. In fact, after Marianne had been living in the house on Dover Street for several months, some of Lucy's more inquisitive neighbors wondered if the couple might actually be gay.

Nothing could be further from the truth. Marianne occasionally went out on dates but, apart from one brief affair while she was still living in Swannington, that ended in a broken engagement, she preferred to remain unattached.

Lucy often invited friends and colleagues to the house but rarely dated the same man twice. That was all about to change with the advent of Vincent Foxworth and Lawrence Welbourne.

3

UNINVITED

MARIANNE HAD ONLY MET LAWRENCE WELBOURNE on a couple of occasions and did not like the man. He was flashy and too cocksure of himself. She even thought he had made a pass at her one time when she met him as she was leaving the house on Dover Street. As he bumped into her on the doorstep, he said, "Careful, love! We've got to stop meeting like this, or Lucy will get jealous." He winked at her and brushed unnecessarily close as he went by.

Lucy was obviously smitten by him, however, and it was only a matter of months before she announced their forthcoming marriage. Marianne guessed, correctly, that there may have been a reason for the expediency, but Lucy hadn't confided in her, and Marianne forbore to broach the subject, feeling it was too personal a matter to discuss.

She was invited to the wedding along with a guest. Marianne asked Ivan Bronowski, a good friend with whom she shared a work studio and who was himself at a loose end that weekend. The marriage took place at the local registry office in Swannington, and the reception was held at an upscale hotel in Birchford.

The food was good, and the drinks flowed freely from an open bar. Marianne had never yet been to a wedding where there weren't at least one or two people who got drunk and made fools of themselves—this one was no exception.

Apparently, Lucy and Lawrence worked at the same place, and nearly everyone there turned out to be coworkers at a place called Vanguard Industries. There were only a handful of relatives, and those were mostly from Lawrence Welbourne's side.

Marianne was introduced to a woman called Maggie, who shared an office with Lucy; a jolly person with an easygoing flow of conversation. There was also a couple whom Lucy introduced as Jackie and Lionel Shellaby.

"Jackie and Lionel are my oldest friends," Lucy explained.

"Oi! A bit less of the old, if you don't mind," the man said, jestingly.

"Well, you know what I mean. I've known Jackie ever since we were children.'"

Marianne laughed and shook hands with them both. "Pleased to meet you. Lionel Shellaby? That name sounds familiar. Are you the same Lionel Shellaby that wrote *Witches Brew*?"

"Yes, I am," the man admitted modestly.

"Well then, I'm doubly pleased to meet you," Marianne told him. "I really enjoyed your latest book and the one before it. I love murder mysteries!"

"Thank you!" Shellaby beamed. "Things do seem to be going rather well, so far."

Loud commentary from the DJ and Whitney Houston asking 'How will I know' at a high rate of decibels, precluded any further conversation. Marianne looked around for Ivan, who had wandered off towards the bar.

Just then, someone backed into Marianne and sent his drink splashing over the woman he was attempting to pull onto the dance floor. "Whoops! Sorry!" Lawrence Welbourne turned and apologized tipsily. The woman giggled, "Ooh Larry! You are a one!" and stumbled, on extremely high heels, after him.

"That's alright. No harm done," Marianne called after them, but she couldn't help noticing a look pass between Jackie and Lionel Shellaby, whose raised eyebrow spoke volumes.

Later, as the DJ put a Lionel Richie record on the turntable, Ivan found Marianne sitting at a table by the dance floor, gazing morosely into an almost empty glass.

"Let's go, Annie. I can't stand any more of this God-awful noise," he said, leaning close and touching her shoulder.

"Yes, perhaps you're right. I'm ready to leave too," Marianne agreed. They made their escape, and no one seemed to notice their absence.

Marianne had the house on Dover Street to herself for the next two weeks while Lucy and her husband were away on their honeymoon in France. Although Lucy had reassured her that she could maintain her tenancy once the couple returned, Marianne had her doubts. Did she really want to share a house with that man? Yet, she had become so accustomed to living there and at such a reasonable rent, too. She had come to look on Dover Street as her home. *I'll be damned if I'll let Welbourne force me out*, she thought obstinately.

When the happy couple eventually returned, Lawrence Welbourne seemed content for her to remain there. For several weeks, life went on as before until an incident occurred that made Marianne seriously reevaluate her situation.

Lucy had gone out to the shops one Saturday afternoon, leaving Lawrence alone in the house with Marianne. He had never come to her room before, and she rarely saw him except for the few times when the three of them shared an informal evening meal in the kitchen. But on this particular day, he knocked on her door.

Thinking that it was Lucy, Marianne answered it and was surprised to see Welbourne standing there.

"Hello, Annie," he smiled at her.

"Lawrence?" He had insisted that she drop the more formal Mr. Welbourne, although she never felt comfortable using his Christian name.

"What do you want, Lawrence?" she asked impatiently as he continued to stand there looking at her. Marianne remained standing in the doorway, barring his way as he looked over her shoulder, evidently seeking an invitation to enter.

"I just wondered if you had a spare roll of film that you could let me have? Luce and I are going out for a drive this afternoon, and I thought I'd take my camera along."

"I may have. Just a second. I'll look in my bag." She went back into her room, and he followed her, uninvited, quietly pushing the door closed behind him.

As she bent down to look in her camera bag, Welbourne crept stealthily up behind her and, putting both hands on her hips, said, "Mm! Very enticing, I must say."

Marianne stood up and turned towards him, delivering a stinging slap to his face.

"That'll be enough of that!" she told him forcefully.

Staggering back and rubbing his cheek, his face red with anger and humiliation, Welbourne was too surprised to speak at first, but then he spat, "You bitch! I think it's about time you found another billet, don't you?" "We'll be needing this room soon. Lucy's expecting a baby."

"Poor thing," Marianne said with asperity. "I wonder if she knows what a two-timing, low-life she married."

"You'd better keep your mouth shut if you know what's good for you," he said, glaring at her menacingly.

"Oh, don't worry. I won't say anything. Lucy's got enough troubles as it is. And I'll be more than happy to leave."

Luckily for Marianne, Vincent Foxworth had already entered her life.

4

VINCENT

VINCENT FOXWORTH, TWENTY YEARS MARIANNE'S SENIOR, was, at fifty-two, the most attractive man that she had ever met. He was not handsome in the conventional sense, but there was something about him that so appealed to Marianne that for the first few weeks of their friendship, she could think of nothing and no one else.

Their first meeting was on a rainy afternoon at Utopia, an upscale art gallery in Swannington. Marianne did not consider herself on a financially sound enough footing to go squandering hard-earned money on such luxuries, but she had been urged by Ivan Bronowski to view the current exhibition. He had insisted that the pieces were well worth seeing even if she couldn't afford the exorbitant price tags, and his enthusiasm was relentless.

"Go and see them, Annie! Just look at them and tell me what you think. Irina won't go. She thinks it's all rubbish, but I tell her, you don't know what you're missing, woman! She is such a Philistine when it comes to art. How can you not love Chagall? And Kandinsky! His work is beyond words. And Dimitri Gurvich! You will love his pictures, darling. Just go and look! You don't have to buy anything. Please, Annie, for me. Tell them I sent you."

Eventually, Ivan's persuasive wheedling, the charming, vocal caressing of his seldom-seen alter-ego won her over as he always knew it would, and reluctantly, she went to see what all the fuss was about.

The gallery, situated off the main thoroughfare, was tucked away in a narrow side street, overshadowed by new shops and restaurants. A building that clung to life by virtue of its age and having few redeeming architectural features, it existed under the constant threat of demolition.

There was very little externally to indicate what was within. The windows were painted over and the sign on the door merely said Utopia. But among the many people who hurried past there every day, on their way to work or just visiting the town to shop or sight-see, there were those who were aware of what lay behind that blank facade. The serious collectors, the connoisseurs who invested large sums of money in works of art, knew with certainty that any purchase was virtually guaranteed to appreciate in value if it was bought at Utopia. Most agreed that the owners of this remarkable gallery possessed an unerring instinct when it came to knowing just what would be sought after in the years to come.

Marianne opened the door and heard a sharp buzz, like the sound of an irate, electronic bee, as she crossed over the threshold. She felt like Alice stepping through the looking glass. Leaving behind the drab and noisy streets of Swannington and entering a serene and crisply vivid world of color, she looked about her in wonder. The white painted walls and high ceilings, the polished wood floors, and carefully angled lights that illuminated the paintings that were displayed in the gallery seemed extremely grand. A piano piece by Neville Wyndham was playing quietly in the background, and a light citrus scent perfumed the air.

Seated at a desk near the door was a young woman, smartly dressed and smiling pleasantly. She greeted Marianne, who explained that her business partner, Ivan Bronowski, had urged her to come and see Dimitri Gurvich's work.

"Oh, Ivan. Of course!" He was obviously well-known there, and on the strength of this recommendation, the receptionist handed her a catalogue, which she accepted with thanks.

"If you have any questions, our associates will be happy to assist you. Please feel free to take your time and look around. Our visitors are encouraged to enjoy the pieces that we have on display here without feeling any pressure to purchase." The receptionist spoke as though she were reading from a well-memorized script.

Marianne thanked her again and began her tour of the gallery. There were three other people in the first room, each looking intently at the pictures displayed on the walls. There was evidently a lot more to Utopia than this one room, and indeed as she went on, she realized that the place covered two floors, each containing two large galleries. The current exhibition featured the works of three artists, one an English painter Joseph Standish, a Russian named Dimitri Gurvich, and a woman, Sandra Dickson, who created modernistic sculptures.

The first floor was devoted exclusively to Standish's artwork. The large, brightly colored paintings were somewhat bewildering and at times overpowering, the colors leaping out and grabbing one's attention in a rather unnerving manner. She could see why Ivan would be enamored. These brash and florid pieces would appeal to his effusive temperament.

As Marianne referred to the catalogue, she compared the description of each item to the piece that was displayed. A massive crimson and black conglomeration of oil paints laid thickly on the canvas was listed as "Poppies in a Field." Standing back a bit and looking at it from a certain angle, she supposed one could see it as that. But the dazzlingly yellow and orange streaks that covered the neighboring canvas and entitled "Sunrise by The Lake" left her unimpressed.

Her knowledge of art up until that point had been limited to an appreciation for the works of the old masters such as Da Vinci, Rembrandt, and Michelangelo and the later paintings of Fragonard and Constable.

Her love of art had also included an intense but fleeting passion for her art teacher at the highly impressionable age of eighteen. Apart from the principles of color and perspective, which she could never quite seem to master, he had taught her the art of lovemaking, which had probably been his greatest contribution to her education. Her amateurish daubs on canvas may not have been much to write home about, but by the time she was nineteen, she had more than a nodding acquaintance with the exotic delights of the Kama Sutra.

Having realized early on that she did not possess the gift required for painting, Marianne turned her attention to another art form, photography, with which she was happily more adept, and the brief romance abruptly came to an end. The master had taught his willing pupil all that he knew and had moved on to enlighten another. Such was life.

Standish's work, although not Marianne's cup of tea, was admittedly colorful, and she could see why Ivan would appreciate the bold and garish interpretation of his subjects. Having given all the pieces on the first floor her careful consideration, she moved on up the stairs to the second floor and the works of Dimitri Gurvich and Sandra Dickson.

After walking about the first room for a while, pausing now and then to look at some sculptures that, to Marianne's untrained eye, defied description, but with which Ivan was much enamored, Marianne moved on to the next room.

The work of Dimitri Gurvich was more to her liking. Though not as colorful as the pictures by Standish, the subjects depicted were recognizable, and she found the catalogue descriptions unnecessary—the pictures spoke for themselves.

Marianne stood looking intently at an ornately framed painting. The principal subject of the piece, a female dressed in the fashion of the 1920s, appeared to stand in imminent danger of being devoured by a fire-breathing dragon. Its magnificent wings stretched across the width of the canvas as it hovered menacingly above her, and in the upper left-hand corner of the picture, a knight dressed in full armor, holding a shining lance aloft, was preparing to do battle. The smoke that issued from the dragon's nostrils swirled about the girl, and her long hair, which seemed to be blown by the creature's fiery breath, mingled with the ribbons that adorned the knight's helmet. Ever the romantic, Marianne's imagination was completely captured by the scene.

Not since seeing *The Death of Chatterton* for the first time had Marianne been so deeply touched by a painting. Henry Wallis had portrayed the young poet, barely seventeen at the time of his death in 1770, his lifeless body draped across the mean bed beneath the tiny garret window. Wallis had made Chatterton more eloquent in death than he had ever been in life. The utter loneliness and finality of the scene tore at her heart, and she had wept silently as though for someone she'd known personally.

She was jerked back into the present by the sudden appearance of a tall, well-dressed, middle-aged man standing beside her.

"Mm, what do you think of it?" he asked, considering the artwork with his head tilted slightly to one side. His voice was deep, soft, and educated. At first, Marianne wasn't sure if this question was directed at her, but looking about to see if there was another person present, she realized that they were alone. She suddenly felt herself tongue-tied.

Being an introvert, she preferred to view life from the safe distance behind a camera. Conversation, even with close friends, did not come easily to Marianne, or Annie as she was usually called. She had never been blessed with the ability to make the timely or witty rejoinder, always finding it necessary to mentally analyze her responses. She was constantly fearful of making a social blunder.

Scrambling momentarily for the appropriate words, she silently prompted herself, *say something, you idiot*, then, *oh God, please don't let me say anything stupid!*

"I...think...it's well done," she finally managed to get out, "Although it's a bit somber. The detail," she pointed tentatively," is rather lost in all those dark colors. You have to look very closely to see the fine work, the dragon's scales, the pebbles in the foreground."

"One can't help but wonder who he was thinking of when he painted it," the man said as he scrutinized the picture. "Gurvich never married, but they say he was passionately in love with a young woman of his acquaintance who spurned his affections. She was, apparently, in love with someone else."

"Perhaps it's representational," Marianne ventured.

"In that case, was he the dragon or the knight?" The hint of a smile appeared on the man's lips.

"And if he was the knight, who was he protecting her from?" Marianne pondered. "The style reminds me of a Burne-Jones painting. *King Cophetua and The Beggar Maid* was always one of my favorites." She smiled weakly and waited for his reply, half expecting him to remark contemptuously on her limited artistic knowledge and walk away. But he remained.

He was silent for a moment, still contemplating the artwork, then he said quietly, bending his head close to her so that she could hear the words.

"Her arms across her breast she laid:
She was more fair than words can say;
Barefooted came the beggar maid
Before the king Cophetua'
So sweet a face, such angel grace,
In all the land had never been.
Cophetua sware a royal oath:
This beggar maid shall be my queen!'"

He straightened, looking at her so intently that she felt her cheeks flush with embarrassment.

"At least that's how Tennyson saw it, but yes, you're quite right," he added. Then, to her total consternation, he took her arm and led her to the other side of the room, saying, "Now this one over here is very different, brighter and more eye-catching, don't you think? The brushwork is excellent, and the detail is certainly there."

Despite the unexpectedness of his actions, which many women might have found presumptuous and possibly even threatening, it seemed to her a natural and welcome attention. He gestured toward the canvas, but she didn't see it. All Marianne could see was his face. She could still feel the touch of his hand, and she was lost.

They spent the next hour or so wandering throughout the gallery, commenting on various pieces and, having given their considered opinions, returned to the desk by the door. Marianne felt rather guilty at having spent so much time there without having actually purchased anything, but she could tell her companion felt no such qualms. He courteously thanked the still-smiling receptionist, who addressed him by name, and held the door open for Marianne to pass through.

Marianne was fearful that this brief acquaintance would end here, but Vincent Foxworth invited her to go and have coffee with him, and before long, they were sitting side-by-side on high stools by the window in the café just down the street. They looked out at the sidewalk and watched the pigeons parading up and down outside, heads bobbing as they pecked at imaginary crumbs on the paving, unafraid of the people passing by.

As they sat drinking their coffee, a familiar figure came into view. Lucy Welbourne was alone, and normally Marianne would have gone outside and called to Lucy to join her. Instead, she watched her walk further along the street and said nothing. She didn't want to share this precious time with Vincent with anyone else.

Just then, the pigeons scattered in a flurry of beating wings as a man, striding along, a large borzoi hound at his side, went past. It seemed, to Marianne's fertile imagination, that he was watching Lucy, who was just a few yards ahead. She felt suddenly cold. She gave an involuntary shudder and turned her attention back to Vincent Foxworth.

They chatted of this and that for several minutes until Foxworth looked at his watch and said apologetically, "I'm sorry. I must dash. I have an appointment across town, and if I don't leave now, I'll be late."

With a few parting words, he left Marianne sitting by the window watching as he hurried away.

5

OVERTURES

THEY HAD AGREED TO GO OUT FOR DINNER in Swannington the following evening. Vincent picked Marianne up at the house on Dover Street on time, looking very debonair. He chose a small Italian restaurant that served good food and excellent wine, and the intimate surroundings seemed, this time, to invite something more than casual conversation.

Foxworth, who was a professor of English Literature at the University in Swannington, mentioned some of his favorite haunts: restaurants, cafes, and book shops, many of which Marianne knew well. She was surprised that she had never seen him before. She was sure she would have recognized him. She found herself strangely at ease in his company, no longer diffident and tongue-tied but confident. She knew so little about him, and yet Marianne felt that she had known Vincent Foxworth all her life.

"My mother wasn't too happy about my move to Swannington," he confided over a soup lightly seasoned with nutmeg and marsala wine and accompanied by sourdough pane Ferrarese. "She and my older sister Judith live in Beckham, up in the Lake District."

Marianne listened attentively as he talked about his home, Stoughton Manor, and his family. When the second course, mouthwateringly-tender beef cooked in Barolo wine, arrived, she in turn described the day-to-day activities involved in her work as a photographer and her association with Ivan Bronowski.

The conversation then turned to their respective tastes in music. It seemed that they both enjoyed listening to classical music, although Vincent admitted to a liking for jazz and a passing interest in Madonna, whose latest song *Like a Virgin* was still doing the rounds.

"I can clearly remember the first piece of music that I ever really enjoyed as a child," Marianne recalled wistfully. "Ketelbey's *In a Persian Market*. I must have only been about five years old at the time. My mother took me to a concert while we were holidaying at a seaside resort. It was the first time I'd ever been introduced to anything of that kind, and I found myself totally absorbed," Marianne recounted. How exotic and evocative the notes had sounded, conjuring up visions of far-away lands and the colorful, extravagant characters alluded to in the stories that her mother read to her at bedtime.

"I was in absolute awe of the grandeur of the theater with its high ceilings and elaborate decorations. Listening to a live orchestra was a new and fascinating experience for me. Until then, I'd only heard brass bands playing in the park," she explained. "This was something altogether different, so many strange and exciting instruments making a sound infinitely more enjoyable."

Vincent nodded his understanding and recalled that he had been introduced to the world of classical music by his grandfather.

"He played the piano remarkably well and taught me to play, too. He particularly admired Neville Wyndham, who was himself an accomplished pianist. Wyndham had a house in Cumbria near where my grandparents lived, and I believe he also rented a villa that grandfather owned in Honfleur. I remember he visited Stoughton on several occasions. He seemed like a very nice man."

Marianne talked, with some reluctance, of her own family; a brother, Matthew, who had fallen out with his father and left home when he was still quite young and who now lived in a flat in London. She told Vincent about her father, Ronald Clay, who lived in Hackney, and a married sister, Clare, who lived in Richmond Upon Thames. Their mother had died several years before Marianne had gone to live with Lucy Rowe in Birchford.

Vincent asked if there was anyone else in her life, a question that would normally have seemed rather forward on first acquaintance, but to which she truthfully replied, "No. No-one special."

"Ivan?"

"Good heavens! No! Oh, I admit he is very good-looking and I was tempted at first, but no. I'm afraid our temperaments are just too incompatible, and besides he has Irina. She's more than a match for him. She has him eating out of her hand even though he likes people to think that he's this tough guy. No, Ivan and I, as they say, are just very good friends. It's much better for business that way."

In turn, Marianne half-jokingly quizzed Vincent about his love life and was relieved to learn that he was not at present involved with anyone. Would she have gone out with him if she thought otherwise? Probably. Truth be told, she was ready to cast aside any scruples that she might have harbored where Vincent was concerned.

It certainly wasn't for the want of admiring feminine company that he had no permanent companion, she was sure. He could have had his pick of any number of adoring and adorable women, but somehow, he conceded, he had drifted in and out of relationships with an inconstancy that Marianne found rather alarming.

At the end of the evening, when the remnants of the meal had been cleared away, the owner of the restaurant, Gianni, approached their table and greeted Vincent, with whom he appeared to be on good terms. He was accompanied by a waitress carrying a tray that held two small glasses.

"Vincent, my good friend! Some limoncello before you and your beautiful companion depart?"

"Thank you, Gianni. The meal was excellent, as always." Vincent accepted the drinks, and Marianne, who was already rather tipsy from several glasses of wine that had accompanied each course during the meal, coughed as the limoncello slid down her throat.

"Sorry. Sorry," she spluttered. "I wasn't expecting it to be quite so strong."

Vincent and Gianni laughed as Marianne wiped her eyes. Vincent helped her with her coat as she tried to recover her poise, and they left the restaurant with Gianni wishing them, *"Buona notte!"*

As they made their way back to Vincent's car, Marianne thanked him for dinner. "I can't remember when I last had such a feast," she said as they walked slowly side by side. Vincent stopped and Marianne turned to face him. Taking her hand in his and raising it to his lips, he said,

"A Jug of Wine, a Loaf of Bread—and Thou

Beside me, singing in the Wilderness–

Oh, Wilderness were paradise enough!"

Marianne found his penchant for quoting these romantic verses charmingly sentimental, so much so that the words combined with the effects of the limoncello overwhelmed her, and she felt an unexpected tide of emotion.

He kissed her fingertips again and laughed. "Don't cry, Marianne, or you'll spoil everything."

Suddenly, Marianne regretted having agreed to go out with him. She felt like a silly schoolgirl. He had made her feel ridiculous, and she wanted nothing more than to run away and hide. Conversation, after that, was one-sided, and Vincent decided it was time to go home.

He drove Marianne back to the house on Dover Street and walked her to the door.

"When will I see you again?" he asked in such a matter-of-fact way that Marianne immediately forgot how upset she was.

"Soon, I hope," she responded. "Will you call me?"

"Of course." He kissed her cheek and left her on the doorstep. She watched as he started the car up and drove away. Although there wasn't much in the way of street lighting, Marianne caught a glimpse of someone moving about on the pavement opposite, and she was rather startled to see that it was the man that she had noticed outside the café. The man with the dog. She felt a sudden chill and, turning the key in the lock, Marianne let herself into the house.

That night, she dreamt of dragons and knights, the man with the dog, and Vincent, who had asked her to a picnic that consisted of nothing but a loaf of bread and a bottle of wine.

6

THE DRAGON'S LAIR

MARIANNE ANXIOUSLY AWAITED A CALL FROM VINCENT, half afraid that it would not come. What if he didn't want to see her again? She could not bear the thought that things might be over before they had even really begun. But when he called two days later, all her fears were set aside. He was giving a lecture that morning at the university but could get away for lunch. Could she meet him there? "There's a café on the corner called The Bolero. Do you know it?"

"Yes, I think so. What time?"

"I should be able to get there by noon."

Marianne arrived at The Bolero fifteen minutes before the appointed time and secured a table in the increasingly busy café. As she waited, she thought, *Here I am again, a thirty-year-old woman feeling like a schoolgirl again. How silly!* But her heart skipped a beat as she saw Vincent walk through the door.

"Hello. Have you been waiting long?"

"No, I just got here," Marianne lied, hoping that he wouldn't notice her almost empty coffee cup.

"I'll go and order. What would you like?"

"Oh, anything. Whatever you're having," Marianne told him.

He went over to the counter and purchased sandwiches and coffee. When he returned, Vincent put the tray on the table and took off his coat, reaching into a pocket to retrieve a small package wrapped in gold tissue paper. He sat down opposite Marianne and handed it to her. She accepted the gift hesitantly and, when she opened it, saw with delight that it was a red, leather-bound copy of *The Rubaiyat*.

"How lovely! She exclaimed. "It really is too kind of you. You hardly know me."

"I hope it will remind you of our first evening together. Now, eat up," he said, airily dismissing the subject. "I have to get back to the university for a tutorial."

They finished their somewhat hasty meal with little time for anything other than small talk and were just leaving the café when Vincent recognized a man hurrying towards them. "Jonathan! Hello!"

"Oh, hello, Vincent. Are you leaving?" The man, shorter and somewhat older than Vincent, stopped at the café door. "I'm just going to grab some lunch. I'll see you later." And with a wave of his hand, he disappeared inside.

As Vincent walked Marianne back to her car, a brightly-colored VW Beetle, he explained, "That was Jonathan Amor. He's a professor of sociology. We've been friends for some time now. His mother was the daughter of a Maharaja of somewhere or other. You'll probably meet him and his wife Lisa again. They come over to the apartment for dinner occasionally."

Marianne took this as a hopeful sign. Did it mean that she too would be invited to dinner?

"There's a film showing at the Rialto that I rather wanted to catch. *The Name of the Rose*. Would you like to go tonight?"

"Isn't that the one with Sean Connery? Yes, I'd like to see it," she agreed.

"Good. I'll pick you up at seven, alright?" Vincent stood waiting as Marianne settled herself in the car.

"Thank you," she called as he closed the door. As she drove away, she looked in the rear-view mirror and saw him standing on the curb, watching with something like a puzzled frown.

Subsequently, they spent many enjoyable hours together but always in circumstances that were not conducive to intimacy of any kind. This didn't concern Marianne, for she felt that it would happen when we were both ready and didn't want to rush either of them into a hasty affair that they might later regret. Vincent hadn't yet taken her to his flat in Swannington and although Lucy Rowe was not in any sense strict regarding her terms of tenancy, still Marianne did not feel comfortable inviting him to her room on Dover Street.

Their meetings, however, served to fortify their relationship as they became acquainted with each other's likes and dislikes. They learned, above all else, to accept each other's friendship in a spirit of easy camaraderie without making demands, setting impractical goals, or unrealistic expectations.

It was so easy to fall in love with Vincent. He was everything that many women looked for but seldom found in a man: considerate, romantic, intelligent, and slightly egotistical, which gave him the self-assurance that made him so interesting and fun to be with. Seldom a day went by without either sight or sound of him. If they weren't together, he would call her or send notes, tucked into bouquets of flowers, quoting Shakespeare, Keats, or Shelley. This rather heady dose of attention affected Marianne's ability to concentrate to no little extent, and Ivan teased her mercilessly as her preoccupation with Vincent became self-evident.

Several weeks later, Vincent asked if he might stop by the studio that Marianne and Ivan shared in Swannington, something he had not done before, and she wondered just how Ivan would react to this first meeting. Despite having made fun of her lapses in concentration, he had shown a rather sneering lack of interest when she told him that she had fallen in love with Vincent. If she did not know better, Marianne would almost have said that he was jealous. Maybe he thought that her love for Vincent would diminish the importance of their friendship in some way, which was stupid. As difficult and quirky as Ivan was, he and Irina were her greatest friends, and she made a conscious effort not to suddenly neglect their time together outside of work.

Her ability to bring about a meeting between Ivan and Vincent had been frustrated largely by conflicting schedules, but also it seemed that Ivan had deliberately seen to it that he wasn't available. To catch him off guard, she had not told him of Vincent's proposed visit to the studio.

As usual when he was in the process of putting together a fashion shoot, Ivan was bullying a bevy of models hired from a local agency, tweaking stray strands of hair, adjusting attitudes and poses, and generally throwing his tall, thin frame about in a frenzy of artistic creativity.

"Oh my God! Liza! Do something about this girl's make-up. It's not right, around the eyes…here and here. Just try to make something of her." Catching sight of another miscreant, he threw his hands up in despair. "Gina! Darling! You've got the wrong outfit on! It's supposed to be that blue thing with the sparkles." Not wishing to leave anyone out, he addressed the last of the three models, running his hands abstractedly through his dark hair, "Show more cleavage, for God's sake, darling!" Then, with mounting fury and not stopping for breath, "We're trying to make these wretched rags look appealing. Think of the poor devils who are going to shell out hundreds of their hard-earned pounds on something that, in all probability, will do absolutely nothing to make them look anything but the drab, plain people that they are." Then, looking round at Marianne for support, screamed out in his thick Russian accent, above the cacophony of music pouring from his stereo, "Can't they ever send us anything but these brainless, flat-chested females?" There was no such thing as 'sexual harassment' in Ivan's vocabulary.

Marianne shrugged theatrically in response. Liza, the stylist who frequently helped Ivan at these fashion shoots, advanced, unperturbed by his outburst, to apply the necessary creams and powders. Gina flounced away to change her dress after deftly gesturing at Ivan's back in a time-honored but unladylike manner. Marta, hauling at the top which had already threatened to spill its contents, muttered dark imprecations as Ivan, unconcerned, went about his preparations.

Vincent entered the studio in the middle of this chaos and, seeing that Marianne was otherwise engaged, helping to set up lighting and backdrops, seated himself in a vacant chair and watched in barely-concealed amusement.

She had not noticed him at first, her attention being temporarily diverted by Ivan's first victim who, taking issue with his remark regarding her makeup, was giving him a verbal lashing, which seemed to bother Ivan not at all. Finally, catching sight of Vincent, Marianne hastily made the necessary adjustments to one of the reflectors and called over to her tempestuous colleague, "That's it. I've finished. Can you manage now? I've got to go."

Bronowski turned, his face frozen in a look of surprise then, catching sight of Vincent, his dark brows knitted in such impotent rage that for a second, she bitterly regretted this fait accompli that seemed to have put him at such a disadvantage. Ivan looked at them for a moment, and Marianne hastened to throw oil on troubled waters.

"This is Vincent," she gestured toward Vincent, mentally wincing at the unpredictability of Ivan's temperament, never quite sure what response would issue from those sardonic Russian lips. His expression had quickly changed, however, to one of smiling insouciance, and he strode forward with uncharacteristic bonhomie, his hand extended to greet the newcomer.

"Vincent, this is my colleague and very good friend Ivan Bronowski."

The handshake between the two men was brief. Marianne breathed a sigh of relief.

Thank you, Ivan, she thought gratefully. *He's making an effort for my sake, to be sociable, bless him!* But Ivan quickly dispelled that notion, unable to sustain the 'Hail fellow, well met!' attitude for more than a moment.

"Hello! So, you are the handsome knight who has come to carry Annie off on his white charger. Just make sure she's back here in the morning to do tomorrow's shoot. She's very busy just now and we have a tight schedule this week." He turned to Marianne, gushing sarcastically, "Annie, my darling! You were right, he's gorgeous!" loudly enough that she was sure Vincent must have heard him, and she felt a warm flush of embarrassment cover her face.

Ivan walked away, his concession to his idea of polite conversation exhausted, and Marianne hastily led Vincent over to the door, calling goodbye to everyone in the studio as they descended to the street below.

"Sorry," she apologized. "He gets a bit over-enthusiastic at times, but he means well." She was trying to excuse Ivan's behavior even though she could cheerfully have kicked the wretched man all the way back to Moscow.

Vincent laughed. "He certainly is a character! How long did you say you've been working together?"

"Sometimes it seems like a lifetime, but actually it's been about six years now. Surprisingly, it's worked out pretty well so far. We share the expenses of the studio and schedule shoots so that we get equal use of the facilities, and sometimes we help each other, like today," Marianne explained. "He does mostly fashion work. The girls call him 'Ivan the Terrible' behind his back. He can be quite a tyrant, and he's upset just about everyone at one time or another, but we've learned to live with it. He gets the most magnificent results; his work is incredible. He's off to do a shoot for one of the big magazines next week, so, apart from Mark,, who does all the film processing, I'll have the place to myself for a few days."

They walked to where Vincent had been obliged to park his car several streets from the studio. He opened the door and held it as Marianne got in. Small courtesies like this, she noticed, came naturally to him. She appreciated such considerations so rarely shown in the fast-paced and emancipated times in which they now lived. Despite her financial independence and firm belief that women were equal to men in all things, she still welcomed the polite attentions of a more chivalrous time.

Vincent expertly maneuvered the car out into traffic, and they began to discuss their plans for the evening ahead, which included dinner and a movie.

"Would you mind if we stopped at my apartment first? I have to check my mail for some important documents that I'm expecting, and I thought perhaps we could have a drink and relax before we go out again. It's been a long day for you as well, I'm sure."

This was an evening of firsts. Marianne had been wondering when she would finally get to see the place that Vincent now called home. It didn't take them long to cross the city despite the lingering rush hour traffic, and they soon pulled up outside a large, old building that had once housed offices but had recently been converted to apartments.

Vincent greeted the concierge at the desk in the lobby while retrieving his mail, and they took the lift up to the third floor. As he ushered her through the vestibule and into the living room, the first thing that caught Marianne's eye was a magnificent grand piano standing before a set of floor-to-ceiling windows that looked out onto the street below.

"I see you still play," she said, remembering what he had told her about his grandfather teaching him to play the piano.

"Just a little, to amuse myself."

She looked around at the large oak bookcases that lined one entire wall. *Natural enough for a professor of English literature*, she thought as she peered at the titles on the shelves. All the giants of the English language were represented there: Shakespeare, Shelly, Keats, Dickens, Jane Austen, and the Bronte sisters. Not so many of the modern-day authors and poets appeared in his collection, but enough to show that he was not entirely absorbed in the past. John Le Carre featured heavily among these, and besides these works of fiction and poetry, there was a vast array of material covering diverse subjects ranging from art, music, and the theater to travel, religion, ancient mythology, and psychic phenomenon.

Vincent, meanwhile, had left her to her own devices and was pouring drinks in the kitchen. When he returned with the glasses, he found her glancing through an autobiography by the great Russian singer Nikolai Dvorkin.

"Have you heard any of his recordings?" he asked as he handed Marianne her drink.

"Yes," she replied, recalling the time at Ivan's apartment when he had plied her liberally with vodka, and they had sat listening in an alcoholic haze to that phenomenal artist's remarkable performance in Mefistofele. She remembered too how, when the music had faded, Ivan had said in melancholy tones, "Sometimes I sit and listen to him and I cry. That a man with such a voice could die. God should have allowed him to live forever. My great-uncle, on my father's side, was related to him by marriage, you know."

Marianne was unimpressed by this blatant piece of name-dropping. That had been the night when Ivan had made his first and only attempt to seduce her, and he was successful. But being made love to by Ivan was all about him: his needs, his wants, his desires. It was like being hit by an express train. You knew something monumental had happened, but it happened so quickly and with such little regard for the person who had been hit that it was hard to say just what had occurred.

Thanks, but no thanks, Marianne thought when she left to go home that night. She already knew that to continue their relationship on that level was out of the question, and when she later told Ivan that she thought it would be for the best if they didn't pursue it any further, he agreed, admittedly with bad grace. And although she felt a slight embarrassment when they were together at the studio the next day, Ivan shrugged the whole situation off with an air of almost callous disregard, as though nothing had happened, which was probably just as well.

Marianne replaced the book on the shelf and resumed her reconnaissance of the room. There was a delicious fragrance in the air that came from several large crystal vases filled with beautiful fresh flower arrangements, the large velvet petals of red and white roses chiefly among them. Vincent watched as she sniffed at them appreciatively and closed her eyes the better to enjoy their heady aroma.

Strange how a perfume could paint such a vivid picture in one's mind, she thought. She remembered walking as a young child in her grandmother's garden after a spring shower, and the peonies, bathed in raindrops, smelled so sweet that she wanted to run and gather them all up in her arms and hug them to her. Her grandmother, disentangling Marianne who was sopping wet and covered with clinging petals, led her reluctantly back to the house but, ever after, the smell of peonies brought back pleasant memories of her grandmother's garden and the happy hours she had spent there in that lush green oasis that had been so aptly named Paradise House.

Vincent, too, had surrounded himself with mementos of his childhood, mostly in the form of framed photos scattered about the apartment. Pictures of his mother with him as a young child, his sister an adorable cherub in a smocking-topped dress and curly hair, his grandparents in a formal portrait. His grandfather, bearing a striking resemblance to Vincent, had evidently passed on his charm and good looks as well as his love of music; his grandmother, smiling beside him, unremarkable in appearance save for a fine head of dark, lustrous hair.

Notably absent from this gallery of family portraits was his father, and without thinking, Marianne remarked upon it.

"My father left home when I was twenty-three. It came as a great shock to us all," he replied gravely. "I don't think my mother had any idea that anything was wrong. We never suspected…that he might have a mistress, anything of that kind. Things always seemed normal. There were never any arguments, nothing to indicate that he was unhappy with his life."

"I'm sorry." Marianne stammered, embarrassed by her faux pas. "How sad for you all. It must have been awful."

"Mother took it surprisingly well, but my sister Judith was devastated. We never heard from him again. We didn't find out about the other woman until Judith discovered some letters in his bureau from her, unsigned but leaving no doubt as to their relationship. I thought he and my mother had been happy, but, apparently, he was totally besotted by this woman, whoever she was."

As he did not appear to be averse to discussing the matter, Marianne asked, "Did your mother divorce him?"

"Yes, on the grounds of desertion. He never responded, and she retained most of the property, including the house in Whitehaven where we lived. Of course, things changed considerably later on. My grandfather did quite well for himself in business, and when he died, my grandmother had predeceased him by several years, he left everything to us. The estate was split equally between my mother, Judith, and I, hence all this."

He gestured about him at the luxurious appointments of the apartment, and she was somewhat taken aback by his forthrightness, not knowing quite how to respond.

Jolly nice! she felt would have been inappropriate, so Marianne merely replied, "I see."

"That was when my mother and Judith moved to my grandfather's house near Penhampton. God knows why they wanted to live in such a huge place, but there they are to this day, doing good works and keeping the local shopkeepers in business."

Vincent made himself comfortable on the large leather sofa, but Marianne continued to stand and look about her with unabashed curiosity. The room had a masculine air about it despite the flowers and object d'art. There were several excellent framed paintings on the walls, but one stood out immediately, and she gasped as she recognized the dragon from the Utopia gallery.

"I had to have it," was all he said, but his eyes spoke for him, and Marianne needed no other explanation. He motioned her to join him, and she settled comfortably beside him on the sofa. Taking her hand, he said, "I think, Marianne, that we know enough about each other now to see in what direction we're headed. Do you have any doubts?"

Her heart was racing, and she felt dizzy with joy as she looked into his hazel eyes. Doubts? She was never more certain of anything in her life. "No, no doubts."

He leaned close and kissed her passionately. There was to be no dinner or movie that night.

On the day she moved into Vincent's apartment, he took her to dinner to celebrate. Upon returning to her new home, he welcomed her with an unexpected gift. Although there had never been any mention of an engagement or marriage—there seemed no necessity for either as what could make things any more perfect than they already were—Vincent presented her that evening with a diamond ring.

"I would like you to have this," he said. "This may sound rather corny, but my grandfather gave it to me before he died and told me to give it to the woman that I truly loved. He said I would know who that person was when the time came, and I believe that person is you." She looked at it in amazement, it was a beautiful piece, not gaudy but exquisite, seven diamonds set in a floral motif on a gold band.

"I…I don't know what to say. I'm overwhelmed. This is the most beautiful thing I've ever seen." She slipped it onto the ring finger of her right hand, and it fit as though it had been made for her.

"The old boy told me confidentially that he had meant to give it to someone who had been very special to him at one time but apparently the lady in question turned out to be something of a disappointment, and it seemed rather presumptuous to ask why he hadn't given it to my grandmother instead, so I left it at that. I suppose you could call it a family heirloom."

"I'll treasure it always. I just wish your grandfather were still alive. I would like to have met him. He must have been a remarkable person."

"You would have loved him," Vincent said wistfully, "and I'm sure he would have adored you. I probably would have had to fight to keep him away from you, the lecherous old rascal!"

"Was he really such a Lothario?"

"Oh, he had an eye for a pretty girl, and I'm sure he strayed from the straight and narrow path of matrimony more than once, but my grandmother tolerated his lapses in fidelity. She knew he'd always come back to her, and because she loved him so much, she turned a blind eye to his roving one."

Marianne fervently hoped that Vincent wasn't hinting that she should do likewise and said as much. He laughed but said nothing. And so, they began their life together, little knowing how much and in what manner their love would be tested in the coming months.

7

A VISITOR

MARIANNE HAD AT FIRST BEEN RELUCTANT TO TELL HER FAMILY about her relationship with Vincent. She only mentioned him in passing when she called Clare or Matthew and on the rare occasions when she visited her father in Hackney. She merely told them that she had moved into a much nicer apartment—presumably alone—and that she had made one or two new friends, including someone who she believed had some connection with the University. She certainly wasn't ashamed of the fact that she was living with a man, particularly one who was so loving and sincere in his affection for her. It was just that she didn't want them to expect more of her than she was capable of giving.

Her father, who was always fiercely protective of her, would not approve of such an arrangement, she was sure. Clare, her older sister, was happily married with a family of her own. Matthew, her younger brother, who, although still a bachelor, fervently clung to the hope that he would one day meet the right girl and get married. Both brother and sister expected Marianne to follow the conventions, too. Marianne found it strange that they should have been so optimistic in their view of matrimony when evidence to the contrary was daily before their eyes. They all secretly suspected that their parents' marriage was not a particularly happy one.

Although they never actually witnessed any major altercations between mother and father, their manner toward each other was, to say the least, potentially explosive, and one could sense that the friction between them was constantly there, just barely hiding below the surface. Marianne tried not to take 'sides' in this ongoing matrimonial disharmony, maintaining a close relationship with both parents. But upon her mother's death, she sensed an air of total indifference in her father that she found rather shocking. Clare, who openly fought with him on many occasions, felt herself vindicated, and even Matthew, who had tried so hard unsuccessfully over the years to win his regard, was appalled.

Her father's attitude toward Matthew was always ambivalent. Marianne could never understand why, but it troubled her to see him treat his only son in so belligerent a fashion. Over the years, she endeavored to bring them closer together but to no avail. And so, as they grew older, they all followed their separate paths, although Marianne continued to play the part of intermediary between her sister and brother and their father.

Despite her reluctance to confide in her family, Vincent eventually persuaded Marianne to write and tell them the real reason behind her change of address. Both Matthew and Clare had seemed genuinely happy for her. Her father reacted much as she had expected. He wrote back, expressing his displeasure with a vehemence that even for him was exceptionally dictatorial. He demanded that Marianne leave Vincent immediately and come home. By turns, he threatened and cajoled until finally she wrote to remind him that as much as she loved him and understood his moral objections, she was no longer a child and was quite capable of making her own decisions. Thereafter, her letters to him went unanswered, and thinking it wise to let his anger subside, Marianne decided to give him time to reconcile himself to the idea that she was no longer his little girl and ceased to communicate with him.

Not long after this, Matthew wrote to say that he was planning to visit Swannington and was looking forward to meeting Vincent and presumably giving his unofficial approval. Although he had planned to put up at a local hotel, Marianne insisted that he stay at the apartment. For her part, although Marianne was loath to admit any faults in Vincent, she knew he could sometimes appear aloof with strangers and looked forward to Matthew's arrival with some trepidation.

Matthew, as a child, had always been a friendly soul, and even when he was older, somewhat naive. His eagerness to please other people and his evident discomfort on the few occasions when he was rebuffed was, she felt sure, directly attributable to their father's treatment of him. She wondered how he would view Vincent's sometimes cool demeanor.

On the day of Matthew's arrival, Marianne watched from the window, waiting to see his car pull up in the street, and when he finally stepped out, taking an overnight bag from the passenger's seat, she ran to the door. The concierge had been apprised of his arrival, and as Matthew emerged from the elevator, Marianne ran to him and threw her arms around her brother, exclaiming, "Matthew! How lovely to see you. How are you?"

He disengaged himself and looked at her as if searching for some unexpected change in her appearance. "Not too bad." He grinned, apparently satisfied that everything was as it should be. "Terrible traffic jams all the way, but here I am at last!" She led him back to the apartment.

Marianne remembered Vincent, who she had temporarily forgotten in the excitement of the moment. He had hung back when she ran to greet Matthew and was standing watching them, a strange, unfamiliar look on his face, hard to define, not exactly jealousy, but curiosity. The expression was fleeting, however, and coming forward, he smiled and shook Matthew's hand warmly.

"Matthew, I'm so glad to finally meet you. Marianne has told me so much about you, I feel I know you already."

"Good Lord! What have you been saying about me, Annie? I hope it was all good."

"Of course, silly! Come on in. Would you like some tea?" As Vincent bent to retrieve Matthew's bag, Marianne grabbed hold of her brother's arm and led him into the living room.

That evening, they sat up late, catching up on all their news. Matthew was full of amusing anecdotes, many of which related to Clare, her husband Preston, and their three children, Sarah, Emma, and Justin. His pride in his nieces and nephew was evident.

They learned that his work as a junior partner in a firm of chartered accountants kept him busy and that he had a moderately full social life.

They reminisced about earlier times too, little vignettes, memories of their mother, grandparents, and other family members and friends or places they had visited when they were children.

"Annie always had lots of imaginary friends," Matthew recalled. "Of course, I was too young to join them in their games, but Annie would introduce them, and I would make believe that I could see them too. We always had such fun at playing pretend."

Marianne vaguely remembered these 'friends' who had shared their playtime. To her, they had seemed so real: the little boy who appeared one morning at their house in Golders Green and later, the young girl who visited them at the house in Hackney. There was another boy who had joined them at their grandparents' home in Kent, but after a while, he ceased to visit. Maybe it was just because Marianne had started to grow up that these phantom children no longer came to play.

Among all these recollections of their past, there was never any allusion made to their father, and Marianne respected Matthew's obvious disinclination to touch upon the subject. Once in a while she would look over at Vincent and, every now and then, when he was unaware of being observed, she would catch that same fleeting look of curiosity as he listened to Matthew's cheerful conversation. For some reason, despite the fact that the two of them seemed on the friendliest of terms, she felt a strange uneasiness.

Matthew had planned on staying for just three days, and Marianne naturally wanted to take him to see the studio where she worked. Ivan was surprisingly well behaved when they arrived the next morning, during one of his shoots for a well-known lingerie catalogue.

Matthew, although of a friendly and easy-going disposition, was rather old-fashioned and guileless in his manner. He appeared self-conscious and ill at ease, surrounded as he was by a crowd of scantily dressed girls. But Ivan, who took these things for granted, soon made him feel at home.

"Don't be nervous, *Tovarich*," he told Matthew with a salacious wink and a hearty dig in the ribs with his elbow. "Enjoy what God has seen fit to give us." And leading him by the arm, Ivan immediately proceeded to introduce him to the giggling models who welcomed any break from Ivan's tirades and especially one that came in the guise of a handsome young visitor whose blushes and stammered greetings tickled their sense of humor no end.

"I've seen some of your work, I think, in Vogue, perhaps?" Matthew told Ivan. "It's very good."

Ivan picked up a simple black dress that one of the models had cast aside and held it up for Matthew to look at. "All smoke and mirrors, my friend. Take this dress, for example. Nothing fancy. Something you could buy at the market for a few pounds. But put it on a beautiful woman, add some bling and colored lights, and you can name your own price. Something like this sells for more than a week's salary in Harvey Nicks." Ivan laughed and slapped Matthew's arm, repeating, "All smoke and mirrors."

Marianne then introduced Matthew to Mark Truman, who was responsible for developing all of the film that Ivan and Marianne used in their work. Ivan sometimes referred to him as the Artful Dodger, a veiled reference to Mark's dodging and burning abilities in the darkroom. Mark greeted Matthew warmly and offered to show him some of his work.

Ivan maintained his friendly manner almost until the end of their visit, but Vincent arrived to take them to lunch, and right away, the feeling of *joie de vivre* evaporated. Ivan reverted to his sullen and sarcastic self, totally ignoring them as they left him to continue his work.

8
THE RAILWAY WOMAN

VINCENT HAD ACCOMPANIED MATTHEW AND MARIANNE on their jaunts about the city the next day, but on the final full day of Matthew's visit, he had business to attend to at the University.

Vincent had suggested a visit to a train museum near Cambridge as a result of a conversation that had taken place the evening before. Matthew and Marianne were talking about the train rides that they used to take to their grandparents' place in Kent, and Matthew waxed nostalgic about the passing of the old steam trains. He admitted to the usual predisposition that most young, male children aspire to when deciding their future employment, and laughingly declared that he still hoped that he might one day fulfill his childhood ambition of being an engine driver.

It was an unusually hot summer, and the day promised to be another blistering record-breaker, the early morning haze still clinging to the fields and hedgerows as they drove out into the countryside. Vincent had provided directions on how to find the place, but even with the aid of his detailed map, Marianne made several wrong turns. It didn't matter. They had all day to get there, and they were in a light-hearted mood.

After they had been driving for a while, Matthew took the opportunity to put a question that had apparently been weighing heavily on his mind.

"Are you really as happy as you look, Annie? I mean, everything seems...I don't know...too good to be true." He smiled apologetically. "I don't mean to pry. It's just that with you being so far away from me and not knowing about Vincent for so long, I wondered, you know…" He trailed off, hoping she would understand his concern.

"Don't worry," Marianne endeavored to reassure him. "I've never been this happy in my entire life. I wish I could have told you sooner. I wish I could explain why I didn't, but there it is. Dad was furious of course, and I know you and Clare probably think we should get married, but honestly Matthew, a little scrap of paper is not going to make the slightest bit of difference. And as for children, Vincent and I are everything to each other. It may seem selfish to you, but we just don't need anyone else in our lives right now and maybe never will."

She could see he was finding it hard to accept. Dear Matthew, always the conventional one. "I know I've made some mistakes in the past, bad choices, wrong decisions, but I love Vincent. We're perfect for each other." Frustration at her inability to persuade and an impatience with Matthew's unwillingness to be convinced were starting to give an edge to her voice. "I wish I knew how to make you see. Please try and understand, he isn't…" She stopped, reluctant to take the thought any further, but he finished it for her.

"Kevin? But you loved him, and look what happened." Matthew was referring to an old flame of Marianne's and one to whom she had not given a thought for several years.

"It was a long time ago, Matthew."

It had seemed like a lifetime. She and Kevin had dated for over two years. There seemed to be an 'engagement epidemic' among their friends. Every week one or the other would parade a diamond ring in front of her envious eyes, for Marianne to admire and gush over. If they could do it, why not her? She almost forced Kevin into proposing, even though in the back of her mind a little voice kept telling her that this wasn't right, that she didn't really want him, for better or worse. And when the diamond ring was finally on her finger, there wasn't the thrill, the exultation that one might have expected. But she kept it to herself, too proud to admit that she'd made a colossal mistake, and when, five months into the engagement, Kevin confessed to a continuing relationship with another girl, someone who she had known at school, they parted. Marianne was secretly relieved.

She never fell in love again, until that moment when Vincent came into her life.

"Things are different now." The vehemence with which she had uttered these last words seemed finally to have convinced Matthew, and he nodded, accepting what once would have been unthinkable.

"I like Vincent, really I do," he said. "And if you're happy, well, that's the most important thing." And with this benediction they continued on their way, in companionable silence.

After a while, Matthew broke the lull in conversation with a piece of news that had evidently slipped his mind earlier. "Grandma's old place in Kent has changed hands again," he said.

"Oh, too bad!" Marianne replied sadly. "I liked the Russells. What happened?"

"His company sent him out to Sweden, so of course they had to sell."

"Who's in there now, do you know?"

"A young couple, I think. I haven't had a chance to go and introduce myself yet, but I will as soon as I get the chance."

She smiled at this. Despite the fact that the property had been out of the family's hands for many years, Matthew maintained a tenuous link with the subsequent owners, unwilling to totally sever the family's connections with a place that held so many happy memories of their childhood. David and Doris Russell had fortunately understood his desire to hold on to that part of their past and had invited Matthew, Clare, and Marianne down to Paradise House to visit on several occasions.

The main feature of Paradise House, at least to them as children, was a clock tower that rose from the roof of the stables that had eventually been converted to a garage. Their grandfather would periodically climb up by means of rickety wooden steps, pulled down from a trapdoor in the floor above, to the cupola perched high atop the garage, to attend to the mysterious workings of this quaint old timepiece. Despite their repeated requests to be allowed to watch this process, the Clay children had never been permitted to venture up there because, as grandmother O'Malley explained, it wasn't safe. That refusal was a constant challenge to Marianne as a child. She remembered her grandfather O'Malley catching her once, half-way up the steps to that elusive sanctum, and giving her the most awful lecture on the sin of disobedience. And although she never again attempted to reach those forbidden regions, she dreamed on many a night, even into adulthood, of creeping up there. She was sure that dark and mystic chamber, a room no larger than a walk-in closet, contained some hidden treasure. But the truth was never revealed to her then, and she had to be content with gazing wistfully up at the large white face, black hands, and numbers of the clock from the safety of the cobbled courtyard or catching a glimpse of it from her bedroom window.

From there she could also look out to where, in the distance amongst the trees, she could see the tops of the old oast houses belonging to a neighboring hop farmer. She and Matthew would often walk over there during their visits to play with the farmer's dogs and feed the chickens that he kept in a barn next to the farmhouse.

Those walks were some of the most tranquil and happy moments of her childhood. The simple pleasures of finding primroses among the grass at the foot of the hedgerows that lined the quiet, narrow country lanes. Listening to the gentle splashing of the cool, clear stream that passed beneath the old wooden bridge on the road to Diffingham and watching the butterflies fluttering lazily from flower to flower in the fields above Paradise House. The muted hum of bees filling the air was among the priceless treasures that enriched their lives then. How they enjoyed those peaceful sojourns far away from the hustle and bustle of city life. Maybe it was just because of the times they now lived in, or maybe because they were that much older and more cynical about life in general, that things no longer seemed so idyllic.

Matthew and Marianne traveled for about two hours that morning, stopping once or twice to get a better look at some scenic view or historical marker along the roadside, before finally arriving at their destination.

The heat, as they emerged from the car, was oppressive. As they walked across the gravel-covered car park toward the entrance, Marianne was already regretting the amount of photographic equipment she had decided to carry around with her. She never missed an opportunity for picture taking and liked to be prepared for all eventualities.

But in this weather, the burden seemed considerable. She finally opted to run back to the car with the tripod and several other items that were deemed unnecessary, leaving Matthew at the ticket booth, clutching a camera and the bag that she used for holding lenses and other vital bits and pieces. She deposited everything else in the trunk and, on second thought, flung off the vest with all those useful little pockets that she usually wore while working outside. Well, that was better! Now she could move around with considerably more ease, and she ran back to Matthew, laughing.

"Okay, big brother. Let's go. I know you're dying to get a closer look at those engines." And having paid for their tickets, linking arms, they went through the gates.

Matthew was in his own little heaven, looking at all the gears and pistons and shining metal plates, but the technicalities of the massive locomotives held little interest for Marianne. Color, shape, and texture were more her stock-in-trade, and she had naturally gravitated toward a bright red baggage car that she knew would look great against the clear blue sky. They spent an hour or so in this manner, Matthew moving from one giant engine to another, the wheels of which stood as tall and sometimes taller than himself, examining in detail all the nuts and bolts, levers and gizmos with avid enthusiasm, and Marianne going slower, looking for that perfect shot and wishing for the hundredth time that it wasn't quite so hot.

At midday they stopped at a garishly decorated food stand to eat slices of limp and uninspired pizza and gratefully gulped at an ice-cold cola. They meandered over to a replica of an old station building and sat outside on a wooden bench, scorching the backs of their thighs, as they finished their drinks. Having consumed their meager lunch, they dutifully looked inside the waiting room and ticket office, which had been faithfully recreated to resemble its original appearance in the early 1850s.

"Where next?" Marianne asked. "Shall we look around some more, or do you want to take a ride? They're running a couple of the trains, I think." And just as she spoke, an old steam locomotive puffed laboriously into view towards the station.

"Rough decision," Matthew replied seriously, "but I'd really like to take a look at some of those old carriages in the sheds first."

"Alright," she agreed. "Let's walk down to the furthest one and work our way back, and then if the trains are still running, we'll take a ride."

They made their way along the path past several of the enormous sheds, each of which must have been some three hundred yards in length, down to the last one, set apart from the others, ostracized from the rest of the collection and surrounded by a field of weeds. Marianne wondered at first if they had trespassed into forbidden ground, but no one came forward to challenge them, and they went inside. They were the only people in the shed. Marianne wasn't surprised—it felt like a furnace. The corrugated metal roof and walls radiated the heat of the day almost intolerably. Matthew was so engrossed that he didn't seem to notice, and, not wanting to spoil his enjoyment, she followed him up the wooden steps to the walkway which was built on a level with and ran parallel to the windows of the carriages.

The interior of the shed was dark, the only light coming from the enormous open doors at either end of the building. It was eerily quiet in there as they walked slowly along, the only sound coming from the aluminum roof as the intense heat caused it to expand, making it creak and snap periodically. As they peered in at the dirt-begrimed windows of the compartments, Marianne supposed that funds had not yet run to cleaning and restoring this once elegant means of transportation. The museum seemed to be manned mostly by volunteers. The ticket prices were minimal, and judging by the sparse number of visitors that they had seen so far, their coffers could not have been overflowing.

There was an unmistakable smell of mildew in the air, and looking down between the rails under the cars, she could see, through the cobwebs that festooned the underpinnings and wheels of the carriages, little mushrooms sprouting amid the gravel.

In the gloomy interior of the carriages, they could vaguely make out seats covered in what was probably once vibrant green plush but were now faded, dusty, and threadbare. There were small lamps mounted in the corners of the cars each with its own little decorative shade, tasseled blinds hung askew from some of the windows and as she looked in, Marianne wondered about all those passengers who had traveled daily back and forth in such luxurious accommodation, all those years ago, and who were now long dead and gone.

45

Halfway along the walkway there was a stand containing a plaque and a brief history of the train and plans for its future. Matthew read the words aloud, but Marianne was ready to continue on, and while he was still digesting this information, she reached the steps at the farther end of the row and had already descended. The heat was becoming unbearable. Just one more, she promised herself, and then she would have to get outside.

Matthew had moved on to the next line of carriages and was making his way along the wooden planking while his sister trudged down to the last row of cars. Wearily climbing the steps, she looked in at what was once a dining car. Someone had begun the task of restoration by covering the table next to the window with a white tablecloth. Two settings had been laid out, white plates, cups, and saucers each encircled with a dark blue trim, plain utilitarian cutlery, and beside each place a stained and faded menu. Marianne wondered if it would be worth trying to take any shots. Lifting the camera to eye level, she looked through the viewfinder but just couldn't seem to get the composition that she needed, and the perspiration was beginning to run down her forehead and into her eyes.

She had taken a few more steps, noticing a filthy, cracked wash basin and toilet in a minuscule cubicle at the end of the carriage, and was peering in at the next compartment, her nose almost touching the window, when it happened.

A woman was standing there, looking back at her.

Startled, Marianne fell back against the railing of the walkway, her heart racing. Then recovering, she looked again. At first, she thought that it must have been her own reflection, but she was mistaken. As she approached the window once more, she saw that there was indeed someone there, probably, she thought with a surge of relief, one of the volunteers. She had no doubt drawn the short straw and had been sent down there to assist any stray visitors. She was even dressed in the style of the turn of the century, wearing a light brown traveling costume, the draped-over bodice forming a V-front, filled in by a high-necked cream-colored blouse and the long skirt narrowed from knee to ankle, accentuating the slender figure that seemed to shimmer in the heat. A dark brown velvet hat, decorated with cream-colored feathers perched atop her elegantly coiffured dark hair, completed the ensemble. A neat touch, Marianne thought, intended to lend an air of authenticity to the proceedings.

Marianne was about to acknowledge her presence when her arm, arrested in its motion, dropped to her side, and her heart gave another lurch. The woman seemed to glide towards Marianne, and as she did so, she lifted the hand that was pressed against her breast, revealing a dark, spreading stain. The sight of the blood that covered the palm of the woman's hand as she pressed it desperately against the dusty windowpane sent a chill through Marianne's bones.

All this happened in a matter of seconds, but it seemed as though everything was moving in slow motion. She must have had an accident or been attacked or...what? Whatever it was, Marianne had to get to her.

Without thinking to call Matthew for help and dropping all her precious photographic equipment on the boards, she climbed over the railing at the nearest entrance to the carriage and ran back along the car, stumbling over broken seats and fixtures in the gloom.

"Hello!" she shouted. "It's alright, I'm coming. Where are you?" The woman was no longer where she had been standing. Marianne hurried back and forth along the entire length of the carriage but could see no one. She was completely bewildered and, going back to where she had entered, climbed out again, looking up and down the path between the trains. All was as still and as silent as the grave.

She began to wonder if she had imagined the whole thing. Maybe the heat was finally getting to her, and she felt sheepishly thankful that there had been no other visitors in there to see her frantic scrambling. She did not even mention it to Matthew when, after retrieving her belongings, she found him reading another informational plaque at the exit. But something in her manner must have given him cause for concern, and putting his arm around her shoulder, he asked, "Are you alright, Annie? You look as though you'd seen a ghost."

"Yes, I'm okay, honestly. Just a little overcome with the heat. Why don't we go for that train ride now?" And not leaving him time to demur, she took his arm, and they strolled back down the path towards the station. But as they went, Marianne looked over her shoulder at the shed, expecting to see someone emerge. No one appeared, however, and she shook her head to try and clear away the image of that blood-stained hand.

Despite the sunny, blue sky, a cloud had passed over the day for her.

They paid for their train ride at the ticket booth and climbed aboard. Matthew, excited as a schoolboy, took in every detail of the brief excursion, commenting on the myriad fixtures and fittings of the carriage and pointing to a pheasant in a nearby field, preparing to fly off as they made their noisy approach. But Marianne couldn't concentrate. That scene in the shed kept playing over and over in her mind. Had she imagined it? Had there really been someone there? She would never forgive herself if she'd left the woman there alone, hurt and afraid, maybe to die, without doing anything for her. The images conjured up by her febrile imagination were beginning to make her head throb, and she fought to suppress the picture of that pitiful figure. *Oh, for goodness sake, stop*, she told herself. It was just the heat. But the more she tried, the less she was able to quell her anxiety.

The train continued on its way for another twenty minutes, the carriage jolting occasionally as they passed over crossings and points. Matthew, in his unremitting enthusiasm, kept up a steady stream of commentary at her side. From time to time, Marianne would nod absently and remark, "Interesting" or "Really?" until finally they pulled into the station once more, and the engine ground to a halt with a mighty blast of steam. Matthew helped his sister down the steps to the platform below, and they walked past the station building toward the souvenir shop.

Matthew stepped into the shop and she followed him mechanically, watching him as he happily browsed among the merchandise, picking out a t-shirt with the logo of the museum printed on the front, a colorful brochure with details of the museum's collection, and a selection from the rack that held the postcards. "Is there anything you'd like, dear?" he asked her.

"No, thanks, really." She patted her camera. "I've got all I need in here."

Having made his purchase, Matthew carefully put his wallet back in his pocket. He took the bag that the young woman handed to him along with an audaciously flirtatious smile, which he acknowledged and returned in his usual good-humored way. As they left, she called out to their retreating backs, "Thank you. Come back and see us again."

They were slowly making their way towards the car park when Marianne stopped and tugged at her brother's arm. "Oh, hold on a minute, Matthew. I've just thought of something. Wait here." She turned and ran back to the shop. The assistant looked enquiringly as she returned to the counter.

"I just wanted to ask you something," Marianne said breathlessly. "Do they ever have people working here in costume? You know the kind of thing, early 1900s dress?"

"No, but it's a good idea. This place could do with a bit of livening up if you ask me."

"Yes, well, thanks."

"Sure. Take care. Enjoy the rest of your day."

She rejoined Matthew. "I just wondered who does their photo work, for brochures and that. You know me. Always looking for a business opening. Not that it's really my kind of thing, but you never know when you might need to make a bit extra here and there."

They walked slowly back past the entrance booth, and as they went, Marianne found herself still wondering about Shed D. What had happened back there in that carriage? Had there really been someone there, or was she merely a figment of Marianne's imagination, a mirage conjured up by the heat of the day?

Matthew was talking to her, asking her something, but she hadn't heard. "Did you?" he was asking, as she just caught the tail end of his question.

"I'm sorry, Matthew. What?"

"Did you manage to get any good shots?" he repeated.

"Yes," she replied, trying desperately to shake off the strange feeling of having missed something, something important that she should have done, but hadn't.

When they got back to the car, Marianne slipped into the driver's seat and frantically tried to drag herself back into the present. Thankfully, Matthew seemed unaware of her distracted state and babbled cheerfully on. "I say, Annie, that was fun! Just like being a kid again. Thanks for bringing me here, dear. You'll be able to come again and get some more pictures when they have the festival in October."

"Possibly, although that's a busy time of year for me usually. I doubt I'll have time to come back again this year."

But as they drove away through the gates, she looked through the rear-view mirror, saw the sheds receding behind the clouds of dust that the car had thrown up, and knew with an inexplicable certainty that she would be returning there soon.

9

SLEEPLESS NIGHTS

AS ATTUNED AS THEY WERE TO EACH OTHER'S MOODS AND FANCIES, it didn't take Vincent long to realize that something had happened during that last day of Matthew's visit and naturally assumed that, despite his apparent liking for him, Matthew had lodged some objection to their relationship. The subject was not broached, however, until Matthew departed for home.

That evening they sat together in companionable silence; Wyndham's music, *The Honfleur Suite*, was playing softly in the background. Vincent was at his desk writing notes on a forthcoming lecture, the lamplight highlighting his unruly blonde hair, and Marianne was curled up on the sofa, reading Hardy's *The Return of the Native*, when Vincent stopped what he was doing and turned to her.

"So, did I pass the test, do think?" His manner was partly jesting, and yet there was a note of genuine concern in his voice.

"Oh yes, absolutely," she replied with conviction. "I'm certain of it. He thinks you're wonderful," she added, getting up and going over to him, "and so do I." Marianne stood behind his chair and put her arms around him. "He said only good things about you."

"It's just that you seemed a bit preoccupied today. I just wondered … if things hadn't gone quite the way you hoped."

She never kept any secrets from Vincent. They told each other their most intimate thoughts and yet she was strangely reluctant to tell him about the episode at the museum, perhaps because she didn't want him to worry needlessly about her health or, heaven forbid, her sanity. Upon further reflection, it had seemed rather like the imaginings of someone who was emotionally unbalanced, and she was in some sense ashamed of that momentary lapse in her rationality. Thus, she mentioned to him in passing the eerily cold sensation that she had felt when she'd seen the man with the dog outside Lucy's house. He seemed rather troubled by it at the time.

"Trust me, you were an enormous hit, and I'm fine. It's just that ... well, no, it's too stupid for words. The more I think about it..." she shook her head and gave his shoulders a squeeze. She ruffled his hair and returned to the sofa, but he followed her, unwilling to let the matter rest.

"What is it, Marianne?" He never shortened her name to Annie as Matthew and the others did, but always called her Marianne. "Tell me." His face held a look of concern, and as he knelt down in front of her, his hands reaching up to touch her, she capitulated and told him what had happened.

"It's silly, I know," she finished, "And I'm sure it must have been the weather. It was unbelievably hot in that shed, but I can't seem to stop thinking about it."

She did not really know what she was expecting him to say. She hoped that he would laugh and tell her not to be so fanciful or dismiss it impatiently as something not worthy of further discussion, but his reply came as something of a surprise.

"Darling, why didn't you tell me about this right away? It must have scared the hell out of you." He sat beside her and held her close to him.

"I don't know. I didn't know what you'd think of me. It seems so senseless, looking at it in the cold light of day, but at the time it was so weird."

"And you're sure there was no-one there? You couldn't have missed her in one of the compartments?"

"No, I looked everywhere and outside too. Besides, I think Matthew would have noticed her if she'd gone past him."

He appeared thoughtful for a moment, and then, seeming to reach a decision, he said softly, "I'm sure it was nothing. You're probably right about it being the heat. Don't let it worry you anymore." He pulled her closer, kissed her slowly, and then more passionately. In the ecstasy of the following hours, the apparition of the Railway Woman, as Marianne had secretly dubbed her, was temporarily banished from her thoughts.

But in the silence of the night, as they lay together, asleep in bed, a nightmare came to shatter her fragile peace of mind. A terrible vision, the woman on the train, staring out of the window, her face deathly white, her eyes pleading desperately for help. Her bloody hands reaching towards her seemed to penetrate the glass barrier between them as though through a curtain of smoke, and she grasped Marianne's wrists in an icy grip.

She woke with a start, drenched in perspiration, her heart beating wildly. She looked about her but could make out nothing of her surroundings. Everything was still. There were no phantasms lurking in the darkness. She turned on her side and reached over to Vincent, who was still sleeping soundly beside her. Not wanting to disturb him, she put her arm gently around him and, drawing closer, sought protection from his nearness, and eventually, she drifted back into an uneasy sleep.

But the dream re-visited her on the next night and for many nights thereafter, until she dreaded the unwelcome onset of sleep and postponed the evil moment for as long as she possibly could, until exhaustion and an overpowering feeling of depression began to take a toll on her health and reason.

Vincent watched her with anxiety during those days but said nothing. Then one morning after a particularly restless night, he looked at her across the breakfast table and said, "This can't go on, Marianne! We've got to do something…about the dreams."

She looked startled. She dreaded any suggestion that he might make about 'seeing someone' in order to delve into the explanations for these nocturnal horrors. She made to get up, but he reached for her arm and held her there.

"I know you don't want to make a big thing of this, but it's obviously getting out of hand. I'm not suggesting you go to a psychiatrist or anything like that, but … we've got to do something." He paused as though searching for the right words. "Would you be willing to try an experiment?" he asked cautiously. He looked at her anxiously, but she trusted him so completely that there was never any question that she would agree.

"Why don't we go back there, to the museum?" His words brought a momentary wave of panic, but he went on hurriedly. "It won't be easy for you, I know, but I thought if you could go there again and see for yourself that there was nothing there. We could even make discreet enquiries, find out if anything has happened there recently. Please, Marianne, let's try it. I'm sure it would help."

He waited for her reply, and although it filled her with a sense of dread, she said in a whisper, "Alright."

He gave her hand a grateful squeeze as she again rose to trail slowly back to the bedroom in order to dress and face the day.

That evening, Jonathan Amor, Vincent's colleague at the university, and his wife Lisa called for them at the apartment. Vincent had made plans to go out to dinner with them, the arrangements being made well before Marianne's nocturnal visitor had become such a problem. He suggested putting them off, but Marianne was adamant.

"No. It will do me good to have an evening out. Jonathan and Lisa are good company, and we really have got into rather a rut since all this railway thing started. Honestly, I'll be alright. I'm looking forward to it."

They went to the restaurant that she and Vincent had visited on their first date together and spent a convivial evening, and although Marianne felt physically drained, she relished the mental stimulation that such intelligent conversation provided. Politics and religion were taboo subjects, Vincent and Jonathan long ago agreeing to disagree on such controversial topics, but everything else was fair game for Jon's dry wit and Vincent's logical mind. And when they became embroiled in a deep and theoretical confabulation about some obscure subject during dessert, Lisa and Marianne turned their attention to more feminine matters such as the latest fashions and the best places to shop for eye make-up.

"What does Ivan think about the clothes for the coming season?"

Lisa always set great store by what Ivan thought, mistakenly in Marianne's opinion, because she didn't think he was really an expert on such matters. He only knew how to make the things look good in print. He didn't really care what the models were wearing and couldn't tell the garments of one fashion house from another.

Marianne told her about the latest collection that he had worked on, fabrics, skirt lengths, colors, and the like, carefully omitting the more obscene comments that he had made as he posed his models and fussed over the drapes and folds of the various dresses and outfits.

Lisa, who owned her own beauty spa in a well-to-do neighborhood, always appreciated being given the inside track on the latest fashions. They discussed at some length the attributes of her latest hair stylist, who she thought could do wonders for Marianne if she would care to visit the salon at any time.

"Not that there's anything wrong with the way you've got it done now," she added hastily, correcting any impression of adverse criticism. "But you've been looking a bit down just lately, and sometimes a new hair-do can perk you up no end. There isn't anything wrong between you and Vincent is there?" she asked as an afterthought, bending her head towards the other woman confidentially.

"No," Marianne prevaricated. "I've just had a busy work schedule the last few weeks. We could probably use a vacation."

This conversational opening prompted a story from Lisa about her and Jon's latest trip to Tuscany. As usual, the story was augmented by humorous observations from Jonathan who described in some detail their unexpectedly less-than-luxurious accommodations and the embarrassing circumstances surrounding his inadvertent entry into the wrong hotel room, catching the current occupant in a somewhat compromising position with one of the maids.

After dinner, the two couples went back to the apartment for a nightcap. Vincent was showing Lisa a book that he had recently purchased at an antique store in Swannington, when Jon, looking at Marianne rather disconcertingly, said, "Lisa's right. You have been looking a tad peaky just lately. Are you feeling alright, Annie?"

"Thanks for the concern, Jon, but I'm fine, really. I was telling Lisa this evening, I've been pretty busy just lately, that's all. We need a vacation."

"Quite right. Get Vincent to take you away somewhere when he has his next break. Do you both the world of good."

"Yes, we'll have to see what we can manage."

Vincent and Lisa rejoined them, and Jon said. "I told Annie you two should go away somewhere on your next break, Vincent. She needs something to bring the roses back into her cheeks."

"Yes, she's been under a bit of a strain lately," Vincent agreed, and Marianne thought for one horrible minute that he was going to tell them about the Railway Woman. For an instant, her eyes, wide in alarm, met his in silent warning.

"Heavy workload," he continued, and she let out a quiet sigh of relief. "You know what it's like. She's got her own stuff to do, and then Ivan expects her to help with his set-ups. Really darling, you should put your foot down and tell him to figure it out for himself."

"Oh, I couldn't do that. I don't mind really." Then, to change the subject, Marianne said, "Did I tell you that I saw Lucy the other day? Lucy Rowe or Welbourne now, of course. She had her little girl with her. Robin, I think she said her name was."

"Lucy Rowe? That name rings a bell for some reason," Amor said thoughtfully.

"Marianne used to room with Lucy in Birchford," Vincent informed him. "Didn't you teach in Birchford at one time?" he asked Amor, who suddenly recollected where he had heard the name.

"Yes, for my sins. I subbed as a music teacher for a year while I was working on my PhD. I remember Lucy Rowe." Amor recalled the time when he had taken Lucy under his wing and, he remembered, that other girl too. "What was her name? Oh, yes!" he recalled. "Rose Cooper, whose father murdered the policeman in Birchford and had been one of the last people to be hanged for his crime. A sad business."

The topic of conversation then changed to other things, and the rest of the evening passed pleasantly enough. But as Jon and Lisa were leaving, Lisa gave Marianne a hug and said, "Take care of yourself now, Annie. You really do need to take a break."

Marianne's lassitude and general appearance did not go unnoticed at the studio either.

"Are you unwell, Annie?" Ivan asked her with an uncharacteristic look of solicitude one morning after a particularly distressing night when her dreams seemed so distinct that she was beginning to have difficulty separating them from reality.

"Just a bit under the weather. Probably a cold coming on."

Ivan immediately backed away in alarm.

"Don't worry. I'm sure it's nothing catching." Marianne assured him.

"You should go see a doctor."

"No. I told you, it's nothing."

"Well, all the same. You should take care of yourself." He continued to look at her, and she could see a thought gradually forming in his mind as he said with horror, "My God! You're not pregnant, are you?"

"No, Ivan!" she said with a touch of asperity. "I'm not pregnant."

"Because if you are—" he continued as if he hadn't heard her.

"Ivan! Are you listening to me? I'm not pregnant. But if I was, would it be such a terrible thing?"

He didn't reply, but she could tell by the look on his face that as far as he was concerned, it would have been catastrophic.

"Well, don't worry, I'm not."

She hadn't told him about the dreams or anything relating to the episode at the museum, knowing that he would probably make light of the whole thing, but she felt a little guilty for withholding the truth when he seemed so genuinely concerned over her health. Or was it that he was just looking out for his own well-being? Either way, she couldn't bring herself to tell him the real reason for her increasingly haggard appearance.

To give the impression that everything was fine, she worked twice as hard that week and positively ran herself into the ground, dashing about with zealous determination in an effort to convince herself and everyone else that there was absolutely nothing wrong with Marianne Clay.

10

A Brief Encounter

It was agreed that Vincent and Marianne would make the journey back to the railway museum that Sunday. After a week of sunny weather, the day dawned, perversely, dreary and wet. They set out in silence, both deep in their own thoughts. Vincent glanced over at Marianne occasionally as he drove the dark blue Lexus through the rain. She studiously avoided his gaze, looking out at the scenery as it flashed by. After a while, he seemed to feel the need to say something, anything to break the silence.

"Are you sure you're alright with this, Marianne?" He sounded doubtful.

"No. Of course I'm not alright with it!" she snapped back. She immediately regretted her words. "I'm sorry. I didn't mean to sound brusque. I'm scared to death, but you're probably right. I should face my fears. We need to do this and get it over with. We'll probably laugh about all this in the future and wonder why on earth we made such a fuss about it."

"Yes, no doubt."

Traffic was minimal, and without making the various detours that she and Matthew had taken on their previous visit, they arrived all too soon at their destination.

As they entered the parking lot, it was evident that the weather had thus far kept most visitors away. There were only two other vehicles parked close to the gates. Vincent pulled in alongside them.

He turned off the engine and reached into the back seat to retrieve the large black umbrella that he kept as protection against the elements on his long treks from the parking lot to his rooms at the University. He walked around to help Marianne out. Closing the door behind her, he put his arm around her shoulders and held the open umbrella over their heads, rather in the manner of the knight with his shining lance in the Gurvich painting.

The girl who had served Matthew in the gift shop was now doing a stint in the ticket booth. "Hello again," she said as she recognized Marianne. "Lovely weather for ducks." She looked at Vincent, who smiled weakly and replied, "Yes. We didn't pick a very good day."

Marianne felt faintly embarrassed. First Matthew and now Vincent. The girl must be wondering at this string of gentlemen friends that she was bringing to the museum. Having paid their entrance fee, they were about to walk away when the girl called after them, "Oh, by the way, I told Mr. Brimley."

"I'm sorry. What?" Marianne stepped back under the awning.

"You know. Your idea about having people dressed in period costume. He loved it! He said we might even have a special day when visitors could dress up too."

At any other time, Marianne might have been flattered that she had prompted such a response to her comment, but now she could only think of one thing. Giving a nod and muttering, "Great!" she and Vincent hurried away through the increasing downpour towards shed D.

Marianne hesitated as they reached the entrance to the cavernous structure, but Vincent, with gentle yet insistent pressure, would not allow her to turn back. He closed the umbrella, shaking the raindrops from its folds, and they stepped over the threshold, making their way to the last row of carriages.

Vincent mounted the steps ahead of Marianne and reached down encouragingly to help her ascend. He held her hand firmly as they made their way along the walkway, inching inexorably toward what, they could not tell. The rain drummed noisily on the metal roof overhead, and a flash of lightning lit up the interior of the shed. This was followed by an ominous rumble and a sudden crash of thunder.

They had got as far as the cubicle that held the washstand when a cold and insidious wave seemed to flood over Marianne. She knew with undeniable certainty that the woman would be there. They took one more step, and her fingers bit into the flesh of Vincent's arm as she let out a horrified gasp.

There, in the compartment, just as before, was the solitary figure of the Railway Woman, standing by the window, the agony plain upon her face, her hand raised in supplication and an ominous patch of blood staining the material of her gown about her breast.

Oh my God! What horror was this? And yet, incomprehensibly, Vincent couldn't see her.

"Look! Look there!" Marianne pointed with a shaking finger at the apparition so clearly visible to her.

Without wasting another second, Vincent shouted, "Wait here! Don't move!" He left her and sprinted back to the carriage door, vaulted over the barrier, and disappeared into the interior of the train. In less than a minute he appeared. Just for an infinitesimal fraction of a second, Marianne saw the two of them, Vincent, dimly outlined in the compartment, and the woman, closer, pressing her bloody hands against the window. Then, as suddenly as an extinguished light, she vanished, and Vincent rushed forward, looking out at Marianne with an expression of wild consternation. Her confused brain could stand no more—she collapsed in a heap onto the wooden planking.

When she came to, Vincent was kneeling beside her, cradling her in his arms.

"I'm sorry! I'm so sorry, my darling. I should never have brought you back here. How could I have been so stupid? Can you stand? We've got to get you out of here."

He helped Marianne to her feet and, careful to shield her from the prospect of looking at that window again, he led her back along the walkway and into the fresh air outside.

The rain was still falling heavily, and they made their way hurriedly back along the path toward the little waiting room that formed part of the train station. Thankfully, it was empty, and they sank down on one of the green-painted wooden benches. Now that the shock of the moment had subsided, Marianne was desperate to know what had happened.

"Didn't you see her?" she asked in disbelief. He shook his head and looked apologetic as if he had failed her in some way.

"But that doesn't mean that you didn't." He looked steadfastly into her eyes. "I truly believe you saw her. There's no doubt. It's the strangest thing. Are you alright?"

"Yes, I think so." And indeed, she felt amazingly calm now. Somehow, the paralyzing fear that had defeated her just moments before had left her, and only a feeling of puzzlement remained.

"I know she was there," she said insistently. "She was as real and as close to me as you are now." She stood up decisively. "I've got to go back! She's trying to tell me something, Vincent. I have to find out what she wants!"

She made to leave, but he pulled her back and held her tightly against him. Pressing his face against her hair, he whispered vehemently, "No, I'm not letting you go in there again. That's enough!"

She struggled against him momentarily, but his embrace was so powerful that she could not break free. She sank against his chest in surrender.

"Let's go home, my sweet," he said softly.

Without further resistance, she allowed him to lead her back to the car through the rain, which had now increased to a positive deluge. Flashes of lightning filled the skies and thunder continued to rumble all around them. In all the confusion they had somehow managed to leave the umbrella behind and were forced to run unprotected through the downpour. He opened the door and helped her to get in, then hurried around the front of the car towards the driver's side. As he did so, she noticed that he gave a fleeting glance back towards the direction of shed D. His expression was perplexed, a frown creasing his forehead.

When he got in, they sat looking at each other, both soaked to the skin, and, despite the heat of the day, she shivered involuntarily. He reached to turn the keys in the ignition and with almost frightening speed, reversed the vehicle out of its space and, slamming it into gear, sped away through the gates back onto the road to Swannington.

They said little during the time it took to reach home, Vincent merely repeating that he was sorry for having taken her back there.

"It's not your fault. We both agreed that it was the right thing to do. I don't know what's happening, but there must be a logical explanation somewhere."

Reaction to what had transpired was finally beginning to catch up to her, and she realized that her stomach was churning and a wave of nausea was steadily rising in her throat.

"Stop the car! Pull over! I have to throw up!" she said, desperately trying to hold everything in until she was outside the car.

Vincent swerved to the shoulder, causing the person in the vehicle behind them to blast his horn. Marianne threw open the door almost before the car had come to a halt and tumbled out, retching and gasping. Vincent followed and helplessly stood by her as the rain beat steadily down on them until she felt that she could safely continue the journey and staggered weakly back to the car.

After they pulled back onto the highway, he kept glancing over at her, and, to alleviate the tension that seemed to be building by the moment, he switched on the radio. The well-modulated voice of a broadcaster was reading the news; something about Prime Minister Margaret Thatcher opening a Nissan car factory in Sunderland and an update on a Pan Am flight from Bombay that had been hijacked earlier in the month with resulting fatalities. The news always seemed so grim, Marianne thought, leaning back against the headrest.

The next piece of news hit closer to home: a high-speed rail collision involving two packed express trains in Staffordshire with, miraculously, only one dead. The mention of trains prompted Vincent to immediately turn the radio off, while Marianne closed her eyes and feigned sleep for the remainder of the journey. She knew that Vincent blamed himself for the outcome of their expedition, but she was also well aware that no words from her would convince him otherwise, and as much as she yearned to relieve his anxiety, it seemed pointless to try.

What to do? They couldn't just forget that all this ever happened, and even if she wanted to, Marianne felt a strange presentiment that the Railway

Woman wouldn't let her. She could tell that Vincent was badly shaken by what had occurred back at the museum. *Think!* Think what was best to be done. She wracked her brain to try and solve the problem, but by the time they reached home, she was not yet resolved upon a course of action.

After Vincent parked the car in the private lot reserved for their apartment building, they made their way through the first-floor lobby, cursorily acknowledging the friendly greeting of the concierge sitting behind his desk. Marianne thought they must have presented a sorry sight as they hurried toward the elevator, looking so wretchedly bedraggled.

Vincent pressed the button impatiently several times as they waited for the summons to be answered, and eventually the doors slid open. An elderly couple stepped out, an immediate look of recognition on their faces as Vincent stood aside to allow them to pass, but he was in no mood for casual conversation, and he quickly ushered Marianne past them and into the elevator.

"Hello, Vincent, Annie! How are you?" the woman enquired as the couple turned, but before Marianne could answer, the doors were already closing, and she was left with a brief glimpse of the woman's face, surprised and offended by their brusque departure.

As they ascended, she looked up at Vincent. Squeezing his hand, she said softly, "It's over, darling. Don't worry about it anymore. It's finished." He made to reply, but she pressed her finger gently against his lips to silence him. The elevator sighed to a halt, the doors parted, and they made their way along the thickly carpeted passageway. He fumbled momentarily with the key to the door but recovering, turned it in the lock, and pushing the door open, allowed her to precede him into the vestibule.

Marianne went directly to the bedroom to change out of the clothes that were still clinging damply about her. He followed and, closing the door, went over to her and began to peel away her rain-soaked garments. "Let me do that," he commanded, and she gratefully allowed his sensuous hands to caress her skin as he did so. His touch, as always, was the magic antidote to all her ills, and she surrendered to his passion, forgetting, momentarily, the strange events that had unfolded a few hours earlier.

11

A LITTLE RESEARCH

THE ENSUING DAYS PASSED, much as usual. Before departing for the University, Vincent lingered a little longer over his morning coffee, seeming reluctant to cut short their time together.

Marianne, meanwhile, filled the hours with routine shooting sessions at various locations interspersed with days spent in the studio poring over prints for numerous publications. She took the occasional portraits for wealthy socialites who knew and liked her work, although they were sometimes put out by her insistence that, "Sorry, I don't work with children." She just didn't have the temperament for it. She could never perform the clowning required to get a toddler to look into the camera and smile, which was usually the kind of thing the client wanted. The best pictures she'd ever taken of youngsters were the candid photos that she had captured of Clare's daughters when they were babies. Unaware that she was lurking in the background with a zoom lens, they behaved naturally, and the resulting shots were, in turn, poignant and hysterically funny. Later, Clare had them sit for regular portrait work, and the results were horrendous, false smiles and grimaces that gave satisfaction to neither mother nor photographer.

Marianne, herself, made a poor subject for portrait photography and refused to sit when Vincent had asked for a picture of her. It wasn't that she was unattractive; when she made the effort to appear at her best, her looks were quite striking with her chestnut hair and green eyes. Marianne just could not bring herself to smile on command.

"No! Don't grin like that, Annie! You look like a Cheshire cat," Ivan had told her on the only occasion that he'd tried to take a portrait of her. She stuck out her tongue at him, and they had both laughed uproariously while Ivan captured the moment, the resulting black and white pictures, now hanging on the studio wall, natural and unposed.

Vincent called Marianne several times during the day at the studio to make sure that she was alright, which although considerate of him, was not always convenient and on more than one occasion evinced a snort of ill-concealed annoyance from Ivan. Nevertheless, she did not have the heart to admonish Vincent, for no matter how ill-timed his calls were, it always thrilled her to hear his voice.

But despite the return to a normal daily working routine, the nights remained, for Marianne, haunted by the nocturnal specter of the Railway Woman. Strangely, however, the prospect no longer terrified her as it had done in the beginning, and as time went on, she found herself willing the woman to return in the small hours in the hopes that the reason for her continued manifestation would reveal itself.

Sometimes in her desperation to find the answer to the mystery, she was the one to reach out through the window to the phantom woman and grasp her icy wrists. The dreams never lasted long enough, however, and the answer remained elusive.

Vincent, meanwhile, maintained a discreet vigilance over her, constantly watchful for signs that her ghostly companion had finally relinquished her hold on Marianne. From time to time, they sat and talked about her, now that the subject was no longer the traumatic issue that it had once been, and their mutual curiosity in this strange phenomenon finally spurred Vincent into further action.

One Sunday in mid-September he informed Marianne that he had arranged to meet Jonathan Amor for lunch to discuss the possible collaboration on a book that Vincent was considering writing. Marianne wanted to catch up on some of the paperwork involved in her day-to-day work, so they parted in the morning to pursue their various activities.

When Vincent returned to the apartment later in the afternoon, he was carrying an armful of books, pamphlets, and the like. He smiled sheepishly and said, "I thought I'd go and find my umbrella. Would you believe it? It was still lying on the walkway." He held it up triumphantly and then tossed it aside, advancing into the room. "Jon had to cancel our meeting. He said he tried calling here, but I'd already left."

"I'm sorry," Marianne said. "I must have missed the call. I went out for a walk."

"That's alright. He called the café and left a message for me," Vincent explained, trying to sound as casual as possible. He laid the stack down on the coffee table and sat beside her on the sofa, giving her a kiss on the cheek. "Fancy doing a little research?"

She laughed. "What a sneaky thing you are."

That evening after dinner they sat down to begin their task and, reaching over to retrieve the leaflet on top of the pile, Marianne saw that it was a brochure from the museum. It detailed hours of operation, dates of special interest, and a plan of the grounds, including the placement of the tracks, the little station, and the sheds. It was in these, and in particular the one designated with a D, that their interests centered.

It was marked as containing cars awaiting restoration, which certainly would explain their state of dilapidation and the reason why so few people had bothered to go in there. There was no further useful information, however, and they moved on to the next pamphlet, which looked more promising.

This yielded a detailed description of the contents of all the sheds, including shed D. They turned to its designated page and began to read.

Vincent went down the list, skipping over the numerous descriptions of the cars they had seen until he came to the one that he thought was relevant.

"Exhibit 195 - Great Eastern Railway. Carriage with toilet cubicle built in 1890 and dining car built in 1899."

The places listed as stops on its old route meant little to either of them, from its point of departure in Norwich to its destination at Liverpool Street

Station in London. Vincent, reading them aloud, looked enquiringly at Marianne as he named each one, but none of them rang a bell until he came to the name Sterling.

"That's it!" Marianne exclaimed. Something had occurred there. What was it? She searched her memory, trying to think back. Why had that name sounded so familiar?

And then she remembered. Several weeks before she had moved in with Vincent, they had taken a ride out into the country, a brief respite from their daily routines. They had no special plans but drove about aimlessly through villages and farmland, enjoying the day and taking pleasure as they always did in each other's company. They stopped at a quaint little restaurant for lunch, where they formulated a route by which they would return home.

The car was running low on fuel, necessitating a detour through an area likely to offer a suitable petrol station, and so they had alighted on Sterling.

A once flourishing town, it had fallen by the wayside. Time and a shift in economic fortunes had left it struggling for survival. "For Sale" signs sprang up outside numerous local businesses that had been abandoned many years before. The once thriving heart of Sterling was now a feeble shadow of its former self. It was evident that some areas had, at one time, been home to the more well-to-do members of the community. The huge old houses, once magnificent, were now mostly shabby boarding houses. They were run down and neglected, paintwork peeling, roof shingles missing, and once carefully tended gardens overgrown and strewn with litter.

One street in particular seemed completely devoid of any human presence. Several large houses looked as though they had been deserted for decades. Most of the windows, like so many sightless eyes, were either broken or boarded up, and once elegant front doors hung drunkenly on their twisted hinges.

As they drove slowly past them, Marianne felt a sudden urge to capture the image of these abandoned buildings and asked Vincent to stop so that she could get out of the car and take a few shots. Always willing to humor her creative urges, he pulled up and, gathering together her camera and equipment bag, things that she never traveled anywhere without, Marianne walked back alone along the empty street.

The first house, a large box-like structure, had at one time been painted a most hideous shade of light blue with dark blue trim. Marianne decided not to waste time on this but took one shot just for the record. The house beyond that, although somewhat older, had at various times been saddled with additions, giving the whole an unauthentic appearance of mismatched miscellany.

Another was aesthetically easier on the eye, although clearly older than the preceding two. Of faded, white painted brick, with a portico supported by two large columns, it was irrevocably in the final stages of decay. It cried out to be saved, but Marianne doubted if anyone would think it worth the expense. It would cost a small fortune to restore it to its original glory.

The last house was not clearly visible at first, the overgrown shrubbery shielding it from view as she walked toward it, but as she drew nearer, she could see that this was no ordinary dwelling even by the standards set by its neighbors. It was far larger than the others, more imposing, and yet had not been spared, for all its one-time splendor, the ravages of time. Marianne peered through a gap in the hedge and looked at the crumbling facade. The two-story house of Italianate architecture was, she guessed, built sometime in the early 1800s. The white painted bricks were dingy and badly in need of tuck-pointing. The black shutters were rotting in place, and large patches of mold could clearly be seen about the eves where years of inclement weather had taken their toll. Marianne felt a sense of profound sadness as she raised the camera and focusing in on the rotting and worm-eaten wood of the half-open door, she began to take picture after picture.

She only intended to stop there briefly, but the subject had so much to offer that she could not tear herself away. It was as though she was becoming mesmerized by the scene, and lowering the camera, she just stood there staring, a most peculiar sensation of being held there by some invisible force.

The moment was broken as Vincent, getting out of the car, had walked back to find her and called out a little impatiently, "We better get going." She ran back, guiltily conscious that she had completely forgotten his existence for that brief space of time, yet feeling satisfied that she had probably got some good material that could be stored away for future use.

The memory faded as Marianne became aware that Vincent was looking at her as though he too remembered Sterling.

"I remember it now," he said. "Where you took the pictures of those old houses."

"Yes, that's right," she replied. "And I know you'll think it's crazy, but there was something about that place."

"I know. I had to practically drag you away. I thought it was because you had found some promising shots, but you weren't even taking pictures. You were just standing there."

"I did use up one roll of film on it. The pictures are in the studio, but you're right. It was the strangest feeling, as though something was holding me there."

"I wonder—" he began, but she already knew what he was going to say and finished the thought.

"Perhaps we could go over to the studio and find the pictures? I haven't seen them since they were first developed, and I think they may well be worth a second look."

And, despite the lateness of the hour, they threw on light jackets, Vincent collected the car keys, and they made their way hurriedly down to the car park.

The trip across town was brief—the streets seemed eerily deserted at that late hour—and finding a parking space was considerably easier than during the turmoil of regular business hours. Vincent pulled in at the curb just a few yards from the entrance to the building that housed the studio. Marianne produced the two keys needed to gain access and they climbed the stairs to the second floor.

Entering, Vincent flipped the switch by the door, and the studio was instantly bathed in light. All the usual paraphernalia stood about, a confusing jumble of cameras, diffusing screens, reflectors, spotlights, and floodlights mounted on sturdy tripods. A container inexpertly constructed by Ivan in a burst of do-it-yourself enthusiasm, mounted against one wall, held large rolls of multi-colored background paper, and a table that served as a stand for still life shots also bore a light box for viewing slides.

Ivan's jacket lay draped carelessly across the wheeled cart used to ferry film, filters, lenses, and other small items, but he was not there in the studio; nor did Marianne expect him to be. He was probably at home in bed with Irina by now. She knew that he and Irina planned earlier to attend a production of Chekhov's *The Cherry Orchard*, put on by a local amateur dramatics group at the little theater on Barnaby Street. That would probably be followed by a meal at Ivan's favorite eating place. This surly Russian exile was still fiercely loyal to his country's culture and cuisine, despite having abandoned his homeland with much difficulty many years before.

A doorway at the far end of the room led to another, smaller room where shelves were ranged around the walls holding box upon box of prints, the labels thereon denoting their various categories. The container, marked Locations S-T, was on a shelf too high for Marianne's five-foot three-inch frame to reach, but Vincent, spurning a proffered step stool, had no such trouble and grasped the required file easily. He took it down and carried it to a table in the center of the room. Pushing it across to her, he watched as she quickly opened the metal clasp that held the lid secure.

"Salisbury ... Seymour ... Spurgis ...," Marianne read the names aloud. Each set of pictures and their corresponding negatives were enclosed in a manila envelope. "Stanbury ... Sterling! Here it is." She extracted the envelope and tipped its contents onto the table, while Vincent turned on the lamp, which incorporated a large magnifying glass, and swung it into position over the photos.

Marianne fanned them out on the surface of the table and looked closely at the glossy 8x10 prints laid out before them.

A shot taken from the end of the road showed an overall picture of the scene that contained the remnants that had once been family homes but which were now reduced to stark and deserted shells. Subsequent views presented the exteriors of the individual buildings, each one different but having in common the same abandoned and neglected look about them.

The bulk of the pictures were those of the house at the farther end of the street, the one that she had stood before in that almost trance-like state. She moved the magnifying lens closer and took in every detail. The cupola that rose from the tiled roof, built to ventilate the home in hot weather, stood sentinel over the house and grounds.

Yes, there was something about that place. She could feel it, even now. Looking intently at the last picture in the pile, Marianne again seemed to be drawn to it by that invisible thread and gave an involuntary start as Vincent touched her shoulder

"Can I see?" he asked, leaning over to take a closer look at the pictures.

After scrutinizing them for several minutes, he asked, "What do you think? Could there be some connection?"

She considered for a moment, then answered, "I'm almost positive that there is. It's hard to explain that odd feeling I got when I was standing in front of the house and now, seeing it again in the picture."

He gathered up the prints and slid them back into the envelope. "Let's take these with us. You've had enough for one day. You need some sleep. We'll go home now, and as soon as we both have a free day, we'll go back to Sterling and take another look at this place."

They returned to the apartment with the hope that they would find further clues that would reveal the identity of the Railway Woman.

For the first time in the two months since her initial visit to the museum, Marianne slept undisturbed. It was as though the ghastly specter was satisfied that she had fulfilled her part of the mission and was now leaving the rest up to Marianne.

12
THE HOUSE AT THE END OF THE STREET

COMMITMENTS TO THEIR RESPECTIVE JOBS kept them close to home for the next two weeks. Marianne had been commissioned to do some work for a museum on a brochure for an upcoming exhibit featuring a display of jewelry. Vincent was teaching classes and working on his book.

On the last Thursday in September, they finally managed to get away. Vincent called for Marianne at the studio where she had been putting the finishing touches to some work she had done earlier in the week. Ivan was there too, preparing for a shoot that he was doing the following day, and he greeted Vincent in the forced and blatantly insincere manner that he had adopted towards him almost since their first meeting.

"Vincent! You are looking excellent today! Annie! I am desolate that you are leaving me." He clutched melodramatically at his chest and then yelled at the top of his voice, "Irina! Here is Annie's charming companion!"

Irina, who had been hidden from their view in the office, came out, a warm smile illuminating her small, pale, heart-shaped face. It wasn't hard to see how she had won Ivan's undying affection. She was a beautiful woman. Her flawless complexion, blond hair, and large blue eyes were only a part of her dazzling allure. How different from Ivan she was, in so many respects. She was always so calm and serene, even in the face of some of his most tempestuous outbursts.

"Vincent! I'm so glad you're here." She came over and embraced him with the customary kiss on both cheeks. "Perhaps now you will settle an argument. Ivan thinks I should go with him to California next week, but I cannot get away from work. He doesn't understand. I can't just leave. I would lose my job."

Irina worked at the children's hospital as some kind of liaison between the medical and office staff. Marianne never fully understood her exact position but she had accompanied Irina once when she went there during her off-duty hours to visit some of the more seriously ill patients one Christmas. Marianne was immediately impressed by the rapport Irina seemed to have with the young ones. It was evident that they loved her, and her presence lit up their faces as much as the gifts that she had so generously brought them.

How tragic that if Ivan had his way, she would never have children of her own. How much she must have loved him to concede this most basic instinct in a woman. Marianne could tell, however, that her work at the hospital, a shadowy substitute for the family she was denied, was not to be taken lightly, and she thought even Ivan realized that she would not willingly give it up. Maybe he felt he owed her at least that. But it didn't stop him from testing her every once in a while, making demands that he really didn't expect her to accept.

"Then lose it! I want you with me!"

"But I don't want to lose it! Vanya, be reasonable. I love my work." She looked at them for support.

Marianne was always reluctant to get into the middle of these periodic arguments, not wanting to offend either side, but she was bound to agree with Irina. "Surely, Ivan, you don't really expect her to give up her job just to come with you. You'll only be away for a week."

"Of course, you would agree with her. You women are all the same. Very well! I can see you have no desire to be with me. Clear off! Go! Leave!" He threw his arm in a wild gesture toward the door and glowered at Irina, who, with utmost calm, collected her purse and jacket and shepherded Vincent and Marianne out of the studio with a phlegmatic, "He'll get over it. He always does."

They descended the stairs as Vincent shook his head in baffled incomprehension. "Why do you put up with him, Irina?"

"That's simple," she laughed. "I love him. What can one do? He is like a little boy. His tantrums are soon over and quickly forgotten. We will be making love tonight as we do every night. He will go to California alone, and I will be waiting here for him when he returns and so it goes on."

They emerged from the building and Marianne turned to hug Irina. "You're amazing! But I think I understand. I wouldn't have the patience, but you are so right for Ivan, and he loves you with every beat of his wicked heart. Bless you both," she told her friend, and they parted, Irina to go home to wait for the penitent lover's return and Marianne and Vincent to pursue their own inescapable destiny.

They made their way out of the city, heading toward Sterling with only a vague recollection of the whereabouts of the house, but certain that once they got there, they would easily recognize the area again.

The weather was cool and sunny, small white clouds dotting the blue sky. The trees had only just begun their transformation to autumn colors and most clung defiantly to the last vestiges of their verdant summer glory. As they got further into the countryside, they passed fields now stripped of their bounty and, here and there, groups of black and white cows standing idly about chewed nonchalantly as they watched them pass by.

After some time, they began to see the name of Sterling on the signposts at intervals along the roadside, and eventually, they reached the outskirts of the town. It had changed little since they were there last. Nothing had come to rescue it from its inevitable slide into obscurity, and the streets appeared as they had before, deserted and forlorn.

Vincent followed their previous route as best as he could remember it, but there was no sign of the houses in the photos that Marianne had brought with her and that were now resting on her lap. With a sinking feeling, the thought occurred to her that the buildings may have already been demolished, but upon further reflection, it hardly seemed likely, as there was no sign of any recent effort at rehabilitation in the area. After a few minutes, they reached the other side of town, and Vincent pulled the car into the petrol station where they had stopped on their first visit there.

"Give me the pictures. I'll see if they recognize anything." He left the car running as he gathered up the photos and walked purposefully over to the cashier's booth at the center of the station. He returned momentarily and maneuvered the car around the pumps, back in the direction of the town center.

"We missed it by a couple of streets," he said. "He recognized them right away. Wellington Street. We make a right, down here, two roads down then left."

On they went, following the directions given, and as they approached Wellington Street, Marianne recognized it instantly.

As they drew slowly to a halt outside the house at the end of the street, she took a deep breath. Vincent came around to open the car door. She slid out and together they stood looking up at number seventeen.

A rusted, black wrought-iron fence, with many of its sections missing, separated the tangle of growth that was the front garden from the cracked and buckled sidewalk. A "For Sale" sign had been thrust into the ground close to where the gate should have been and as they squeezed through a gap in the surrounding shrubbery, they brushed against the branches of a still-blooming buddleia that encroached upon the path, its purple florets continuing to entice bees and butterflies despite the dwindling summer days. The once meticulously manicured lawn was now the home of myriad weeds and alien grasses, growing, thanks to its continued neglect, in wild profusion. In what had, at one time, been carefully tended flower beds, Michaelmas daisies fought tenaciously for position with the wildflowers that had now invaded their domain.

An enormous oak tree dominated the whole; its gnarled and weathered appearance and sheer size suggested that it had been there long before the house had ever been built. The spreading branches almost touched the windows in the upper part of the building, and the breeze gently rustled the leaves as they waited for the change of the seasons.

They made their way cautiously along the path, up to the four steps that led to the verandah that wrapped around the house. The door, which was partially open when they had seen it last, was now boarded up and several of the windows on the first floor were similarly covered.

Vincent was the first to mount the steps, and Marianne followed him, looking furtively around as they ascended. The boards of the verandah creaked as he stepped onto them and a large crow, which had been watching them with bright, beady eyes, from its perch on the surrounding balustrade, flapped noisily away on glossy, black wings, startling Marianne and sending her heart momentarily into her mouth. She stood still for a few seconds and then recovering her equanimity she went to the farther end of the verandah to examine a window that was yet to be boarded up. Vincent went in the opposite direction.

"I can't see a damn thing," he exclaimed as he pressed his face close to one of the few windows that remained unbroken, and which, beyond the dirt and dust of the glass, bore the tattered remnants of a lace curtain.

"I don't think anyone's been here for years," Marianne said, peering in at the window, which, although similarly grimy, was not obscured by any form of drapery. "I can't make out anything either."

As they stood there, she thought she could faintly catch the strains of some music being played, distant and muffled. Although so quiet that she could barely detect the notes, it nevertheless sounded familiar, and for an instant, she wondered if they had left the car running, the cassette tape still continuing to play.

"Do you hear that?" she asked Vincent.

"What?"

"The music. *The Honfleur Suite*. Did we leave the car running?"

"No, we couldn't have." He jingled the keys in his pocket. "I don't hear any music."

And neither could Marianne now. She thought she must have imagined it, or perhaps another car had driven past.

"There must be another entrance somewhere. Let's take a look around the back," Vincent suggested, and they descended the steps again.

Any path that may have existed leading to the rear of the house was totally overgrown, and they made their way with difficulty along the side of the house. Vincent pushed aside wayward branches of hydrangea and lilac shrubs and stepped gingerly over pieces of disintegrated brickwork, guttering, and shingles that the house had shed rather like a snake shedding its skin. Marianne followed with equal caution, noticing several dangerously jagged pieces of broken glass amongst the undergrowth.

Eventually, they reached the rear of the building, which opened out onto what must have once been a beautiful and much-loved garden. A line of trees bordered the end of the property and, as with the front of the house, the lawn and herbaceous borders were now all one mass of uncultivated growth. But here and there were reminders of better times, remnants of dainty trellises that once supported the luxuriant growth of climbing roses, partially shattered remains of lichen-covered statuary, and a small stone fountain in the center of a now empty ornamental pond. While Marianne was taking in the scene, Vincent climbed the steps of the verandah at the back of the house and was unsuccessfully trying to turn the handle of the door.

"Locked tight, I'm afraid," he called down disappointedly.

Looking around, she could see away to the left, a small cottage that might have been a guest house at one time or perhaps served as accommodation for one or more of the staff that must have been employed at the big house. The roof had fallen in at one end and there was not one window that remained unbroken. The door was missing altogether and ivy covered most of the crumbling brickwork, its creeping tendrils reaching as far as the chimney which had lost its crowning pot.

Having taken in the scene, her eyes traveled past it towards the line of trees that bordered the far edge of the property and, without really knowing why, she began walking towards it, slowly at first, because of the vegetation that threw up obstacles at every step, but then more urgently as she stumbled over fallen branches, mounds of earth and the detritus of decades of neglect, till she reached the trees and shrubs that enclosed it, and desperately pushing her way through, she let out a gasp. There in front of her was a grassy bank at the top of which ran a disused railway line.

Vincent watched her progress from the steps but was now running to catch up to her. Making his way through the dense thicket, he arrived breathless at her side.

He stood there dumbstruck for a moment, looking at the scene before them, and then said, "Oh my God! This is it! This is the connection. The railway."

He threw his arm around Marianne's shoulders, and they stood gazing up at the huge wooden ties and rusty tracks. She was filled with a sense of elation. They had unraveled another segment of the mystery, or so it seemed, but it still left them with many unanswered questions. Marianne felt that although this was an amazing discovery, it was only the beginning.

She climbed to the top of the bank and looked up and down the long-abandoned tracks. Thistles grew rank among the railroad ties and there was no sign of life or movement. The bank on the further side sloped down toward a narrow dusty road which ran parallel to the tracks and on the other side was a slow-running stream.

They turned again toward the house and began to retrace their steps, but as they came close to the deserted cottage, they suddenly heard something fall to the ground with a dull thud. They stood still and waited, their ears straining to catch any further sound, but there was nothing. Not satisfied, however, Vincent decided to investigate further, and they approached the building cautiously.

The light inside was dim but sufficient to show them the complete desolation of the place, dirt and dust everywhere and the smell almost overpowering. Some of the local wildlife had made use of the available shelter, the odor of fox prevalent, and as they moved forward, two or three birds that had made their home there flew up and out of the open doorway.

Marianne was climbing over some fallen timbers that were blocking the way through to the kitchen when something darted beneath the wood, past her into the room from which she had just come. She let out a startled shriek. It was a cat, a large mangy looking tortoiseshell with malevolent eyes, that stopped in mid-flight to turn and look back at her, curious to see who had come to disturb its peace and, having scrutinized the intruder, blinked, turned, and stalked away with feline stealth.

"It's alright!" she called to Vincent who had braved the broken boards of the stairway to look upstairs. "It was only a cat. No spirits here, as far as I can see. I..." The words froze before they were uttered. A hand reached out, roughly gripping her arm and she let out another, more sustained scream. But this was no ghost. It was a man of flesh and blood, weather-beaten and dirty, with prematurely grey hair and stubbled chin. His clothes were creased and soiled and the hand that held her was grimy, the nails broken but the strength in the fingers formidable. Pushing his face forward to look more closely at his captive, he peered at her, his breath reeked of alcohol, and her first instinct was to land as hard a blow as she could muster with her free hand to the side of his head. At that moment, Vincent, who heard her cry of alarm came tumbling down the stairs, running in to see what was the matter. Startled by Marianne's show of resistance, the tramp let go of her and was backing away, and taking advantage of the seconds afforded him by Vincent stopping to see if Marianne was alright, made good his escape, scrambling agilely out through the open door.

The episode had unnerved them both but, in a sense, it was more with relief than anything that they watched the tramp as he ran helter-skelter through the garden and out of sight behind the house.

"It looks like he's been making his home here for quite a while," Marianne said pointing to a pile of empty cans, bottles, and paper bags. There were candles too, half burned, the wax melted into convoluted puddles on the floor.

"He might have burned the place down." Vincent was indignant. "The building should be demolished. It's really not safe leaving it in this condition. Anything could happen!"

"Well, I suppose that's up to the owner, whoever he is. It's not our problem, but *that* is," she said, pointing toward the house.

"We've got to see inside," she said emphatically. "It's probably too late now to get a hold of the agent but we could make a note of the number on the board in front and give them a call in the morning."

Vincent agreed and they returned to the sign posted by the fence. Taking a notepad and pen from her purse Marianne copied the number and taking one last look at the house they went back to the car. Vincent turned the key to start the engine and seconds later, the music continued where it had left off; Wyndham's *Honfleur Suite*, the tune Marianne thought she had heard as they stood outside the door of Number 17.

13

A PERILOUS ENCOUNTER

PLANS TO CALL THE ESTATE AGENT WERE PUT ON HOLD, however, when Marianne, who was sick all that night, developed a bad case of influenza the day after their trip to Sterling. The doctor and, more importantly, Ivan, who would on no account allow Marianne to come into the studio, ordered her to rest in bed and drink plenty of fluids, which she reluctantly did. Vincent was rewarded for his constant care by coming down with the same malady once Marianne had sufficiently recovered and both found themselves having to catch up with work that was necessarily neglected during their illness. Marianne chaffed at the delay in pursuing their investigations, but Vincent assured her that a few weeks probably wouldn't make any difference. It was almost the last week in October when they finally called the estate agent.

After expressing some interest in a possible purchase of the property, which Marianne hoped sounded tolerably plausible, they agreed to a date and time for viewing that was convenient for all. Both she and Vincent looked forward to this next step with a heightened sense of anticipation, rather like two naughty schoolchildren planning a particularly daring escapade. If they had only known the tragic events that were about to overtake them, they probably would not have embarked on so foolhardy and dangerous a mission in so cavalier a fashion. But it was as though, once begun, they could not hold back.

The viewing was set for that Wednesday and on Tuesday night they just finished dinner when the phone rang and Vincent went to answer it. He came back a few moments later with a look of annoyance mixed with apology. "That was Jonathan. He's been doing some research for the book, over at the college library in Cambridge. He's found some very interesting material and wants me to go there tomorrow to take a look. Damn! I hate to turn him down, darling. He's been working so hard on this. But the appointment…"

"Don't worry, I'll call in the morning and re-schedule," Marianne assured him. "The book is more important, and you can't let Jon down. As you say, he's done a lot of work on this already and I'm sure this Mrs. Anderson will understand. I'll just tell her that I've had to schedule a last-minute doctor's appointment or something."

"If you're sure."

"Yes. It's alright. As you said, there's no big rush. I'm sure they're not inundated by people wanting to look at the place, and whatever's in the house is not going anywhere," she reassured him.

Early next morning Vincent left, carrying his briefcase. "I'll probably be back by tomorrow evening at the latest. See if she can manage Friday instead." Marianne followed him to the door, and as he was about to leave, he turned, kissed her, and said in a serious tone, "Don't go without me. I mean it!"

"Don't worry, I'll wait."

She closed the door but as she walked slowly back to the kitchen, Marianne began to feel a familiar spark of rebellion. He thinks I'm helpless without him, she thought indignantly. She could handle it on her own just as well. She began to formulate her plans for the day. She would go ahead and drive to Sterling, meet Mrs. Anderson, and go with her to look at the house. She didn't anticipate anything very much untoward happening, just a feeling maybe, something to indicate that the Railway Woman had been there at one time. If he could go to the museum without her, she could certainly return the favor and take care of the Sterling trip herself.

The drive was uneventful, but when she reached the agent's office in Sterling, Marianne suddenly realized that she'd forgotten to tell Ivan that she wouldn't be in to work that day and swore aloud, "Damn!" Oh well. It didn't matter. He wasn't her boss, and she wasn't obliged to inform him of her every move, but she would try and call, all the same. Perhaps she could use the phone in the agent's office.

Reaching across to gather up her purse and jacket, Marianne peered through the car window at the small storefront of the agent's premises and, with mounting excitement tinged with a feeling of guilty apprehension, got out and made her way across the pavement to the entrance.

"I have an appointment to view a property with Mrs. Anderson this morning," she informed the receptionist, a young girl with bobbed hair and scarlet fingernails.

"Name?"

"Clay."

The girl consulted the book in front of her and ran her finger down the page. "Oh, yes," she drawled, inspecting her nails and looking up at Marianne with weary disdain. "Mr. Clay, it says here."

"No," Marianne corrected her. "Ms. So if you wouldn't mind telling Mrs. Anderson that I'm here. Thank you." For some reason she had taken an instant dislike to the girl. Her condescending manner irritated her.

"Well, I'm afraid Mrs. Anderson isn't here," the girl informed her with a degree of malicious satisfaction. "She tried calling you at home, but you must have already left."

"Well, really!" Marianne exclaimed, with some annoyance. "This is most inconvenient!"

The receptionist rolled her eyes. "Well, she called in earlier this morning to say her daughter is sick with the flu and she won't be able to get in until later but the key to the property is here," she added reluctantly, "And she said to tell you that if you'd like to go ahead and look at the house, she'll meet you back here as soon as she can get away."

"Thank you," Marianne responded rather contritely. After all, it wasn't Mrs. Anderson's fault if her daughter was ill. "I can sympathize. I've only just got over a bout of flu myself. Yes, I'll take the key then, if that's alright."

The girl gave a heavy sigh and wrenched open her desk drawer, which raised Marianne's hackles once again.

"I certainly didn't expect to drive all this way for nothing," she couldn't restrain herself from saying.

The receptionist handed over a key attached to a large tag which had the address written in black marker and, despite her earlier bravado, Marianne accepted it with some misgivings. She had not intended to go there alone, but she couldn't lose face and back out, so she took the key and dropped it into her purse.

"Thanks," she said peremptorily. "Perhaps you could call Mrs. Anderson, if you have a moment to spare from your busy work schedule, just to let her know that I arrived. I may be some time. I'll return the key when I'm finished, and please tell her not to worry about coming in unless she really has to. I'll take a look at the place, return the keys here, and get in touch with her tomorrow."

And with that, she retreated through the door and out to the car, somewhat ashamed at her loss of sang-froid. "Damn and blast!" In her hurry to leave, she'd forgotten to call Ivan.

Marianne sat there for a moment debating whether to just fake a visit to the house and return the key later in the day unused, or risk going there alone. She recalled Vincent's admonition to wait for him, and her obstinate decision to assert her independence. Well, she had come this far. She couldn't weasel out now. She'd have to go on. She started the car, and taking a deep breath, drove the few blocks to Wellington Street.

The house stood there as if it were waiting for her, confident of her return. It almost seemed to breathe a welcome as she walked up the path, passing under the branches of the oak tree, whose leaves had now turned color. Some of them were floating lazily to the ground, and where the wind had caught at them, lay in small heaps against the side of the house. Clutching the key tightly in her hand as if to draw some hidden strength from it, Marianne made her way to the back of the house. Thoughts of the tramp who they had encountered on their previous visit flitted in and out of her mind as she looked around, fearful that he might still be in the neighborhood, an added misgiving that had not been thought of until now.

After stopping frequently to convince herself that there was no one about, she eventually reached the verandah and climbed the steps. The silence was in itself unnerving. She trembled as she stretched out her hand to put the key in the lock and turn it.

There was a soft click and Marianne looked warily about her as she turned the handle as stealthily as a burglar who had no right to be there. The door, after many years of disuse, was difficult to open, the wood warped and the hinges rusty. Marianne pushed it with her shoulder and it finally flew open with a loud crack, which made her heart jump. Looking into the dim interior of the kitchen, she stepped across the threshold, leaving the door partially open to give much-needed light and also as a means of speedy egress if circumstances dictated.

The light switch, when she found it, yielded nothing, and she had not thought to bring a torch. Well, she would have to manage as best she could. The wooden floorboards creaked as she walked across them, and she stopped to listen as the faint scuttling sound of tiny rodent feet told her that she had disturbed at least one inhabitant of Number 17. She looked about, hoping desperately that she wouldn't see the horrible creatures running about, but there was no sign of them. She went on, looking cautiously around at the whitewashed walls and varnished wood floor.

Against one wall, sitting on a platform of whitewashed bricks, was a large, black cast-iron stove, the double doors of the oven left open. Evidently, the previous owners had made little effort to modernize the appliances, she thought. By the window stood a sink, the porcelain basin supported by an ornate stand decorated with metal tiles along the front and sides. Inside lay several dishes waiting to be washed and a large black spider scurried on long hairy legs beneath the safety of an upturned saucepan. At first, she did not find the presence of these innocuous household items at all incongruous. It merely seemed to her that the last people to live here had left suddenly without taking any of their possessions with them. A drawer left open revealed a few items of cutlery, including several long and extremely sharp-looking carving knives, and a jug standing on the table held a simple bouquet of autumn flowers. A dainty porcelain cup and saucer stood next to it.

But the longer Marianne remained there, looking at these domestic arrangements, the more she began to suspect that this wasn't the abandoned home that she had first supposed it to be. Feeling more of an intruder than ever, she crept out into the hallway which led to the front of the house. The carpet, which ran the length of the passage, muffled the sound of her footsteps, but she found herself going on tiptoe past a marble-topped console toward the rooms up ahead. The walls were hung with several paintings, landscapes mostly, but with one or two portraits thrown in for good measure.

Faintly, in the distance, she thought she could hear music playing, but it was barely audible, and Marianne discounted it as either the breeze blowing through an open window somewhere in the house, or perhaps someone's radio playing nearby. She pushed hesitantly at the first door that stood ajar and entered what looked to be the dining room. She found the scene even more puzzling. Beyond the large polished table and eight chairs surrounding it, at the far end of the room, stood a massive mahogany sideboard with intricately carved dolphins at its four corners. She made her way around the table to get a closer look. The base supported by scrolled feet had four cabinet doors and a drawer with a marble-topped serving area upon which stood covered silver dishes and an elegant porcelain dinner service. It was backed by a large beveled mirror which reflected the rest of the candle-lit room and Marianne's own image back at her. Surely Mrs. Anderson had told Vincent that no one had lived there for many years. How could this be possible?

Marianne marveled at the notion that although at one time they had clearly seen the front door hanging open, thus making it easy to gain access to the house, no one had attempted to ransack these antique and undoubtedly valuable furnishings. And who had lit the candles? If the house had been uninhabited for so long, the picture that this scene presented was extremely puzzling and, once again, the unwelcome image of the tramp came to mind. Had he availed himself of these luxurious accommodations?

And there it was again! The music, just as she had heard it before, muffled, but coming from somewhere within the house. Alarmed by this sound she moved on down the hallway toward the boarded front door.

Outside the entrance to the next room, the door of which was closed, stood an elegant walnut hallstand, its arched mirror topped with a crest carved in high relief and must have been at least seven feet tall. Sturdy hooks on either side were provided for visitors to hang their coats, and Marianne was disconcerted to see that there was a large, black overcoat there. Not only that but also an umbrella that stood in one of the two cast iron drip pans at the base of the stand. The appearance of these items made her wonder if perhaps someone else had come to view the house.

"Hello! Is anyone here? Hello!"

She waited, hardly daring to breathe, but there was no reply. The silence was broken only by the music that seemed to be coming from the room beyond. The atmosphere in the house was almost oppressive and feeling that she must find out who was there, she reached down and turned the ornate brass doorknob.

The heavy wooden door opened slowly and the music, which had been heard only as a muted noise somewhere in the background, came to meet her as she stepped into the room and then, just as quickly, stopped. Wyndham's *Honfleur Suite*. How strange! The room was deserted. The lace curtains hanging at the windows through which Vincent had vainly tried to see, blocked much of the light, but even so, Marianne could make out the complex curving forms of the rococo-style furniture within.

Turning around to survey the room she gradually took in her surroundings and noted the various items therein: the piano which she could have sworn she'd heard playing just moments before; a rosewood triple-backed sofa upholstered in red satin and two armchairs of similar design, built for show rather than comfort, stood on a large Persian rug in the center of the floor. A rosewood cylinder desk with mirrored upper doors and foliate carvings stood against the wall by the entrance to the room; a bookcase filled with elegantly bound books to her right; an étagère holding delicate porcelain figurines and bric-à-brac over by the windows and a serpentine shaped table with acanthus leaves carved upon cabriole legs.

On this table, lying face down, was a picture frame. Pulling her coat more closely around her—she was feeling distinctly chilly by then—Marianne reached out and stood the frame on end. Although she had almost expected it, recognition of the Railway Woman brought a startled cry to her lips. Staring at her from the sepia-toned photo, surrounded by an ornate gilt frame, the woman appeared seated, dressed in a soft, graceful afternoon gown, the square collar joined at the lower edges forming a fichu effect. The sleeves of the dress followed the outline of her slender arms, culminating in dainty frills at the wrists and the trim raised waistline was encompassed by a satin sash. Her fresh complexion and luxuriant raven hair should have made her a pleasing model for whoever had taken the picture, but her expression was devoid of any emotion, just a blank, withdrawn stare as though her thoughts were miles away. Beside her was a man, older, stern of aspect, his hand placed possessively upon her shoulder. Marianne lifted the picture and examined it more closely in the dim light. She felt a pang of pity for the woman. Was this her husband?

The answer to that question presented itself shortly, in the form of an album that lay open on the desk. Inside, several pictures of a bridal party indicated that they were indeed man and wife. Underneath the first portrait was written in bold copperplate lettering: "Our Wedding. October 15th 1890." The bride, wearing a white satin dress trimmed with ribbon rosettes, a magnificent veil crowned with an orange blossom headpiece, and a double-stranded pearl choker at her throat, was seated beside her husband, the pair flanked by two bridesmaids and two groomsmen. The three women carried enormous bouquets of roses, carnations, and baby's breath, with attendant greenery that trailed lavishly to the floor. All the other women in the group wore tailored costumes with high-necked blouses and fashionably large hats with broad feather or silk flower-trimmed brims. The men, dressed in frock coats, wore their short hair uniformly parted at one side, all of them with mustaches, including the groom who sported a floral boutonniere in his exquisitely tailored morning coat. Despite this last concession to the occasion, he appeared sullen and detached. Had she chosen him willingly? Surely not! There was not a shred of happiness or love to be seen on either of their faces.

Marianne thought of how she and Vincent must appear to others, their feelings for each other transparently obvious, but there, in that picture there was no such emotion, nothing but an empty shell of humanity staring out at the world with no hope for the future or pleasant memories of the past. Poor girl!

Marianne stepped carefully around the dimly lit room, looking with great interest at all the things that spoke so eloquently of the lifestyle that this couple had led. The fireplace surrounded by an ornate marble mantelpiece still held the remnants of a fire, the ashes laying thickly in the hearth, and the two high-backed armchairs standing on either side like sentinels, their tufted cushions still seemed to hold the impression of their former occupants.

Marianne shivered, thinking that a fire would not be unwelcome now. The temperature since she had entered the room appeared to have dropped considerably. She rubbed her hands together as if she were about to hold them up to some imaginary flame, and then her heart skipped a beat. She thought she detected a noise, very faint, in the room above. Marianne stood still, listening intently, but it was not repeated, so she continued her exploration.

A newspaper lay on the floor by one of the chairs. She picked it up and read the date at the top of the first page, October 6th, 1892. The bold headlines proclaimed that infamous criminal, Adam Worth, the man who had stolen Gainsborough's celebrated portrait of Georgiana, Duchess of Devonshire, and was wanted by the police of the United States of America, Europe, and South Africa, had finally been captured in Belgium during the attempted robbery of a money delivery cart. Incredibly, the pages of the newspaper were not, as one would have expected, brittle and faded with age, but on the contrary, the print appeared fresh and the paper pliable. Marianne wondered briefly if it was a reproduction of some kind.

She placed the paper on the chair and tip-toed across the rug. On a side table by the other chair, a crystal wine glass lay on its side, the lace cloth beneath it stained a ruby red. Next to it, a little calf-skin bound book lay open, the edges of the pages having soaked up some of the spilled wine. She picked it up and saw at once that it was a diary, written in a neat feminine hand. Despite the poor light, Marianne could see the writing quite clearly, and overcome by a desire to discover its contents, she sat down in the chair and turned back the pages to the fly leaf and began to read.

The year 1892 was written at the top of the page.

The next page began: *January 1st. Last night we were invited to a party at the Weatherall's. I did not think that Arthur would wish to attend but was surprised when*

89

he changed his mind at the last minute. How wonderful! I Have not been out to visit in ages and have spoken to no-one other than Arthur, cook and the maid since Arthur's family was here at Christmas. John and Jane Weatherall have the most beautiful house and the furnishings are very elaborate. Jane Weatherall wore a stunning gown. I did not dance, as Arthur does not approve of such things, but watched the others, who seemed to be having an enjoyable time. Jane introduced me to several of her friends including Daisy Hargrove who has rather a scandalous reputation, but who seemed very nice, and Desmond Renard, an artist who lives in Sterling and who, I am told, has been commissioned by John Weatherall to do a portrait of Jane this year. I so wished that we could have stayed to see the New Year in with the others, but Arthur had one of his headaches and so we had to leave early.

The next few entries held nothing of interest, merely cataloging the mundane domestic duties of the household and a brief allusion to the fact that Arthur had been unwell and had kept to his room. Nothing of any significance occurred until the end of February when the entry for the 23rd read: *Jane Weatherall came to visit today. She brought Mr. Renard with her. She is to begin sitting for her portrait tomorrow and has asked me to go over to the house to keep her company and talk to her. Jane says she will be bored, having to sit still for so long. I told her I would come to keep her company, but when I mentioned it to Arthur this evening, he was quite angry and said I was on no account to go, and that she is a foolish woman who is as vain as she is stupid.*

Then on the next day: *February 24th – Sent a message to Jane giving an excuse for my absence. I hope she is not too cross with me. I have so few friends; I would not like to think that I had given her any offense by not keeping my promise to go over there.*

May 10th - Jane Weatherall arrived this morning, very excited, to say that her portrait was finished and would I go back with her to the house to see it. I knew Arthur would not approve but Jane was insistent and we drove back to Maple Street together in her brougham. Mr. Renard has done a very creditable job with the picture. In fact, he was there at the house when we arrived and I congratulated him on his excellent work. Jane suggested that he should paint me, which is ridiculous, but Mr. Renard said he would be happy to do it. Arthur would have a fit if I were to propose any such thing.

At this point she seemed to become more circumspect in her entries, leaving much of what was most important in her life unsaid. The next significant entries were in August.

August 23ʳᵈ - Portrait finished. How I wish I could bring it home but Desmond says it must stay with him and he is right, of course. Arthur must never know.

August 24ᵗʰ - Desmond wants me to continue our visits even though the picture is finished. But it is becoming increasingly difficult. I am fearful that someone who knows me may see me and tell Arthur.

Then, a more ominous entry: *September 30ᵗʰ - Arthur suspects and watches my every move. Desmond has urged me to go away with him. I can tell he is nervous and fears discovery but how can I leave? He says he is going with or without me, but dare I risk flight? What a dilemma!*

And then, as though reaching a monumental decision: *October 2nd - I have agreed to go away with Desmond. He has left me no alternative. I can't live without him and must, therefore, go with him. God help me! I am so afraid of Arthur. I don't know what he will do when he finds out.*

The final chilling entry read: *October 4ᵗʰ - Leaving the day after tomorrow. Thank God! Will no longer have to endure this life. Desmond will meet me at the station. He has not told me where we are going but has made all the arrangements and I must trust him.*

How incredibly naive she must have been to think that her husband would not search for evidence of her suspected duplicity. Arthur had undoubtedly found these damning accounts of his wife's infidelity.

Marianne was so lost in thoughts and conjectures that the sound did not immediately register, but it came again, the distant voice of a man shouting, the words indistinguishable but clearly coming from inside the house. The cold was biting at her now, her fingers almost numb so that she could scarcely hold the diary, and she shivered as she strained to catch the angry phrases that were being uttered in the room above. As terrified as Marianne was, she nevertheless felt an overwhelming urge to seek out whoever was there on the second floor. The compulsion to go on and confront whoever was in that room pulled her forward, into the passage, and toward the staircase.

As she put her foot on the first step, the voice came again, clearer this time. She could make out the words, "Whore! Filthy whore!" and the sound of a woman sobbing. Then the man shouted again, "Desmond Renard! You were going to leave me for that common dauber, that miserable mountebank!"

She climbed halfway up the stairs when the unmistakable sound of a slap reached her ears and a sharp cry from the woman. Spurred on, Marianne took the last few steps with a bound and reaching the landing, ran toward the room at the end of the corridor, the door partially open. The man's voice continued its vitriolic assault, the woman, crying out passionately, "Stop Arthur! Please stop!"

Without any thought of danger, Marianne burst recklessly into a room that seemed filled with a swirling mist. No longer in control of her actions, she was drawn into whatever drama was being played out in that gloomy interior. What she saw there, as the smoky veil gradually dissipated, brought her up with a start. The woman was sprawled across a large four-poster bed, the man astride her, pinning her body beneath him, had one hand around her neck and the other was raining blows on her face and head.

Marianne found herself shrieking at him, "Stop! Leave her alone!"

At that, the man ceased his assault and released his hold on the woman. He sprang from the bed and spun around to face Marianne, his face livid, spittle running from the corners of his mouth, his eyes bulging with rage. Then in a split second, before she could stop him, he had reached his hand toward something that lay on the counterpane at the foot of the bed, and in an instant his right arm raised, a knife blade flashed and descended downward into the body of the woman who was screaming for mercy.

Too late, Marianne rushed forward and tried to pull him away, her hands grasping ineffectually at his jacket. *Stupid!* she told herself. She should have known that she couldn't change what had already happened. The woman had stopped screaming, and the man turned again to face Marianne. A terrifying look of murderous insanity distorted his cruel face, and Marianne knew in that instant that he would not let her leave that room alive.

She was relatively fit, and they struggled briefly, but his size and strength overcame her efforts. She felt the blade strike home between her ribs. A searing pain shot through her and she felt as though she had been turned to ice. As the mist once again seemed to form before her eyes, the figure of the man appeared to dissolve and Marianne fell to the floor, clutching the bedcover that inexplicably melted into nothing as she lay there.

She felt that she was dying, and with her final breath called to the only person she knew could save her, "Vincent!" and then felt herself slipping away into oblivion.

14

THE ROAD TO RECOVERY

SOMEONE WAS WHISPERING, "MARIANNE," very close to her ear. The voice was calling her back. Her eyes were closed and she couldn't move, but she could hear the voice. It was Vincent. Marianne tried to answer, but it was as though she were drowning in a dark pool. The water was swallowing her up and she sank deeper and deeper into nothingness once more.

Was it minutes, hours, or days later when she heard the voice again? Vincent was calling her. Marianne struggled to make her way to the surface, but when she got there, she could not distinguish the shapes that swam before her. She could feel someone touching her hand, stroking it and Vincent's voice again, softly in her ear, "Marianne."

She couldn't speak, the words just wouldn't come, and her eyes, weary with such a little effort closed again.

The next sound that came to her, sometime later, was that of a door closing. Slowly opening her eyes, Marianne realized that the mist had finally cleared, and she was able to focus with some difficulty on her surroundings. She was in a hospital bed, that much was evident. An IV pumping something into her veins, dripped silently at her side. Her body felt bruised and sore and at each intake of breath, there was a dull pain. What was she doing there? What had happened? She remembered vaguely, going into a house, somewhere that she had never been before. The effort of trying to recall made her head swim and she gave it up. Then she noticed a familiar figure, that of Vincent, his body slumped uncomfortably in an armchair by a window speckled with raindrops. He appeared to be asleep.

Sleep, yes, what a good idea. She must sleep too and, exhausted from the arduous climb back into consciousness, she slipped gratefully back into sleep once more.

When she woke again, the room was in darkness except for a meager light that filtered through the small square window in the door from the corridor outside. The pain that she had experienced earlier had eased somewhat. Just then the door opened and Vincent, entering, seeing that she was awake, moved quickly to the bed, momentarily blocking her view of the person who had followed him into the room. He bent over her, an inexpressible look of relief on his face.

"Darling. Thank God!" he said, kissing her forehead. He stepped aside, revealing his companion. "Look who's here, Marianne." And there was Matthew, gazing down at her, his face unusually haggard and drawn.

He pulled a chair close to the bed as Vincent watched, and sitting down, leant over so that his face almost touched hers.

"Annie, it's me, Matthew. How are you feeling, dear?"

Marianne barely found the strength to whisper, "Alright," which she obviously wasn't, but it didn't matter. Everything would be alright now that Vincent and Matthew were both there.

"I got Vincent's call early yesterday," Matthew went on, "And drove up here straight away."

She looked at Vincent, bewildered. Why on earth should he call Matthew? Vincent, seeing that she was perplexed, said, "Just rest now, Marianne. I talked to the doctor earlier. He says you're doing well, but you need plenty of rest. We'll let you sleep now and come back first thing in the morning."

Matthew leaned forward to kiss her cheek. "Good night, dear. God bless. We'll see you tomorrow and you'll be home before you know it. He stood up, and he and Vincent walked softly to the door. Vincent looked back at her as he went, lifting his hand in a brief wave of farewell. He put his other arm around Matthew's shoulder. And they were gone.

Left alone, Marianne now began to recall those last moments in the house. She had a clear recollection of climbing some stairs. Yes, it was all coming back to her now. There was a room with a bed, and a woman screaming. And the man, holding a knife.

The next day, a doctor who she could not recollect seeing before came to visit her. "Good morning Ms. Clay. My name is Doctor Parmenter," he told her. "I'll be taking care of you while you're here at the hospital. How are you feeling today?" He reached over to feel her pulse and nodded with satisfaction.

"Do you remember what happened?"

"I was in a house. Someone was screaming, maybe it was me, and then this pain..."

"Well, it's clear that someone attacked you while you were in the house. You were there to view the premises; do you remember? When you didn't return the key to the estate agent's office, they thought something must have happened to you. Someone from Grey and Walters went to the house and found you there. The ambulance brought you here to the emergency room three days ago. You had been stabbed." He paused and looked at her inquiringly. "Do you remember it now?"

Of course, she remembered. Arthur coming at her with the knife, the struggle, Adele already stabbed to the heart, lying across the bed, her life's blood pouring out upon the pink quilted counterpane. But in that moment of recall, something cautioned her to remain quiet, and she shook her head.

"No, I'm sorry. There's nothing there."

"It will come in time, but for now, we must concentrate on getting you healthy again. You lost a lot of blood and we had to do quite a bit of work to repair some things internally. But you seem to be doing nicely now and I think by tomorrow we will be able to move you from intensive care to a room down on the next floor. I'm changing some of your medication, but I'll leave all the instructions with your nurse and she will take care of you. I'm glad to see you on the road to recovery. I'll look in on you tomorrow."

He began to walk towards the door but as a thought occurred to him, he turned back, "Oh, I almost forgot, I'm afraid the police have been waiting to speak to you. I've managed to keep them at bay so far, but they need to ask you some questions, about the attack, you know. Of course, there's not much you can tell them yet, but I'm sure they will want to see you anyway, as soon as possible. Perhaps tomorrow—" he trailed off and, smiling, he left the room.

The police! How could she tell them? How on earth could they possibly understand that she had been attacked by someone from the past? Someone who no longer existed. Impossible! Marianne could hardly believe it herself. But it had happened. She remembered it all so clearly now. She must see Vincent; tell him what had happened.

He arrived later that morning, holding a bunch of red roses, and accompanied by Matthew, who looked considerably refreshed by a good night's sleep. They exchanged greetings and Vincent kissed her, Matthew standing discreetly back, not wanting to intrude.

"How are you darling?"

"Better. thanks. The doctor said they'll probably move me tomorrow. Hello Matthew."

He stepped forward and grinned. "You're looking much better, dear." He moved around to the other side of the bed and looked down at her.

They talked for a while, Matthew telling Marianne how he had spoken on the phone to Clare and she had sent her love. Marianne still felt very weak and after a while, the conversation languished.

Matthew said, "I think we'd better let you get some rest. Ivan called to ask if he could visit, but I thought better not. I told him maybe in a day or two. Was that alright?"

She laughed weakly. "Yes. I don't think I could survive his histrionics in my present condition, as well intentioned as they might be."

"Quite! Well, goodbye for now, dear. We'll be back later. I'll bring some magazines, shall I?" Mathew asked.

She nodded gratefully, and he walked away toward the door. Vincent bent to kiss her and she whispered hurriedly, "I've got to talk to you, alone. Make some excuse and come back. I have to tell you something."

"Yes, alright darling," he replied. Then, more loudly so Matthew could hear, "Bye for now, I'll look in again later." They left the room together but, in a minute or so, Vincent returned.

"I told Matthew I wanted a word with the sister in charge of the ward. He's waiting for me out in the car. What is it, Marianne?"

She had reached out and grasped his sleeve, pulling him nearer.

"I saw them, Vincent. In the house. They were there. Her name is Adele and her husband killed her. I saw him! He stabbed her and I tried to stop him."

Vincent looked at her in bewilderment. She could tell that it wasn't that he didn't believe her, but events were racing now at such a pace that he seemed unable to keep up with them.

"And he attacked you?" he asked incredulously.

"Yes! Yes!" She was exhausted now. Reliving those last few horrific moments in Wellington Street had sapped what little energy she had, but she had to go on. "The police, they're waiting to talk to me."

"I know. They've been to see me too," he replied.

"You didn't tell them, did you, about what we suspected? Not about the woman on the train? Any of that, did you?" She was desperate to know.

"No. No, it's alright. I thought someone had come in, possibly that tramp, while you were there. I had no idea … Why did you go alone?"

"I know. I'm sorry! I should have waited, but I thought I could handle it."

"When the police come, say nothing about what you saw," he warned her.

"Of course not. They'd think I was crazy."

He kissed her again and said, "I'll have to go, but I'll come back on my own later, this afternoon or this evening. I love you."

He left, passing a nurse who had come into the room to bring some new medication.

Thoughts were going round and round in Marianne's head like a swarm of angry bees. How could all this have happened? It was incredible! To see these apparitions was one thing, disturbing enough, but to actually suffer an injury inflicted by one of them was frightening. She couldn't begin to fathom how this could have occurred. But Vincent was right. She mustn't divulge what had happened. She must tell no-one else, not even Matthew. Vincent was obviously the only one she could trust with her secret.

Later that afternoon, after the promised visit from the physical therapist, Marianne had another visitor, a detective sergeant from the Sterling police department. Young, dark-haired, good looking, and accompanied by a strong aroma of after-shave, he came into the room and immediately apologized for his intrusion. He was accompanied by a policewoman in uniform.

"I'm sorry to bother you Ms. Clay, but the doctor said you'd probably be up to seeing me now and there's a few questions I need to ask you. I'm D.S. Ince and this is W.P.C. Samuels." He pulled a chair toward the bed and sat down. "About what happened the other day. Do you mind just going over it for me?"

"Well, I'll try, but I'm not too clear about most of it. I went there, to Wellington Street, to see a house that we were thinking about buying."

W.P.C. Samuels made some notes on a pad that she had taken from her pocket and Marianne continued. "Vincent, Mr. Foxworth, that's my partner, was supposed to come with me, but he was called away on business at the last minute, so I went there alone. I stopped at the realtor's office, but she wasn't there. Her daughter was sick, but she'd left the key for me, so I took it and went over to the house."

"On your own?"

"Yes."

"Was there anyone there, when you got to the house. You didn't see anyone hanging about outside?"

It would have been so easy there and then to point the finger of suspicion at the tramp. He would have been a perfect scapegoat, the evidence of his presence for anyone to see in the remains of the cottage, but her conscience wouldn't allow it.

"No. It was very quiet. The place was deserted."

"You weren't afraid, to go in, alone, I mean?" he asked.

"No. I didn't think there would be any problem. I went round to the back of the house and let myself in. The front door was boarded up, you see.

I looked around, as well as I could. There was no light. The electricity was off."

"You're sure?

"Yes, I tried the switch but there was nothing."

He looked puzzled, and she continued. "I looked around the kitchen and then went down the hallway to the dining room." Marianne hesitated, wondering whether to mention the fact that she had been curious about the presence of the furniture and everything, but she thought, on the whole, it would be better not to.

"What made you think it was a dining room, Ms. Clay?"

"I don't know." Marianne faltered then went on, "I thought it must have been. The position in relation to the rest of the rooms. I assumed that's what it was because it was nearest to the kitchen. Then I went on to the front of the house and into the drawing room."

"And all this time you were alone, yes?"

"Yes, quite alone."

"And you didn't hear anything, no one moving about, nothing like that?"

"No."

"And then what?"

"Then I went upstairs, looked around, but it was hard to see anything properly. I went into the room at the front and ... I think ... I heard something behind the door as I went in. I turned round to look behind me and someone jumped out. I felt this pain," she indicated in the direction of her ribs and went on, "And that's it. I don't remember anything else until I woke up here in the hospital."

"You didn't get a look at the person who attacked you?"

"No. No, sorry. As I said, the light was poor and everything happened so quickly. I don't think I can really tell you anything that would be of any use."

He looked at W.P.C. Samuels, and she nodded, tapping the pencil on her notepad to indicate that she'd got everything down.

"Well, something may come to you, later on. If it does, please call me at this number." He placed a card on the bedside table and appeared ready to leave, but stopped in the doorway and W.P.C. Samuels produced her notebook again with alacrity.

"Just one more thing. Where did you say Mr. Foxworth had gone?"

"He was in Cambridge with a professional colleague, doing some research for a book they're writing."

"But you had originally planned to go there to the house together?"

"Yes, but this meeting with Professor Amor was more important, so he went there instead."

He considered for a moment and then put one final question, "You can't think of anyone, I suppose, who would want to do you any harm, someone with a grudge, someone you may have had an argument with, say?"

"Well, of course you're bound to have disagreements with people, but no, nothing on that scale. Honestly, I can't think of anyone who dislikes me that much."

"It's just that ... well, whoever did this ... robbery wasn't the motive. Your purse was still there, on the ground where you'd dropped it. It didn't look like anything had been taken, but perhaps you've checked and noticed something missing?"

"No, I hadn't given it a thought, to tell you the truth."

He stepped over to the bed again and bent to open the cabinet in the bedside table. Extracting a brown leather purse, he handed it to her.

"Perhaps you could look, just to see if anything's missing."

She opened the clasp and checked the contents. "No. It all seems to be here. Nothing missing."

Marianne thought then of Adele's diary and wondered if that, as well as the contents of the house, had merely been a figment of her imagination or whether she had really slipped it into her coat pocket. The detective said goodbye, leaving her with as many unanswered questions as he had himself.

That evening Vincent returned, alone this time, and having just awoken from a long nap Marianne felt refreshed and eager to talk. She related to him exactly what had occurred at Wellington Street and finished, "Is my jacket here at the hospital?"

"It must be. I haven't taken anything home." He went across to the long cabinet that was provided for the storage of patients' clothes and additional pillows and bedcovers and took out a brown, sheepskin-lined suede jacket. He reached into one of the capacious pockets, pulled out the little book, and held it up triumphantly. Adele's diary!

"Yes! That's it! Vincent, you must read it. I skimmed through it at the house and it explains everything. Arthur killed her because she was having an affair. She was going to leave him and he killed her!"

Vincent sat down and began to read, shaking his head occasionally and muttering, "Amazing!" and "Incredible!" When he came to the final page, he looked up at Marianne and said, "She was supposed to take the train. The one that we saw at the museum."

"And she did take it, Vincent! Her spirit was there even if her body wasn't. She had to tell someone what had happened, and I think that someone was me, although God knows why."

"And you're sure you've never had anything happen like this before?"

"No, I told you, never."

"Well, I think we should keep mum about it, as far as the police are concerned. For now, anyway."

"Right, I agree. How's Matthew doing, by the way?"

"Oh, he's OK now, now that he knows you're going to be alright. But he was a wreck when he first got here."

"Poor Matthew!"

"I know, darling, but what could I do? They told me you might not regain consciousness. I had to call him, just in case. Promise me you'll never go to that house again. Whatever happened there is in the past, for them and for you. You can't change it," he pleaded.

She was reluctant to give a promise that she felt was not within her power to keep. Despite everything that had occurred, she still believed that she had not fulfilled the task that Adele had set for her. But to put his mind at ease, she agreed, and he seemed satisfied.

"Ivan and Irina will be here tomorrow afternoon, so I'll wait till the evening to come again. Is there anything you need?"

"No, thanks. I just want to come home."

"Soon, darling, soon."

Ivan and Irina arrived the next day with arms full of flowers, fruit, and reading material. Irina was smiling and calm, while Ivan looked ill at ease in an environment that, to his cautious mind, was running rampant with communicable diseases.

"Darling, how are you?" Irina kissed Marianne, but Ivan contented himself with a kiss to his long fingers that was blown to her from a safe distance several paces from the bed.

"It's alright, Ivan. I don't have anything catching, at least I don't think you can catch a stab in the ribs."

"Darling Annie! What on earth happened? No, don't talk about it if it's too upsetting, but I'm just bursting to know." Irina settled in the chair and Ivan plunked himself down on the end of the bed, causing Marianne to wince.

"I knew something like this would happen," he said sourly. "Ever since you've been living with that man, things have not been right."

"How can you say that? This had nothing whatever to do with Vincent." As anticipated, Ivan was already sending Marianne's blood pressure soaring.

Irina gave her beloved a warning glower, and he raised his hands in submission.

"Alright, alright! You know best. But why did the police come to the studio and ask me a million questions about him? Tell me that."

"When?" Marianne asked in surprise.

"Why, the day after they found you, of course."

"What did you tell them?'

"Nothing. What could I say? I know nothing about the man, only that he persuaded you to go and live with him, that he is making you so unhappy that you are coming to work looking like death warmed over every day."

"Oh Ivan, that's not true! How could you tell them that? It's ridiculous."

"But it is true!" he retorted defensively. "You can't tell me there hasn't been something wrong with you for weeks now."

"But it's got nothing to do with Vincent!"

"Vanya, please!" Irina intervened. "You're upsetting Annie."

He got up and paced restlessly about the room, finally stopping by the window, his hands thrust deep into his pockets, and looked out toward the parking lot down below.

"I'm sorry, Annie," Irina said apologetically.

"It's alright. It's good of you both to come, really. I appreciate it tremendously and I know I haven't been quite myself lately, but honestly, Ivan, it hasn't anything to do with Vincent. We're very happy together." This evinced a sound that was suspiciously like a derisive snort from Ivan.

"Of course, you are," Irina said emphatically. The conversation from there on took a turn toward Marianne's treatment at the hands of the hospital staff, which she assured them was excellent and her return home which she said she hoped would be in the not-too-distant future. She thanked Ivan for the magazines and he pointed out with a self-satisfied smugness the layout that he had worked on, in the largest and glossiest of the periodicals that he had carelessly flung on the bed.

After an hour had passed, Marianne felt exhausted and was not sorry when Ivan finally declared the visit at an end, practically dragging Irina from her chair.

"Good bye, darling. Let us know if there's anything we can do. Get well soon."

Irina kissed her, and Ivan, waiting until Irina had left the room and momentarily forgetting his preoccupation with not catching anything, bent down and kissed her hurriedly on the lips.

"I'm sorry," he said suddenly, and the admission stunned her. He had never once, in all the time that she had known him, apologized for anything, and the words scared rather than pleased her. Was he sorry for what he had said, or was he sorry about what had happened, or worse yet, was he sorry for what he thought had happened? And just what had he thought when they'd told him that she had been found stabbed and close to death in the house on Wellington Street?

"I have something else for you." He reached into his pocket and drew out a small book.

"Please, Annie! I insist! Take the book and read it." He thrust it into her hands. "It will help pass the time. You will appreciate it, believe me."

He hurried from the room and Marianne looked down at the book. She turned the pages, idly glancing at the verses, and realized it was Ivan's favorite book of poems. Some of the pages were badly dog-eared and Marianne smiled to herself. Many a time she had reprimanded him for doing the same thing to the books that she had lent him. It was one of her pet peeves, but in typically obstinate fashion he continued to mark anything of note in the same manner, and she wondered curiously what he had found so interesting on these particular pages.

The poem was *The Demon* by Mikhail Lermontov, but although Marianne was familiar with the story as presented in the opera, she had never actually read the work that had inspired it. She looked more closely at the words. Ivan had underscored several of the lines with black marker, another transgression for which she had often had cause to admonish him, and her eyes immediately went to them.

This was no angel to befriend her,
This was no heaven-sent defender:

And further on, another dog-eared page with more lines marked:

He set her blazing.
He gleamed above her like a spark
Or like a knife that finds its mark.
That devil triumphed!

And finally, another page, desecrated in the same manner:

Again, he stood before her eyes,
But God! - too changed to recognize!
So evil was the whole impression,
So full of poison and aggression
And endless hatred;

She wondered why he had been at such great pains to emphasize the words in this fashion. Why were they so important? What was there about them that had merited his attention? Or was it her attention that he had wanted to draw to these strangely unsettling lines? Was that why he had urged her to accept the book in an almost feverish burst of generosity?

Marianne guessed at the message that it conveyed. The thinly veiled allusion to Vincent was disturbing, but she put it down to Ivan's prejudiced and macabre imagination. Her mind was already seething with suppositions and conjectures and there was no room for someone else's fantasies.

Meanwhile, back in Cambridge, D.S. Guy Ince was reporting back to his boss, Detective Inspector Parks.

"I've interviewed Marianne Clay, sir. She doesn't think she can identify the man who attacked her."

Parks harrumphed, "Tcha! Nothing? Young? Old? Tall or short? She must have seen something, man!"

"I think she was still rather shaken up by the whole thing, sir. Something may come to her once she's had time to reflect."

"Reflect, be buggered! We can't have things like this happening on our patch, Ince. Have they done a house to house?"

"Naturally, we would have, sir, but Wellington Street is almost deserted. Most of the houses are empty except for one or two at the other end of the road. They did check on those but no one saw or heard anything, except a little old lady rooming in one of the houses thought she saw a tramp hanging about in the place next door, and they did find signs that someone had been sleeping rough in one of the outbuildings at number seventeen."

"He must be your man, then," Parks rumbled. "He was probably making himself at home there and the woman startled him."

"It's possible. We're looking for him now, sir. He shouldn't be too hard to find."

"Let's hope you're right. We can't have someone like that going around terrorizing the neighborhood," Parks rumbled.

"No. Well, I'd best crack on, sir, if there's nothing else." Ince tried to make his escape.

"Alright, Ince. Cut along." Parks sounded like a benevolent headmaster, and the D.S. felt as though he was back in school.

"Thank you, sir," he said, and made his exit.

15
READING BETWEEN THE LINES

SOME DAYS LATER, Marianne was released from the hospital to complete her convalescence at home. Matthew had stayed at Vincent's invitation, and was still at the apartment where he fussed around her like a mother hen, Vincent watching sometimes in amusement and sometimes in irritation. Matthew was grateful to his senior partner for understanding the situation and allowing him time off, and although occasionally they found his presence a trifle wearing, his inestimable help when Vincent was absent from the apartment was more than welcome.

In the days immediately following her return home, Marianne received several calls from Clare who explained, during the course of one of them, that she had spoken to their father, informing him of what had happened. Marianne was gratified to hear that, despite their estrangement, he should express concern for her well-being. Upon her assurance that Marianne was over the worst, Ronald Clay did not think it necessary to call his youngest daughter, and the silence between them continued.

Ivan and Irina and Jon and Lisa Amor had all paid visits at various times. On one particular occasion, Irina came alone and Marianne was surprised to see her usually calm and placid manner disturbed.

"How are you, darling?" her friend asked her solicitously.

"Much better, thanks Irina. It's good to see you. How's Ivan?"

Irina sat quietly for a moment, looking down at her pale, tremulous hands that twisted nervously in her lap.

"Irina, what's wrong?"

"It's just that … I'm sorry, Annie. Will you forgive me if I ask you something that may seem, how you would say, out of line?"

"Of course. What is it? Irina, we're friends. Good friends, I hope. Ask what you like. I don't know if I'll have the answer, but whatever it is, it can't be that bad, surely."

"You and Ivan," her friend said hesitantly. "There's nothing between you is there? He told me that you and he had once been lovers."

"Wait, Irina," Marianne laughed, then when she saw that Irina was serious, she asked, "He told you that?"

"Was it not true?"

"No! At least … well, I'll be completely honest with you, Irina, because I've nothing to hide from you. We made love once, you understand? It was just one time, a long time ago, when we first met. But there's nothing now. We never really felt anything for each other, not in that way. We work together and we are very good friends, just as you and I are. I'm sorry if he led you to believe there was anything more between us. He was probably trying to make you jealous. You know what he's like."

"He's seemed so distracted, ever since you were hurt. As though you were more than just a friend."

"And you thought—"

"Yes. I asked him if he loved you and he went crazy. Oh, I can't repeat all the things he said, but he told me that you had given yourself to him, that you adored him and he couldn't send you away."

"How typical!" Marianne said indignantly, although she couldn't help laughing again. "Really, Irina, he is the most awful liar. Please believe me. There's nothing, truly. I'm sure he was upset when he heard about what happened to me, but that's only natural. I'd feel the same way if anything happened to either of you. But as a friend, that's all. Nothing more. Vincent is the only man in my life. Ivan knows it and it annoys him. He's never liked Vincent; I don't know why."

"It's true. He never has a good word to say about him. Oh, Annie, I shouldn't be telling you this."

"Don't worry. I know it. I think he's just looking out for me, like a brother, like Matthew would. It's just that he carries it to extremes. Everything that Ivan does is over the top, as you well know. He can't say or do anything without making a huge production of it. Everything is so dramatic."

"You're right, of course, darling. And I believe you. If you say there is nothing more between you, then it must be so."

"Of course. If I thought that you doubted me for an instant, I'd … well, I'd have to leave the studio. I couldn't go on working with Ivan if I thought it gave you a moment's uneasiness. You do believe that?"

"Yes, but please," Irina looked genuinely frightened, "Please don't leave the studio. Ivan would be furious with me if he thought I had caused you to leave. You won't tell him that I told you all this, will you?"

"No, of course not."

Irina had left feeling easier in her mind, Marianne hoped. Of all the idiotic things! Ivan really was the limit!

Meanwhile, things gradually returned to normal and Matthew began to think about going back home. Marianne was ready to resume work and there seemed no reason for him to remain, so he told them he would be leaving in two days' time.

It was then that a disturbing incident occurred. Marianne had retired early to bed that evening, feeling the tiring effects of an unusually long walk that she and Matthew had taken earlier in the day. Vincent was working late at the University with Jon, and so Marianne left Matthew watching the TV.

She had been asleep for some time when she was awakened by a noise. She must have inadvertently left the bedroom door ajar and the sound of two male voices raised in argument came clearly from the living room.

Her mind, still blurry with sleep, could not at first catch the words, but as her head began to clear, she could distinguish Matthew saying, "What on earth can you want with these? You surely don't expect her to go back there?"

And Vincent replying with suppressed anger, "What I don't expect is you to go looking through my private papers! They don't concern you!"

"But Annie's safety does! Surely you can have no further interest in that place after what happened."

"I'm as concerned for Marianne's safety as you, but she's stubborn. She won't let it go! I've told her I don't want her going back there, but she insists on knowing what happened."

"But what can all this possibly have to do with it? All this happened more than eighty years ago."

She wondered then if Vincent had told Matthew about Adele and her untimely demise. But it didn't seem likely. He had been insistent that it should be kept secret, and she certainly hadn't divulged it to anyone, despite a continuing barrage of questions from the police.

"I don't intend to discuss this any further. We are enormously grateful for the help you've been to Marianne since she came home, of course. And I realize you're only thinking of her welfare." Vincent's voice was placating now. "But she is fine now and I wouldn't dream of letting any harm come to her again. She's far too precious to me for that, believe me."

Matthew's anger appeared to have subsided, and she heard him say, "You're right. I'm sorry. I shouldn't have blown up like that. It's just that I wish they could catch the person who did this so that things could be wrapped up. I'm sure Annie must be going through hell with all these questions from the police and everything. I'd just like to see the whole thing over and done with."

"I know. It's a mess, but they'll figure it out eventually, and until then I'll see that she stays out of harm's way."

The conversation seemed to come to an amicable enough conclusion, and not long after, Vincent crept into the bedroom. Marianne closed her eyes, not wanting him to know that she had overheard them, and she felt him climb into bed beside her.

The next morning, everything was calm. By their demeanor, Marianne would never have guessed that there had been any discord between lover and brother, if she had not heard them for herself the night before. She said nothing and made preparations to go back to work as soon as Matthew left for London.

The following morning, Matthew said his goodbyes. Marianne thought he seemed rather on edge and, smiling reassuringly, told him, "I'll be alright, really."

"Yes. Don't worry, Marianne. I'll make sure everything's okay," came his cryptic reply.

He got in his car and drove away while Marianne stood at the curb, waving and frowning slightly. Now what had he meant by that she wondered?

Meanwhile, Vincent was zealous in his promise to take care of her and hovered about her constantly. He said very little about the episode at Wellington Street since Marianne's return from the hospital, although she knew the Sterling police had been in contact with him several times.

But that evening, he broached the subject once more. "He got away with it, you know."

"Who?" she asked.

"Arthur Hemmings. They never did find her body."

"We don't know that, do we?" We know very little about them at all other than the fact that she was unhappy and had decided to take a lover."

"Actually, I have found out a few things about them." Vincent sounded pleased with his efforts. "I looked in the county records office to find out who had owned the house in 1892." He retrieved some papers from the drawer of his desk and handed them to her. "As you can see, the building was owned by Arthur Edward Hemmings. It remained in his possession until 1930. The records show that he died in October of that year. I couldn't find any mention of Adele's death, only the certificate of marriage issued in 1890."

Marianne looked at the sheaf of photocopies in her hand. Vincent had been methodical and thorough in his research. "It says here that he was a banker," she said, pointing to a copy of an article that had appeared in the local newspaper.

"Yes, and a very important one at that. There were three banks in Sterling originally. Two closed down, including Hemmings' bank and the last one, the Bank of Lockstone and Sterling, has been in business almost from the town's beginning. The name of Hemmings crops up quite a bit in Sterling and the adjoining village of Lockstone. Apparently, he owned quite a lot of property there, and he seems to have donated a considerable amount of money to various worth-while causes, the hospital, library, and even the local museum, amongst others."

Marianne was staggered by the amount of information that he had been able to unearth in such a short space of time. "This is amazing, Vincent! How on earth did you manage it?"

"Oh, just digging about. Years of doing research helped, I guess. There are several references to him in books on local history in the library. Of course, they all mention his philanthropy."

"Ha!" Marianne gave a derisive laugh, remembering how she had seen him as perhaps no one else ever had, at the moment when, mad with jealousy and rage, he had plunged the dagger into his wife's heart.

"I did find this little book." Vincent produced a volume, the pages brittle with age and stained with damp. "This gives a bit more insight into the life and times of Arthur Hemmings. It was clearly written by someone who knew the family well. Someone who moved in their social circles. Actually, I found it amongst a pile of old donated books that were being sold to raise funds for the library."

She took it and sat down, turning the pages carefully.

This was indeed a remarkable find. The book contained the biographies of three of Sterling's most prominent inhabitants, Frederick Lockstone, Lord John Lockstone, and Arthur Edward Hemmings.

Born in 1850 in Manchester, into a family already steeped in banking history, Arthur Hemmings had moved with them to Sterling in 1881 and they quickly became a force with which to be reckoned. At the comparatively early age of thirty-six, Arthur Hemmings succeeded his father as head of the Hemmings Bank and continued to direct the company toward an ever-increasing fortune.

During this time, he became acquainted with a young woman by the name of Lady Adele Lockstone, younger sister of Lord John Lockstone, and Frederick Lockstone, who was chairman of the second largest bank in Sterling. Because the Lockstone family had encouraged the match and despite the fact that Adele had expressed a reluctance to marry, in 1890, Adele and

Hemmings were wed. It was not difficult to read between the lines, knowing what they did about the outcome of this disastrous union. In those days, a young woman was expected to marry, and Adele had no doubt been under considerable pressure from her family to ally herself to the Hemmings fortune.

After suffering a miscarriage in 1891, Adele maintained a low profile in the community until, in 1892, she was introduced to a young artist named Desmond Renard who had inherited his own fortune from a father who had amassed great wealth as a major shareholder in the East India Company.

Marianne could imagine Jane Weatherall gossiping maliciously to her friends about Adele and her supposedly secret assignations with the young artist. How she would have enjoyed making such veiled allusions to her friend's infidelity, the treacherous cat!

In October of that year, much to Arthur's chagrin, it became common knowledge that Adele had left him and, because of the simultaneous disappearance of the artist and his fortune, causing much scandalous speculation, it was assumed that they had indeed run away together. Hemmings had appeared distraught by his young wife's flight and, after waiting for several days in the hopes that she would return of her own volition, made exhaustive efforts to trace the couple in order that he might offer to forgive and welcome her back home. This magnanimous gesture was thwarted, however, when all attempts to locate them proved fruitless. Enquiries made at Renard's home showed that the place had been vacated, and all his personal possessions removed, leaving no forwarding address.

After a year of searching, Arthur reluctantly conceded his wife's defection and once more devoted his full attention to business and his position in the community. He continued to live alone at the house in Wellington Street, having never remarried. The book listed his achievements up until his death in 1930. The narrative concluded that Arthur Edward Hemmings had been one of Sterling's most munificent benefactors and respected citizens.

She closed the book and looked over at Vincent. "So, no one ever knew the truth of what happened to Adele."

"No. There was some speculation that they'd gone to live on the continent and one or two people thought they might have left for America." He shook his head and came across the room to take the book from her. "I wonder what he did with her body."

"She's still in the house, I'm certain of it," Marianne said with conviction. "Don't ask me to explain how I know. I just felt it when I was there. Oh Vincent! It angers me so much to think that he got away with murdering her." Marianne appeared pensive for a while and then said, "But there's another question that hasn't been answered. We know that he killed Adele, but what happened to Desmond Renard? Did Hemmings kill him too?"

"It's possible. I couldn't seem to find any record of his whereabouts after 1892," Vincent replied.

"How awful! What a brute Hemmings must have been." Marianne suspected that Vincent was going to offer the typical male excuse justifying a cheated husband's revenge, and went on quickly, "Oh I know, she was having an affair but look at the facts. He took advantage of her naivete when he married her. He didn't really love her. He didn't want her, but he kept her shut up in that house and when she finally found the happiness she'd been longing for, he couldn't stand the fact that someone else had stolen her. She was a possession that he had no further use for, but he would rather kill her than allow another man to possess her."

Vincent laughed and put his arms around her. "You're right, as usual. But I can't help feeling a little sympathy for him. I would certainly kill anyone who tried to steal you away from me." Despite his levity, there was an underlying seriousness in his words.

"But you forget there's one big difference," Marianne replied. "I love you. You surely don't still need to be convinced of that fact."

He pulled her closer and, with a playful smirk, answered, "Yes. Please convince me," and in one swift movement, lifted her up out of the chair and, carrying her through to the bedroom, unceremoniously dropped her onto the bed. He stood looking down at her and just for a moment, an expression passed across his face that she had not seen before, a look of uncertainty as though not sure of his welcome there. How could he ever doubt that? She held out her arms to draw him down.

16

CONFLAGRATION

THE FOLLOWING DAY, although it was cool, the weather was sunny and, being a Sunday morning with no special commitments on hand, Vincent proposed a day out. Marianne said she thought it was a good idea, and they set out to drive into the countryside for one of their mystery tours. Vincent kept up a lighthearted banter as they went along, his manner unusually effervescent. It seemed as though the cloud that had hung over them since that first trip to the museum had finally lifted and the relief made them positively lightheaded.

Marianne was not taking much notice of the direction of their progress, too much absorbed in the pleasure of being with Vincent in this joyful mood and so it was with uneasy surprise that she found herself approaching the outskirts of Sterling. They had been discussing his book, and she stopped in mid-sentence to exclaim, "What? What are we doing here?"

Vincent hastily attempted to reassure her. "It's alright. Don't panic. If you don't want to stop, we'll go right back home now, honestly. But aren't you just in the least little bit curious to know where she is?"

Of course, Marianne knew who he was referring to and, truth to tell, she still harbored, despite all that had happened, an overwhelming desire to discover Adele's final resting place.

"I'll be with you every step of the way this time," he assured her.

She was not inclined to refuse, and despite her reluctance, they continued their way to Wellington Street.

Once again, the place was deserted, although Marianne was surprised to see that the "For Sale" sign was no longer posted in the front garden. She was wondering how they were to gain entrance to the house, when she was surprised to see Vincent produce a key from his pocket and precede her up the path. It was evident then that this trip had by no means been a spur-of-the-moment thing, but was planned with the obvious intention of entering the house. He must have been confident of her compliance, Marianne thought with a stab of resentment. Well, no matter. He knew her too well, that was all. And shrugging off any objection, she followed him to the back of the house.

Minutes later, he was turning the key in the lock, but just as he was about to open the door, a thought occurred to her.

"You do understand that when we get in there that, well … I know it sounds crazy but I may see things that you can't, so I think it would be best if you let me lead the way and you just stay back a bit." He made to argue, but she was adamant. "We'll do it my way or not at all."

"Okay! Okay! But I want you to tell me what's going on. I don't want you making any sudden moves without telling me."

"Alright, just don't be surprised if I start talking to thin air," she warned, half-jokingly. To tell the truth, she was doubtful if anyone or anything would manifest itself while he was with her but it was better to be prepared for all eventualities. He pushed open the door and, with a theatrical gesture, ushered Marianne in ahead of him.

She stepped in to a place that was totally unfamiliar to her. The kitchen, far from looking as it had done before, now appeared to her as others must see it, an empty room covered in dust and hung about with cobwebs. The table with its little posy of flowers had gone. The pots, pans, and other accouterments were no longer hanging from the walls or lying in drawers or cupboards. Even the bulky cast-iron stove had disappeared, leaving the sink with its ornate tiling as the only recognizable object in that once well-scrubbed and efficient hub of domestic activity. Even the mice seemed to have deserted the place, it was so silent. Marianne made her way across the room with Vincent following a few paces behind her.

"Everything looks so different," she whispered. "I can't believe it. When I came here before, it was as though they were still living here. I wish you could have seen it then," she exclaimed, and realized with a sudden sinking feeling that he probably wouldn't have seen the same thing anyway.

She led the way along the corridor, noticing, as their footsteps sounded noisily against the wooden floorboards, that the carpet was gone and the walls were adorned now only by large irregular-shaped patches of damp. She stopped at the first door and they looked in. As with the kitchen, the dining room was empty. Only footprints in the thick dust of the floor, probably those of D. S. Ince and possibly W.P.C. Samuels, as well as her own, showed that anyone had been there recently. Vincent shook his head in amazement. "It's incredible! That you were able to see all those things," he said, remembering her earlier description of the ornate Victorian furniture that had adorned the room on her previous visit.

On they went down the hallway to the drawing room. Here the image of abandonment seemed complete. Nothing remained of the elegant scene that had been laid out before her eyes just a few weeks before. The interior smelled musty and damp with decay. Not a single vestige of the former occupants remained. All trace of Adele and Arthur Hemmings had been obliterated by the passage of time, the photos, newspaper, wineglass, all gone; only the diary of a desperately unhappy woman remained, tucked safely away in a drawer in their apartment.

Marianne walked slowly around the room, remembering clearly the contents and its position, here the desk, there by the window, the étagère with its bibelots and bric-à-brac. She wondered darkly if the restless and possibly vengeful ghost of Adele had ever come back to haunt Arthur Hemmings as he sat there night after night amid the material splendor of his accumulated wealth.

She led the way back through the room, out into the hallway, and they climbed silently to the floor above, making their way to the bedroom at the front of the house. Vincent knew from Marianne's account of what had happened here, that this was the room in which Adele had met her death. He reached forward to stop her from entering but she turned and whispered, "It's alright, I don't think they're here now." They went in and looked about the room. As she had suspected, there was no one there. The scene of Adele's bloody demise was, like the rest of the house, empty and covered in dust.

Nothing was to be gained by remaining there. Marianne felt that if they were to find Adele's body, it would be in another part of the building, and after a cursory inspection of the rest of the second floor, they returned downstairs. As they reached the bottom step, Marianne became aware of a cold wave of air that she sensed was not wholly attributable to the time of the year or lack of heating inside the house.

They were here, somewhere within these walls, despite the absence of all other external evidence of their tenancy. Adele and Arthur Hemmings were still in residence. She could feel their presence as surely as she could feel Vincent's closeness to her in that dark hallway. She walked rapidly back in the direction of the kitchen and straight to the door that she had assumed on her first visit would lead to the cellar, Vincent still following a few paces behind. The doorknob felt icy to the touch and Marianne shivered as she turned it and pushed the door open. She had become accustomed to this eerie sensation of extreme cold whenever she came into contact with either Adelle or Arthur Hemmings. Its manifestation warned her that they were on the right track.

A light shone from the depths of the cellar, illuminating the steps sufficiently for her to descend safely, but Vincent, who was still crossing the kitchen floor, called out, "Wait! Hold on, I've brought a flashlight with me." He clicked on its broad, penetrating beam and followed her cautiously down the stairs.

On an upturned cask at the bottom of the steps Marianne discovered the source of the light, an oil lamp, which projected its glow about the damp walls of the cellar, casting eerie shadows and flickering occasionally as a draft from somewhere in the house caught at the flame. The presence of the lamp was strange. Had the tramp, no longer satisfied with the shelter that the ruined cottage afforded, managed to find a way into the house? Someone had been here before them and recently, but whether a living, breathing person or a shadow from the past she couldn't tell. All she knew for certain was that the cold was almost tangible in that subterranean vault.

Boxes filled with papers and piles of old tattered draperies littered the earthen floor. A shelf against the far wall contained objects such as old cans of paint, glass bottles holding various cleaning agents, and miscellaneous items of an indeterminate nature.

The center of the floor had been cleared and the earth, different in color from that surrounding it, appeared to have been newly dug. This supposition was enforced by the presence of a shovel, earth still clinging to the metal blade, leaning against a large wooden chest close by.

Vincent was descending the stairs, but Marianne motioned him to stay back. She remembered how Adele had vanished when he'd entered the carriage at the museum, and she was fearful that any interference on his part would jeopardize their search. Determined to pursue this thing to its conclusion, she went on alone as Vincent stood watching halfway down the stairway.

Picking up the lamp, Marianne went towards the newly turned soil and putting the lamp down on the ground and grasping the shovel began to scrape at the surface, carefully removing the layers of dirt. She didn't have to go far before she reached what she knew would be there.

Flinging the shovel aside, Marianne dropped to her knees and began to scrabble at the earth with her fingers. Gradually there began to appear the light brown material of Adele's traveling clothes, the skirt, and the blood-stained bodice. With trembling hands, she removed the last of the earth and uncovered the bruised neck and finally the pallid face, once beautiful but now battered. Adele's dark hair lay loose about her shoulders.

"She's here!" Marianne cried triumphantly.

Vincent ran down to the foot of the stairs and came a few steps toward her, peering through the gloom as Marianne got to her feet.

Just then, a noise reached their ears. This was evidently not otherworldly, but someone who had either already been in the house when they arrived, or worse yet, witnessed their entry and followed them in. Marianne fervently hoped that it wasn't the police. Could it possibly be the tramp?

They both looked up toward the top of the stairs as the door was suddenly flung open and, to their utter amazement, there stood Matthew, breathless and disheveled.

"Matthew!" his sister exclaimed. "What on earth are you doing here?"

He came stumbling down the stairway, his eyes not yet accustomed to the dim light. They both went forward to assist him, but he regained his balance and came on with a look of anger on his face that Marianne had never seen before. They backed away from him in alarm, wondering what could have upset him to such an extent.

Marianne watched, stupefied, as he made directly for Vincent and without any warning, drew back his right arm and aimed a blow with a tightly clenched fist to his jaw that sent Vincent staggering backwards. He came on relentlessly and had grasped hold of Vincent's coat lapels, all the while shouting, "You! You brought her back here! You rotten bastard!" as he struck again. But Vincent, despite the disadvantage of his years, was still athletic and agile enough to retaliate and the two fought savagely amid the boxes and debris that lay about the floor.

Marianne made an attempt to separate them, but they were oblivious to her presence, so engrossed were they in their conflict. She was inadvertently knocked to the ground, tipping over the oil lamp that had been left standing at the foot of Adele's grave. The flame quickly ignited the cloth of the dead woman's gown and rapidly spread to the papers that had been scattered about the ground by the two combatants. Marianne had twisted her leg as she fell, and as she tried to stand up, a surge of pain shot through her, making her stagger and cling to the railing at the bottom of the stairs for support.

At that moment the old familiar icy-cold wave engulfed her and, looking up through the smoke, she saw the dark, menacing figure of Arthur Hemmings coming slowly down the stairs towards her. She screamed but neither her brother nor her lover could hear her, for they were too much embroiled in their own private battle. On he came, and Marianne was powerless to move. An enormous crash caused Hemmings to pause in his descent, as Matthew, throwing Vincent against the shelving, had caused the whole unit to come smashing down on top of them. But it was only a temporary reprieve as Hemmings quickly dismissed their struggle as of no consequence and continued his descent.

The fire was now burning fiercely and the flames, fed by the highly flammable contents of the bottles, greedily consumed everything in their path. They had already reached up as far as the wooden floorboards overhead. The smell of burning and the noise of the various bottles and cans cracking and exploding mingled with the acrid black smoke that was filling the cellar was appalling. As Marianne watched helplessly, Arthur Hemmings took one final step toward her and grabbed her by the hair, dragging her backward until his arms encircled her in a vise-like grip.

Arthur's voice came in a whisper, cold as the grave, "You've come back to interfere for the last time."

One icy hand closed about her mouth, stifling the scream that had again risen to her throat as he dragged her struggling toward the stairs. As she looked back towards the cellar, Marianne could see through the flames, Vincent, venturing one last effort to fend off Matthew's attack, landing a blow that sent the other man reeling backwards, hitting his head on the corner of the chest. Vincent, exhausted, collapsed to his knees, choking from the smoke as Matthew fell senseless to the ground.

As Hemmings pulled Marianne up the stairs, Vincent finally seemed to become aware of what was going on around him and staggered to his feet. She saw him look desperately around the mounting inferno as if he were searching for something.

As they reached the top of the stairs, Hemmings pulled Marianne through the doorway, and she caught a final glimpse of the cellar as the flames that had now taken hold of the stairway itself licked upward towards them. Vincent made a desperate rush at the burning steps and, with the boards barely sustaining his weight, flung himself upward through the door. As he reached out to grasp Marianne, she felt Hemmings relinquish his grip, and he vanished as she and Vincent lay there gasping for breath on the floor. Then an explosion, emanating from the region of the cellar, rocked the whole house, which had now become filled with smoke, and the flames that had already escaped from the cellar threatened to engulf the entire building.

Barely able to speak, Marianne clutched at Vincent and rasped, "Matthew! He's still down there!"

Vincent shook his head, hardly able to draw breath. "It's too late. We can't do anything!"

Staggering to his feet, he dragged her through the flames back along the burning hallway. As they reached it, the smoldering front door was split apart, and an unearthly figure appeared amid the dense smoke, a fireman helmeted and masked, to lead them to safety.

17

AFTERMATH

ONCE OUTSIDE, THE SCOPE OF THE DISASTER BECAME APPARENT. The entire building was a solid mass of flame. Hurrying them away from the conflagration, their rescuer yelled, "Is there anyone else in the building?"

"Yes! my brother. He was down in the cellar," Marianne screamed, frantically clutching his arm.

He looked back at the house and hurried away, leaving them with two paramedics who helped them to the back of an ambulance that was drawn up at the curb. Vincent was burned about the arms and legs, having narrowly escaped from the cellar before the floor above had come crashing in upon it. Marianne's injuries had ironically been less severe, in part because of Hemmings timely intervention. If he had not dragged her up those steps when he did, she would have undoubtedly been caught in the inferno. Although what he had planned for her, once they had attained the first floor, she dreaded to think. Nothing short of death, she suspected, would have satisfied him.

But now Marianne was in an agony of mind, wondering desperately what had become of Matthew. She tried to see over the shoulder of the man who was administering first-aid to them, to get some glimpse of what was happening. Was there any possibility that he could have survived? She knew deep down that there was little hope and was sickened by the thought.

Vincent had at first declined any assistance. The shock of what had happened had made him oblivious to his injuries. He was trying desperately to console Marianne, for she was by now becoming frantic in her anxiety over Matthew. He was eventually persuaded that his injuries were serious enough to warrant treatment, and he reluctantly submitted as he was whisked away in the ambulance to the hospital from which Marianne had so recently returned home.

Marianne was torn between her desire to be with him and the overwhelming need to stay at Wellington Street in the faint hope that Matthew might be rescued. But at least she knew Vincent was safe, and so she waited and begged every person who passed her for information regarding her brother's fate. But they either couldn't or wouldn't tell.

What seemed like hours later, she felt a tap on the shoulder and spinning round, almost believing hope against hope that it was Matthew, she saw D.S. Ince standing before her.

"Matthew? Is he alright? Did they find him in time?" she pleaded.

He shook his head regretfully. "I'm very sorry Ms. Clay. He didn't make it. They tried to get in there, but the fire was just too far advanced."

"I see," she said numbly. "Yes. Of course. I understand. I'm sure they did their best."

"You really should go to the hospital" he insisted. "You're probably suffering from shock. They can give you something to help."

She couldn't think. She couldn't comprehend what had happened. Her mind was a complete blank. Nothing could help her now. Oh Matthew! What on earth had occurred to make him come after Vincent like that?

In a daze, she allowed Ince to lead her back to his car, and she got in, mechanically closing the door and fastening the seat belt. He was silent during their journey to the hospital, although Marianne was certain his natural instinct to pepper her with questions must have been uppermost in his thoughts. However, whether in deference to her devastating loss or because he realized that in her present condition, she was in no fit state to answer anything coherently, he refrained.

Arriving at the emergency room, Ince showed his identification to an attendant, and they were ushered through the doors to where people were awaiting treatment. They quickly located Vincent who, bandaged and with a look of sheer exhaustion, threw his arms around Marianne, grimacing with pain.

"Darling! I'm so sorry that I couldn't save Matthew. Sorry that I ever suggested going back there."

She was alarmed at his appearance, and despite her own misery at the loss of Matthew, her heart went out to him.

"Don't talk about it now. You're safe. That's all that matters."

Ince, who had been standing discreetly to one side during this tearful reunion, now stepped forward.

"I hate to bother you at a time like this, but it really would help if you could just give us some idea of what happened back there at the house."

Marianne remained silent, but Vincent was in control of the situation now.

"Yes. Anything we can do to help. We went there, the three of us, Ms. Clay, her brother and myself, to Wellington Street to see if we could jog some memory of what happened there in October. We thought perhaps Marianne might remember something that would give us a clue as to who attacked her."

"And were you successful?"

"I'm afraid not," Marianne said. "I couldn't remember anything that would have been of any use. We wandered about for a bit. It was becoming dark in there, so Matthew found some candles in a cabinet and lit a couple of them."

"Yes." Vincent took up the narrative, obviously aware that she was carefully steering Ince away from what had really happened. "He wanted to take a look in the cellar, so he went down there."

"We stayed upstairs. I knew there was nothing much down there except some cans of paint and a lot of old newspapers. He'd only been gone for a minute or so, and all of a sudden there was an explosion. The candle must have touched something off. We tried to get to him, but it was useless. There was nothing we could do," Marianne explained.

"Did you notice any kind of smell in the house, gas fumes, anything like that?"

Vincent appeared to think for a moment and said, "No, nothing other than just what you'd expect from a house that's been shut up for so long."

"No," Marianne added, determined to back him to the hilt. "Nothing out of the ordinary."

"It all happened so quickly," Vincent explained. "Before we knew it, the whole place was in flames."

The tale sounded thin in the telling and Marianne could see that Ince didn't think much of it, but for now he would have to be satisfied with their account.

"May we leave now?"

"Yes. Yes, of course, we'll notify you as soon as we are able to … find the body." The detective hesitated, not wanting to upset Marianne any further. "You'll want to make arrangements."

"Yes. Thank you," she replied and left him scribbling notes in his little book, as a doctor came to examine her.

Once they were discharged, she and Vincent made their way to the hospital lobby.

"I'll call for a taxi to take us back to Wellington Street to pick up the car," she said, and left him while she went to make the call.

Back at Wellington Street, the picture was one of absolute devastation. The house was nothing but a pile of burnt and twisted rubble. Even the oak tree had been reduced to a charred stump. Having deposited them on the sidewalk outside the remains of number seventeen, the taxi driver sped away, leaving them to gaze at the smoldering ruins. The fire department was still there, hosing down the last of the glowing embers. They would soon begin the grim task of searching through what remained of the building for Matthew's body.

Marianne shuddered and felt a rising surge of nausea. Trying hard to put the thought out of her mind, she urged Vincent towards their car. "Come on, let's get out of here. I'll drive. You're in no fit state." She nodded toward his bandaged hands and he agreed.

Before leaving, she looked across the street to where Matthew had left his car and while Vincent was getting settled, she ran over to it to see if the doors had been left open. As she suspected, the doors were unlocked, the key still in the ignition. He must really have been distracted for him to do such an uncharacteristically negligent thing. She opened the driver's door and removed the key. Then, on second thoughts, checked the glove compartment and seats to see if he had left anything there. There was nothing, so she locked the car and went around to the trunk. Marianne had half hoped that there might be some clue to Matthew's irrational behavior, but there was nothing there and having checked once again to make sure everything was secure, she re-crossed the road and got into their car. Vincent looked at her questioningly.

"I just thought I'd look to see if he left anything," she explained. "But there's nothing."

He didn't reply and she could think of nothing to add, so she started up the car and they left.

No music now. Nothing but a silent drive home through the night, each thinking about what had happened. What on earth had possessed them all? Why had they been so determined to discover Adele Hemmings' whereabouts, and what on earth had prompted Matthew to act as he had?

Then a terrible realization hit her. Clare! She would have to call her, tell her what had happened. How to tell her sister that because of her obsession with the past, she had led their brother into a death trap, that she and Vincent had escaped and had left Matthew there to perish in the flames?

By the time they arrived home, the sun was beginning to rise, and they were both exhausted, but Marianne knew she would never be able to sleep. Vincent, however, was so loaded with painkillers that sleep was inevitable. He had hardly flopped down on the bed before he was dead to the world. Marianne sat and watched him for a while, then got up and went to the kitchen to make strong coffee, something to fortify her for the task ahead.

Time and time again Marianne went to the phone only to replace the receiver in a cold sweat, dreading the moment when she would hear Clare's voice at the other end of the line and be compelled to deliver the worst of all possible news. The burden of telling her of Matthew's death lay squarely on her shoulders, but she just couldn't bring herself to do it.

It wasn't until nearly mid-day that she finally summoned up the courage to complete the call to her sister and the summons was answered immediately, leaving Marianne no further time to consider her words.

"Hello. Who is this?"

"Clare? It's me, Annie."

"Annie? Is everything alright?"

Marianne began to find her nerve failing her and could say nothing at that moment.

"Annie! Are you there? What's happened?"

"Clare, I've got some terrible news. Are you on your own, or is Preston there?"

"Yes. He came home for lunch. For God's sake, what's happened?"

"It's Matthew. Clare, there's been an accident."

"Car accident? What's happened?" Clare repeated, the panic rising in her voice.

"No, a fire. We were at someone's house last night. There was a fire."

"Oh my God! Is … is he hurt?"

There was no easy way to say it. "He's dead, Clare. He didn't make it out in time."

Marianne could hear a muffled cry and the sound of the receiver as it must have fallen from Clare's hand to the floor.

"Clare! Clare!" she shouted. "Are you alright?"

The next moment Preston had picked up the receiver.

"Annie? What's happened? Wait a minute. Hold on!"

She heard them as she imagined Preston trying to calm Clare. Then, after what seemed like minutes, he was back on the phone. By this time, Vincent, who had woken at the sound of her voice, had joined her.

"Clare?" he asked in a whisper.

She shook her head. "Preston."

Vincent, feeling that one explanation was about all Marianne was capable of handling, took the receiver from her and said calmly, "Preston? This is

Vincent. I'm sorry this has been a terrible shock for Clare. I'm afraid its Matthew. He's been killed in a fire."

He listened for a moment and then said, "She's okay. Some minor burns and smoke inhalation, but we're home now. Listen, Preston, I can't go into details now, but they won't release the body yet. Proof of identification and all that. But we'll let you know as soon as we can. One last favor? Would you mind breaking the news to your father-in-law? I don't think Marianne is up to it right now, and for one reason or another, hearing it from me would just make matters worse."

Again, he waited. "Thank you! I'm tremendously grateful. Please tell Clare, I'm very sorry and we'll be in touch tomorrow. Let me know if there's anything I can do." Vincent paused as Preston said something and then finally, "Thanks. Goodbye."

He hung up the phone, and Marianne looked at him questioningly.

"Clare's alright. Preston said he'll call their doctor. Get something to calm her down. But what about you darling? Are you alright?"

"Yes. At least—"

The floodgates opened and the tears came pouring out. Nothing was held back and Vincent, cradling her in his arms, absorbed the grief and bitter self-recriminations that flowed from her. He sat with her until, absolutely drained of energy and emotion, she went to sleep.

18
REVELATIONS

THE DAY FOLLOWING THE FIRE had already been productive for D.S. Ince. He received a call from one of the patrol cars to say that a tramp, answering the description given to them by the old lady in Wellington Street, had been picked up and was now being transported to the station.

Shortly thereafter, he confronted the man seated across from him in the interview room and began to question him.

"It says here that you refused to give your name, and that you have nothing to identify you on your person."

"That's correct." The voice was surprisingly cultured, if a little tipsy.

"Can you tell me where you were yesterday?"

"Why?"

"Just answer the question."

"I was over at Lockstone Grange."

"Oh, yes? Tea and crumpets in the drawing room, no doubt," Ince scoffed.

"I was spending a pleasant afternoon with a friend, actually, officer."

"Don't make me laugh! Which friend would that be, then? Lord of the manor maybe?"

The tramp gazed back at Ince stoically, but didn't reply.

"Can anyone verify your whereabouts?"

"As it happens, yes. I was enjoying a little tipple with the head gardener, Jerry Dunster. Why? What am I being accused of?"

"There was a fire on Wellington Street yesterday. Someone reported seeing you in the area recently."

"And why would that have anything to do with me?"

"Can you account for your whereabouts on the 28th of October of this year?"

The tramp appeared to think. "I believe I may have been here in Sterling. Yes. It's pointless to deny it since someone evidently saw me. Why?"

"Did you enter the house at 17 Wellington Street on that date?"

"No. Not the house. I'd been kipping down in the cottage in the grounds for a while. It seemed like a safe billet. No one around to bother me."

"Did you happen to see a young lady there?"

"Not then, No. I'd seen her there a few weeks earlier. She was with a man. They were poking around in the grounds and she caught me unawares."

"But you didn't see her after that?"

"No. I laid low for a bit after that. I was afraid they might come back, so I let myself into the empty house next door and stayed there."

"Did you see anyone else hanging around number seventeen?"

"No. As I said, I kept a low profile. Kept my head down."

"And no one can vouch for your whereabouts on the 28th?"

"No. I'm afraid not."

"In that case, I must detain you on suspicion of assault and attempted murder. I must ask you again, for your name, sir."

The tramp was clearly rattled. "Very well, D.S. Ince.

If it's absolutely necessary. My name is Francis Frederick Lockstone and, apparently, the new owner of Lockstone Grange."

Later that afternoon, Marianne received a call from D.S. Ince. Would it be possible for her to return to Sterling immediately? They had located a body, and they needed her to identify some items that had been found with it. She told Ince that she would drive over right away.

Vincent offered to go with her, but Marianne felt that she needed to make the trip alone and set out for Sterling unaccompanied.

As she entered the austere premises of the Sterling police department, Marianne received one or two curious glances and was ushered through to Guy Ince's desk.

"Ms. Clay, how are you?" He seemed genuinely concerned and his clasp of her hand lingered fractionally longer than was altogether necessary.

He motioned her to a seat and resumed his place behind the desk. He looked at her for a moment, his dark eyes searching her face for signs of what? Misery? Anger? Guilt? She felt all three, but tried to remain calm under his penetrating gaze.

"I would be lying, detective sergeant, if I said I was fine."

"That's understandable. You've just lost your brother, after all. This must have been a very traumatic experience for you, and I really hate to add to your troubles right now, but as I explained on the phone, I need you to identify some items that we recovered from the house on Wellington Street this morning. Of course, we'll have to get confirmation of identification through dental records and such, but for now, if you could just take a look at these."

Marianne winced at the gruesome image that Ince's words had conjured up.

He opened a drawer, took out several plastic evidence bags, and placed them on the desk in front of him. He looked at her again, a long hard stare, as his fingers lightly touched the bags. Marianne sat mesmerized as she watched him slowly lift the first, hold it momentarily suspended, then place it carefully on the desk in front of her. Her hands began to tremble. The thought of seeing something belonging to Matthew caused a wave of panic to wash over her.

"May I?" she indicated the bag and Ince nodded.

Marianne picked it up and scrutinized the contents through the clear plastic. Inside lay a gold ring. She recognized it immediately. It was the ring that her mother had given Matthew shortly before she had died, a man's gold signet ring with 'Love Forever' inscribed inside the band. Up until that time, Marianne had only seen it, hidden away under some handkerchiefs, in the small drawer of her mother's dressing table. At first, she wondered who it had belonged to. Perhaps it was her grandfather's, although it didn't seem likely. In the end, she preferred to think of it as belonging to someone her mother had known long ago, before her marriage to Marianne's father. And so, it was passed on to Matthew and although it was too large for him to wear until he had grown older, he kept it safe through the ensuing years.

She nodded her head and said quietly, "Yes, that's Matthew's."

Ince's hand closed again on the bag and replaced it with another that contained a man's watch. Marianne thought she had seen Matthew wearing it, although she hadn't paid particular attention to it, so couldn't be certain. A third bag held a St Christopher's medallion on a chain that she did recall seeing about his neck.

Ince returned the bags to the drawer and continued to gaze into its interior as though there was something he had yet to show her. He reached in and slowly withdrew another bag, this one containing a long silver chain from which hung a heart-shaped locket. Marianne had seen it before, but not on Matthew.

She looked alternately from the locket to Ince and hoped that the recognition did not show on her face. She reached forward. "May I?" She took the bag and, gazing down at it, thought about how she had seen the locket hanging around the neck of Adele as she appeared that day in the train carriage. She returned it to Ince, who continued to look at it speculatively.

"I'm sorry, I don't remember seeing that before. It might have been Matthew's, but I don't recognize it."

"No, I don't think it was his. You are certain that there were only three of you who went into the house that afternoon?"

"Yes."

"And no one came in there after you entered?"

"No, I'm sure we would have seen them."

"Could there have been someone already in the house when you entered it?"

Marianne could see where this line of questioning was headed now, but she refused to concede that other presence in the house and looked blankly at her interrogator.

"No, there was not a living soul in there when we went in," she said truthfully.

"And you have no idea who this locket could have belonged to?"

"No idea at all. I'm sorry."

"That's too bad," he said disappointedly. "You see, we were hoping that you could shed some light on the other body that we found in the cellar."

"Other body?" she asked tremulously.

"Well, when I say body," Ince corrected himself, "There wasn't much left. We discovered the remains alongside those of your brother. The only thing left to give us any clue to the person's identity was this locket." He continued to hold it out for her inspection and waited for her to reply, but she remained silent.

"No? Nothing suggests itself? Do you still claim, even in the face of what I've just told you, that there was no fourth person in the house at the time of the fire?"

"I'm sorry. I can't tell you. I don't know who she was."

"She? What makes you think it was a woman?"

"Well, the locket … I naturally assumed."

"Yes, of course." Ince stood up and walked around to Marianne's side of the desk. "Was she already dead when you got there?" The question shot out and made Marianne jump.

"No!" her response came too quickly and Ince leapt upon it.

"So, she was still alive, then?"

"No!" Marianne was becoming confused.

"Well Ms. Clay, it must be one or the other. She was obviously there, unless you're suggesting that the fire department somehow put her there after the fire."

"No! Of course not! I'm not suggesting any such thing. Don't be ridiculous!"

"So, which is it? Was she dead or alive at the time of the fire?" he persisted.

Marianne put her hands up to cover the desperation in her face and shook her head. "I … can't say."

He suddenly changed tack and put his hand solicitously on her shoulder. "Would you like some tea, Ms. Clay? I think we need to calm down a bit and think about what's going on here." Not waiting for Marianne to respond, Ince picked up the phone and asked for someone to bring two cups of tea from the canteen.

He resumed his seat behind the desk, and the two sat looking at each other in silence. Marianne couldn't decide whether to tell him the truth behind their visit to Wellington Street, but it was beginning to look as though she would have no other choice. The claim that they had been totally unaware of Adele's presence was too implausible. She weighed up the consequences of telling Ince about Arthur and Adele Hemmings against the continued denial of all knowledge of the second body. She wished she could talk to Vincent; to seek his advice, but doubted she would be given the opportunity.

The tea arrived, strong and hot. Marianne took a sip and placed the mug carefully on the desk. It was then that she decided to relate at least a partially truthful rendition of what had occurred at the house.

"Alright, I'll tell you," she agreed. "She was there."

"And who was she?"

"Adele Hemmings, and she was already dead when we got to the house. In fact, she's been dead for eighty years or more," she said. "And if the Sterling police department had looked into the case a little more thoroughly at the time of her disappearance, they might have discovered that fact," Marianne couldn't help adding recklessly.

Ince looked incredulous, and she hurried on with her explanation. "You will of course be able to confirm most of this. I know it sounds very melodramatic, but it's quite true. We were doing some research, Vincent and I, into the history of Sterling and naturally, the name of Hemmings came up. Vincent discovered an old book detailing Arthur Hemming's role in the community and there was also mention of his wife, Adele." Marianne looked at him, trying to gauge whether he believed her or not.

"Vincent thought the explanation for her disappearance was questionable, and we got more and more into the whole idea of finding out what happened to her. We couldn't believe our luck when we realized that the house was still there and for sale."

Ince shifted in his seat, a look of puzzlement on his face, whether real or put on for her benefit, Marianne could not tell.

She resumed, "We didn't want to say why we were really interested in looking at the place, so we pretended to be prospective buyers. That was when I went there to look around inside."

"Yes, you went there alone, if I remember rightly. Mr. Foxworth was unfortunately called away on business that day. And you still insist that you don't know who attacked you then?" He referred to the report that was before him on the desk.

"No. Maybe it was someone who didn't want the truth to come out about Adele's disappearance, although I don't know how anyone could have known that I was there for that reason. Anyway, the attack made us more convinced than ever that there was something there in the house, some clue to Adele's whereabouts."

"When you went there the first time, you said that you tried the light switch, but the power was off?"

"Yes, that's right."

"And yet—" Ince referred once more to the file. "When our officers arrived on the scene, they reported that the light in the kitchen was on. How do you explain that?"

"I can't. The power was out when I got there."

"So, it's possible then that the person who attacked you knew you were going to be there, turned the power off before you arrived, and turned it back on after he'd taken care of business, shall we say?"

He waited for Marianne to reply, but she was baffled. Arthur Hemmings hadn't known that she would be going there that day. How could he? But she couldn't tell Ince that. How could she possibly explain seeing Hemmings in the act of brutally murdering his young wife, the look of surprise and rage on his face as he had turned on her with a knife that was already dripping with Adele's blood?

Ince sat watching Marianne, his fingers idly twirling the pencil that he had been using to make the occasional notation in his little book.

"Well, anyway, despite what happened, you decided to go back there?"

"Yes," she went on. "After I got home from the hospital and had got back on my feet, we decided to go and take another look at the house. Matthew was staying with us; he had come over to help take care of me and he came with us to Sterling. We went to the house and Matthew suggested that we should take a look down in the cellar. He was joking, really, but he said that if Arthur Hemmings had done away with his wife, he would most likely have buried her down in the cellar. So, we all went down there, not actually expecting to find anything, and Matthew started digging about in the dirt floor with a shovel. That was when we found her."

"Adele Hemmings?"

"Yes! She was buried there in the cellar, just as we had surmised."

"So, what happened then?"

"Yes, the fire, that was when it happened. I had gone back upstairs to get some more candles. The light down there in the cellar wasn't really good enough for us to see what we were doing, and just as I was taking them out of the cabinet in the kitchen, there was this tremendous explosion. The whole place shook, and I was knocked off my feet. It stunned me for a few minutes, I think." Marianne tried to keep her voice steady and her hands from shaking.

"I knew something dreadful had happened down there. Flames were coming through the floor in the kitchen and I had trouble getting back over to the entrance to the cellar. The door had been blown off its hinges and smoke was pouring out of the opening. I could see the stairway was beginning to burn, but Vincent managed to climb up before it collapsed. He thought Matthew was following him, but he must have been knocked out in the explosion. He was still down there and we couldn't get to him."

Ince stopped twirling the pencil and put it down carefully on the desk. He closed his eyes as though trying to summon up a mental picture of what had happened.

"I see."

"Perhaps we hit a gas line or something when we were digging around?" she suggested.

"Mm, possibly."

He sat considering what Marianne had told him for a moment. "Okay, Ms. Clay, perhaps you wouldn't mind waiting here for a moment." He got up and strode down the room between the desks into the corridor outside and disappeared from sight.

Had he believed her? Surely tests would prove conclusively that the fourth person was Adele. Marianne wasn't too worried on that score. And there had been no need to tell him about the fight between Vincent and her brother. It was the fire that had killed him. No one was to blame for the outcome except perhaps Arthur Hemmings, and he was beyond the reach of justice now.

After what seemed an interminably long time, Ince returned and, resuming his place behind the desk, asked, "Were you aware that someone was outside in the grounds, someone who saw you enter the house?"

The tramp! So, he had been there after all.

"No, I didn't know."

"He says that he saw only two people enter the house."

"He was obviously mistaken," Marianne protested.

"Obviously." The detective looked skeptical. "He also told us that he saw the two of you there on a previous occasion. He can't remember exactly when."

"I wouldn't have thought he was a totally reliable witness," Marianne countered, reluctant to implicate the tramp in any way.

Ince made a motion as though lifting an imaginary drink to his lips and raised his eyebrows questioningly.

"Precisely." Almost as soon as the word had left her lips, Marianne knew she had blundered.

"So, you know who I'm talking about. You did see him."

"The first time we went there, I did see him, yes."

"You didn't mention it."

"No. I didn't think it was important."

"Not important?" Ince was incredulous. "You were stabbed by someone. You knew there was a vagrant hanging about the place and yet you didn't think he was worth mentioning?"

"Believe me, I had close contact with the man on that first visit. I would have known if it was him, just by the smell."

"Right." The detective slapped his hands on the desk and rose from his seat.

"Well, thank you, Ms. Clay, for coming here today. What you have told us has certainly been very helpful, but of course you understand we will have to verify one or two facts before we can release your brother's remains."

"Yes, I understand. I'm sorry that I wasn't more forthcoming at the outset. It's just that we hadn't wanted to make it public knowledge, you see, about what we had suspected. The good name of Hemmings. But naturally, when I realized that you knew there had been another person in the house, I had no option but to tell you the truth."

A thought suddenly occurred to her. "The house. Was the property insured? Will we be held responsible for the damage?"

Ince seemed puzzled by this question and took some moments before replying, "I shouldn't think there'll be a problem. After all, Mr. Foxworth owns the property. He was quite entitled to be there, and I'm sure the place was well insured."

He seemed surprised by Marianne's look of incredulity. "You really didn't know that he owned the house on Wellington Street?"

"No. I had no idea."

Vincent owned the place? Marianne was totally nonplussed by this latest revelation. There must have been a misunderstanding. Surely, she would have known. He would have told her. No, it wasn't possible.

Ince appeared to digest this piece of information and, having ruminated on it for a moment or two, said, "There's just one more thing, Ms. Clay. We think we have apprehended the man who attacked you on the 28th of October, but we need you to identify him. We want to be sure we've got the right man before we charge him."

"As I told you at the time, D.S. Ince, I didn't really get a good look at him."

Marianne was starting to panic. She didn't want to accuse an innocent man. But then, of course, the simplest recourse was to tell them that she couldn't identify him. They would let him go, surely.

"Well, let's see, shall we? If you wouldn't mind waiting here for a moment."

Ince left the room and was immediately accosted by Superintendent Richard Robson. "What the devil's going on, Ince? Parks tells tell me you've got Frederick Lockstone's son cooped up in a holding cell."

"Yes, sir," Ince replied blandly.

"Good God, man! I hope you know what you're doing. You've got your inspector's exam coming up soon, haven't you? A mistake like this could cost you any chance of promotion."

"Yes, sir. I realize that, sir. We didn't know who he was when we brought him in. Nevertheless, he's being held here pending identification."

"On what charge?"

"Assault and attempted murder."

"Impossible! Frederick Lockstone passed away recently. I was at his funeral and I didn't see his son there."

"I have to admit, I thought he was pulling my leg when he told me, sir. This man claims to be Francis Frederick Lockstone. Do you know him, by any chance, sir?"

"We all thought he'd gone abroad. He was a young man when he left Cambridgeshire. I'm not sure I'd recognize him now."

"I'd welcome your opinion all the same, sir. He didn't have any papers on him. Nothing to verify who he is."

"Very well. I'll take a look," Robson agreed and followed Ince downstairs to the holding cell where he peered cautiously through the opening in the door.

"My God!" Robson exclaimed. "He looks like a tramp!"

"Precisely, sir. As I said, he had no identification on him and no visible means of support."

Just then, a constable came to tell Ince that they were ready for the lineup. They escorted the disheveled suspect upstairs where he was issued a number and told to stand in a line with several other vagrants who had been rounded up earlier that morning in the local park.

Ince went to fetch Marianne and led her to the other side of a window, where she could view, without being seen, the men who were lined up before her.

"Look carefully, Ms. Clay, and let us know if you see the man who attacked you on October 28th at 17 Wellington Street."

Although she had no intention of picking anyone out, she took her time and was momentarily startled to see the tramp, who had accosted her at the cottage, looking back at her. She was not about to point the finger at him, however, and after several minutes she turned to Ince and said, "I'm sorry, I don't recognize any of these men."

Ince shrugged off his disappointment and said, "Well, if you're certain, we won't detain you any further. As I said, we'll need a little time to be sure of our facts and get positive identification on the remains found at the house. I'll call you as soon as I can. Thank you for coming in."

They shook hands and again she felt his eyes bore into her as though he were trying to divine some fragment of evidence that had escaped him during their conversation.

As Marianne drove back to Swannington, her mind was in a turmoil. So much had happened in the past few months; the appearance of Adele and Arthur Hemmings, the attack, Matthew's death, and now this. What did it all mean? Had Vincent always known about the history attached to number seventeen, and how long had he owned the house on Wellington Street? Had he cared so much about discovering the truth that lay buried there that he had spared no expense to secure the building and its gruesome contents? But why hadn't he told her? And was the reason for Matthew's assault on him tied to all this? Had he known about Vincent's involvement? They kept no secrets from each other—at least she thought not, until now. Should she confront him with this evidence or keep silent and let him tell her in his own time?

Oh, Vincent! She had never doubted him before. He had never given her the slightest reason to believe that he was anything but truthful, but her faith in him had been dealt its first real blow. Although she was determined to accept whatever explanation he should give without question, Marianne couldn't help but feel that the rock-solid walls of their relationship had received a devastating hit.

She returned to the apartment to find Jonathan Amor there, thus forestalling any immediate questions that she might have put to Vincent regarding Wellington Street.

Amor stood as she entered the room and came over to greet her. "Annie, I'm so sorry about Matthew! Vincent's been telling me what happened. I just couldn't believe it. You poor thing! What a terrible experience for you both."

"Thank you, Jon. It's good of you to come over."

"If there's anything we can do to help, please, let us know."

Vincent remained silent during this exchange, but watched Marianne intently. Seeing nothing immediately untoward, however, he asked, "Can I get you anything to drink? Have you had anything to eat?"

"No, I'm fine right now, thanks," Marianne told him.

They sat for a while making polite conversation, trying not to touch upon recent events but about things that seemed mundane now, in comparison. All the time, Marianne could feel Vincent's eyes on her and where once she would have welcomed this attention, she now felt uncomfortable and ill at ease. Finally, pleading extreme fatigue, she withdrew to take refuge in the bedroom.

Sometime later, after Marianne had fallen into an uneasy sleep, Vincent came silently into the room. He slipped into the bed next to her and she could feel the closeness of his body as he put his arm around her, kissing her hair and neck and whispering her name. Despite her earlier misgivings, Marianne felt the familiar stirring within her that left her powerless to resist his advances, and she turned to respond to his embrace. His kisses, if anything, were more passionate than ever. The urgency of his lovemaking, despite his injuries, was so unlike his normally slow and seductive approach that it was almost as though he didn't want to give her time to reject him. As if she could!

In the morning, they awoke to the sound of the phone on Vincent's bedside table. He reached reluctantly from beneath the covers to answer it. The conversation was brief, and he replaced the receiver after just a few moments. Propped on one elbow Marianne looked at him enquiringly as he stretched his arms and ran his fingers through his tousled hair.

"D.S. Ince," he announced. "He's coming to pay us a visit."

"Oh?" His words brought her back to earth with a thud. *What now?* Had Ince some new revelation to spring on them? She doubted he was coming just for the pleasure of their company, and her heart sank at the prospect of more questioning. Vincent, however, seemed unperturbed and rolled over on his side to look at her. His slow smile and raised eyebrow suggested that the last thing on his mind was unexpected visits from detectives, but she put her hand against his chest to fend him off and asked, "When will he be here?"

"He's on his way. About an hour he said?" he replied nonchalantly.

"What!" Marianne sprang out of bed. "Listen, Vincent. I have to tell you something, she said hurriedly as she got dressed. "I didn't have a chance yesterday with Jon being here and everything, but when I saw Ince yesterday, I had to tell him about Adele."

"You did what?" He suddenly became serious.

"Oh, not about seeing her at the railway museum," Marianne added hastily. "Only that we suspected that something had happened to her. I had to tell him, Vincent. He knew! They found her in the cellar with Matthew." She was on the verge of panic and close to tears.

Vincent did his best to calm her, listening as she told him everything that had happened the previous day in Sterling. When she came to the part about his ownership of number seventeen, she sensed his body stiffen, but she needed to know.

"How long, Vincent? How long have you known about what happened at Wellington Street?"

"Only since the attack. When I read the diary, after you'd told me about what you'd seen there, I was determined to keep anyone else from going to the house. The only solution seemed to be to buy the place outright. Then we would have plenty of time to investigate further and not worry about someone coming in and taking the place away from under our noses before we'd discovered the truth."

"But why was it so important to you? I can't believe you'd go to such lengths."

"It's difficult to explain. I just got so immersed in the whole thing, especially after what happened to you. But I had no clue that things would go the way they did."

"But why did Matthew come after you like that?"

"He came across the papers detailing my purchase of the house. I think he was always rather suspicious of my intentions towards you, and I believe he even suspected I had something to do with the attack on you at Wellington Street."

"But why on earth would he think that?" Marianne asked, struggling to make sense of all that was happening.

"I don't know, but he was livid when he thought I was preparing to take you back there. He was just trying to protect you. I wish now that I'd listened to him, but I was so caught up in everything. It was as though I was just being pulled along from one decision to the next without really being able to stop."

"I know how you feel," Marianne agreed.

They were startled to hear the door buzzer. "Damn! That must be Ince!" Vincent jumped up. "Take your time. I'll keep him busy."

When Marianne joined them, she saw that D.S. Ince was accompanied by another man who was introduced as Detective Inspector Parks. Ince had already produced his notebook and was making copious entries as she heard Vincent go over, once again, the events of the past few weeks.

"The book that you say you found at the Sterling library, do you still have it here?" Parks asked. He apparently felt it necessary to take a more active interest in the case because of Francis Lockstone's involvement.

"Yes, would you like to see it?" Vincent asked.

"If it's at all possible, sir, yes."

Vincent went to his desk and, taking out the book, handed it to Parks.

The D. I. looked at it for a moment and said, "Thank you. I wonder if I might borrow it for a day or two. You understand, I don't have time to go through it now, but I'd be very interested to read. I'll give you a receipt and let you have it back as soon as I've finished with it."

"Certainly," Vincent said obligingly, fetching pen and paper from his desk.

Not to be outdone in this show of courteous cooperation, Marianne added, "You might also be interested to see something else that I found at the house on the day that I was attacked."

She left the room and returned shortly, holding the diary. Marianne felt that if they were looking for proof of Arthur Hemmings' foul deeds, this would be as good an indication as any of what had happened all those years ago.

Parks accepted the diary and looked at it with interest. Anticipating his request, Marianne said, "You can take it."

"Thank you. Technically speaking, it belongs to Mr. Foxworth, as part of the contents of the house. But I'll return it just as soon as I can."

Parks extended a hand in farewell and Ince did likewise. Vincent walked with them to the door and Marianne could hear the detective inspector say, "Thank you once again for your help, Mr. Foxworth. I hope we can resolve all this as quickly as possible. I realize this must be very distressing for Ms. Clay. I'll contact you once we tie up all the loose ends."

The door closed and Vincent returned.

"Well, that's over, thank goodness!"

"Do you think they believed all that?" Marianne asked, dubiously.

"They must. We've done nothing wrong. He'll see that when they prove that it was Adele."

"But what about Matthew?" she persisted.

"What about him?" Vincent replied rather indignantly. "He was the one who came after me, remember? I had to defend myself. If it hadn't been for the fire, things would have been alright, but there was nothing we could do."

"Yes, I know that!" Marianne replied impatiently.

"We've got to try and stay calm. It's terrible, but there's nothing we can do to change it. If we stick to what we've told them, there shouldn't be a problem. Darling, don't worry. Everything will be alright."

But he was mistaken. Just how wrong he was, did not become immediately apparent, but things were about to take another dangerous turn.

19

IN MOURNING

SOME DAYS PASSED BEFORE INCE CALLED to say that everything had been cleared up.

"I wanted to let you know, myself, that Matthew's identification has been confirmed," he told Marianne. "I'm very sorry." His sympathy sounded genuine.

"Thank you," Marianne was saddened and yet at the same time relieved by the news. "And Adele?"

"I probably shouldn't be telling you this, but although we can't be absolutely certain, the other body could possibly be that of Adele Hemmings," Ince reluctantly conceded. "They haven't yet determined the reason for the explosion and fire," he went on. "But the possibility that it was caused deliberately has been ruled out."

"I see. Well, thank you again for letting us know."

"Of course. We'll be in touch again regarding the return of the book and the diary, but it may take some time."

"Yes. I understand. One more thing, D.S. Ince. I would be grateful if you could let me know if you are ever able to confirm that it was Adele who you found at the house."

"I'll see what I can do," Ince replied.

After a further exchange of information and phone numbers, Ince rang off, and Marianne was left to officially mourn the loss of her brother.

Clare made all the arrangements for the funeral and invited Marianne and Vincent to stay with the family in London for the duration.

"It will be so much easier if we're all at the house together. No need to go to the trouble of booking a hotel room, and we can spend some time together," Clare insisted.

Quite apart from the emotional stress of the funeral, Marianne dreaded the forthcoming meeting with her sister. She had heaped most of the blame for what had happened to Matthew on her own head and was sure that if she knew the truth of the matter, Clare could not fail to do the same. Marianne had decided, therefore, not to elaborate on the explanation already given for the circumstances of their brother's death. A coward's way out, no doubt, Marianne thought bitterly, but one that seemed to be, by far, the least upsetting to everyone concerned.

It was, as Marianne expected, a somber reunion filled with tears and mournful voices.

"How are you, Annie? You look terrible," Clare greeted her sister when she and Vincent arrived at the Fanthorpe's home in Richmond upon Thames.

"You don't look so good yourself," Marianne retorted, half-jokingly.

"Well of course it's all been a terrible strain, but Preston's been marvelous, and the children have been a tremendous help. But how are you coping with it?"

"I'm okay, but I couldn't have got through it all without Vincent."

Clare turned to look over her shoulder at the two men who were also deep in conversation a few paces behind them in the hallway.

"He seems very nice and we're very grateful for everything that he's done," Clare whispered. "It's too bad that we had to meet him for the first time under these circumstances. It's quite late," Clare observed, looking at her watch. "Do you two want to go and eat somewhere, or will a sandwich and coffee here be alright?"

"I'm not that hungry. A sandwich will be fine, if that's alright with you?" Marianne replied.

"Yes, I think that would probably be best." Clare seemed relieved by her sister's choice. "By the way, I hope you two will be comfortable tonight. I've put Sarah in with Emma and given you her room while you're here."

"I hope they didn't mind being moved around?" Marianne asked anxiously.

"Good heavens no! This is all rather an adventure for them, seeing you again and meeting Vincent for the first time. Of course," Clare added, "they are absolutely devastated about Matthew. They were very close, but children are so adaptable and easily distracted."

"Matthew thought the world of them," Marianne said. "He talked about them all the time when he was with us."

Clare dabbed at her eyes with a tissue hastily retrieved from her pocket. "They worshiped him. He was such a good sport. He took them out to all sorts of places, brought them presents. There wasn't anything he wouldn't do for them. He spoiled them terribly."

They lapsed into silence for a while, then Preston said, "I don't know if Clare told you, but your father won't be coming to the funeral. I'm sorry, Annie. I did call him after all this happened and Clare tried talking to him."

"It's no good. He won't come. I thought he would make the effort, show some sign of remorse, but there was nothing," Clare added.

"Well, let's not worry about that now. I expect it's all been a huge shock for him. Perhaps he'll change his mind when he's had time to think about it," Marianne said, making excuses for her father as she had always done. "I didn't really expect him to come. Let's forget about him for now. We both want to thank you for everything you and Preston have done, making all the arrangements," Marianne said gratefully.

"Everything's set for the day after tomorrow," Clare explained as she led the way into the kitchen while Preston took Marianne and Vincent's bags to their room. "The service, as I told you on the phone, will be at our old church, St Simeon's, and the burial at Abney Park. I wanted him to be near Mum. Matthew was always her favorite," she added ungrudgingly.

"Who else is coming to the service?" Marianne asked as she filled the coffee pot while Clare was busy making sandwiches.

"Matthew's business partner, David Wheeler, of course, and the secretary, what's her name? Lee-Anne, is it? Aunt Isabelle and Uncle Mort, and oh yes, Mr. and Mrs. Russell. Can you believe it? They're flying in tomorrow."

"My goodness," Marianne expressed her amazement. "All the way from Sweden?"

"Yes! Isn't that kind of them?" Preston answered as he and Vincent joined them in the kitchen. "I thought I'd better let them know. Matthew went to stay with them a few times down at Diffingham, as he probably told you. But I never dreamed they'd travel all this way for the funeral. They must have thought a lot of him to do that."

"He was very fond of them," Marianne recalled. "He told us all about going down to Paradise House and how welcome they made him. It was very good of them. I remember them as being very nice people."

"Everyone will be coming back to the house after the service. I'm having Marshall's cater lunch," Clare informed them. "The Russells are staying nearby and are going on to visit relatives while they're over here.

As they continued talking, Marianne looked around her. It wasn't long after their marriage that Clare and Preston had moved from their flat in Cricklewood to their present home in Richmond upon Thames. Sarah had been born soon after, and Emma two years later. Justin was something of an afterthought and had arrived on the scene two years after Marianne had gone to live with Lucy Rowe in Birchford.

She had seen the children only rarely, and Marianne couldn't help wondering how she compared to Matthew, the one who had lived close by and had lavished so much love and attention on them for the past ten years. Her experience with children was minimal at best, and she realized that she could never in a million years live up to the standards that Matthew had set. Well, they must take her as they found her, she thought defensively.

A genial, middle-aged, and obviously capable woman bustled into the room and was introduced as Louise, a dear friend and neighbor who sometimes took care of the children. She had taken them out for the day and was now delivering them back home safe and sound. Justin had been packed off to bed, after much protest, but Sarah and Emma were just washing their hands and would be in shortly, she informed them.

"Thank you, Louise! That was so good of you. They needed cheering up, and I'm sure they had a wonderful time."

Louise smiled, said her goodbyes, and hurried off.

After making small talk for a few more minutes, Clare stood up and said, "I expect the girls are in the family room. Why don't you come through and see them?"

As they walked through the door to the family room, the TV, which had been tuned in to some inappropriate late-night show, was hastily switched off and two young faces turned to peer at Marianne over the back of the sofa. They looked at her with all the unabashed curiosity of youth, making her feel rather like a specimen under a microscope as she advanced toward them.

"Sarah, Emma. You remember Auntie Annie," Clare prompted, as the two girls smiled and sprang up to greet her. Marianne gave them each a hug and looked at them in some amazement. Sarah had been four and Emma three when she had left London for Birchford, and with visits to the family in London sporadic at best, the intervening years had wrought a dramatic change in their appearance. Sarah was tall for her age and looked a good three years older. She had inherited the O'Malley red hair, the legacy of Grandfather O'Malley passed on to her mother, and in features resembled Clare. Emma, on the other hand, favored Preston's side of the family. Both were polite, well spoken, not exactly precocious, but certainly they showed a maturity beyond their years. They each took Marianne by the hand and led her to the sofa where they took up strategic positions on either side of her, relegating Clare to a nearby armchair.

"Well, you two have certainly grown," Marianne said. "How's school?"

"Alright." Sarah replied nonchalantly. "I was top of the class last year. We're learning French this year, and Mummy says we can go over to Paris when I'm more proficient, so we can go shopping."

"I'm going too," Emma added. "I'm going to go up to the top of the Eiffel Tower and I'm going to go for a boat ride on the Seine. Daddy said we could, right, Mummy?" She looked to Clare for confirmation, and Clare laughed.

"Yes, probably. We'll see."

"You like to go shopping then," Marianne said, remembering how she and Clare would spend countless hours browsing among the racks of clothes in the Oxford Street stores during their teenage years.

"Yes!" the girls answered enthusiastically.

"Well at least you're starting out on the right foot," Marianne laughed.

At that point, the girls' interest transferred from Marianne to Vincent, who had seated himself in an armchair near the window. He gave them one of his rare but melting smiles. "It was very good of you, Sarah, to give up your room for us. We're very grateful."

"Oh, that's alright," Sarah simpered and gazed at him goggle-eyed. Emma, always the bold one, stood up and, taking his hand, led him to where Marianne was sitting. "You can have my seat, Uncle Vincent," she offered, and in this cunningly strategic move, placed herself next to him, perching on the arm of the sofa, leaving Sarah to maintain her place on the other side of her aunt.

"Can I get anyone a drink?" Preston volunteered. "Annie? A sherry?"

"Yes, that will be fine," she said.

"Vincent? Beer or scotch?"

"A scotch would be most welcome, thanks."

Preston went away to get the drinks, and once again the two girls monopolized the conversation. They wanted to know everything about life in Swannington and peppered the two with questions until Preston returned and Clare finally put her foot down, insisting that it was well past their bedtime.

"Off you go, you two! You'll see Auntie Annie and Uncle Vincent tomorrow. It's very late." After a token show of resistance, they departed and left the four adults to more serious topics of conversation.

"I didn't want to say anything in front of the children," Clare began, "and you don't have to, if it's too painful for you." She added, looking pointedly at the burns on the back of Vincent's hands, "But do you think you could tell us again what happened, you know, with Matthew?"

Marianne turned to look at Vincent and he nodded. Once again, she related the story that they had told D. S. Ince. Vincent held her hand as she did so, and because she had become word perfect in her narration, it came easily to the tongue. She had almost fooled herself into believing the watered-down truth that she so convincingly dispensed to others.

By the time Marianne finished, there were tears in Clare's eyes. Preston, his arm around her shoulders, consoled her as best he could. "Chin up, old girl. He wouldn't want you crying. Poor old Matthew. Terrible! A horrible experience for you two as well."

"I think if you don't mind," said Clare sniffing, "I'll go to bed now. It's been a long day."

"Yes," Marianne agreed. "I think we could all do with a good night's sleep."

Clare led the way upstairs to what was temporarily to be their bedroom. "Here we are," she said. "I hope this will be alright."

"Lovely!" Marianne said, though she secretly wondered how Vincent would adjust from sleeping in their king-size bed at home to the much smaller full-size one in Sarah's room. Well, no matter. It would only be for a few nights.

The room itself was quite sizeable and contained what Marianne assumed were the usual accouterments of a ten-year-old girl whose parents could afford to be indulgent. There was a computer on the desk by the window, something that they had never owned when they were youngsters. Next to it was a well-stocked bookcase with many of the classic children's stories that she and Clare had read when they were of a similar age. The walls were liberally decorated with a strange assortment of posters, several showing currently popular groups of young musicians and one that seemed to resemble a scene taken from 'A Midsummer Night's Dream' with fairies and elves cavorting about the sleeping figure of a young man. In stark contrast, a small religious picture of the Virgin Mary hung above the head of the bed, which reminded Marianne that the family still adhered to the rigid catholic upbringing that she had been so eager to escape when she was growing up.

She gave Vincent's arm a squeeze as she saw him cast a rueful glance at the bed. She knew from experience that he liked to spread himself, which on a large bed was not a problem, but on the present accommodations might well result in her being pushed ignominiously to the edge. However, they would no doubt deal with that problem when they came to it, she thought.

Marianne sat down on the bed exhausted, her face buried in her hands.

"You handled it all beautifully, darling," Vincent said, sitting beside her. His long gentle fingers began to massage her shoulders and she felt the grief and tension slip away as if by magic. "I know these next few days are going to be hell for you, but I'll be right here with you. Whatever you need me to do, I'll do."

"Right now, I need you to hold me and tell me that everything will be alright," she answered.

"You know it will be, as long as I'm here with you," he whispered close to her ear.

That night, surrounded by a voyeuristic gallery of stuffed teddy bears, pigs, and rabbits who watched over them in glassy-eyed silence, the two slept fitfully.

Marianne's dreams were peopled by familiar faces; Matthew, deathly pale, his eyes sad and accusing; her mother following him through a swirling cloud of smoke looking at Marianne reproachfully as if to say 'Look at what you've done.' And Adele was there too, her long black hair loose and blowing about her, intermingled with the smoke billowing about her shoulders. She passed before Marianne and then, from out of the depths emerged another figure that so terrified her, she tried to scream but nothing would come out. She tried to run but found herself rooted to the spot. Arthur Hemmings came slowly toward her, the knife stained with Adele's blood held high above his head. On he came, nearer and nearer.

Again, Marianne tried to cry out, and just as she felt his icy breath on her face, she finally broke through the barrier of silence and screamed and screamed until she felt her lungs would burst.

The dream dissolved immediately and her eyes flew open. Vincent was instantly awake and holding her.

There was a frantic knocking on the bedroom door, and Preston burst in, flooding the room with light as he found the switch. "What happened? Are you alright Annie?"

Marianne was trembling and bathed in perspiration. Vincent answered instead. "Just a bad dream. Sorry. She'll be alright."

Clare was by now peeking over Preston's shoulder, much agitated by this sudden commotion and turned to usher the children, who had followed her, back to bed. Marianne had evidently roused the whole house with her nightmares. What a thing to happen! With everyone's nerves already on edge, they would now be as taut as bowstrings.

After they had all returned to their rooms, Vincent said, "It was Hemmings, wasn't it?"

"Yes," Marianne admitted. "I feel like I'll never escape him."

"I'll never let him hurt you again, my darling." Vincent tried desperately to reassure her. "You do believe that, don't you?"

"Yes. I know as long as I have my knight in shining armor, nothing will happen to me."

"Good! That's my girl!"

But despite her professed confidence, she did not sleep again that night, and neither did Vincent.

The next morning at breakfast, Marianne received another shock. Walking into the kitchen, she was startled to see a diminutive figure sitting, waiting patiently at the table for his scrambled eggs. She hadn't seen him since he was a baby, and in those four years, he had grown into a carbon copy of Matthew as he was at that age.

"Hello, you must be Justin," she said, pulling herself together. He didn't reply.

"Oh, there you are Annie. Are you alright, dear? You gave us such a scare last night. I wondered what on earth was happening." Clare was busily preparing breakfast at the stove.

"I'm sorry," Marianne apologized. "A really bad nightmare. I'm afraid I get them every now and then. I hope the children weren't too badly frightened."

Justin looked at Marianne curiously. He found the woman who had inexplicably woken everyone up in the middle of the night with her screaming and yelling strangely fascinating. He didn't say anything but continued to study her as he ate his breakfast. Sarah and Emma joined them and were not so bashful.

"Did you have a bad dream, Auntie Annie?" Sarah asked.

"Was it awful? Were there monsters chasing you?" Emma asked hopefully.

"That's enough, you two," Clare admonished them. "Get on with your breakfast. Annie, will you have some eggs and bacon? Vincent, you'll have some breakfast?" she added as he came into the kitchen.

"Yes, please! I'm starving!" Vincent sat at the table opposite Justin.

"Yes. Thank you, Clare," Marianne said.

"All that screaming probably made you hungry," Emma interjected, but Clare glared at her, and she subsided over the remains of her breakfast.

"So, what's the program for today?" Marianne asked of no one in particular.

"Preston's going to the airport this afternoon to meet the Russells," Clare answered. "Do you need to get anything for tomorrow? I mean, clothes, anything like that?"

"No, I'm fine. I brought everything with me."

"Well in that case I thought we might go to Letchworth's Funeral Home and Saint Simeon's, just to make sure everything's ready for tomorrow. The girls will be off to school soon, and Justin can come with us. Vincent, will you come too, or would you rather wait here, unless you have other plans?"

"No, I'll come with you and Marianne if that's alright?" Vincent was doggedly sticking to his vow to stay by her. Only the two of them knew how important that was right now, for they both sensed that although last night's episode had only been a dream, there was a very real danger.

"That's settled then. Come on Sarah, Emma! Get a move on! You'll be late for school." The girls reluctantly left the table, but Justin remained, slowly and thoughtfully chewing bacon and occasionally casting sidelong glances at Marianne, while Vincent sat looking at the boy with that same expression of curiosity that Marianne had seen when he had first met Matthew.

When the morning meal was over, they made preparations for the day's excursions. Before too long, the four of them, Clare driving, with Vincent beside her in the front seat, and Justin and Marianne together in the back, were headed for their first stop which was the funeral home.

Unlike his two sisters, Justin was, for the most part, silent. Still, one felt that, as young as he was, he was taking note of everything and inwardly digesting all that was said.

When they arrived at the funeral home, Clare parked the car and they all made their way to the entrance, but before going in, Marianne suggested to Vincent, "Maybe you could take Justin to the park across the street, while Clare and I take care of things here."

She could see that Vincent was reluctant to leave her, even for a short period, but she persisted, "I'll be alright, honestly. And I think it would be better for Justin, really. We won't be long. I'm sure you'd rather go to the park, wouldn't you, Justin?" she petitioned the boy, and he nodded with a measure of tempered enthusiasm.

"Well, alright then." Clare agreed. "I suppose it would be better, if you don't mind, Vincent?"

"If Justin's agreeable, certainly. Come and get us when you're ready to leave," Vincent replied, and the two of them departed. Vincent held Justin's hand as they made their way across the street to the park. Marianne felt a pang of gratitude tinged with sadness as she watched them go. Would there ever be a time when Vincent would lead his own child about in such a manner? He had never voiced a desire for a family, and she had seldom given the matter any thought. But seeing him with Justin, she wondered, was the old biological clock ticking or was she merely looking for a replacement for Matthew? A son for a brother?

"Come on, Annie. We've got a lot to do this morning," Clare reminded her.

They were greeted at the door of the office by a rotund, jovial looking man who seemed to Marianne rather out of place as a funeral director. For some reason, she was expecting someone more along the lines of a *Uriah Heep,* and she smiled involuntarily at her preconceived notion. They shook hands and Clare explained the reason for their visit.

"Yes, Mrs. Fanthorpe. Would you like to visit the casket? It's already in the west chapel, if you would like to come this way." He led them along a short corridor and into the chapel, where a closed casket was mounted on a raised dais at the far end of the room. The lighting was subdued, and the heavy, cloying perfume of lilies, the traditional flowers of death, hung in the air.

Marianne sensed, rather than heard, a quick intake of breath from Clare. She put her arm around her sister's shoulder as they made their way between the two rows of high-backed chairs that stood in silent regiments facing the dais.

Already floral tributes had begun to arrive, and as Clare knelt, her forehead leaning against the casket, her shoulders shuddering with grief, Marianne stepped aside to look at the cards attached to the wreaths and bouquets. There was one, from Matthew's partner, another, a large ostentatious arrangement from Aunt Isabelle and Uncle Mortimer, and, at her feet, a simple bouquet of white roses and red carnations that she saw with an almost overwhelming surge of gratitude, from Ivan and Irina. There were more, but Clare had recovered her composure and beckoned Marianne to join her.

"Do you think he suffered much at the end?" she asked quietly.

"No, I don't think so. They said he'd been knocked unconscious by the explosion. I'm sure he didn't know anything. Don't torture yourself with thoughts like that, Clare. He didn't suffer, really."

"I can't help it. You can't possibly understand how hard this is for me, how I feel," Clare mumbled through her tears.

Couldn't understand? Marianne understood alright. She knew just what it felt like to watch as Mathew and Vincent had tussled amid the flames and smoke down there in the cellar. Knew how it felt to watch as he'd fallen, been knocked out by the blow as he'd hit his head against the heavy metal-bound chest that stood next to the body of Adele. She knew, all too well, that it had been her fault, and Clare's words cut her as deeply as Arthur Hemming's knife. But Clare didn't know what had happened. Marianne couldn't blame her for what she was saying.

She touched the casket briefly with the tips of her fingers and said, "I think we should go now." They turned to retrace their steps back to the office, where they were once again met by Mr. Letchworth.

"Just to go over the arrangements for tomorrow," he said. "Everyone will assemble here at 11 a.m. There will be a few words and a brief prayer delivered by Father Raymond, then over to Saint Simeon's in Islington for the mass. And after that, the drive to Abney Park. I think that's everything. Have you any questions Mrs. Fanthorpe?"

"No. You seem to have everything very well organized. Thank you, Mr. Letchworth."

He looked at Marianne enquiringly, but she had nothing to add, and they took their leave, returning once more to the fresh air outside where Marianne felt herself breathe easier.

They made their way across the street to find Vincent and Justin and discovered them in the park, each sitting on a swing, barely moving, deep in conversation. Justin spotted them first and jumped up to run to his mother. Vincent remained on the swing and watched the boy intently as he grasped his mother's hand and whispered something in her ear as she bent to catch his words. Marianne went over to Vincent, and he got up, a little stiffly, and put his arms around her.

"Everything alright?" he asked.

"Yes. Everything's ready for tomorrow. Oh, and there's a lovely little bouquet there from Ivan and Irina."

"Good, good," he said absently. He still seemed a bit preoccupied as they walked behind Clare and Justin back to the car. Their next stop would be at Saint Simeon's church and a meeting with Father Raymond.

It wasn't until they arrived at Saint Simeon's that Marianne felt a strong and inexplicable aversion to entering the old church. Although they had been brought up in a strict Catholic household and despite the fact that her mother had willingly adopted her husband's religion before their marriage, Marianne had always viewed her faith with a somewhat half-hearted acceptance.

As a child, she had attended services on Sunday mornings along with all the other worshipers in the congregation, not understanding the words that she mumbled automatically as she knelt in what she hoped was knee-numbing reverence. She lived in constant terror of being struck down by some almighty, invisible hand when she had inadvertently eaten meat on a Friday. And stuttering out her humble confessions, "Bless me Father for I have sinned...sworn ten times, had impure thoughts," and had fervently prayed that she wouldn't be condemned to the eternal fires of hell for having said "bugger!" every time she'd fallen off her bike.

But as the years went by and she was no longer a child, Marianne began to question the perceived rigmarole and hypocrisy, until finally her conscience would no longer allow her to participate in what she thought of as a lot of mumbo jumbo. Despite her parents' vehement objections, she abandoned their faith to follow her own code of ethics and morality. It was a standard with which she was infinitely more comfortable. To her mind, it was truer to the expectations of whatever God there may or may not be out there.

Since then, Marianne had rarely seen the inside of a church except for the occasional wedding, funeral, or rarer still, christening. These were times when she couldn't back out or turn down an invitation without offending someone. She would invariably arrive late, find a seat way at the back, and sit stoically looking about her when all the others knelt, heads bowed as the priest intoned the appropriate prayers and incantations. Were their thoughts any more pious or well-intentioned than hers? She didn't think so. She didn't consider herself a bad person, at least, not then.

There was only one time when Marianne doubted that she had made the right decision in casting off the suffocating blanket of religious autocracy. It was on the day of her mother's funeral. She naturally abstained from any input regarding the arrangements. The family were, by then, well aware of her repugnance for such rituals, and only sincere love and respect for her mother induced Marianne to go with the others to St Simeon's. On that occasion, Marianne could not isolate herself from the rest of the congregation and sit unobserved in the pews at the back of the church. She was obliged to take her place under the watchful eye of Father Raymond in the front row. That was the only concession she was prepared to make, however.

As the others responded to the priest's exhortations to prayer, Marianne remembered gazing ahead of her at a beautifully sculptured statue of the Virgin Mary. Looking at it from a purely artistic point of view it was a lovely piece; the serenity of the face, the graceful gesture of the hands and superbly crafted folds of the gown were most pleasing. But as Marianne sat there, she began to feel something more, difficult to describe, a oneness with the figure before her, as though she had been absorbed into the very material of its construction. At that moment nothing and no one else existed, not the people who were gathered together to honor her mother or Father Raymond, whose booming voice had earlier intruded itself upon her thoughts. Not even the church itself, with its cold stone walls and high-arching, stained-glass windows, was there. She was totally alone, a part of the figure before her, in a heavenly void that held her completely enthralled. She didn't know how long this feeling had lasted. It was probably only a matter of minutes, but it seemed to her as though it had been several lifetimes.

Could she, an avowed agnostic, possibly have had a religious experience? Looking back on it, later that night, Marianne didn't believe so. She was certain in her own mind that it was not prompted by any feelings of Christian reverence. She didn't feel as though she had been converted back to the fold. Her beliefs and opinions were still intact. But something had happened there at the foot of the altar steps, something that she couldn't explain. After several months of trying to analyze and dissect the experience, she gave up and just accepted it as being the result of a stressful situation brought on by the illness and death of her mother.

And now, here she was, back at Saint Simeon's. The prospect of walking through those imposing wooden doors filled Marianne inexplicably with a fear so daunting that she found it impossible to go on. She stopped and looked up at the towering church spire.

"I think, if you don't mind, Clare, I'll wait out here. I'm not feeling all that well. I need some air."

"You'll be alright once we get inside," Clare made to argue, but Vincent was insistent.

"You go ahead, Clare. I'll stay with her. We'll walk up and down for a bit."

"Well, alright … but are you sure you wouldn't rather come inside and sit down?"

"No, really Clare, I'll be fine. I just need to be outside for a while."

"Thanks," she said gratefully to Vincent as Clare and Justin disappeared inside the church.

"Of course. I could tell by the way you were gripping my hand that you didn't want to go in."

"Oh! Darling, I'm sorry. I didn't realize." Marianne looked at the already injured hand in dismay. "It's true. I couldn't face going in there. Tomorrow will be hard enough, but I'll cross that bridge when I get to it."

"And I'll be there with you," he reminded her, as if she doubted that he would be.

"I know. My knight in shining armor."

"That's right."

They walked slowly along the road, looking in at shop windows and stopping briefly at a small café to enjoy a cup of freshly-brewed coffee. They headed back to the church in time to meet Clare and Justin as they were coming out.

"Feeling better?" Clare asked.

"Yes, thanks. Alright now."

"Good." Clare sounded relieved. She had more than enough to cope with. "Well, we've only one more stop to make and then we can go home. I want to go to the cemetery to take some flowers for mum's grave. Things will be too hectic tomorrow, and I think there should be flowers."

"Yes, that's a nice thought," Marianne agreed. Her mother was buried in the family plot in Abney Park, where so many O'Malley and Ward relatives had been laid to rest.

Abney Park, one of London's 'magnificent seven' cemeteries, dated back to 1840. The headstones and effigies, many of which were cracked or broken and covered in lichen now, stood in silent homage to the dead.

Marianne remembered, when she was a child, her mother would occasionally bring her to this somber and hallowed ground on a Sunday afternoon to place flowers on the graves of great-grandparents, aunts, and uncles. A morbid place, some might think, for a young child to be brought for an afternoon's recreation, but Marianne didn't find it in the least incongruous. Her mother would read the names on the headstones, some of whom were very famous people, and Marianne would repeat the names with a kind of awed fascination.

Justin too, seemed at ease here as he skipped ahead of them, along the tree-lined pathway between the rows of graves, and Marianne wondered if Clare had perhaps brought him here already, to visit grandparents who he never known.

The plot covered a considerable area and already contained the remains of Marianne's mother along with her younger brother, their mother and father, her mother's unmarried sister Aunt Ethel, and many other family members besides. A few of the stones were comparatively new and were still clearly legible. Clare placed the flowers, purchased at a local florist, at the foot of the headstone marked, *Here lies Rosemary Anne Clay. Beloved Wife and Mother.*

Marianne sighed as she remembered her father's cold indifference when they had told him about the engraving on the stone that they had chosen. He had not even been there for her funeral. And he wouldn't be there tomorrow either, to witness the interment of his only son. What bitter recriminations had induced such behavior, she could not begin to imagine. Only her father knew, and she doubted whether they would ever learn the truth from him.

Matthew's grave had already been prepared, and wooden boards lay across the ground, the area doubly protected by a temporary awning.

Having satisfied herself that everything was in readiness for the morrow, Clare took Justin's hand, and they walked slowly back to the car park. They said very little during their time in the cemetery, in order to keep a tighter rein on their emotions, but when they were finally back in the safety of the car, they no longer seemed to feel the need for restraint, and let out a collective sigh of relief.

"Well, everything seems to be ready," Clare said, thankfully.

Marianne knew that the burden of organizing the funeral must have been a tremendous ordeal for Clare, who was always such a stickler for getting things right. She felt a surge of love and admiration for her sister. Of course, Preston was there to comfort and support her, just as Vincent was there for her, but Marianne wondered sometimes if he was as much of a tower of strength as Clare sometimes made him out to be. A very nice man, granted, but despite Clare's declaration that he had taken care of everything, Marianne still got the feeling that she was the driving force behind all the preparations.

Marianne was beginning to feel desperately tired now. Lack of sleep the night before and the emotional stress of all that had happened recently were once again catching up to her, and she longed for nothing more than to collapse somewhere and lose herself in dreamless slumber. But would it be free from the old nightmares? She doubted it.

Despite their apparent solution of the Wellington Street mystery and the discovery of Adele's body—and at what horrific cost—it felt like fate had not yet finished with them. They were still bound up, somehow, with the past, and now, more than ever, she was filled with a fear of what was still to come.

20

LAID TO REST

THE NEXT MORNING, THEY ALL ASSEMBLED IN THE KITCHEN, a somber group. The children were dressed in their Sunday best, Clare and Marianne in stylish but unadorned black dresses, Vincent and Preston in dark suits. No one was hungry, but they picked at the toast, cereal and fruit that Clare had laid out on the table because they felt they should eat something. Coffee, however, was a most welcome addition to the bill of fare. It was strong and hot, and the large glass carafe was empty by the time they had cleared everything away.

Marianne wondered if the children had ever participated in the rituals of a funeral service before, and when she and Clare were finally left alone, she asked her.

"No, but Preston has explained everything to them, and I think they'll be alright," Clare answered optimistically.

"Good. I wasn't sure."

"Louise is coming over later, to let the caterers in and help set everything up."

"That's nice of her."

"I hope the weather holds up," said Clare doubtfully, looking out of the window at the clouds that scudded across a wintery sky.

An hour or so later, two shiny black limousines arrived to take them to Letchworth's Funeral Home. The children, who had never ridden in anything quite so grand before, showed a brief flash of excitement until Clare reminded them of the solemnity of the occasion. Chastened, they climbed in and took their places. Marianne and Vincent got into the second car, and they moved off in silence.

When they arrived, Mr. Letchworth escorted them to the west chapel where he left the family alone with the casket, which was now surrounded by a sea of flowers. It wasn't surprising that Matthew had been loved and respected by so many people. He was such a dear, kind person who had never done anyone any harm. There probably wasn't a living soul who had ever had reason to say a bad word about him, and the truth of the saying 'only the good die young' seemed acutely apposite in this instance.

Clare and Preston remained standing by the casket, their heads bent in prayer. As Marianne and Vincent took their places in the front row of seats with the children, they heard the door open and turned to see Uncle Mortimer and Aunt Isabelle enter. Marianne watched as they made their way towards them, and she thought how little they had changed since she had last seen them at her mother's funeral. Mortimer O'Malley, their mother's brother, was as unlike her in appearance and behavior as any brother and sister could be. He was, she knew, a good deal older than her mother, probably by now in his early eighties and still carried his tall, somewhat overweight body erect. His hair had thinned and greyed a little, but he had retained the luxuriant moustache that had always irritated Marianne's skin when he had planted ebullient, avuncular kisses on her cheeks when she was a child. The years had produced little effect on Aunt Isabelle either, although Marianne suspected her hair coloring had more to do with the ministrations of a beautician at the salon rather than Father Time's lenient hand.

Despite the solemnity of the occasion, Mortimer found it impossible to keep his voice from booming out, "Well, well, my dears! A sad day! First your mother, now Matthew. A sad day indeed!" He hugged both Clare and Marianne and enveloped the children in their turn, pausing first to shake hands with Preston. He then turned his attention to Vincent and, as Marianne made the introductions, grasped his hand warmly. "Vincent! Dear boy! I'm so immensely pleased to meet you. Of course, Clare has told us all about you but we little thought to meet you under these circumstances. A sad day!" he repeated.

Aunt Isabelle, as quiet and timid as Mortimer was loud and effusive, added a few words of condolence and subsided into a chair in the row behind them, while Uncle Mort went up to the casket to slap his giant hands upon it, shake his head, and sigh gustily.

Uncle Mortimer had always seemed a larger-than-life personality to the Clay children. His visits to their house, accompanied by timid, docile Aunt Isabelle and two large, excitable boxer dogs who were neither timid or docile and which inevitably caused havoc within the first few minutes of their arrival, was always an occasion much anticipated.

Their mother worshiped her brother and relied heavily on his friendship and good sense when things between her and Ronald Clay were at their worst. His sojourns at their house were usually timed to coincide with the absence of their father—the two did not get on—and their mother always seemed to gain enormous strength from his blustering heartiness, which in turn made the children very happy. Marianne remembered how he had doted on Matthew. Uncle Mort would willingly allow the boy to climb upon his broad back as he crawled about the threadbare carpet in his smart Saville Row suits, making bellowing noises, which would transport the dogs into renewed frenzy. This would send furniture and ornaments flying, while the three children laughed hysterically and their mother watched unperturbed and smiling. None of them, in those days, could have foreseen the darkness and misery that would fall upon them, least of all the genial giant who now stood looking morosely down at the floral tributes.

The next people to arrive were David and Doris Russell. Not having seen them for several years, Marianne couldn't at first place them, but when Clare went forward to greet them and introduced them to Vincent, she recognized the former owners of Paradise House.

"Mr. and Mrs. Russell. It was very good of you to come all this way. Matthew so enjoyed his visits with you at Paradise House," she said with sincerity.

"We were shocked when we heard the news of his death," Doris Russell said in hushed tones. "We couldn't believe it. He came to see us last year and spent a few days in Diffingham. We were always happy to have him at the house. He was such a likeable young man."

Her husband agreed. "We didn't have a chance to say goodbye before we left for Stockholm, but I did mention him to the people who bought Paradise House from us."

"Yes, he said he was planning on going there to introduce himself when he got home," Marianne replied. The door opened again to admit a man and woman who, once again, she did not recognize, and the Russells sat down as she and Clare turned their attention to the newcomers.

Clare made the introductions once more. "Annie, this is David Barton, Matthew's business partner. David, this is my sister Annie and her friend Vincent Foxworth."

They shook hands and David Barton presented the woman who had accompanied him into the chapel. "This is Lee-Anne Jones. She is, or was, Matthew's secretary."

"We're very pleased to meet you, Ms. Jones. Thank you for coming." Marianne said, shaking her hand.

She was beginning to realize how little she knew about Matthew's life since she had moved away to Birchford. Seeing all these people with whom Clare had obviously been in close contact over the years made her suddenly regret her self-imposed exile from the family. She felt like an outsider.

Meanwhile, Preston was escorting another couple, who she recognized as Mortimer and Isabelle's daughter, Renee, and her husband, Ronald Marchmont, down toward the casket, where they were met by the O'Malleys. Having exchanged greetings with them and standing for a few moments in silence by the casket, they came over to Marianne and Clare.

"Clare. Annie. My dears. How sad this is," Renee said, hugging both of them in turn.

"Terrible," Clare replied. Then, turning to her sister, she added, pulling Vincent forward, "This is Vincent Foxworth, Annie's friend. Vincent, these are our cousins, Renee and Ronald Marchmont. Oh, here's Father Raymond," she added and hurried away, leaving them to exchange a few murmured words of commiseration with the Marchmonts. Marianne's attention, however, had now drifted towards Father Raymond; he who had heard the family's most intimate thoughts at one time or another in the secrecy of the confessional. What revelations had he been privy to over the years, she wondered?

"Annie, I'm sorry I missed you yesterday. Are you feeling better?" he enquired as he came over to where she was standing.

"Yes. Yes, thank you," she stammered guiltily, feeling that he somehow knew her absence from Saint Simeon's yesterday had not really been caused by ill health but by a severe bout of cowardice.

"Good, good. Is everyone here, Clare?" he asked, taking in the chapel at a glance.

"Not quite, Father. Just two more people, Matthew's friends, James and Grace Crowe. They should be here shortly." Clare looked anxiously at the door, no doubt praying that nothing would interrupt the carefully planned time schedule that had been laid out for them.

As if on cue, the door opened and James and Grace Crowe came in. Clare went to meet them, and the last few introductions were made.

Now that everyone was assembled, the time had arrived for the elderly priest to say a few words and offer a prayer before departing for Saint Simeon's. He stepped forward to address the gathering. Resting his hand lightly on the casket, he looked at everyone for a moment and then began.

"Knowing Matthew as I did, I'm sure the first thing that he would have said to you all would be, 'Don't be sad. Remember all the good times that we had; the happy times.' So let us thank God now for bringing Matthew into our lives and for all those happy times."

Father Raymond's words opened up a multitude of such moments, and they all came crowding in upon Marianne's thoughts, leaving the remainder of his invocation to fall on other ears.

Preston, Vincent, David Barton and Ronald Marchmont had readily agreed to act as pallbearers, carrying their precious burden solemnly out to the waiting hearse while the others followed. They divided into various groups to form the cortege that would make its way to Saint Simeon's church.

Once there, Marianne and Clare, accompanied by the three children, made their way toward the wide-open doors of Saint Simeon's. Again, Marianne felt some misgivings at the thought of entering the old church. She involuntarily slowed her pace, and Clare, who was holding her arm, adjusted her step and gave it a gentle squeeze. Marianne had determined to look straight ahead at the large stained-glass window above the altar, to focus on that and nothing else, in order to get through the ordeal, so she returned neither the gesture nor the glance that Clare gave her as they crossed the threshold.

As they made their way slowly down the aisle, Marianne couldn't help looking to the right, at the pew closest to the alter rails. She stopped, holding up the procession of mourners as it filed through the doors behind them as she saw two figures, sitting close together, a man and a woman. And as she stared, in utter astonishment, the woman turned to face her, her mother, her youthful looks restored, her flaming red hair cascading about her shoulders. But the man remained facing away from her so she couldn't see his face, although he looked familiar, his blond hair and broad shoulders, his whole demeanor although only glimpsed from behind was almost that of ... No! How could it be? It was impossible!

In the few seconds that it had taken for her brain to register all that her eyes had seen, Marianne had unconsciously let out a gasp. Clare once again squeezed her arm. As Marianne looked again toward the alter rails, the figures disappeared. Clare, solicitous but no doubt hoping that Marianne would not make a scene, almost dragged her to their place in the pews. The children helped her to her seat—the very one that had been occupied moments before by those ghostly apparitions—and they watched nervously as Marianne sank down, leaving a space where Vincent would eventually join them.

The solemn cortege passed silently up the aisle and placed the casket gently on the dais at the top of the steps leading to the altar.

Marianne saw Clare tug at Vincent's sleeve as he returned to his seat, and he bent his head towards her as she urgently whispered in his ear, probably warning him that her sister was on the verge of hysteria. He hurriedly squeezed past the others to her side.

"What happened?" he asked Marianne, but she just shook her head. Silently, she found herself asking a God who she thought had forsaken her long ago, *why is this happening to me?*

After the interminable Mass finally came to a close—the words and ceremony barely registering amid Marianne's frenzied thoughts—they followed the casket down the aisle, back through the mighty oak doors. As they left, Marianne glanced back, almost expecting to see those two figures again. But seeing only empty seats, she joined the others at the car.

Vincent returned, having fulfilled his duties as pallbearer and immediately asked, "Are you alright?"

"Yes. I just felt a bit faint. That's all. Nothing more."

"This will soon be over," he said encouragingly. "Not long now. I'll be with you all the time now."

They proceeded to the cemetery where everything went smoothly. At least Marianne managed to get through it without any repercussions of what had happened at the church. Uncle Mortimer sniffed audibly as the coffin was lowered into the ground, and Sarah cried quietly at her mother's side, while Preston stood with a hand on Emma's shoulder.

Ever since their time together in the park, Justin had considered Vincent his special friend, and now he was confidently holding his hand as they stood listening to Father Raymond intone the words that ceremony demanded. As the moment of interment approached, the boy tugged gently at Vincent's sleeve, to which he responded by stooping and picking Justin up, holding him comfortingly as Clare and her sister, their arms around each other's waist, watched as the coffin was lowered deep into the ground.

Strangely, at that moment, Marianne's mind was not on what was happening there but far away, as she wondered who would be around to watch over Adele's ultimate journey to the grave. No one, probably. No one would remember her now. She made a mental note that when they returned home, she should make enquiries as to the whereabouts of Adele's final resting place and take flowers.

The last prayers having been offered, the proceedings came to an end and after lingering for a few moments by the open grave, Marianne and Vincent joined the others as they all trooped back to the line of waiting cars. Everyone had been invited to returned with them to the Fanthorpe's house for lunch, and Marianne hoped for Clare's sake that everything was well in hand. She was sure that Louise could cope, but she knew her sister's reluctance to leave things to other people. If she could have been in two places at once, she would have willingly done it. As it was, Marianne imagined that Clare would constantly be expecting the worst and knew she would not relax until she saw for herself that everything was going smoothly at the house.

Louise greeted them at the door and immediately put Clare's mind at rest. Yes, the caterers had arrived, and everything was set out ready in the dining room. She was about to leave, but Preston insisted that she stay and have lunch with them, which she agreed to do.

The conversation amongst friends and family now began to flow more easily. The worst was over, and Father Raymond, who had accompanied them back to the house, appeared to be enjoying a joke with Mortimer O'Malley, their laughter no longer seeming out of place. The children were tucking into the food laid out on the buffet table, and Preston wandered around carrying a tray laden with sherry glasses. Isabelle O'Malley was sharing some reminiscences of Matthew with the Russells and David Barton, while Matthew's secretary, Lee-Anne Jones, was exchanging anecdotes with the Crowes.

Marianne went from one group to another, joining in their conversations, and from time to time the various clusters merged and dissolved rather like the intricate steps of an old-fashioned dance, forming new patterns and new partnerships.

But finally, everything had been said. Every phase of Matthew's short life had been recalled, from his birth, which Aunt Isabelle remembered as though it were yesterday, to the moment when Clare and Preston had seen him off the day before he had gone back to Swannington to be with Marianne. There was nothing left to say, and gradually they all departed.

Father Raymond, the first to leave, came over to say goodbye. "I know that you believe you have abandoned your faith, Annie, but it's never too late to come back. I sense that something is troubling you, deeply, not just Matthew's death. If you ever want to come and talk to me, please feel free to do so. Don't worry, I'm not pressuring you into returning to the church, although of course, I would be delighted if you did, but I really would like to help, if I can. So please, do come and see me at Saint Simeon's if you have the time."

"Thank you, Father Raymond. I appreciate the offer, but I don't think…"

"Well, I'll leave it up to you."

"Thanks. Goodbye Father."

He meant well, but she still felt very uneasy in his presence and couldn't visualize herself going back to Saint Simeon's under any circumstances.

David Barton and Lee-Anne Jones left soon after, and the Crowes and Russells took their cue from them.

That left Uncle Mortimer, Aunt Isabelle, and the Marchmonts, who all seemed inclined to stay on. They had made themselves comfortable in the living room, the children having been sent upstairs to play, and Mortimer began the conversation in lugubrious tones.

"Well, your father didn't come, then. I didn't think he would, but it's a shame. I don't know what the situation was there, and I don't want to pry, but the least he could have done was see the poor boy one last time."

"We did ask him, but he just said he wasn't interested," Clare explained morosely.

Mortimer shook his head sadly. "His only son."

No one felt inclined to add anything and the subject was dropped.

"So, what are your plans now, Annie?" Renee Marchmont asked.

"We're driving up to Beckham in a few days' time to visit Vincent's family, his mother and sister.

Mortimer appeared to search his memory. "Beckham, Beckham. Ah yes. Little place in the Lake District, right?"

"Yes," Vincent replied. "The house is just outside the town."

"We went through Beckham once. Do you remember, Isabelle? The time we went to visit somebody or other."

"I don't remember, dear, but if you say so, then I'm sure you're right," Aunt Isabelle agreed affably.

"Rather dreary at this time of the year, of course, but the weather doesn't matter when you're visiting family. How long is it since you've seen them?"

"It's been a while. Just before I met Marianne."

"Good luck, my dear," Mortimer said rather cryptically, raising the glass of scotch and soda that he had been nursing in his hand. Marianne smiled. Did he anticipate that she would meet with some opposition in that quarter?

After another hour of desultory conversation, their visitors left. Preston and Vincent gave the two women a hand to clear up the remnants of the earlier lunch, Clare fastidiously tipping Uncle Mortimer's cigarette ends into the trash bin and liberally spraying the rooms with air freshener.

Later that evening they all went out to dinner, sparing Clare the necessity of cooking a meal at the end of a hectic day. As they sat around the table, Marianne began to realize just how much she would miss them all when she and Vincent went back to Swannington. Family seemed so much more important now as their numbers gradually dwindled, but would family ties be sufficient reason to return to London permanently? Would Vincent ever consider it? One thing was certain, she couldn't leave Swannington without him. Wherever he was, that was her home; her safe haven.

21

A Shared Secret

THE DAY BEFORE THEY WERE DUE TO MOTOR UP TO THE LAKE DISTRICT to visit Vincent's family, Marianne decided, after much soul-searching, to pay a conciliatory visit to her father. Despite his refusal to attend Matthew's funeral and the acrimonious tone that he had adopted in his letters to her earlier that year, she couldn't believe that he would coldly allow her to return home without some gesture, some little sign that there was still a spark of affection left between father and daughter. She was willing, if necessary, to make the first move. She hadn't called him, fearing that he would refuse to see her. But after discussing her proposed plan of action with Vincent, who was dubious about its success but prepared to stand by her, she descended on the old family home unannounced.

Marianne had asked Vincent to go with her, for she felt that this would be her only opportunity to prove to her father that he had been mistaken in his assessment of their relationship. She very much wanted him to see that Vincent was everything that he could possibly hope for in a partner for his youngest daughter. She felt sure that once he met and had a chance to get to know him, things would come right, that somehow, he would see his way clear to accepting the situation. Vincent had agreed to go, rather reluctantly, but to be fair, Marianne realized that this confrontation would not be easy for him. He never was one to bow and scrape to people and never felt the need to ingratiate himself with anyone who did not readily take to him. It would cost him dearly, she knew, to make any effort to 'sell himself' to her father, and she loved him all the more for his willingness to see the thing through despite any reservations that he might have.

They arrived at the house just after ten o'clock that morning, and Marianne felt a pang of nostalgia seeing her childhood home once again. The old terraced house in Hackney had not changed much since she'd last been there. After her mother died, her father made little attempt to keep up appearances and only tidied the miniscule front garden after the neighbors complained about the overflowing rubbish bins and the overhanging trees and shrubs in the wilderness that was now the back garden. He made a half-hearted attack on the paintwork just before Marianne left for Birchford, a project which she was only too happy to encourage, but she could tell his enthusiasm was paper-thin, and by the time it was finished, he showed little or no interest in the results. He always talked about what he was going to do when he retired, but when the moment came, he sank into a stagnating morass of inactivity. According to Clare and Preston, he had done very little with his time, visiting them only occasionally and seldom receiving them in the house that had been the Clay family home for almost as long as Marianne could remember.

She pressed the doorbell. Would he be home? He must be. His car was parked outside on the street, and she thought she had seen movement behind the drapes as they climbed the steps to the house. But it was several seconds before there was any response. She was just about to press the bell again when a figure appeared behind the opaque glass windows of the door, and it opened to reveal her father.

My God! How he had aged! Marianne was shocked at his appearance. His face was lined and pale, his hair grey and uncombed.

"Annie?" He looked at her in puzzlement, not seeming to comprehend her presence there. "What are you doing here? I thought you were in Swannington."

"Dad." She made to embrace him, but he stepped backward in alarm, into the hallway. "Don't you remember? I came home for Matthew's funeral?" She took a step forward and followed him as he turned to walk away from her, back into the house. His vagueness frightened her, and she looked anxiously after him as they made their way into the living room. Vincent had hung back, waiting in the hallway, so Marianne and her father were alone in the room when he turned around to look at her once more.

"Funeral? Oh, yes, the funeral." He seemed to pull himself together with an effort. "Well, Annie, how are you, after all these years? How is life treating you in Swannington?"

"Dad! I can't believe that you didn't come to the funeral." She forgot for the moment her original purpose for their visit and could only think of her bitter disappointment that he had stayed away from the family in its hour of sorrow. "Why weren't you there? What did Matthew ever do to you that was so terrible?"

She was angry and upset, and she was crying, her father continuing to look at her impassively, untouched by her emotion. Then, in an instant, his look of disinterestedness changed. Hearing her voice, Vincent had come into the room, and her father, on seeing him, gave a sudden gasp, a look of hate and anger draining what little color there was from his cheeks. His eyes, so recently vacant and lacking any animation were flashing now with undisguised loathing.

"What's he doing here?" He pointed toward Vincent.

"Dad! Please! This is Vincent. He's come here to meet you."

"Get out! Get him out of here!"

"But Dad, won't you just…"

"I said get out!" He had backed into the desk in his blind fury, but feeling the solid object behind him, he grasped the handle of the drawer. Wrenching it open and scrabbling frantically, he found what he was searching for. He turned again to face them, holding an old army revolver, pointing it unwaveringly at Vincent. "I swear to God, Annie, if you don't get that bastard out of here, I'll shoot him where he stands!"

Marianne had put herself between them, but Vincent grabbed her arm and pulled her aside.

"We're going, Mr. Clay. I'm sorry that you feel this way. I love Marianne."

"Shut up! Just shut the fuck up!"

He took a step towards them, and Vincent, seeing that argument was useless and that her father was beyond reasoning, put his arm around

Marianne and hurried her out of the room, leaving the old man standing there, the hand holding the gun hanging limply at his side.

"I'm sorry, Vincent," she sobbed as they got back into the car. "I don't know what's wrong with him. I've never seen him like this before. I know he was against us living together, but this is just insane."

"Matthew's death may have upset him more than anyone realized," Vincent said consolingly as he wiped away her tears.

"Maybe," she said, but Marianne wasn't convinced. There was something more behind this outlandish behavior than just plain grief. But she was in no mood to sit there and analyze her father's motives, so they headed back to Clare's house.

When they arrived, Clare could tell immediately that something had happened and ushered them into the living room, looking anxiously at Vincent as he took Marianne's coat.

"Sit down and relax," he told her. "Any chance of a cup of tea, Clare?" he asked as she was about to question her sister. Taking the hint, she postponed her interrogation and disappeared into the kitchen, Vincent following her.

When they returned, Marianne guessed that he had told Clare about everything that had happened at their father's house.

"I'm sorry, Annie. I knew it wouldn't work, but I didn't think you would believe me, so I thought it best for you to go ahead," Clare said as she sat down next to Marianne. "I never dreamt he would take it so badly. How rotten for you, Vincent. I feel so awful that he treated you in such a shameful way. I really can't understand why he objects so strongly to you."

"Don't worry, Clare. It's not your fault. You couldn't possibly have known that he would act so irrationally. I don't know why he feels the way he does, but I think Marianne can see now that any hope of reconciliation is out of the question. I would suggest, however, that you keep a close watch on his health if you still care about him. I'm no medical expert, but he doesn't look at all well, and I'm afraid this latest incident may have been too much for him," Vincent said calmly.

"Yes. Yes, of course. I'll give him a day or two to calm down, then I'll go and see if he's alright."

Marianne was alarmed. "Don't go there alone, Clare. Have Preston go with you. Really, I mean it."

"Alright, if you think it's necessary. But are things really that bad?"

"I think he's losing his mind. He must be, to behave the way he did. Try, at least, to get that gun out of the house. He may do himself an injury or, God forbid, shoot someone else. I'd go with you but I think it would only make matters worse."

"Don't worry, dear. We'll manage," Clare reassured her, patting her knee. "I'm sure everything will be alright. Preston and I will go there this weekend and take care of everything."

Later that afternoon, Vincent and Preston had gone out, ostensibly to run errands for Clare, although Marianne suspected that the expedition might encompass a stop at Preston's club for some liquid refreshment. The children had also been whisked away by Clare to a pre-arranged appointment with their dentist.

Left to her own devices, Marianne decided to go out. She thought that some exercise would clear her mind and help her to relax. She walked for a while before boarding a bus that took her through Hammersmith and Kensington. It was good to be back in London. She hadn't realized just how much she missed the place, and she wanted to savor the moment, taking in every sight and sound.

She left the bus and walked again for quite some time. Then, looking ahead, she realized that she was nearing St. Simeon's church. A light rain started to fall, and a chilly breeze sprang up, but she was dressed warmly, and the seasonal nip didn't bother her unduly.

She walked unhurriedly with no real plan or intention, but as she drew near to the church, she thought about Father Raymond's parting words. Despite her reply to him on that occasion, she found herself turning in at the gate and walking up the path that led to the rectory.

At the door, her hand paused in its movement toward the bell, stopping for a second as she wondered why she had come. What had she intended to say? Marianne hardly knew, but in that moment of hesitation, Father Raymond must have caught sight of her from the window, for as she withdrew her hand and made to retreat, the door opened and he called out.

"Annie, don't go, child. Come in for a while and have a cup of tea. The weather's miserable."

How could she refuse? "Well, I can't stay long. They'll be wondering where I've got to."

"You can call them from here. Come in, child," he repeated, and obediently she followed him inside. A few minutes later they were sitting by the fire, a tea tray set out on the little table between them.

"Now tell me, Annie," he said as he poured steaming hot tea into mugs, "How are you holding up? I know this has been a terrible experience for you, and God knows without the support of faith to help you through these troubling times, I really wonder how you are coping with it all."

"I have sometimes found myself wondering the same thing just lately, Father. It hasn't been easy but I have been blessed, if you want to call it that, with the friendship of a very special person who has helped me."

"Vincent?"

"Yes. He has been my strength throughout this ordeal."

"Is it enough, do you think, forgive me for asking, to place your reliance solely on the shoulders of this man. Can he truly sustain you? Bring you the comfort and peace of mind that Our Lord is able to provide to those who are willing to accept his love?"

"I think so. I've never doubted it. He has always been there for me, my knight in shining armor."

"Always? Surely not always. When your mother died? He wasn't there then, was he?"

"No. I didn't know him then, but I feel as though I've known him all my life; as though he'd always been there, out of sight but watching over me, waiting for the right moment to make himself known. Does that sound ridiculous to you?"

"No, but I find it rather unsettling. Forgive me for asking, do you live together?"

"Yes," Marianne answered defiantly.

Father Raymond shook his head sadly. "Without the benefit of marriage. It's a sad fact that so many of you young people have chosen to follow that path these days."

"But what about all the people that married and then found themselves desperately unhappy? If they're Catholic, they're stuck with it," she said, thinking about her mother. "And if not, they get divorced."

"Do you feel so uncertain of your relationship that you're unwilling to put it to the test?"

"No. I'm more certain of my love for Vincent than anything else on this earth."

"Your love for him, yes, but what about his love for you?"

"There's no question!" she replied hotly, but even as she said the words, she felt a curious sinking feeling inside. Damn the man! What right did he have to try and plant these seeds of doubt where up till now only love and trust had bloomed?

"What does your family think about this relationship?"

"Clare and Preston like him. They're fine with the idea of us living together."

"Really? I'm surprised." Father Raymond's bushy eyebrows rose.

"Well, if they have any objections, they haven't voiced them," Marianne said, testily. "It's not always easy to tell what people are thinking. My father, on the other hand, you will no doubt be pleased to hear, was quite vocal on the subject. In fact, he threw us out of the house this morning."

"You may not believe me but I'm sorry to hear that, truly. What happened?"

"We went there to try and mend some broken fences, figuratively speaking, but he ... well, suffice it to say he would have none of it."

"I have tried to see him over the past few months, but with no success," the old priest said. "He stopped coming to church some time ago, and naturally I was concerned."

"Vincent believes he is unwell, mentally unbalanced if you like. He certainly acted very irrationally when we were there today. We've had our differences over the years, but I am worried about him."

"Is there anything I can do to help?"

"I don't know, Father. Clare and Preston are going over there at the weekend to see how he is. Perhaps if you were to call on him next week. But do be careful."

"Of course. What did Matthew think about Vincent?"

The question came suddenly and caught Marianne by surprise. "Matthew? I ... I think he liked him. They got on well together when he stayed with us." *Liar!* Marianne found herself recalling how her brother and Vincent had argued. "Matthew was happy for us, relieved, I think, to see that we were so right for each other." *More lies!* "He understood, you see, that we asked for nothing more than to spend the rest of our lives together. He accepted the fact that Vincent means more to me than life itself."

Could Father Raymond see the truth in her eyes? She could visualize Matthew and Vincent so clearly as they had been on that final day, fighting to the death in the cellar on Wellington Street. It was almost like watching a scene caught on film, so real that she felt she could reach out and touch them. Looking into her soul, as she felt sure Father Raymond was, could he too see them in that deadly struggle?

"Do you believe that people come back from the dead, Father?"

"Are you thinking of Matthew?"

"No, not specifically."

"Well, it's a difficult question, and one that I may not be able to adequately answer. I believe we can love a person so much that we feel their presence even when they are no longer physically with us."

"But can we feel it so strongly that we actually believe we can see them?"

"As to that, I really cannot say. Have you experienced such a presence?" he asked with ecclesiastical curiosity.

"I believe I have, but sometimes I wonder if I didn't just imagine the whole thing."

"And did it trouble you, this manifestation?"

"Yes, but it wasn't just one person," she admitted to him now, relief flooding over her at the prospect of finally sharing this knowledge that up until now she had only shared with one other person. "There have been several incidents, and I feel as though this ability is becoming stronger as the weeks go by."

"You are still experiencing these episodes?"

"Yes. On the day of Matthew's funeral. When I came into the church, I saw my mother, sitting there in the pew in front of the Holy Mother's statue. She was sitting with someone whom I thought I recognized but…"

Just then, the phone in the hallway rang, and Father Raymond, excusing himself, went to answer the summons. He was gone for several minutes, and during that time Marianne began to question the wisdom of telling him all that she had. Why on earth had she unburdened herself to this man? Admittedly there was a certain measure of relief in revealing her fears to someone else, but had she gone too far? Said too much? Was this tête-à-tête subject to the same oath of secrecy as the confessional? She was afraid that Father Raymond might repeat these confidences to Clare and Preston. Surely not, but one never knew. Far better to leave now. Marianne stood up just as Father Raymond re-entered the room.

"I'm sorry, Father Raymond. I really must be going. Vincent will be wondering what's happened to me."

"Call him." The priest gestured towards the hallway.

"No. No, I must go. Many thanks for the tea," she said hurriedly, making her escape down the hallway and out onto the street. She turned as she reached the pavement and saw that Father Raymond had followed her and was standing in the doorway watching as she left. His face showed concern, and Marianne wondered, *Will he be praying for me tonight?* And despite her lack of faith, she hoped that he would.

That night the dreams were as vivid and terrifying as ever. They were no doubt exacerbated by the stress of the past few days, but as horrible as they were, Marianne tried to persuade herself that they were no longer a portent of things to come, but merely a residue of the times that lay behind them. Hopefully now, with this trip up to Beckham, they would be escaping the dolorous atmosphere that seemed to hang about them in London.

As they prepared to leave for Beckham, Sarah and Emma begged them to come back and see them. Marianne even rashly suggested that they might one day be able to come and stay with them in Swannington, a notion that evidently delighted them.

Vincent's attachment to Justin remained firm, and when they made their final farewells, he hugged the boy to him. Marianne found the moment poignant but somewhat disturbing. Had he really looked on him as he might a son of his own, or was it something more—a tenuous link between the child and Matthew?

22

ONE OF THE FAMILY

THEY MADE THE DRIVE UP TO BECKHAM without incident the following day. Marianne often visualized the moment when, for the first time, she would meet Vincent's family. She hoped that she would not be a disappointment to his mother, although, as she thought wryly, what woman could ever truly hope to live up to the expectations that a mother has for her son? But at least she must see that, despite whatever imperfections she might find in Vincent's partner, they were truly happy together.

Of course, Emily Foxworth must have had her doubts about the longevity of such a relationship. After all, hadn't she known about, and even met, many of the women with whom he looked to find permanent happiness? She must have wondered countless times, is this the one or maybe this one, and each time, thinking that he had finally found the right person, would see another prospective union fall by the wayside. How could she help but view their romance with a skepticism born of years of frustrated hopes for her son's future happiness?

Vincent often spoke of his family and had shown Marianne photos of his mother, his sister Judith, and their place in Beckham. But as they entered the imposing gates of Stoughton Manor, it was brought home to her just how well-to-do the family really was. The driveway wound through several acres of parkland covered with a fine coating of sparkling snow.

As the car crunched along the gravel drive, she saw a woman appear at the doorway and wave in their direction. She was too young to be his mother and Marianne concluded that this must be his sister, Judith. As they emerged from the car, she came toward them with arms outstretched, and Vincent greeted her with warm affection.

"Judith! How are you?"

"Fine! Never better!" she said, embracing him and turning immediately to Marianne.

"Marianne, my dear. I am so happy to meet you at last. But so very sorry that it should be under these circumstances." She put her arms around her and kissed her cheek. "Come in, dears."

She led them up the steps and into the house. It was magnificent; a storybook Manor House with all the trappings of a stately home.

"Mother will be down shortly. Would you like some refreshment, Marianne? I'm sure you would." Judith took her hand and led her into a large, sunny room, a roaring fire burning in the hearth of a huge stone fireplace. "Make yourselves comfortable and I'll get Mrs. Roper to rustle up some tea and cake. Vincent, help yourself to a drink if you want one. You know where everything is." She went away to see to things and left them alone in the drawing room.

Their arrival seemed to have come upon a whirlwind, leaving Marianne almost breathless. Vincent looked at her and grinned. "So how do you like it so far?"

"I'm absolutely overwhelmed. I never expected anything on this scale."

"And Judith?"

"I love her already!" She turned to embrace Vincent, but they quickly parted at the sound of someone approaching.

The door opened and Marianne watched apprehensively as Vincent's mother came into the room. What an impressive figure of a woman she was. Tall and still erect, even at some eighty or more years of age, her silver hair immaculately coiffured, her clothes of impeccable taste. Her movements were graceful and unhurried, and her face, although lined with age, still showed signs of the beauty that must have captured many hearts when she was younger. And yet all that had not been enough for Vincent's father, who had looked for happiness elsewhere and had found it with another woman.

She came towards Marianne and held out her hands. The fingers, long and well-manicured, wore several large rings, and Marianne took care not to squeeze them in her attempt to impress this woman with the sincerity of her feelings. She held the cool hands gently and looked into her still-sharp hazel eyes. Here was no emotional greeting, but a calm yet warm and honest welcome.

"Marianne," she said in a voice still strong and steady. "I am very pleased to meet you. And I was most sorry to hear about your brother's death. A terrible blow for you."

"Thank you," Marianne replied meekly, for in truth she felt rather gauche in the presence of this dignified matriarch. Vincent came to her rescue, however, stepping forward to kiss his mother's cheek and leading her to one of the comfortable armchairs.

"Good to see you again, Mother. How are you?"

"Very well, thank you, Vincent. One doesn't expect too much at my age, but happily, I am still able to get about."

Marianne thought that this was probably very much an understatement as she looked as though she was at least as fit as any one of them in the room.

Emily Foxworth settled herself into the well upholstered comfort of the large armchair and although she didn't exactly stare openly at her, Marianne felt that she was being subjected to a most critical scrutiny.

"Tell me, Marianne, did you find London much changed since you were there last?"

"A little. Rather noisy," she said. "But you are so lucky to live in Beckham. It's such a gorgeous spot! And please..." she added shyly, "Call me Annie. Everyone does, except for Vincent of course."

"Very well, Annie, and you must call me Emily. Yes, thank God the countryside is still as beautiful as ever, but it's shrinking. The towns are spreading out and gobbling up the land. Beckham seems to creep nearer and nearer to Stoughton every day." She shook her head sadly.

"Well, you have enough property around you to keep them at bay for quite a while, Mother," Vincent replied encouragingly.

"Yes, that's true." She gave a little smile, which quickly gave way to a look of concern. "But Vincent, how are you, my boy? You look tired, and your hands... !" She had noticed with dismay the bandages that covered his hands and forearms, and Marianne realized that he had not told her the full extent of his injuries.

"It's nothing," he said and, pulling them from view, adroitly changed the subject. "What have you and Judith been up to since I last heard from you?"

Judith, who had just joined them, said, "We were up in town last week to see *Mefistofele* at the Garden."

"And how was it?" Vincent asked.

"Excellent," replied his mother enthusiastically. "Poor Faust! I always think he was such a chump, not to have gone off with the devil and enjoyed himself. How deadly dull being surrounded by a heavenly choir for all eternity." She laughed. "Marguerite was pathetic, but Mefistofele sang his heart out and whistled enough to bring the roof down when they hauled him off during the finale," she added with gusto. For all her dignified appearance Marianne found, with a welcome measure of relief, that Emily Foxworth could be surprisingly down-to-earth in her speech, a trait which she found rather endearing.

"And then we spent last Thursday at the Tate Gallery," Judith continued. "There are some beautiful pictures there. Speaking of which, we finally had some of Grandfather's old paintings restored. You know, Vincent, the ones that sat up in the attics for so many years, wrapped in blankets and gathering dust. I had no idea they were such beauties! They just came back from the framers and they look wonderful. Mother is getting Mr. Adams to come and hang them tomorrow, so you'll be able to see them while you're here."

"My father-in-law was something of an artist, Annie," Emily Foxworth told her. "Of course, we didn't think much of it when we were younger, he only did it as a hobby, you understand. But now that I see his work, after all these years, I realize that he was jolly good and could have been quite famous if he'd put his mind to it."

"He didn't do too badly," Vincent sprang to his grandfather's defense.

"Oh, he did very well financially, of course. After all, this was his home, and everything you see here was his, but that was all in the commercial line. No, I'm talking about making a name for himself in the world of art."

The conversation had taken a turn that caused Marianne to revise her thoughts. Until now, she always assumed that when Vincent referred to his 'grandfather' he meant his mother's father, but such was evidently not the case. The grandfather who had taken such an interest in his education and upbringing was the father of the man who had deserted his family. Had he felt a measure of responsibility for the wife and children who had so unexpectedly been left by his son for some unknown woman?

"Vincent often speaks of him," Marianne said. "I understand he taught Vincent to play the piano."

"He was such a clever man, my dear. He played the piano beautifully, but we never fully appreciated how gifted he was." She gave a wistful sigh and shook her head thoughtfully. "He took his own achievements so lightly, downplayed his abilities to such an extent that they were all but forgotten. But now we have these wonderful pictures and I think, as a celebration of their resurrection, I will give a little party and Vincent can play for us. You will still be here on Sunday, won't you Vincent?"

"Yes Mother, of course. We'll be here for another week at least, if you can bear it."

"Splendid! Then this is what we'll do. Judith, you'll call Adrian Penworthy, the Anstruthers, Nick and Denise, Reverend Forsythe and, of course, Dr. James and his wife, and ask them all to dinner on Sunday evening. Annie, you must come with me to Beckham tomorrow. I want to order some new flower arrangements to be sent up to the house and Taylor's has the new table linen that I ordered. Vincent, be a dear boy and check the contents of the cellar. See if there is any decent wine down there. Parker has been serving up the most awful muck just lately and I can't possibly give it to our guests. Get whatever you think we need from Harvey's in town." Her eyes sparkled with delighted animation as she planned the forthcoming festivities, but suddenly she looked crestfallen and put her hand on Marianne's arm.

"Annie, my dear! How awful! I'm most dreadfully sorry! What a wicked woman you must think me. To have totally forgotten that you are in mourning, I mean. Cancel everything!" she ordered imperiously to the room in general.

"No, no, please," Marianne hastened to reassure her. "There's nothing I would enjoy more, truly. We have had enough sadness to last us a lifetime."

"Are you sure, my dear?" Emily Foxworth looked at her with renewed hope, and Marianne nodded.

"Absolutely! I think the idea of a party to celebrate the return of Grandfather Foxworth's pictures to their rightful prominence is perfect."

"How wonderful! Then full steam ahead!" Emily said, clapping her hands together in delight.

Marianne spent the remainder of the day looking around Stoughton Manor with Judith acting as tour guide. The house itself was impressive and the garden, although the winter months were upon them, was still beautiful and full of life. The lawns sloped down toward the east and a small lake where ducks dabbled about in the as yet unfrozen water, occasionally tipping on end, their heads submerged, tails pointing up towards the sky, as they looked for food.

"We used to come fishing here when we were children," Judith explained. "Grandfather would bring us down, early in the morning just as the sun was rising, and we'd catch tadpoles and tiddlers in our nets and put them in jam jars." She laughed as she remembered. "Vincent caught a frog once and took it up to the house. He let it loose in the kitchen and scared my grandmother half to death. She gave him such a telling off, but grandfather said, 'Don't make such a fuss, Daphne. Leave the boy alone,' and he and my mother spent the rest of the day trying to find it, while grandmother left the house, refusing to return until it was removed."

"And did they find it?"

"I discovered it in grandfather's study under the desk. The poor thing was terrified, so I scooped it up and brought it back down to the lake," Judith replied.

That evening, after dinner, they sat and talked late into the night. Vincent's mother recalled the frog incident and several other anecdotes involving the children when they had come to visit Stoughton Manor and, in particular, a potentially disastrous moment one Guy Fawkes night.

"Derek and Vincent had built a huge bonfire in the vegetable garden," Emily Foxworth recounted. "Judith and I made a guy with one of Derek's old suits stuffed with newspaper."

"And very realistic it looked too; I might add," said Judith proudly.

"We stuck it on top of the bonfire and that night when it got dark, Jenkins, who was our head gardener at the time, lit the fire and we all went outside to watch the fireworks and eat roasted chestnuts," Emily Foxworth continued. "Derek bought a whole boxful of rockets, roman candles, Catherine wheels, every kind of firework imaginable. Well, things went swimmingly for the first few minutes. The children were standing waving sparklers and cheering as the rockets showered over the greenhouse, when suddenly a spark from one of the roman candles got into the box." She laughed heartily at the memory. "We had left it too close to where Derek and Jenkins were letting them off, and the whole thing went up in the most spectacular manner."

"Yes, I remember," said Judith. "There were fireworks and rockets going off in every direction. We didn't know which way to run. We were all screaming, especially grandmother. Grandfather just stood in the middle of it all convulsed with laughter."

"Thank goodness no one was hurt. It was a miracle that someone didn't lose an eye or worse," Emily Foxworth said. "Pounds-worth of fireworks that should have lasted an hour or more went up in a matter of seconds."

"But we did manage to rescue the chestnuts from the fire," Vincent added. "When all the tumult died down."

"Yes, they were delicious," Judith reminisced, as she almost seemed to taste the succulent morsels, piping hot from the embers of that bonfire long ago.

The next morning dawned bright and clear and they assembled after breakfast in the drawing room to await the signal to begin the day's activities. Martin Adams arrived from town and had already been given instructions as to which pictures should go where. Judith, armed with her address book, was preparing to call the people that her mother had suggested as guests for the party to be held in two days' time. Marianne wondered how successful she would be. It was rather short notice and most probably some of them would have prior engagements. But Emily seemed confident that there would be no problem in persuading them to come to the Manor. Judith would also be in charge of planning the menu and discussing the arrangements with Mrs. Roper, the housekeeper.

Vincent had already been dispatched to the cellars and returned with a shopping list that would undoubtedly light up the eyes of the local vintner. His mother, seeing that they were all ready to spring into action, buttoned her coat, pulled on a pair of fine leather gloves and marched ahead of them, out to an enormous, ancient Rolls Royce that was waiting in the driveway

"Good morning, Parker," she addressed the person who stood to attention at the foot of the steps.

"Good morning, Madame." The man who acted as chauffeur, butler and handyman to the household touched his cap deferentially and opened the car door. Emily slid into the rear seat and Marianne climbed in beside her.

She later learned that Emily Foxworth had inherited Parker along with the Manor. He had worked for Derek Foxworth for many years as a young man and, as one of his most trusted servants, had been with him on the morning when the old man had been carried dying to his bed. He had taken it upon himself to send for the daughter-in-law, believing that his employer would wish her to be there. But by the time she had dashed from her home to be by his side, he had already passed away, leaving Parker to carry out the task of handing her a letter that Derek Foxworth had entrusted to him some time before. When Emily Foxworth moved into the Manor, he remained to take care of her, although, as he too was quite elderly, Marianne wondered just who was taking care of who.

"Benson's the florists first, Parker. Then we need to stop at Taylor's."

"Very good Ma'am."

As they pulled away down the driveway, Marianne looked over her shoulder at the receding figure of Vincent, standing waving as he watched them depart. Turning back, she found Mrs. Foxworth gazing at her with a slightly troubled look, which quickly turned to a smile as she placed her hand on Marianne's. "How lucky Vincent is, to have someone who is so devoted to him," she said with genuine happiness.

"Oh, I'm the lucky one," Marianne responded truthfully.

Emily Foxworth nodded approvingly, a mother's natural pride in her son shining through her eyes. "He is rather a catch, isn't he? He's so much like his father. They were as alike as two peas in a pod. So handsome and clever." She seemed to have sunk back into the past, remote and dreamy, and then mentally shaking off her reminiscences, she looked at Marianne again. "Has he ever mentioned his father to you?"

"Only once," Marianne answered hesitatingly, wondering if she should admit to being aware of that part of the family history. "Vincent told me that he had gone away."

Mrs. Foxworth released a little sigh almost, it seemed, of relief. "Well, my dear, that's rather a charitable way of putting it, but yes, he did leave. Lewis ran away with another woman and we never heard from him again."

"How horrible for you," Marianne said sympathetically.

"My pride was hurt, but one learns to get over these things. We managed quite well without him and, of course, my father-in-law made sure that we were taken care of financially. The dear old duck was always there for us. Always." Marianne saw what looked like the suspicion of a tear glistening in the old lady's eye. Emily turned her head quickly and looked out of the window at the passing countryside. After a moment, regaining her self-control, she continued, "I'm very lucky to have such a caring family. Of course, I miss Vincent terribly, but I hope one day you will both come back to Beckham to live. And of course, I have Judith who takes great care of me. Too much, sometimes, I think. But I'm grateful and there will come a time, no doubt, when I will need her help, much more than I do now."

By this time, they had reached the town and Parker threaded his way through the busy streets, it being market day, and pulled up outside the florist's shop. "We'll only be a moment, Parker. Wait here for us."

"But it's a no-parking zone, Ma'am. I told you before, they gave me a summons the last time we left the car here."

"Phooey, I can't believe they'd do that. We'll only be a moment," she repeated. Parker shook his head resignedly and awaited the inevitable wrath of the local constabulary while Emily led Marianne into the store. Inside was a veritable cornucopia of floral arrangements, bouquets, gifts, and colorful balloons.

The young woman behind the counter looked up as the bell on the door tinkled, announcing their arrival, and she greeted them enthusiastically. "Mrs. Foxworth! How are you? We haven't seen you for a while."

"I am very well, thank you, Doreen." Then immediately getting down to business, "Now pay attention as we are rather pressed for time and I need to order some things that must be sent up to the Manor on Sunday morning." Marianne could see that Doreen was about to say something, but Mrs. Foxworth forestalled her, raising a hand imperiously. "Please! You are going to tell me that you don't make deliveries on Sunday. Rubbish! Morris Benson will do anything to make a few extra pounds. Tell him it's imperative that I have these things delivered on Sunday morning."

Doreen nodded, conceding defeat. Mrs. Foxworth was not a person to be trifled with, and after all, the order was probably the largest and most regular that Mr. Benson had on his books.

"I need one large and two smaller centerpieces for the dining table, whatever flowers you think would look best. I'll leave that up to you, but traditional, you understand. I do not want any of that modern look you tried to fob off on me last Easter with bits of tree branches and feathers stuck in," she admonished. "I also need four large vase arrangements with plenty of roses, and not the cheap ones that wilt as soon as they get up to the house. And would you make one of those lovely little bouquets with the ribbons, for Annie's room. I forgot to order it last week, which was very remiss of me." She turned to Marianne apologetically. "So many things to remember. I think that's it. Thank you, Doreen. I'm sure you'll do a most splendid job as usual."

And with that part of business taken care of, they left the store, returning to Parker, who, as he had predicted, was in earnest discussion with the long arm of the law. The constable turned as they approached, and his fresh young complexion flushed crimson as he beheld the formidable figure of Mrs. Foxworth bearing down on him.

"Archie Tremaine! What on earth do you think you're up to, you young upstart?"

"I'm sorry, Mrs. Foxworth, but you can't park the car here."

"I told him it was only for a moment," the elderly chauffer tried to explain, but the indignant owner of the Rolls shushed him and continued her harangue. "Clear off, young Archie! Put away your blasted parking tickets. We're leaving. Good God! What is this place coming to?"

She brushed past the youthful guardian of the law and he stepped backwards, tongue-tied. Evidently this was not the first time he had come into conflict with the dowager of Stoughton Manor and discretion being the better part of valor, he allowed the party to proceed, merely muttering under his breath, "Daft old bat."

Marianne couldn't resist smiling as she imagined trying to pull that kind of stunt on one of Swannington's boys in blue on any of the many occasions that she had been issued with a ticket for leaving her car in a prohibited zone.

Parker resumed his place in the driver's seat, shaking his head and sighing, but evidently resigned to the vagaries of his indomitable employer. Putting the car into gear, he carefully pulled away from the curb as Archie Tremaine stood helplessly watching his quarry escaping down the road.

After some minutes navigating the narrow streets of Beckham's main shopping district, they arrived outside the draper's shop. The proprietor himself bustled forward to attend to them when he realized who the customer was. They were of a similar age, and Mrs. Foxworth showed a sympathetic tolerance as he dithered about behind the counter, looking for the table linen that she had ordered.

"I know it's here somewhere. It came in just the other day. Now where did I put it? Ah, yes, here it is." He produced the package triumphantly and opening it, spread the contents out for his customer's approval.

The gleaming white tablecloth and napkins were inspected, the embroidered pattern at the corners closely scrutinized, and Marianne saw Emily Foxworth's lips compress slightly as though something were amiss. But the look quickly passed and she smiled at the little draper. "Thank you,

Mr. Taylor. These are perfect." He gave a slight bow of relieved gratification and re-wrapped the items carefully. As he did so, they took the opportunity to look around the shop. It was an old-fashioned little place, packed with stock in every conceivable space. The lighting, so subdued as to be almost negligible combined with the uneven wooden floorboards, caused one to move cautiously about the aisles. Not finding any further purchases, however, they collected the package and bid farewell to Mr. Taylor, who accompanied them to the door.

Once outside, Emily Foxworth gave vent to a certain amount of frustration. "Really! He gets worse by the day, the silly old fool! The pattern is totally wrong. Not what I ordered at all. But what can you do? I suppose his mind's going. He must be eighty if he's a day."

Marianne found this observation rather amusing, as Emily was his senior by at least a couple of years. But Emily Foxworth's reasoning didn't work that way. She was still the vigorous and dynamic woman who had come to Stoughton Manor, confident, alert and with an enduring panache that remained undiminished.

After visiting the stationer's, the post office, and the confectioners where she obtained an enormous box of her favorite chocolates, Emily Foxworth suggested that they stop at a local restaurant for lunch. It was an idea with which Marianne was quite agreeable, as she was beginning to feel hungry despite the large breakfast provided by Mrs. Roper. Parker was sent to deposit the Rolls Royce in a place acceptable to any passing officer of the law and they made their way along the busy pavement to The Bluebell Restaurant. They knew Emily here too and the two women were shown immediately to a table by the spotlessly clean latticed window overlooking the street.

"This is my favorite table. I like to see what's going on out there; who's coming and going. It's not that I'm nosy, just inquisitive. There is a difference," Emily told her companion.

As they looked out, Marianne saw, immediately outside the window, a young woman, heavily pregnant, stooping with considerable difficulty to retrieve a package that she had dropped on the pavement. As she rose and straightened, she turned to stare at them and froze as her eyes met Emily Foxworth's. She put her hand up to brush aside the long blonde hair that hung loosely about her face and in that look and gesture Marianne saw recognition and defiance. She also could not help noticing the lack of a wedding ring on the young woman's finger.

She looked at Emily to gauge her reaction, but the older woman had already turned her head away from the window to speak to the waitress who had brought a pot of coffee and was setting out the cups. When she was gone, Marianne said, "Did you know the woman who was outside? She seemed to recognize you."

"She used to help up at the Manor, but Parker didn't have a very high opinion of her. She was very temperamental, always arguing with Mrs. Roper, and she left after a slight contretemps over a valuable piece of porcelain that was carelessly broken."

Marianne could imagine the feathers flying after such an incident; the fury of Mrs. Roper, who looked on the family's possessions with as much personal pride as she would her own. Emily Foxworth's intolerance of any shortcomings in someone entrusted with her prized pieces, pitted against the volatile temperament of this young miscreant, would have culminated in more than just 'a slight contretemps' Marianne felt sure.

"The father of this expected little bundle of joy," Emily Foxworth went on, "is the most dreadful oik—a motor mechanic by trade—though I wouldn't have him touch the Rolls if he was the last motor mechanic alive." She leaned back in her seat as the waitress brought the rest of their order. When they were alone once more, she continued, "When I was a young girl, we would have said that the man should do the right thing and marry the girl, but nowadays I am apt to believe that she would be a lot better off going it alone."

She began to eat the salad that had been placed before her and after a few minutes resumed, "I would never mention something like that to anyone, but you are one of the family … almost." She couldn't help making the final qualification, but Marianne was happy, nevertheless, that she considered her 'almost' family.

By the time they returned to the Manor, later that afternoon, the paintings had already been hung in their respective places and each was covered by a draping of red velvet.

"I thought it would make the event a little more dramatic," Emily explained. "There are four pieces in all, one in the dining room, which I thought we would unveil directly after dinner, then one in the morning room, one in the drawing room where Vincent will play for us, and one in the library. Judith, dear, will everyone on the list be here?"

Judith was delighted to report that her mission had been a complete success. "Yes. They all said they would love to come and are looking forward to seeing grandfather's paintings."

"Excellent! Well done! And Vincent, did you take care of those little tasks I gave you?"

"Yes, Mother. They'll be delivering the order tomorrow."

"Mrs. Roper and I have been working on the menu for Sunday evening and I think you'll be pleased with the result," Judith added confidently. "We've ordered enough food to feed an army, and Mrs. Roper is positively bursting to show what she can do in the kitchen. It's been a while since we've had so many people to dinner at one time," Judith told Marianne excitedly.

Her eyes were shining with pleasurable anticipation of the coming festivities, and Marianne wondered if her days here sometimes seemed dull to her. Did she ever yearn to be out on her own in the world, experiencing all the highs and lows of life, something that she would never know here in the safe haven of Stoughton Manor? Or was she content to watch the months and years glide gently by, secure in the knowledge that she would never want for anything, always have this beautiful home, stay close by her mother and never know what it was like to have had a family of her own?

Vincent had told Marianne that Judith only ever had one romance in her life when she was in her early thirties. The man, who was a local solicitor, had courted her for several months, and just when it seemed that a proposal may be hovering in the wings, he had informed her that he had been offered a position with a Canadian law firm. Judith, reluctant to leave England and her mother, sadly declined to accompany him. Did she ever regret her decision? Marianne thought she must have done, at times, although she seemed serene and happy with her lot. And she must have felt her presence here at Stoughton even more essential when Vincent, the only surviving male member of the family, had decided to leave and move to Swannington.

Did she miss her father, Marianne wondered? She must have been about twenty-one years old when he left home, just emerging from awkward adolescence into adulthood, just beginning to learn the ways of the world and about to discover firsthand that things were not always as they seemed. What were her thoughts then, Marianne wondered, when her father had so unexpectedly deserted them, without a word of explanation? Was she bitter? Did she blame him for abandoning his family or was she, like her mother, soon resigned to the vicissitudes of life? And how had she viewed the move from their own home to the regal elegance of Stoughton Manor, when her paternal grandfather and by all accounts, guardian angel, had died some three years later, leaving everything he had in the world to Emily Foxworth and her two children?

Marianne liked Judith, not only because she was Vincent's sister but because she admired her calm acceptance of the hand life had dealt her, both the good and the bad aspects of it. She wasn't snobbish or boastful of the wealth that surrounded her. Nor was she self-pitying or embittered. Of course, there was still the chance that she might meet someone, fall in love and marry. But start a family? Impossible now. The sands of time had run out all too quickly for Judith. Marianne felt that she would be content to remain as she was, deliberately not looking for romance, turning a blind eye to any possible suitors and avoiding any temptation to leave this cocoon that had she had spun about herself.

23

THE UNVEILING

WHEN SUNDAY EVENING ARRIVED, it found the family and the house decked out in all their finery. Parker, with the help of two young girls from Beckham, had buffed and polished Stoughton Manor to a sparkling finish and deliciously savory smells had wafted from the kitchen all day, whetting their appetites to no little degree. Judith and Mrs. Roper could be seen walking around with self-satisfied smiles on their faces as they inspected the contents of the pots and pans that bubbled away on the stove. Every once in a while, Marianne caught sight of Emily Foxworth pacing about the rooms, clasping her hands together in eager anticipation of the evening's celebrations.

The Reverend Forsythe, the first to arrive, had been a young curate when he had first come to St Anselm's church in Penhampton just after the war, and was totally dedicated to his calling. Now, in middle age, he had remained unmarried and unselfishly devoted his life to God and his flock. He administered to them, seeing them through births, marriages and deaths, with a kindly eye and a gentle, reassuring hand. Beloved by all, this worthy and self-sacrificing servant of God may not have gained wealth from his position in the world, indeed he was considerably poorer than most of his neighbors in Beckham, but he was truly rich in the friendship and good opinion of his fellow creatures. He seemed to want nothing more from life than that he should be welcome at any time, in any home in his parish, which he undoubtedly was.

"Dear Emily," he said, grasping his hostess's hands warmly. "Thank you so much for this kind invitation. So very kind, dear lady."

"Always a pleasure to see you here, Arnold. How are you? I noticed during the sermon last Sunday you sounded a bit nasal."

"Yes. I'm sorry about that. So embarrassing. I got caught in the rain during one of my visits to a parishioner in Penhampton and developed rather a nasty cold, but it seems to have run its course, thank goodness. Mrs. Beaminster very kindly provided lots of hot chicken soup, which still seems to be the best remedy, despite all the pills and syrups one sees in the chemist's shop in the High Street."

"Absolutely. You don't want to go taking any of that muck. Mrs. Beaminster has the right idea. Plenty of hot soup, and I also recommend a splash of whisky mixed in with your porridge in the morning. It does a world of good."

The Reverend Forsythe looked a bit dubious about the latter cure, but thanked his hostess for her suggestions and subsided into the depths of a nearby armchair.

The next person to arrive was Adrian Penworthy, a short, stocky octogenarian, in rather old-fashioned evening dress who, despite his years, was as energetic and alert as Emily Foxworth.

"Annie, I would like you to meet Adrian Penworthy, the family's solicitor, and an old and valued friend. Adrian and I have known each other since the days when I used to bring the children here to visit Derek and Daphne. Adrian, this is Vincent's friend, Annie. They are staying here for a few days."

"How do you do." Mr. Penworthy shook Marianne's hand. "Hello, Vincent. How are you, my boy?"

"Very well, thank you, Mr. Penworthy. You're looking very dashing this evening."

"Well, you know it's not often I get the opportunity to dress up for such a special occasion as this. I lead a very quiet life these days," he told Marianne confidentially. "I turned over most of the practice to my young partner a few years ago, but I still take care of the Foxworth estate."

"And I don't know what we would do without him," Emily Foxworth exclaimed. He got me off of a very nasty charge of reckless driving when I tried to drive the Rolls through Upper Bletchford last year. Admittedly, I don't get to handle the thing very often, but I was doing quite well," Emily explained. "Parker was there, right next to me and said I was driving beautifully when a wretched cat ran out in front of us, and the next thing I knew, we were up on the pavement, knocking down signs and bollards left and right."

"Mother! You never told me about this!" Vincent was appalled.

"Don't make a fuss. No one was hurt, and I was completely exonerated thanks to Adrian. The owner of the cat was severely reprimanded and rightfully so."

Adrian Penworthy gave a slight shrug and looked at Vincent as much as to say, *the woman is incorrigible*. In an aside, he murmured, "It didn't hurt that old Dicky Dunster was on the bench at the time."

Vincent shook his head disapprovingly, but Emily Foxworth had already brushed the subject aside.

The next guests to arrive were Doctor John James and his wife Felicity, the former hobbling into the room with the assistance of a walking stick.

"Hello John. What on earth have you been up to?" Emily Foxworth greeted her old friend.

"He fell down the steps in the garden last week and twisted his ankle," Felicity said with some exasperation. "I've told him a million times to be careful out there, but will the man listen? No!" She kissed Emily's cheek and turned to assist her grumbling husband to a chair.

"Did you get someone to look at it?" Emily asked the doctor as he lowered himself into the depths of the armchair.

"What? The step?"

"No, of course not. Emily means your ankle." Felicity fluttered around him, readjusting cushions while he scowled and made feeble attempts to avoid her ministrations.

"For goodness' sake woman, don't fuss," he told his wife.

"No, Emily, he won't see anyone. I told him to let Leonard Robinson check him out, but the obstinate old fool won't go."

"I don't need to go to a doctor. I am a doctor. I can take care of myself."

"Physician, heal thyself. Oh well, have a whisky and splash." Emily summoned Parker, who was standing to attention by the drinks tray.

"Now, John and Felicity, I want you to meet our special guest. This is Annie, Vincent's friend. Annie, Dr. James delivered Vincent when he was born."

"Couldn't wait till his mother was back home to London," Doctor James said cheerfully.

"Yes, he arrived a little sooner than we expected. Lewis and I were here for a visit and nature took its course before we had a chance to return home. Luckily John was already here, paying a call on Derek."

"Yes, he used to get the most awful headaches, I remember. I gave him pills, but they didn't do much good. Anyway, I was just leaving that day when Lewis came running in from the garden and said your mother had gone into labor out there. We only just managed to get her back into the house and up to her room in time. You were in a hurry to get into this world, Vincent."

They all laughed and Judith, who had been talking to the Reverend and Mr. Penworthy, came over to join them.

"Ah, Judith my dear, how are you?" Doctor James asked her.

"Very well, thank you, Doctor James."

"I was just telling young Annie here about Vincent and his premature arrival at Stoughton Manor. It was almost as though he were meant to live here. It caused such a commotion. I don't know who was more agitated, Lewis or his father. Everyone was running around in a flap, but Daphne, bless her, was as calm and sensible as ever. Took control of everything and the two of us brought Vincent kicking and screaming into the world. And an ugly little brute he was, too."

"John!" his wife admonished him, but Emily agreed. "Yes, who would have guessed he would turn out to be such a handsome specimen? Not at all like the red and wrinkled little squawker that almost arrived among the roses."

To hide his embarrassment at these reminiscences by the senior members of the group, Vincent went away to check on the status of the wine being served with dinner.

Emily, who had gone to greet the final four guests who had just arrived, led Gordon and Florence Anstruther, and Nicolas and Denise Arundel back to where Marianne was standing with the others.

"Late as usual," observed Doctor James as the newcomers exchanged hugs and handshakes with those already assembled. Everyone seemed to be on the most familiar terms. Marianne imagined these elderly friends, all growing up together, meeting here at Stoughton Manor, first hosted by Derek and Daphne Foxworth and after they had gone, by their daughter-in-law, Emily, who now stood beaming as her companions swapped stories and recalled times long past.

Parker, meanwhile, sidled up to Emily and whispered something in her ear, to which she nodded and said, "Dinner is ready, everyone." They all trooped into the dining room led by Emily on the arm of Adrian Penworthy. Marianne and Vincent were the last to be seated at the table, and Marianne found herself placed next to the Reverend Forsythe, who turned out to be an amiable table companion. Vincent, sitting opposite, next to Florence Anstruther, was doing his best to make himself understood, for that lady was evidently hard of hearing.

Mrs. Roper had definitely done the house proud. The food, although not haute cuisine, was delicious and well prepared, and very little was left uneaten by those gathered around the large dining room table.

As dinner continued, they had all occasionally glanced toward the picture that awaited its ceremonial unveiling, and with the exception of Emily and Judith, who already knew the content of the five paintings, they each took turns guessing what the subject matter would be.

"He did some very nice landscapes, I remember," Dr. James remarked.

"I recall he was working on a painting of the Manor when I came to visit once," added his wife. Felicity James closed her eyes in an effort to recall the scene and she went on. "He was sitting at an easel in the middle of the lawn, I remember. I believe you were here too, Emily, with the children. They were very young then, and Vincent was standing next to his grandfather, watching him mix the colors on his palette."

"Yes, I remember that!" Vincent exclaimed. "I was fascinated by the paints and the way the colors blended to make different colors. To my young eyes it was like magic."

"We often wondered if Vincent would grow up to be an artist," Felicity James observed. "He seemed to take after his grandfather in so many respects."

"Well, Felicity, you win the prize this time," Emily congratulated her as she arose from her seat, stepped adroitly to the draped picture and whisked away the velvet material to display a remarkably lifelike painting of Stoughton Manor.

"Stoughton Manor, it is!" she exclaimed. "You were exactly right, Felicity. Derek painted it when we came to visit one summer. He captured the old place marvelously, didn't he? It was one of the last things that he ever painted. His eyesight was starting to go then. That and the arthritis which pained his poor hands so badly put an end to his art and his piano playing."

The men tutted and shook their heads as if in sympathy with the man who had suffered the infirmities of old age, as they did now.

"It's almost like a photograph," Florence Anstruther declared as she, too, left her place at the table and went to take a closer look at the picture.

"Ah, Parker," Emily summoned that worthy man as he hovered attentively nearby. "Would you serve coffee in the morning room?"

"Yes Ma'am. Brandy and cigars for the gents, Ma'am?"

"By all means." Emily led her guests through to the morning room where two more pictures awaited presentation. Parker distributed the coffee and brandy and Gordon Anstruther, Adrian Penworthy, and Nick Arundel puffed contentedly at enormous, pungent cigars.

"Now who would like to take a guess at these?" Emily asked her guests as they tried to visualize what lay behind the folds of velvet swathed about the paintings. "Reverend, you should know this one." She smiled at the Reverend Forsythe, who was the youngest of those assembled.

Aided by this obviously pointed clue, he replied, "It must be St Anselm's. Am I right?"

"Well done, Reverend!" said his hostess, removing the velvet to reveal the familiar features of the old parish church in nearby Penhampton.

"How splendid!" exclaimed Reverend Forsythe. He stepped forward to examine the minute details on the canvas.

"I remember Vincent's christening there," Felicity James said. "I thought poor old Ambrose Fortescue was going to drop him in the font. It wasn't long after that that he retired," she added.

"And not a moment too soon," Emily Foxworth commented. "His sermons were becoming more and more rambling."

"I didn't much care for the man who took his place though," Florence Anstruther said. "Too modern by far. We were rather relieved when he decided to go and do missionary work in Africa and you took over, Vicar."

Forsythe shook his head reprovingly. "I'm sure Reverend Carmichael had his good points. And he was very young. New ideas, you know." He hesitated to remind them that he too had been very young when he had arrived as curate, to assist the Reverend Carmichael. But he soon learned that the parishioners were averse to change, and when he took over from the departing Carmichael, he gradually set aside the more radical changes that his predecessor had initiated, thus endearing him to his flock.

"I can't be doing with all that newfangled stuff," Doctor James grumbled, but his wife silenced him with a sharp nudge.

"I'm guessing that the next one will be another landscape, maybe something down by the stream near Penhampton," Denise Anstruther volunteered.

But she was wrong. The third picture was that of a young man, who appeared to be a gardener in shirt-sleeves, leaning on a shovel, taking a brief respite from his labors, his complexion ruddy, his eyes sparkling.

"That's Ronald Jenkins from the village, surely," Dr. James said.

"No, although you are almost right," Emily replied. "That's Ronald's father. He used to work here many years ago as head gardener. He was a very knowledgeable man, and the gardens always looked beautiful under his care."

"That would be young Monica's great-grandfather, I suppose," Dr. James speculated.

An uncomfortable silence filled the room for several seconds, until Judith asked if anyone would like more coffee.

They sat for a while, discussing the pictures and life in general, back in the times when they had been painted.

"The good old days" Gordon Anstruther bemoaned. "I'm afraid they're gone forever. We made our own entertainment back then. Do you remember, Florence, how we all used to get together at Charles Worthington's house and everyone did their own party piece?"

"Speaking of party pieces, Vincent has agreed to play for us," Emily announced, "So perhaps you will join us in the drawing room."

"Splendid! Splendid!" Reverend Forsythe said delightedly, and offered Emily his arm as they all made their way to the next room. When everyone was seated, Vincent took up his place at the piano and, dispensing with the aid of sheet music, he began to play, *The Honfleur Suite* by Neville Wyndham.

Although Marianne had heard him play before, at home, or sometimes when they visited Jonathan Amor and his wife, she had never seen him put quite so much of himself into his performance as he did that evening at Stoughton Manor. It was as though the spirit of his grandfather, the one who had taught him to play, was urging him on. She could almost see him, standing there beside his grandson, saying, "That's it, my boy, put your heart and soul into it!"

As he played, Marianne's mind drifted back to the house on Wellington Street where she could have sworn she'd heard someone playing this same piece, *The Honfleur Suite*. Was it just a co-incidence that he had chosen it tonight? He had claimed not to have heard anything when they went to the old house in Sterling. Marianne was so engrossed in her own thoughts that she failed to notice when the music had ceased and everyone about her was clapping appreciatively. As an encore, Vincent had chosen a more light-hearted piece, and he dashed it off with masterful virtuosity.

Once more they applauded, and rising from the piano stool, he gave a little bow, embraced his mother, who had come forward to congratulate him, and then shook hands with Dr. James, who exclaimed, "Just like your grandfather! Well done, Vincent, well done! I always enjoyed Wyndham's music. The chap had a house near here, if I remember rightly."

"Yes. Wasn't he the young man who rented that place in Honfleur that Derek used to own?" Gordon Anstruther remarked.

"Yes, indeed. And now," Emily Foxworth broke into these reminisces, "there is just one more picture in the library, so if you'll all come with me." And she led the way once more, to a room that Marianne had not yet seen during her stay at Stoughton Manor.

The library still had a masculine air about it, and she guessed that it had been altered very little since the time when Derek Foxworth had claimed it as his sanctum. The large mahogany desk, kept immaculately polished, held many mementoes of Derek Foxworth's tenure at Stoughton Manor. His photo, the likeness to Vincent uncanny, a silver cigarette case, a favorite book, all kept just as he had left them. The room had been maintained almost as a shrine by the women who now inhabited the Manor, and Marianne wondered, not for the first time, about the man who had so readily assumed the responsibilities of the son who had deserted his family. It was because of his generosity and concern for their well-being that they had to come to live here after his death.

Emily Foxworth made her way to the fireplace, at the far end of the room, and the fifth and final painting which hung above the mantelpiece. She turned to address the gathering while grasping a corner of the cloth that concealed the picture.

"Well, dear friends, we have come to the last painting, but before I unveil this final work, I want to thank you all for coming here tonight at such short notice."

Her guests nodded and murmured their acknowledgments, and she turned to look at Vincent.

"As you know, Vincent and Annie are only here for a few days, and I so wanted to include them in this tribute to Derek's accomplishments."

Vincent smiled and stepped to her side, putting his arm around his mother's shoulders as she reached up to remove the velvet cover, revealing a most unexpected and startling spectacle.

They had all been unprepared for what they now saw before them, and it took their collective breath away. Each of them had reason to stare in amazement at the picture, and Marianne, in particular, was dumbfounded. There, reclining on a chaise lounge, was a beautiful young woman, nude and sensually alluring. Adele Hemmings! Marianne saw the room swim before her eyes and felt her legs buckle under her as she groped for the nearest chair. Luckily the others had been gathered around the picture, but Marianne had held back, and so this faintness had gone unnoticed as they each commented on what they saw.

"I think I'm correct in saying that this one dates back to before Derek came to Beckham," Emily Foxworth explained. "He brought it with him, but we're not sure who the young lady was. She may have just been a paid model, but somehow, I think there was more to it than that. He never spoke of her, of course. Daphne was very jealous of his earlier life and he was always very careful not to allude to it."

"Well! Foxy Foxworth, the old devil! Oh, excuse me, Reverend," Gordon Anstruther apologized, but he could not help ogling the portrait as did all the men in the room.

The old fox, Renard! The artist, Desmond Renard, had become Derek Foxworth. Marianne glanced up and while they were all still fluttering around the picture, she saw Vincent turn and look at her. Did he know who the woman was? Her mouth had gone dry, and she got unsteadily to her feet, walking almost trance-like toward where they all stood.

Emily's guests parted as Marianne advanced and stopped in front of the picture, looking up at it in disbelief. Adele! How absolutely incredible! It was her without a doubt, the dark flowing hair, the silver locket at the throat, the face that she had seen looking out at her from the carriage in the Railway Museum.

She stared and as she took in every exquisite and voluptuous detail of the canvas, it seemed to change before her very eyes. Adele's face was no longer smiling, but had changed its expression to that of an agonized grimace. What had begun as a single spot of red on the alabaster skin of her breast was spreading, the blood running down her body, down the entire length of the painting, splattering on to the floor below. The others, who evidently had not noticed the change, were continuing to chatter and laugh, their interest in the picture already subsiding, while Marianne felt an overwhelming surge of nausea, and clamping her hand to her mouth, bolted from the room and up the stairs to the bathroom, where she lost dinner, lunch, and breakfast in an agonizing bout of heaving and retching.

Vincent had followed her almost immediately, and Judith came in soon after to see if she could help.

"Is she alright?" she asked Vincent as he helped Marianne to her feet.

"I think so. Just a bit of an upset stomach."

Judith wiped Marianne's face with a wet cloth and with her arm around her shoulders, led her the few steps along the corridor to their room, where Vincent, picking Marianne up in his arms as they reached the doorway, carried her the last few feet and lay her gently down on the bed, sitting down beside her.

"Thanks Judith, she'll be alright now. Tell Mother not to worry, and assure Mrs. Roper that it wasn't anything she ate. I'll be down later."

"If you're sure there's nothing else I can do." Judith's face showed genuine concern as she hovered by the door.

"I'm alright now," Marianne assured her. "Really. I'm sorry to have put a damper on the party. I don't know what came over me."

"Well, get a good night's sleep, Annie. That always works wonders. We'll see you in the morning, dear." And with that, Judith returned to the gathering downstairs.

Vincent and Marianne looked at each other in silence for several minutes then, when she felt that she could no longer stand the tension between them, Marianne put the question that had been pounding at her brain from the moment that Adele's painting had been unveiled.

"Did you know it was her, right from the very beginning?"

He glanced down at his hands as though deciding whether to tell her everything, and then looking up, he nodded his head. "My grandfather told me about Adele when I was just eighteen, the day that he gave me the ring."

Marianne looked at the diamonds sparkling on her finger, and despite a desire to wrench them off her hand and throw them as far away as possible, she left them there, unable to bring herself to do it.

"He didn't know what had happened to her. I think he loved her. When she didn't show up that day at the station, he was desolate, but he went on with his plans. Remember, he had told her he was leaving with or without her. He came here to Beckham, changed his name and started over, a fresh new life. I often wondered about the woman he'd left behind. Although I loved him very much, I felt rather ashamed at what he'd done.

"God knows, after everything that's happened, you deserve to be told the truth. Many years after my grandfather told me the story about Adele, I decided to do some research. I was convinced that something had happened to her, but I didn't know where to begin. He never told me her last name, only that she lived in Sterling.

"Even after what happened to you at the railway museum, I didn't make the connection. But when we went to the studio that night and found the pictures that you took of the house in Sterling, I remembered how I saw you standing outside the house. I knew that something must have happened there. Then when you started having the nightmares I got really scared. I was afraid I'd opened up some terrible Pandora's Box, and I felt wretched that I'd got you involved. No one was more surprised than I was when we went to the house to look around and saw the railway tracks."

"So, when I suggested that we contact the realtor, you jumped at the chance."

"Yes, but I was apprehensive about taking you there. When Jon called that night, I was almost relieved. I agreed to go and meet him. It was an ideal excuse for backing out of the trip to Sterling, but I wanted to be sure that you wouldn't go without me."

"Which was why you warned me not to go alone."

"Yes." He gave a bitter laugh. "I should have known you wouldn't let that stop you. But things would probably have been alright if Mrs. Anderson had been there with you."

"That was my bad luck," Marianne said caustically.

"When I got home from the meeting with Jon, and you weren't there, I knew something had happened. I tried calling the office in Sterling, but they were closed, and I was on the point of setting off to go there when the police showed up on the doorstep to tell me what had happened. I was beside myself with worry and self-loathing for what I'd done. When they told me at the hospital that you would be lucky to survive the attack, they asked me if there was any member of your family that I felt should be notified of your condition, and I thought right away of Matthew. I called him, and naturally, he came back to Swannington immediately."

"What happened between you and Matthew when he came back?"

Vincent looked surprised, and Marianne went on, "I heard you two arguing the night before he left for home."

"Yes. When Matthew realized that they were continuing to question me about Wellington Street, he began to draw his own conclusions and decided to do a little investigation of his own. He looked through my desk and discovered the articles that I had found about Arthur Hemmings and the book. He also found the papers from the purchase of the house that I'd signed at the solicitor's office the day before. He confronted me that night and demanded to know what was going on. I was furious!

"At first, I told him to mind his own business but I soon realized that I had taken a wrong tack, making him more suspicious than ever, so I tried to convince him that everything would be alright. I didn't want him worrying you with all that he'd discovered, and he seemed willing to let things lie, for the time being, at least."

"But why did you take me back there, to the house, when you knew the danger?"

"I hadn't meant to. When we went out that day, I had no intention of going there, I was just driving about aimlessly, but when I realized that we had drifted near to Sterling, I just … I don't know how to describe what happened. It was as though I had no control over what I was doing. And Matthew must have been following us. Oh God, Marianne! If I could only go back and changed what happened that day."

She should have hated him. She should have blamed him for everything that had happened, but she couldn't.

"Can you ever forgive me, Marianne?"

"There's nothing to forgive," she said with resignation. "You were right when you said I was becoming obsessed with Adele's fate. I couldn't have turned back any more than you. We were both chasing the same ghosts, and Matthew got in the way, poor boy. I'll always feel responsible for what happened, even now, after everything you've told me."

Vincent gave a sigh of relief, but if they thought that the ghosts had finally been laid to rest, they were sadly mistaken. The revelations of the past months would be as nothing compared to those that awaited them. The final truth would reveal just how much their lives were bound together by the unbreakable thread of destiny.

24

DIRTY LITTLE SECRETS

THE NEXT MORNING AT BREAKFAST, Emily and Judith showed considerable concern over Marianne's hasty exit the night before and were eager to know if she was feeling better.

"Much better," she told them reassuringly. "And I'm very sorry for spoiling the party."

"Nonsense!" Emily sprang to her defense. "It's no wonder you were upset. With everything you've been through these past weeks and then to be pressed into a social gathering with a bunch of old fogies, well ... really. I hold myself completely to blame."

"No! Absolutely not! I won't hear of it!" Marianne exclaimed. "It's true, the last few weeks have been awful for both of us, but it's been a real tonic for us to spend this time here with you and Judith. I'm very grateful for the hospitality you've shown me, and last night, apart from the conclusion, was most enjoyable, truly."

They both seemed satisfied with her answer.

"So, what did you think of the paintings?" Judith asked, adroitly changing the course of the conversation.

Marianne could see that Vincent was about to intervene but she answered truthfully, "They were remarkable. You were right, Emily, about your father-in-law being an accomplished artist. They are most lifelike. I'd rather like to look at them again in the daylight, now that I can give my full attention to them. I'm afraid last night I was not feeling my best."

Vincent looked hesitant, but Judith seemed only too happy to oblige.

"Of course, Annie. Why don't we go and look at them now if you've finished breakfast?" And Judith accompanied Marianne as she went from room to room, looking a little more closely at the paintings.

The picture in the dining room of Stoughton Manor was masterful but it wasn't so much the subject of the portrait that fascinated Marianne so much now as the man who had painted it. She stood gazing as the scene opened up before her, and she imagined she was there, the day that Derek Foxworth, or Desmond Renard as he had once been, had sat at his easel, dressed in an artist's smock and wide brimmed hat, perched on a camp stool, mixing paints while his grandson stood by his side, looking on in awe as the pigments transformed into different shades and hues upon the palette. She could see the elderly man look from the canvas to the Manor and back at Vincent as he patiently explained the process, even letting the child stir the oils with the palette knife.

"That's it. Gently does it. We don't want you getting paint all over your best clothes. Your grandmother would skin me alive."

And Vincent, chuckling, carefully agitating the colors as his doting grandfather looked on. Did Marianne just imagine that she could see Daphne looking out of the window, watching the two of them as they went about their artistic labors, or had he actually incorporated her in the picture? And there was Vincent's mother sitting under the oak tree, looking cool and beautiful, reading a book and glancing up now and then to watch her son as he handed his grandfather his brushes.

Desmond Renard! It was hard to imagine that grey-haired patriarch as the same man who had seduced Adele Hemmings all those years ago, who had run off and started life again in the guise of Derek Foxworth. She jumped as Judith broke into her thoughts, touching her arm and saying, "Would you like to see the others now?"

"Yes, yes. I'm sorry, I was miles away," Marianne replied.

They strolled through to the morning room, and looked again at the painting of the young gardener, his work-roughened hands bearing traces of the soil that he had recently turned over with the shovel, his hair ruffled by an invisible breeze.

The other painting in the room, that of Saint Anselm's Church, had been painted on a gloomier day. The sky was overcast and the shades and tones of the scene were more somber than Marianne remembered from the previous night. The churchyard in the foreground with its ancient tombstones and monuments looked bleak and cold. The trees were bending before a gusty wind and there was the vicar, his cassock blowing about his legs, running from the church, down the path toward the shelter of the nearby vicarage. Above the sound of the wind, she could hear the church organ playing, and someone calling.

"Derek! Derek! Are you there?"

The voice was swallowed up by the wind and once again she was pulled back into the present by Judith who had linked arms with her and was leading her from the room, chattering as they went.

They passed into the library and on to the portrait of Adele. It wasn't difficult to understand why Arthur Hemmings had found her so enticing or why Desmond Renard had succumbed to her charms. Any man would have longed to possess her, as she appeared here, resting against the pillows, languorous and wanton, her naked body inviting, her eyes with their heavy lids and long lashes gazing at the artist as he fought to maintain concentration on his work.

Had she been such an innocent victim after all?

Marianne wondered if Derek Foxworth hadn't sometimes thought of Adele as he lay beside his wife, here at Stoughton Manor. It set her thinking about the former mistress of the Manor, and she asked Judith if she had many memories of her grandmother.

"Oh yes, Grandmother was very good to us. Of course, she worshiped my grandfather. Quite honestly, I think she had rather a lot to put up with."

"Oh, why?"

"Well, one couldn't help overhearing bits of conversation. Children tend to be overlooked in the general hustle and bustle of life, and more than once when no one realized I was listening, I heard some rather ribald comments about grandfather. How he wasn't averse to pinching the occasional bottom.

But I dare say it was all harmless fun. Anyway, Grandmother didn't know, or if she did, she overlooked it, and at least grandfather stayed with her, which was more than my father did."

This was the first indication that Judith harbored any bitterness at her father's desertion and almost immediately she seemed to regret her words, brushing them hastily aside.

"Well, anyway, Grandmother was a gem. Vincent and I used to put on plays when we came down here as children and she would always find suitable costumes and props. Nothing was impossible with her. If she couldn't find the exact thing, she would improvise, taking down curtains to drape over Vincent's shoulders as some fantastic cape or hanging crystals from the chandelier over my ears like giant diamond earrings.

"And she could sing. My God, she could sing! I used to wonder if she had ever sung professionally, but she never discussed her early life. I asked grandfather once and he said, 'It was a long time ago, before we were married. Your grandmother gave up that life when she became my wife and came to live at Stoughton Manor.' And that was it. He wouldn't elaborate, so I just left it alone, but of course there were the photos.

Grandmother kept dozens of albums and we would sit for hours looking at the pictures, the fashions and hairstyles. It's funny though, we never actually saw any pictures of her until after she and grandfather had died. Vincent came across some old albums in a trunk in one of the spare rooms when we moved here and showed me. The pictures were all of Grandmother when she was a young woman. She was beautiful. and many of the photos were of her in costume: Tosca, Marguerite, Lakme. There was a picture of her with Nikolai Dvorkin. She must have sung with him in one of those operas. She looked stunning! I wished I'd known before. I would love to have asked her about her experiences."

"Perhaps she preferred to forget. There must have been some reason why they never discussed her singing career."

"I think it was just that grandfather expected her to sacrifice all that when she married him in exchange for the life he had to offer her here at Stoughton. She loved him so much that she did it willingly."

"Do you think she ever regretted it?"

"No, I don't think so. At least, not to my knowledge. Of course, we only saw them occasionally, three or four times a year at most, although grandfather used to come and visit us more often after Grandmother died. I think he was lonely, and he always made a great fuss of Vincent and I."

"Did he ever talk about his son?"

"They didn't get on very well. I think my father was something of a disappointment and it just seemed to confirm my grandfather's opinion of him when he ran off. The only thing he had inherited from my grandfather, apparently, was his looks. None of the artistic abilities or business acumen were there. I think they must have been rather surprised when he brought my mother home to meet them. She was attractive, intelligent, and cultured, and they would have wondered what on earth she saw in my father other than his good looks. Oh, I know what you're thinking. It must have been the money, but it wasn't that. My father was making his own way then. Grandfather had refused to support him, saying he'd got to learn to take care of himself.

"You never found out who the other woman was, the one your father ran away with?"

"No. I used to think that if I ever found her, I would kill her for wrecking our family, taking my father away. I hated her so much. But I was much younger then. I must have been very naive in those days, not to have seen how things were. As time went by, I realized you can't make people love you, no matter how much you love them. He couldn't have loved my mother, or he wouldn't have left. And I believe now, that she didn't love him. Not really. She didn't seem to mind so very much that he had gone away. Vincent wasn't surprised either." Judith looked about the room and sighed.

"I was the only one that was silly enough not to have seen how things were between them. Of course, Vincent was away at college at the time, but I remember that when I called him to tell him that father hadn't come home and that we hadn't heard anything from him for days, he was very phlegmatic and matter-of-fact about the whole thing. He just told me to stay calm and he would come home right away," she said, picking up a glass paperweight from the desk and looking at it as though for the first time.

"We reported father's disappearance to the police, and of course, right away they jumped to the conclusion that he had run off with someone. I didn't want to believe it but after a week or so had gone by and he still hadn't returned or contacted us, I went and searched in his room, looked through cupboards and drawers. I believe I thought he must be in some kind of trouble: money, gambling debts, or something of the kind. That was when I found the letters, addressed to him at his club, from his lover. They made me sick, literally. I read them; I had to, and my stomach just turned over. How could he do this terrible thing, cheat on my mother, leave us without a word for this this other person? I was beside myself." Judith closed her eyes for a moment as if to shut out that brutal discovery.

"I showed them to Vincent, and he gave them to mother. She seemed almost relieved. Well, that's past history. We must seem a very strange family to you, Annie. I hope you won't hold that against Vincent."

Marianne laughed. "Of course not. Every family has its problems. Mine wasn't exactly the most loving group of people you could ever wish to meet, but we made the best of it. Of all of them, I think I'll miss Matthew the most. We got on very well together most of the time. Of course, I loved them all, but there was always that feeling of something simmering, like a volcano waiting to erupt, and every now and then the sparks would fly. But this is too depressing," she said, taking Judith's hand. "Let's forget all the bad things and enjoy the rest of the day."

Emily had informed them at breakfast that the Reverend Forsythe had issued an invitation to lunch that day, a request that she had felt obliged to accept, and at mid-day, Parker dutifully drove them over to the vicarage at Penhampton.

"I hope you don't mind," Emily said a little belatedly as they made their way up the path to the vicarage door. "He's such a dear man," she added hurriedly, as an unseen hand rattled the latch and the door opened. It was not the Reverend Forsythe, however, but the young woman they had seen in Beckham, wearing a coat that no longer reached across her swollen stomach and a wooly hat pulled down about her ears, preparing to leave in what appeared to be a less than cheerful frame of mind. She seemed taken aback momentarily and glared at Emily, who had already mounted the step.

Emily too showed signs of discomposure but nevertheless managed to address the girl with a curt, "Monica." The salutation was not returned and the woman pushed roughly passed Emily and Judith and scowled at Vincent who had stepped forward as if sensing impending trouble. Marianne had taken a couple of steps backward, giving Monica room to exit down the path without further hindrance. At that moment, the Reverend Forsythe arrived on the scene and ushered them inside.

For those few seconds, everyone's attention was directed away from the departing visitor, but as she drew level with Marianne, Monica stopped and looked back. Grasping Marianne's arm, she pulled her further from the door and whispered, "Watch yourself. They're a mean, grasping lot up at the Manor. Liars and cheats! Every one of 'em is sick, up here." And she tapped a finger meaningfully at her head.

"Annie." Emily had turned to see Monica holding Marianne back, and she said abruptly, "Vincent, bring Annie in out of the cold."

Vincent retreated back down the path and took Mariane's hand. Monica stiffened and cried out after them as they went to enter the vicarage.

"Sick! That's what they are, sick! Think they're better than everyone else, but I know their dirty little secrets!"

The Reverend Forsythe, appalled by this spontaneous outburst, hastily shepherded them inside and called out beseechingly, "Go home Monica, there's a good girl. Please!"

The poor man was mortified and apologetic in the extreme upon his return. "I'm most dreadfully sorry for that unfortunate scene. The poor girl is, as you may have noticed, in a delicate condition."

"Please don't blame yourself, Reverend," Judith hastened to reassure him. "It wasn't your fault. The girl was obviously distraught."

"Yes, poor child. One misfortune after another. A pathetic case. But do come into the parlor and make yourselves comfortable. Lunch will be ready in a few minutes. Mrs. Lund has excelled herself today I think."

He bustled about, no doubt relieved that Emily had not taken umbrage at the recent confrontation. The rest of the visit proceeded without further allusion to that wayward member of his flock.

But Monica's words kept coming back to Marianne, and while the others chatted over lunch, she wondered what the girl had meant. Sick? Dirty secrets? Could it merely be on account of the accident with the porcelain piece and the subsequent firing of this unfortunate girl, or was there something more that had provoked her and induced such a venomous tirade?

Later, when they returned to Stoughton Manor, Marianne found herself alone with Judith in the morning room and decided to question her as discreetly as she could about the young woman.

"Oh, it was nothing. She used to work here, but she wasn't very reliable ,and mother let her go. That's all. Well…" She seemed to consider for a moment, then went on, "She did have a bit of a crush on Vincent, but of course he wasn't interested. She threw herself at him quite shamelessly the last time he was here. It was quite embarrassing for him, poor boy. And I told her so. Of course, she reacted much as one would expect from someone of that type, accused me of being a jealous old maid and so on. She said some very derogatory things about the family. Her behavior was really quite unforgivable. She came back to the house about a week later, to ask for her job back, I suppose. I was surprised that mother even saw her. She spent a long time talking to her in the library, but it was no good. Mother must have turned her down, and she went away again.

Just then Emily entered the room with Vincent, and Judith, looking as though she had been guilty of an indiscretion, dropped the subject and sat down by the fire, studying her hands intently.

"Well, Annie," Emily walked over to her and put her hands on her shoulders, "I'm sorry that we are losing you both so soon. Call me a selfish old woman, but there's nothing I would love more than to see Vincent come home for good. Oh, I know things are going well for him in Swannington, but … well. I'm sure you understand."

Vincent kissed her cheek. "Maybe, soon, Mother."

"Don't wait too long Vincent. I may not be here if you wait too long."

"I think you are putting Marianne in rather a difficult position, Mother," Vincent said.

"Am I? I'm sorry my dear. It wasn't intentional. When you get to my age, you tend to say things without always thinking."

"No, I understand. I'm not totally opposed to the idea," Marianne began, trying to be as diplomatic as possible.

"But we won't discuss it now," Vincent interposed gently as he led his mother to her chair.

"Judith, you're very quiet," he declared as he stood with his back to the fire.

"I was just thinking how nice it's been to have you here. You will come back and visit us again, even if you don't decide to come back permanently, won't you Annie?"

"Of course, I'd love to. You've made me very welcome."

"Well, after all, you're almost one of the family now." Emily was like a terrier, unwilling to let go of its quarry, shaking the idea back and forth with a ferocious persistence that was unrelenting.

Almost but not quite, Marianne thought and smiled. Was this a none too subtle hint directed at Vincent, to make an honest woman of her?

"We'll cross our bridges when we come to them, dear," Vincent told her. "And now," he said as if to escape Emily's allusions once and for all, "You girls must go and put on your glad rags. I've made reservations at The Monmouth for dinner this evening. Don't worry. Everything's arranged. I told Mrs. Roper yesterday, so you can give her the rest of the day off."

"What a lovely surprise! The Monmouth! I haven't been there for ages," Judith exclaimed.

Despite their wealth and social standing, Marianne suspected that the Foxworth women lived, apart from the occasional trip up to London, a quiet life, and the prospect of an evening out, for Judith, was a welcome treat.

They had only been seated in the bar at The Monmouth for a few minutes and were sipping the cocktails that Vincent had brought back to their table, when they were surprised to see the arrival of a couple who had dined with them the night before at the Manor, Dr. and Mrs. James.

"Emily, how delightful. I had no idea you would be here," Felicity James exclaimed.

"I didn't know myself until this afternoon. This was Vincent's idea."

Vincent invited the couple to join them, and the James's accepted with alacrity. When they had settled into their chairs, the doctor's wife opened the conversation. "Did you know, that girl who used to work for you, what was her name? Oh yes, Monica Jenkins, she's been left in the lurch by that young man of hers. They'd planned to be married next week, and I heard from Mrs. Potts, who comes in to clean for us, that he ran off last week."

She was oblivious to the silence that greeted this piece of news but ploughed on. "I never did like the girl, especially after that business at the Manor, but I felt rather sorry when I heard that she'd been abandoned by that rogue."

If she'd expected any echo of sympathy from the Foxworths, she was disappointed. There was none forthcoming. They were rescued from any further discussion on the subject by the maître d' who came to tell them that their table was ready and, bidding farewell to the doctor and his wife, they followed him into the dining room.

Towards the end of the meal, Marianne excused herself and paid a visit to the ladies' restroom. She was standing by the wash basin, pumping soap from the dispenser when someone came in, and she saw that it was Mrs. James.

"It's been so nice to meet you, my dear. Vincent is such a sweet boy."

It tickled Marianne that his family and Emily's older acquaintances always referred to Vincent as a boy, even though he was in his fifties. They still thought of him as that blonde, hazel-eyed child who had roamed about the Manor many years ago, when Derek and Daphne were still alive.

They stood side-by-side, looking into the large mirror above the basins. Marianne re-applied lipstick and powder while Felicity James watched her.

"Emily will miss him when he leaves."

"Yes, I'm sure she will, but she has Judith." Marianne was beginning to feel that people were blaming her for his prolonged absence from home and was getting a little tired of it.

"Oh yes, Judith's a good girl, but Emily needs a man about the place."

"There's Parker," Marianne suggested.

"I meant someone from the family, dear. She needs a man there to advise her."

"What about Adrian Penworthy? He's her solicitor. Doesn't he advise her?"

"A good man, undoubtedly, but not on the spot."

"But surely she can contact him at any time if she needs help."

"It wouldn't have done her much good when Monica Jenkins came to the house. The girl was in a rage, and I was quite afraid for poor Emily. I didn't like to leave her alone with the wretched creature, and when they went off to the library, I could hear the Jenkins girl yelling at the top of her voice. Of course, I couldn't actually hear what she was saying, you understand." Mrs. James did not want to be accused of eavesdropping. "I knew they were both very angry. Judith was very upset.

"Wasn't Mrs. Roper there?"

"No. She'd gone to visit her daughter, and Parker was off on an errand somewhere, so we three were left alone to cope with her. I did wonder if I should call the police, but just as I was about to do so, everything went quiet. Monica ran out of the house, and Emily came out after her, looking very calm although she was as white as a ghost. When she saw me, she just said 'Oh! You're still here.' And I said yes, I thought she might need some help, and she just said, 'It was just a storm in a tea cup.' Well, that was an understatement if ever there was one, but Emily was very cool about the whole thing and never mentioned any more about it. It's times like that when I think she misses having Vincent there."

"Yes."

"Well anyway, it was nice to have met you," the old lady repeated.

Marianne snapped her purse shut. "Nice to meet you too," she replied ,and left Felicity James standing watching her speculatively.

When Marianne and Vincent were alone, later that evening, she wondered if she should repeat the story that Mrs. James had told. What if something more untoward happened once they left? Marianne would blame herself for not having told Vincent. Could Judith cope with further trouble from that quarter, should it present itself? Emily didn't seem outwardly bothered by it, but deep down Marianne wondered if these emotional scenes were taking their toll. After all, she was an elderly woman, in good health, admittedly, but at that age anything could happen. The possibility of a heart attack or stroke could not be discounted. She decided to approach the subject with him indirectly.

"I've really enjoyed this visit to Stoughton. I'm beginning to feel like things are getting back to normal, now that I know all about your grandfather and Adele and everything. And meeting all those people who knew him. Listening to them talking about the old times. I almost felt like I'd been there with them. The Reverend is a nice man, isn't he. I felt sorry for him this afternoon, when there was all that fuss at the vicarage. Judith told me what happened with Monica."

"Did she? It was all so stupid. She was working here at the Manor when I came here last time, and well, it sounds conceited, but I knew she'd taken a liking to me. I tried to avoid her but it was difficult. She was always around, popping up all over the place, until she got quite brazen about it. I think she even imagined, poor girl, that I felt the same way about her, although I swear, I never gave her the slightest cause to think that I was interested.

"I didn't want to say anything about it to mother or Judith, although I think they could see for themselves how things were, and I didn't want to make trouble for the girl. I'd be gone soon enough, and I decided to just steer clear of her as much as I could. Then one night, just before I left to go back to Swannington, she turned up in my room, and not to put too fine a point on it, made quite a spectacle of herself. I bundled her out, just as Judith was passing in the hallway. Poor Judith didn't know which way to look. She must have thought I'd finally been hooked. She told me afterwards there had been the most awful row, where insults weren't the only things that were thrown around. Mother sacked Monica on the spot. Judith wrote later that Monica had come to ask for her job back, but mother refused. I thought that was the end of it."

"I think you should know, there's more," Marianne told him. "The day after we arrived, when your mother took me into Beckham, we saw her, outside the restaurant. She spotted us and if looks could kill ... well. Of course, then I didn't know who she was, and your mother just said she was someone who used to work at Stoughton, and that she'd had to let her go. Then after the episode at the vicarage this afternoon, I asked Judith about her, and she told me the whole story. Then at The Monmouth this evening, when I was in the ladies' room, Mrs. James came in and started talking about Monica again. How she had been with your mother when Monica had come to the house. She said things got pretty heated, to say the least, although according to her, she didn't know what it was about."

"Nosey old bat!"

"Well to be fair, I do think the old girl was worried. She said she even thought of calling the police."

"Oh, for heaven's sake!"

"Is that so surprising? You saw the way the girl behaved today."

"Yes, you're right. I must admit it has got me a bit bothered."

"Do you think we should stay longer, just to make sure that nothing happens?"

"Oh, I don't think so. No, Judith's here with her, and I'm sure she will be on her guard. And mother's no fool. She won't take any unnecessary risks. I'll have a word with Parker too, before we leave, just to be sure."

"Do you want to come back home permanently to Stoughton, Vincent?" Marianne asked suddenly.

There was silence for a minute or two. She was sure the subject had been on his mind more and more these last few days and she thought it might be good to bring it out into the open.

"I don't know. Would you mind?"

"I'm afraid I'm not much help. I don't know, either. It would mean giving up so much."

"Would that be such a bad thing? I could go on teaching here."

"And what about me? I'd have to start all over again."

"But you've got plenty of contacts. It wouldn't be so difficult, would it? I could get you a studio in Beckham or even Windermere, if you didn't mind traveling a bit."

"No! I'm sorry but if I did it, it would have to be with my own money. I know you're concerned about your mother, and I can understand it, but despite everything that's happened, I am worried about my father too. I don't like leaving Clare to cope with him alone. I feel like I'm running out on her. Living up here would put me even further away from the family. If only we could see into the future and then we'd know if we were making the right decision." *God! What a dilemma!* Marianne thought.

They spent their last evening at Stoughton Manor quietly. Emily, content to have both her children with her, if only for a few days, was playing solitaire at a small table near the fire. Vincent was playing the piano, soothing, quiet melodies. Judith and Marianne sat together on the couch looking at Daphne's albums. The pictures, unlike the stiff and formal portraits that Marianne had seen in Adele's album, were full of life and gaiety. Derek Foxworth, looking so much like Vincent, appeared most frequently in the collection, oftentimes smiling, occasionally serious, always elegantly dressed, even in the most casual and off-guard moments, when the camera captured his every expression and mood.

Daphne, on her wedding day, appearing radiant and joyful beside her husband, both looking at each other with adoring eyes. Marianne couldn't help comparing it to that picture of Adele and Arthur, with their solemn faces and passionless pose. How different things would have been if Adele had met Desmond Renard earlier, before she precipitously committed herself to that doomed marriage with Arthur Hemmings. If she had married Desmond instead, he might never have left Sterling. His son, instead of meeting Emily, would have no doubt settled down and married someone else. Vincent and Judith would never have known the splendors of Stoughton Manor, for it might never have existed. But then, she thought, she probably would never have met Vincent.

There, in the album, were so many of the people who had been bound together by fate. Derek, Daphne, Vincent, Judith, and Emily, the only absentee being Vincent's father. All traces of him had been expunged from this collection of memorabilia. Had it been Judith's hand that had removed his likeness from the pages, or perhaps Emily had preferred to wipe the slate clean, sweeping away all traces of the man whose devotion had been so brittle and short lived? But could she look at the father-in-law without being reminded of the husband?

At each turn of the page, his magnetic personality stood out, here surrounded by his contemporaries, men of his own age and social background, or again with a much younger group, Gordon Anstruther, Dr. James, and Adrian Penworthy, all looking jovial and in high spirits. But most touching of all, a candid shot of him with Vincent as a young child, sitting on his knee, the two of them engrossed in a book that Derek Foxworth was holding in his hand, that same book that Marianne had seen on the desk in the library. It was not hard to see why Vincent had so looked up to this elderly head of the Foxworth family.

Strange, how life played out. Its twist and turns leading them all along by the nose. How little control they had over their destiny. It moved them about like pieces on a chess board, while they, helpless pawns in the game, went from square to square, passing other pawns, capturing castles, bowing to bishops, conquering kings, or perhaps losing oneself to a knight, as she had fallen to Vincent, her knight in shining armor.

25

A SENTIMENTAL JOURNEY

MARIANNE HAD PROMISED HERSELF ONE LAST DETOUR before they returned to Swannington, and when she called Clare, the day before leaving Stoughton Manor to tell her of their plans, her sister greeted the news with tempered enthusiasm.

"I wanted to visit Paradise House," Marianne explained. "I feel like I owe it to Matthew to see it one last time. He said that he had intended to make the acquaintance of the new owners."

"What will they think when a total stranger comes knocking at their door, claiming some tenuous link with their home? You can't demand to be let in. Will they understand?" Clare, always the practical one, didn't sound too hopeful.

"Possibly not, but it's worth a try. I just need to see it one last time, to fix it in my mind. And then I won't ever need to go there again."

"Well, good luck with that," Clare told her skeptically. "We're going over to Dad's this afternoon, to see how he's doing."

"Do be careful," Marianne cautioned her. "You know how he was when we went there."

"We'll watch our step, although to be honest, Annie, we've never had a problem with him. He must have just been having a bad day when you went. I'm sure everything will be alright. We'll give him your love. I'm sure he'll be interested to hear all your news."

Marianne wasn't so sure, but she let it go.

Vincent had called ahead to The Three Poachers in Diffingham and reserved a room for two nights, so they were under no pressure to hurry,. Avoiding the busy highways, they made their way south by means of the narrow winding roads that linked the picturesque villages and hamlets, thus bypassing the congestion of the larger towns and cities.

Despite the events of the past weeks, they were in a light-hearted mood. Now that she knew the story of Vincent's grandfather and Adele Hemmings, Marianne was in some sense relieved that she had finally been able to put some closure to their story.

As he drove, she noticed that Vincent had been checking the rear-view mirror more than was his usual custom, and she asked him if there was a problem.

"Don't tell me we're going to get copped for speeding. We've been positively crawling along for the past hour."

"No, it's not that. It's just that ever since we left Beckham, I've had the feeling that we were being followed. At first, I thought it was just co-incidence, but the same car has been behind us for quite some time. I've only caught glimpses. He's stayed well back, so I can't be certain but ... well, just a feeling."

"Why don't you pull in somewhere and see if he catches up to us."

After rounding a curve in the road, Vincent spotted a narrow lane almost hidden from view by trees and shrubs and quickly pulled in, coming to a halt several yards from the road. He switched off the engine, and they both turned in their seats, looking through the rear window, waiting to see who could be following them. No one came. They sat there for several minutes and then both laughed.

"False alarm. Well, Sherlock, I'm afraid your powers of detection are slipping. There's no one there," Marianne told him.

"No. My mistake. Well, let's get going. I'm starving. Isn't it about time for lunch?"

Vincent backed the car out into the road once more and they continued on their way, but Marianne saw that more than once he gave a surreptitious glance at the mirror as though not totally convinced that he had been mistaken. As if to put more miles between him and his imagined pursuer, he applied slightly more pressure to the gas pedal as they headed toward their destination.

Marianne was thrilled to discover, as they arrived at the outskirts of Diffingham, that it had hardly changed since the days when Matthew, Clare, and she had been taken there as children. Time seemed to have missed this quaint little village and left it untouched. In those early days of their childhood Marianne's parents had not owned a car, and the visits to Diffingham had always been made either by train or bus. Marianne remembered how they had watched through the window as the countryside went flashing by. They would excitedly point out cows, horses, and sheep, animals that were in short supply in the city, unless you counted the horse-drawn cart that belonged to the 'rag and bone' man who occasionally made his way down their street looking for unwanted items of clothing or household goods.

They always knew they were getting close to Diffingham when they saw the tops of the oast houses amongst the trees, and the fields of hops where migrant workers from the city would come to gather in the harvest and then move on to the next farm.

When they stepped from the train, it was like stepping into another world. The station master would recognize them without fail, despite the fact that they only made the journey two or three times a year. Marianne and Clare would tussle for the honor of handing him their tickets as they made their way along the deserted platform, and the beaming official, resplendent in his British Railways uniform, would touch the peak of his cap as their mother greeted him in her usual friendly manner. He would bend down to smile at Matthew, who, holding his mother's hand, would submit to having his hair ruffled.

Their father rarely made the trip with them. He found country life dull and preferred to stay at home. They were not sorry, for they found these vacations far more enjoyable without the strained atmosphere that always seemed to hang over them when their parents were together.

Once outside the station, they would make their way up the hill, as Marianne and Vincent were doing now in the car, only then they were on foot, her mother carrying the heavy suitcase that contained all the necessities that traveling with three young children entailed. But she never complained. In fact, she always seemed to gain a new lease on life when they were in Diffingham. The very air seemed to rejuvenate her and, looking back, Marianne believed that she was only truly happy during those sojourns away from her father.

When they reached the top of the hill, Marianne pointed out to Vincent a golf course where they had, all those years ago, taken advantage of a short cut through to the village on the far side. The place had nearly always been deserted, and they would dash about like mad things, unrestricted, shouting and laughing. Clare had once discovered a 'fairy ring', a circle of gleaming white mushrooms and they all took it in turns to stand in the center and make a wish. Of course, they couldn't tell what their wishes were, or they would not have come true, and Marianne kept silent, never divulging her fervent plea that a handsome knight in shining armor would someday come along and sweep her off her feet. Who said that wishes made in 'fairy rings' never came true!

The road that they followed now, kept to the perimeter of the golf course and then diverged slightly to encompass the woods where the family had once gathered bouquets of bluebells, only to watch them quickly droop and die long before they could get them to their grandmother's house and the safety of a vase of water.

Finally, the road dipped down toward the village, and there before them lay the sleepy village of Diffingham. Everything about it, so well-remembered, so dearly loved. The first building, as you entered Diffingham, was the village pub, The Three Poachers, and they pulled in to the parking lot that, being mid-day, was crowded. Vincent retrieved their suitcases from the trunk of the car and the couple walked into the unmistakable atmosphere of a country pub, the cigarette smoke and smell of good English ale heavy in the air.

The landlord welcomed them and escorted them up the wooden staircase to show them to their room. The accommodations were small but adequate, although it had no bathroom. Marianne remembered the days in her childhood when, staying at various guest houses and hotels they had been forced to furtively grope along unfamiliar, dark corridors to a bathroom shared by several other visitors. These places had always been kept scrupulously clean, however, and the inconvenience of such an arrangement had never, in those days, occurred to them. They always accepted it as part of the 'holiday experience.'

Having deposited their suitcases on the floor of their room, checked the bed for comfort and the view from the window which looked out onto the village green, they made their way back down the stairs and into the bar where they fortified themselves with glasses of warm lager and huge slices of ham, bread, and cheese freshly cut by the landlord's wife. The inhabitants of the snug were, as usual in these country inns, friendly and hospitable, elderly villagers passing the time of day with their friends over a game of dominoes, farmers stopping in for a liquid lunch on their way to town, and young men resting from the labors of the day, all chatting cheerfully. After some unabashed questioning by a weather-beaten octogenarian sharing a game of dominoes with some of his cronies at the next table, it soon became common knowledge that Marianne and Vincent were visitors and were here to see Paradise House.

"Aaah! They got new people there now. Mr. and Mrs. Russell moved out, you know. Went to Swindon or some such foreign place."

"I think you'll find it was Sweden, but yes, Matthew told me." Marianne couldn't help laughing to herself, to think that the old man considered Swindon as a foreign place. "He used to stay with the Russell's. My grandparents owned Paradise House a long time ago."

"Not Mr. and Mrs. O'Malley?"

The old man's eyes twinkled as he gazed at Marianne with renewed interest.

"Yes. Do you remember them?"

"Do I remember them? Of course! I used to do odd jobs for them." He peered closer and burst into good natured laughter. "My Lord! Are you little Annie?"

"Yes! Charlie Pierce? Is that you?"

Their mutual recognition brought back a flood of memories, and she couldn't resist the impulse to throw her arms around him and hug him, a move which elicited hearty chuckles and a few ribald comments from his friends.

Charlie Pierce! He had seemed ancient even in those days, to her young eyes. How long ago it seemed, the time when he had sat on a tree stump in the courtyard at the back of Paradise House, singing in his rasping voice, a country song, clapping his hands to beat out the rhythm as Marianne danced and twirled upon the cobblestones, her four-year-old legs taking her up and down the length of the courtyard, in an uninhibited display of her newly learned ballet accomplishments.

"Well, well! I never thought to see you again. What brings you to this part of the world?" the old man asked.

"Oh, just reliving old times, Charlie. I wanted to show my friend Paradise House." Marianne touched Vincent's arm and drew him forward.

Charlie looked at him and a brief look of recognition seemed to pass across his face. "I know you, too, don't I?" he said as he struggled to recall a name.

"I don't think so," Vincent replied, smiling and offering his hand, which Charlie shook vigorously. "My name is Vincent Foxworth and this is my first visit to Diffingham."

"Funny, I could have sworn I'd seen you here in the village before. Right here, in fact, in The Three Poachers. You sure you've never been here before?"

"Certain." Vincent's answer was rock solid. Marianne had wondered at first if Charlie had caught him out in another deception, but the reply had the ring of truth about it.

"Well, if you say so. Of course, it was a while back, now, so I may be mistaken, but I'm usually pretty good at remembering faces, though the names sometimes get lost."

Charlie pulled up a seat and joined them at a table. "So, tell me, Miss Annie, how's your Ma, and your sister, and that little scamp of a brother?"

She knew the question would come and dreaded having to tell him, especially about Matthew.

"Mum died several years ago, Charlie. She was ill for quite some time and, in the end, it seemed a merciful release."

"I'm truly sorry to hear that, Miss Annie." He shook his head sadly.

"Clare is married and has three children of her own. They still live in London."

"And the boy? I sat with him, here, the last time he came to visit, just before the Russells moved out of Paradise House, last year."

Marianne hesitated, reluctant to speak of the recent events, but she couldn't avoid the inevitable and, Charlie Pierce had a right to know, if not all the details, at least the one stark fact that was responsible for their return.

"Matthew's dead, Charlie. He was killed in an accident last month. That's why we're here. I wanted to take one last look at Paradise House."

The old man looked aghast. "I can't hardly believe it," he said incredulously. "He was so young, so full of life. Such a nice chap, friendly … I … don't know what to say, Miss Annie. I'm that stunned by what you've told me."

"I know, Charlie. It was a terrible blow to us all. And that's why I want to visit Paradise House one more time. Matthew had meant to go there, to meet the new people, so I'm going instead. Have you met them, Charlie? What are they like?"

"A young couple, I believe. I haven't spoke to 'em. They've got a local boy doing the garden and some clod from Lowminster to do odd jobs. The missus does her shopping mostly in town. He's some fancy executive from Maidstone. Comes in here with his mates but always in the saloon, doesn't mix much with the locals. Not like you and Mr. Matthew." He shook his head morosely.

"Are we likely to catch them at home this evening, do you think, Charlie?" Marianne asked hopefully, for even though he had professed not to have had much contact with the new owners of Paradise House, she knew enough about village life and its residents to realize that he would be familiar with their comings and goings, as there was little that went unnoticed in such a small place as Diffingham.

"Aye, probably. She goes up the Women's Institute on Thursday evenings, weekends they're mostly out, but they should be there tonight."

"Great! Thanks Charlie. Well, we better get going. I'm giving Vincent the grand tour this afternoon. It was lovely to see you again."

They stood up to take their leave, and Charlie Pierce reached out his hand to Vincent with a look that told Marianne that he was still unconvinced he had not seen him there in Diffingham at some time in the past.

"What a genial old soul," Vincent remarked as they made their way out into the afternoon sunshine.

"Yes, he's a dear. I'll never forget the look on his face when Matthew dug up all his carrots in the garden one summer. He went absolutely purple with rage and then almost choked with laughter when Matthew tried to put them back in the ground. I think he was in love with my mother but 'worshiped from afar' as they say. I know she was always very happy when she came down here to Diffingham. She seemed like a different person, but I don't think Charlie Pierce was the reason."

Visiting Diffingham as children meant not only escaping the city and the suffocating blanket of discord that seemed to hang over them when their parents were together, but also the rigorous Catholic upbringing that their father had imposed upon them when they were at home. Marianne's mother was quite willing to allow them to forego the torment of Sunday services; at least they never, to the best of Marianne's recollection, visited the nearest Catholic church in Maidstone, but would sometimes accompany their grandparents to St Peter's Church, where the atmosphere seemed totally different, more friendly, presided over by a God far less wrathful and demanding.

St Peter's was a beautiful old church full of history and damp. Marianne always enjoyed the sound of the bells that rang out in tumultuous welcome every Sunday morning. They were real, honest-to-goodness bells, not the electronically taped recordings that were currently favored by the more modern houses of worship. Their solid peals summoned the people of the village to Sunday prayers, the occasional wedding, or more seldom yet, a booming toll would announce the funeral of one of the inhabitants.

The Clay children nearly always celebrated Christmas at Diffingham. Their father, more often than not, would remain at home in London, which left them free to enjoy the holiday, and as always when they were there, their mother seemed to glow with happiness. They basked in the reflected sunshine of her mood, soaked up the Christmas spirit in abundance, and learned to appreciate early on those precious days of harmony.

As Vincent and Marianne came nearer to the church, the door opened and a woman came out. She carried a basket and a pair of scissors and had probably been arranging flowers.

"Let's go and take a look inside," Marianne suggested as she tugged at Vincent's arm and they made their way through the arched wooden gate set in the stone wall that surrounded the churchyard and up the gravel path to the ancient oak door of the church.

It was dark and cold inside, and silent, until the sound of their footsteps on the stone floor echoed and filled the old place. They skirted the carved stone font and looked about. Now that the sun had gone behind some clouds, the stained-glass windows had lost some of their brilliance, but they were still beautiful. Marianne remembered the times when as a child she had sat between her mother and grandmother in the pews, staring up at the reds, blues, greens and yellows that had been so cleverly worked and pieced together to form familiar scenes, sparkling like gems in the sunlight.

Vincent had picked up a brochure detailing the history of the church, from the wooden rack by the door, and was sitting in the pews reading it while Marianne tiptoed down the nave towards the altar. It certainly was cold in there. She pulled her coat around her, and as she approached, she thought she could hear someone whispering. She looked to either side, but there was no one visible. Yet the whispering continued. Marianne began to shiver, the chill air reaching into her bones and the whispering now seemed to fill her ears, the words becoming more distinct even as she put her hands up to block the sounds.

"Why don't you tell him?" a man's voice whispered urgently, and a woman answering, "I can't. I daren't."

"We can't go on like this. It's madness! I want you. Come away with me. We'll go abroad, anywhere you like."

"But the children."

"Of course, we'll take them with us."

"I can't think. Give me time. I have to think."

"For God's sake! What is there to think about. You love me, don't you?"

"Yes, Yes, but it's such a big step, to leave everything, uproot the children."

"I love you!" The man's voice repeated urgently over and over in Marianne's ears, filling the entire church with his protestations intermingled with the woman's cries, "Give me time," echoing against the stone walls.

The sound was overwhelming her, forcing Marianne to her knees, and she leant her forehead against the altar rail, squeezing her palms against her ears in an effort not to hear what was being said.

"Stop! Please stop!" she cried out, and the whispering suddenly ceased. Vincent, hearing her, had hurried across the aisle to where she knelt.

"Marianne, are you alright?"

"Yes, Let's get out of here. It's cold and damp in here."

"Right." He knew something had happened, but he didn't question her, and they left the church, emerging into the November air, which seemed comparatively mild.

They continued their walk around the green, past several cottages and up the country road that ran past Paradise House. It was, as most byways in that area, narrow and flanked by hedges interwoven, when in season, with honeysuckle.

The first building that they passed was the village smithy. Marianne was saddened by the sight of the old place that was abandoned and overgrown. To her, this place had been the heart of the village. It was an anachronism that had clung to life until Tony Waites, the blacksmith who had inherited the business from his father, could no longer make a living from it. How sad! An era had passed them as they grew up and disappeared in the blink of an eye. It had left only the crumbling, ivy-covered red brick building that had once reverberated to the clanging of the blacksmith's hammer and his cheerful singing as he beat metal against metal, rasped the big file across the horse's horny hooves, or plunged the glowing red-hot horseshoes, hissing into the water trough.

Back then, it was a magical place, at times full of sparks and noise, at others peaceful, the only sound coming from Mr. Waites as he talked lovingly to the animals that waited patiently to be shod.

Charlie Pierce was often to be found there and he and Mr. Waites would share jokes and stories, some of them rather risqué, when they hadn't realized Marianne was within hearing distance, and would laugh, full, deep throated bursts of mirth that made her want to laugh too, even though she had been too young to fully comprehend the words that had passed between them.

Walter Waites, who had been Marianne's idea of what she could have most wished for in a father, had died when she was fifteen years old. His passing saddened her immeasurably, although she had to admit that she had been consoled somewhat by the fact that his son, a sturdy, extremely good-looking young man, had taken his place at the forge. Marianne continued her visits there right up until the time that her grandparents had died, within six short months of each other.

So many of the people that she loved, grandad and grandma O'Malley, her mother, Matthew and Walter Waites, the blacksmith, all gone! If only she had realized what little time she had to enjoy their company, to savor every moment with them.

Just a few hundred yards further on, around the first bend in the road on the left side was Paradise House. Set back from the road behind a screen of trees and shrubs, it had changed little in the intervening years. No wonder Matthew had been so reluctant to let the dear old place slip from their lives. At the time of their grandparents passing, Uncle Mortimer and her mother had agreed to sell the house, as they couldn't afford to maintain it, and it had passed to the Russells.

There was, as Marianne had expected, no sign of the new inhabitants, so she and Vincent merely contented themselves with the view of Paradise House from the road, planning on returning later, when they considered it more likely that they would find the new owners at home.

26

PARADISE HOUSE

LATER, WHEN THEY WERE BACK AT THE THREE POACHERS, Vincent was searching among their luggage for the road map. "It's not here. I must have left it downstairs in the car. Won't be a minute. I'll just run down and get it."

He left Marianne to go and retrieve it. When he returned a short time later, he was looking puzzled.

"Something wrong?" she asked.

"No ... it's just that when I was in the parking lot, I could have sworn ... well, I thought I saw your father."

"No. Surely not. What on earth would he be doing here?"

"I don't know. I'm probably wrong. It was only for a second, and after all, I only met him that one time, which was quite enough, I might add. No, my darling, I seem to be seeing a lot of things that aren't there just lately. Perhaps your abilities are starting to rub off on me." He laughed jokingly. Marianne laughed too, but neither of them really saw any humor in his observation, and they made their way silently downstairs to the dining room.

During dinner, conversation lagged and Marianne noticed that they both looked around them in seemingly casual fashion every few minutes as though they expected to see someone they knew at any moment. The meal over, they got up to leave, and Marianne's heart gave a lurch as a hand touched her shoulder. She turned around, slowly, to come face to face with a tall, heavy-set man with prematurely greying hair and a broad smile on his face.

"You probably don't remember me, but I recognized you as soon as you walked in. Tony Waites from the forge," he reminded her.

"Tony! Of course!" She hadn't recognized him at first. After spending most of the day remembering people as they had been, some twenty or more years ago, it was something of a shock to see these same people as they were now, and she thought, with some regret that they must think the same about her.

"How are you, Tony? I thought you'd moved from Diffingham."

"Only as far as Bearsted. I still come over to The Three Poachers once in a while. I met Charlie Pierce as I was coming in. He told me about Matthew and your mother. I'm very sorry."

"Thank you. We're just on our way over to Paradise House." Marianne looked over to the door where Vincent stood waiting for her. "We took a walk along there earlier and saw the old forge. Do you miss it, Tony?"

"Sometimes, but it was a hell of a struggle, and after Pauline and I got married and the baby came along, well, I realized I couldn't keep the old place going. I'll always be grateful that Dad sent me off to college before I joined him in the business. At least I had other prospects when things got too slow to go on. Well, I won't keep you. It was nice to see you again Annie. Perhaps I'll see you before you leave." They shook hands and she hurried to rejoin Vincent, who had already gone outside .

The evening was mild, but Marianne was eager to get to Paradise House so they didn't dawdle and, cutting across the green, they soon arrived there. The garage door was open, and a car parked inside. Lights shone from the house and Marianne could see a figure moving about in one of the rooms on the first floor. She stepped resolutely to the door, and using the heavy brass ring of the door knocker, announced their arrival. It was some moments before a man of about her own age answered the summons and he looked at her enquiringly as she stood on the doorstep. Marianne had gone over in her mind, time and time again, how she would explain her reason for being there. She prayed that they would believe her.

"Good evening, Mr. Morris?"

"Yes. Can I help you?"

"I hope so. My name is Annie Clay. This is Vincent Foxworth. We're staying at The Three Poachers. I wonder if you could spare me a few minutes?"

Greg Morris shook his head as though he were about to turn them away. He didn't want whatever it was they were selling. She hurried on, "Please, let me explain. My grandparents used to own Paradise House many years ago. I have some photos here that show the house and my family." She reached into her purse for the proof, and Morris looked at the pictures that she handed to him.

"I know this must seem like a very strange request, and I wouldn't blame you for being cautious, but there are people in the village who can vouch for me. Charlie Pierce, and Tony Waites who was the village blacksmith at one time. He's over at The Three Poachers right now."

Mrs. Morris had come to see who her husband was talking to and joined him at the door.

Marianne continued, "My brother Matthew used to visit David and Doris Russell when they lived here, and he had planned on coming to introduce himself to you this summer, but he was killed in an accident recently and …"

"Yes, we had heard. David Russell called us a few days ago to say they had come over for a funeral. That was your brother?" the woman asked, sympathetically.

"Yes." Marianne breathed a sigh of relief. Her task had been made so much easier by the fortunate intervention of David Russell's call.

"Please come in." The young woman ushered them in, through the narrow passageway, that Marianne knew so well, into the living room at the back of the house.

"We were just going to have a cup of coffee. Would you like one?" she asked.

"Please, let me help," Marianne was quick to reply as she followed Mrs. Morris into the kitchen while Vincent remained talking with Greg Morris.

The two women made polite conversation for a while as Gillian Morris arranged cups and saucers on a tray, and then Marianne asked, "Does the clock in the tower over the garage still work?"

"I don't think so. I went up there once when we first moved in, but Greg doesn't really have time to take care of it. Nor do I. I suppose we could get someone in from the village but … well, you know how these things get overlooked, with so many other jobs to take care of."

"I wonder; would you think it an awful cheek if I asked to take a look over there?" Marianne explained about her fascination with the clock tower and how she had been forbidden to go up there. Even in the Russell's time she had never quite got up the nerve to investigate.

Gillian Morris laughed. "I don't see why not. It's quite safe, I should think." They left the house and made their way across the cobbled yard, lit by several outdoor lights, to the garage.

"Oh, Greg's forgotten to close the door again. Well, that's alright since we're going in anyway." She led the way up the wooden stairs that led to the loft above the garage. The Morris's had utilized the space as a storage area.

Mrs. Morris pulled open a trap door in the ceiling that creaked on its hinges and let down a second flight of steps with a clang. The distance leading up to the clock tower seemed a lot shorter to Marianne now than it had done when she was a child. She followed Gillian Morris with the same feeling of trepidation that she had experienced when she tried to creep up there all those years ago.

As Marianne mounted the steps, an icy wave began to envelope her, heralding the now familiar feeling of another presence. Mrs. Morris climbed up and disappeared into the interior, the light from the torch flickering as she pointed it back towards Marianne. "Come on. It's quite safe," she repeated, but Marianne wasn't so sure. She was shivering, the intense cold biting into her bones and, as she ascended the stairs, she detected a smell, the smell of death. Faint at first, but as she reached the top of the steps it became almost overpowering, the stench filling her nostrils. She climbed up on to what was little more than a platform among the rafters.

"Are you alright? Gillian Morris, sensing something untoward, shone the torch in Marianne's face and touched her arm. "My goodness! You look as pale as a ghost! Let's go back to the house. There's nothing much to see up here anyway." She waved the torch around and its beam revealed nothing more than the dusty workings of the clock and a few old rags on the wooden floor.

The woman was evidently oblivious to what had happened here in the past. Someone had met their end in this perch above the garage at Paradise House and Marianne doubted if anyone knew but her. But surely this could have nothing to do with Arthur and Adele Hemmings. As far as Marianne knew, they had no connection with Paradise House.

Gillian reached the top step and began to descend, leaving Marianne without the benefit of the light from the torch.

She felt her way gingerly across the floor, but as she turned to take one last look about her, she saw a swirling eddy of grey smoke in the center of the floor, and the outline of a figure, gradually appeared.

"Are you coming?" Gillian Morris appeared again at the foot of the stairway, holding the torch to light Marianne's way down. In that instant, the figure vanished, leaving the clock-tower empty and dark.

"Yes, sorry. I was lost in thought for a moment. I'm coming." When they reached the ground once more, Marianne said, "Thanks, for taking me up there. I've always wondered what it looked like. My grandfather would never allow me to climb up there."

"It was locked when we first came here. We had to get someone in to open it. Greg thought there might be some hidden treasure up there, old paintings or something, but there was nothing. Or at least, there was a ring; a woman's gold ring. I remember we called Doris Russell to ask her if she'd lost it but she said it wasn't hers." Gillian seemed to consider a moment and then said brightly, "I say! Maybe it belonged to your grandmother. Wouldn't that be wonderful! I'll see if I can find it and you can have it."

Marianne followed her back to the house and they rejoined the men who were looking at a collection of Roman coins.

"Just a minute. I'll go and look for that ring. Greg, give Annie a drink, would you. I think she got a bit of a chill out there."

At these words, Vincent immediately looked up, but before he could say anything Marianne raised a finger to her lips, as she received the glass of sherry that Greg Morris handed her.

"So, you saw the old clock tower. Funny old place. Was it your grandfather who built it?"

"No, I believe it was already above the stables when they bought the house. Grandfather converted the stables to a garage, but he left the clock tower as it was. He called it his toy."

After some minutes, Mrs. Morris returned holding something in her hand. "I've found it. The ring, it's here. Take a look. See if you recognize it." She held it out to Marianne, who held it under the lamp to get a better look. She couldn't remember seeing it before, a small gold ring with a floral pattern engraved on the outside of the band. There was an inscription on the inside, however, that might provide a clue as to its owner. *Love Forever.* At first it meant nothing, but then Marianne realized that they were the same words that were inscribed on the ring that her mother had given Matthew.

"I can't say for certain," she said honestly, "but I believe it may have been my mother's."

"Well, take it," said Gillian Morris generously.

"Are you sure? Finders, keepers, after all."

"No, no. Please. I insist!"

"Thank you. It's very kind of you."

"Nonsense! You've every right to it, if it's your mother's, after all." Marianne slipped the ring into her purse and looked at Vincent. "Well, I think we've trespassed on your time long enough. Thank you so much for showing us around. I wanted Vincent to see the place. I've told him so much about the times we had here when we were children. I'm enormously grateful to you."

"Our pleasure," Greg Morris said. "It was lucky you came when you did. We're leaving in the morning for a holiday in Barbados. Just a week, but it would have been a pity if we had missed seeing you. Do come back and see us if you're ever over this way again."

"We will. And thanks again." She and Vincent made their way across the yard, past the old stables and the clock tower that stood silently overlooking Paradise House. Marianne looked up and could not suppress a shiver. Whatever had happened there all those years ago, she was certain that it involved her family in some way. The ring and the death were bound together.

When they were out on the road once more and out of sight of the house, Vincent stopped and gripped her arm. "What happened?"

"I don't know. At least, I knew someone was up there, the minute we started climbing the stairs, the cold, you know, and there was a smell, a terrible odor. At first, I couldn't see anything because Gillian was standing in front of me, but when we came down, she left ahead of me. When I looked back, there was a man standing there."

"Who was it?"

"I don't know. He had his back to me. But it was the same man that I saw in the church. The one who was sitting next to my mother, at Matthew's funeral, I'm sure of it."

"You want to go back?"

"Yes. But not tonight. They'll be gone tomorrow. We'll go then. Will you come with me?"

"Of course. You don't honestly think I'd let you do anything like that on your own. We're in this together."

"Oh, Vincent. I have a strange feeling that this is the answer, that I'm about to find out something that will put an end to all these horrors. I'll finally be rid of the ghosts."

"I hope so, Marianne. Oh God, I truly hope so," he replied fervently.

27

ALARM BELLS

CLARE WAS INCLINED TO BELIEVE THAT MARIANNE'S ACCOUNT of her recent meeting with their father was nothing more than hysteria brought on by the death of their brother, Matthew.

Despite her father's absence from Matthew's funeral, Clare couldn't say that she had noticed anything remarkable in his behavior of late. Mention of the gun, however, had caused her some concern. Bearing this in mind, she and Preston went to visit him several days after Marianne and Vincent had left for the Lake District.

Despite ringing the bell and knocking several times on the door of the terraced house in Hackney, Clare received no reply. She thought it was strange as his car was parked outside and, fumbling in her purse, Clare produced a key that she had retained in case of emergencies.

As she stepped across the threshold, the smell of stale cigarettes, moldy food and body odor wafted out to meet her. Clare wrinkled her nose and called out, "Dad! Dad, are you home?"

There was no reply, and Preston suggested that Clay may have walked down to the local pub. But then they heard a clink; the sound of bottles falling together.

Clare walked into the living room and saw her father, slumped in an armchair, his clothes disheveled and hair uncombed. He had an empty glass in his hand, and he waved it unsteadily at his daughter.

"Well, Well! Look who's here. C'mon in." Clay was clearly drunk.

Clare entered the room closely followed by her husband who, truth be told, was rather afraid of his belligerent father-in-law.

"Oh, I see you've brought reinforcements," Clay mocked. "Hello, Preston. What brings you here?"

Clare went up to her father and gave him a quick peck on the cheek.

"Dad. It stinks in here! Why don't you open a few windows." Clare was clearly undaunted by her father's less than cheerful welcome. She moved to let in some fresh air and picked up several empty beer bottles that lay about the floor. An ashtray nearby was filled to overflowing and she scooped it up and went to empty it in the garbage bin in the kitchen. Dirty plates were stacked in the sink and she set to work, filling it with hot water squirted liberally with Palmolive.

Meanwhile, Preston was left to make desultory conversation with a man who obviously had no desire to join in.

"The funeral went off OK," Preston ventured.

Clay merely made what sounded like a snort of indifference.

"I understand Marianne came to see you."

"What of it?" Clay responded, staring at the empty glass in his hand.

"She thought you didn't seem too well. She asked us to look in on you," Preston soldiered on.

"Oh, yes?"

"They've gone up to the Lake District, her and Vincent, to visit his family. I must say, we did take quite a liking to him," Preston persevered. "I believe you met him. They're going to stop off at the O'Malley's house in Diffingham on the way home. Marianne wanted to show him the old place," Preston babbled on.

Clay suddenly threw the glass across the room, missing Preston by inches, shattering it against the far wall.

Preston stood dumbfounded as Clare rushed in from the kitchen, her hands wet with soapsuds.

"What on earth's happened? Preston, are you alright?" She looked at the broken glass that lay shattered on the carpet.

"I never want to see him in this house again, ever!" Clay shouted. "I don't know why you came here, any of you."

"Because we care about you, Dad," said Clare as she picked up pieces of broken glass, cutting her finger in the process.

"I might as well be dead, for all you lot care," Clay said, morosely, slumping back into his chair.

"That's not true," Clare cried, wrapping her finger in the handkerchief that Preston hastily supplied.

"Leave me alone. Just go. Clear off!" Clay reached for a bottle that stood by the armchair and aimed it at the startled pair.

"Alright. We're going," Preston held up a hand in submission. He pulled at Clare's arm. She was not ready to give up, but her husband was insistent.

"Come on, Clare. We can't do any good here. We'll come back later when he's had time to calm down." They left the room, closing the door behind them; a split second later, the sound of an object came crashing after them.

As they left the house, Clare reluctantly agreed that Marianne had been right. "I can't understand it. He's never been this way with us before."

"It's the drink," Preston said sententiously. "You must admit, dear, that he's sozzled every time we come here. It's addling his brain."

Once they were back in their car and heading home, Clare said, "I think I'm going to go and see Father Raymond tomorrow. Perhaps he'll be able to help."

Well, if you think so, but the mood your father's in right now, I don't know if it would do any good."

"We have to try something. I can't just let him go on like this."

Preston remained silent.

The following day, Clare visited Father Raymond at St. Simeon's Church.

"I'm very worried about him," Clare concluded after explaining the situation.

"I can understand why," the elderly priest said, sympathetically. "Marianne expressed similar concerns when she came to see me."

"What did she say?" Clare asked, burning with curiosity.

"I don't think I can tell you, really. Our conversation was confidential, but I will go to see Ronald. Put your mind at rest. Trust in God. And you can be assured that I will do all I can to help."

"Thank you, Father. You don't know how relieved I am to hear that."

Clare felt as though a great weight had been lifted from her shoulders. She would wait and hope that Father Raymond could get through to her father. But she was already too late.

Father Raymond was as good as his word, but the next evening, when he arrived at Ronald Clay's house, he found the front door ajar and Clay's car gone. Bearing everything that Clare and Marianne had told him in mind, the priest was more than a little concerned. And although by no means a brave spirit, he pushed the door open and went inside.

He called out, but there was no answer and he ventured into the living room. Pieces of the shattered glass still lay on the carpet and empty bottles that had once contained beer, whiskey, and vodka were strewn about. Given the amount of alcohol that he must have consumed, Father Raymond would not have been surprised to find Ronald Clay lying in a drunken stupor. But after searching the rest of the house, he was nowhere to be seen. And there was the missing car.

The desk drawer was open, and remembering that Marianne had mentioned a gun that Clay kept there, he hurried across the room to look inside. It was empty all except for a single bullet that lay ominously on top of a few papers. What had he told Clare? *I might as well be dead.* Was the man really suicidal?

Alarm bells were beginning to sound in the old priest's mind. Where could Clay have gone? And in his condition?

Returning home, he called Clare, who, despite the late hour, answered the phone immediately.

"Hello, Clare? This is Father Raymond. Have you heard anything from your dad?"

"No. Nothing," Clare answered, concern making her voice quaver.

"I've just been round to the house. He's not there and his car's gone. He must have left in a hurry. The front door was open, so I took the liberty of going in. There was no sign of him. I closed the door when I left. I do hope he has his house keys with him." The priest sounded concerned.

"I don't know what to do, Father. Should I go to the police?" Clare asked anxiously.

"I don't think there's much they can do yet. They won't consider him missing for a day or two at least. Wait until tomorrow and we'll see if he shows up," the priest counseled.

He didn't want to mention the missing gun. No need to worry the poor woman any further. Hopefully, Clay would return with no harm done.

28

LAST ORDERS

"LAST ORDERS PLEASE, LADIES AND GENTS!" the barman made his familiar plea, and there was the usual rush to get in the final round. Marianne and Vincent were sitting in the bar with Charlie Pierce, who had looked in to 'wet his whistle' for an hour or two. A weekly darts tournament had promised to be hotly contested. The players had miraculously hit their target more often than not, despite the numerous pints of beer that had been downed between rounds. The cigarette smoke had made visibility a dubious commodity. The crowd, appreciative of the skills demonstrated by their respective teams, had cheered vociferously as the darts unerringly found their mark with a soft thud as they penetrated the cork board.

But now many of the people had gone back to their homes, Charlie Pierce among them. The couple watched as the last few customers, draining their glasses and bidding each other goodnight, straggled through the doors and out into the cold night air. They waited until the last of them had departed and then followed.

"Just going for a breath of air," Vincent called back to the landlord.

"Okay, Mr. Foxworth. But perhaps you'd better take a key for the side door, in case we've closed up by the time you come back."

Vincent went back and collected the key. The night was clear and the moon cast a silver light over The Green. Because of this, they did not take the shortcut across the grass, for they wanted to remain as inconspicuous as possible. Instead, they followed the road past the shuttered shops and houses with their curtains drawn against the night. The place was deserted now, and as they made their way past the last cottage, the silence seemed unnerving. An owl hooted in a tree high above them as they made the turn into the lane and something rustled in the undergrowth as we walked past the old smithy. A few more steps and there was Paradise House. They looked furtively about them but there was no one there to witness their movements as they crept up to the large garage doors.

As Marianne had hoped, Greg Morris had once again been negligent in his task of closing things securely. In his haste to leave, he hadn't bothered to engage the padlock that was attached to the hasp. Vincent pulled cautiously and the door came open with a rattle, just enough to allow them to slip inside. He had come prepared with a torch, but he dutifully handed it to Marianne as she insisted on leading the way up the stairs to the loft. Once in the loft, she turned the beam of the torch on the trapdoor and Vincent released the steps that led to the clock tower platform.

The floor creaked, and little noises, mice maybe, could be heard as they paused at the foot of the stairway. Just for an instant Marianne thought she had caught the sound of someone's labored breathing. She knew it wasn't Vincent. He was as fit as a man half his age. And now there was the cold! It was stealing down from the floor above. It hovered around her like a shroud, enveloping her in an icy embrace that told her most assuredly that they weren't alone. Someone was there, awaiting their arrival.

She mounted the last few steps, and a voice called weakly, "Rosemary? Is that you?" As Marianne's line of vision began to encompass the clock tower floor, she saw that there was indeed someone there.

One, two, three more steps and she was standing, dumbstruck, looking down at the figure that half sat, half lay, slumped against the far wall beneath the workings of the clock. He had been shot, the blood from the wound in his chest had spilled out, soaking his once white shirt. His eyelids heavy with the weight of approaching death flickered and opened, the hazel eyes trying desperately to focus, the blond hair falling across his forehead.

It was Vincent!

Marianne cried out as a voice near her said, "What is it, Marianne? What's happened?"

"No, don't come up! Wait there!" But it was too late. She could feel Vincent's body close behind her, a living, breathing person, while she stood gazing in horror at the dying figure.

It wasn't Vincent but his father, laying there in a pool of blood, his face so much like that of the man she loved, smiling up at her, the voice almost a whisper. "Rosemary. You came back. Be careful darling, he's still here." Lewis Foxworth tried to get up, but there was no strength left, and he fell back. Marianne wanted to help him but she knew it was already too late.

Vincent touched her arm, startling her, for his father's dying words were still sounding in her ears. "He's still here. He's still here."

"What did you see Marianne?"

She couldn't tell him. Not yet. Not here. As soon as he had touched her, the body of his father disappeared, and Marianne turned to beg him to come with her, away from that accursed place. But as she did so, she saw another person standing at the head of the stairway, and at her sudden intake of breath, Vincent turned away from her.

"Dad! What are you doing here?" Marianne was not only surprised to see her father standing there but alarmed, for he was holding the gun that he had brandished so menacingly at the house in London, and it was pointed once more at Vincent.

Did he plan to kill her too? He would have to if he wanted to achieve his goal, for she threw herself in front of Vincent.

There was absolute silence for a moment as they looked at each other searchingly.

Then her father spoke. "Stand away from him, Annie!"

"No! For heaven's sake Dad, what are you doing?"

"He took your mother away from me, and now he's come for you. I won't let him take you away, Annie. Not you as well."

"But Dad, it wasn't Vincent."

"Of course, it was. Don't you think I'd know that face? Ha! I used to look at Matthew and think this bastard is that man's son. But I wasn't going to give her up, as much as I hated her. No! I wasn't going to make it easy for them."

He stared at Vincent with a puzzled look. "I thought I'd killed you. That night I followed you here, watched you both go into the garage and up here to the clock tower. I could hear you making love, and I wanted to kill you both right then and there. But I waited. I wanted her to suffer for a lifetime as I had. She came down later on and I watched her go back to the house. But you were still up here. How surprised you were when I came in."

He laughed, a half-crazed cackle that changed to a cough. Vincent, taking advantage of the momentary lapse in her father's attention, pushed Marianne behind him. Her father, pulling himself together in an instant, leveled the gun once more at Vincent's heart.

"But I don't understand. I thought I killed you. I remember distinctly. I pulled the trigger and you fell back against the wall. There was blood, a lot of blood, so I know I hit you. I thought you were dead. What a joke I played on them all. I carried you down and buried you in the garden amongst the peonies. I used to laugh when I thought of Rosemary going out in the garden and smelling those precious flowers. She never knew, you see. She thought you'd gone back to your wife or run off with someone else." He laughed again, the gun wavering as again his body was wracked with coughing.

Suddenly Vincent made a lunge for the older man. But he wasn't quick enough. The gun went off, and Vincent fell back. Marianne made to go to him but her father was not finished. He turned the gun towards her.

"Stay away from him, Annie! I mean it!"

"Dad! Please, stop this! You're wrong. You must know it."

But he didn't know anything of the kind. He was beyond knowing the truth. He was mad. A madness brought on by passion, jealousy, and the knowledge that he had done murder. A madness compounded by the sight of her half-brother Matthew living in his house year after year.

Vincent groaned and moved, struggling to stand.

Clay looked at him in alarm. "I'll make sure this time, that you don't come back."

He snarled with deadly determination, and Marianne knew that she must act now if she was to save Vincent's life. She rushed forward and grappled with a man who, weak with age and ill health, still put up a fight with the strength that only a madman could muster. She tried to pull the gun away from him, and they tussled dangerously close to the opening in the floor. Suddenly, the gun fired, and before she could save herself, Marianne pitched backward, down the steps into the darkness. The pain was excruciating, but only for a moment before the night closed in on her, blotting out all sight, sound, and feeling.

Sometime later, a voice called out, "There's three of them up here. Hurry up! We may be in time to save this one. He's still breathing. I'm not sure about the other one. He doesn't look good."

Marianne was being carried away on a stretcher, but she wanted to tell them that there was a fourth person in the clock tower. They must not have seen him, surely, but she couldn't speak, couldn't move, a prisoner of a body that refused to function and a mind that had become lost in its own torment.

29
DISCOVERY

IT WAS ONLY BY THE MEREST CHANCE that they had been discovered. Greg Morris, at his wife's insistence, called the local constabulary to ask if someone could check to make sure that the padlock on the garage door was secure. Later that night, a constable, who was cycling home from his shift and had offered to look in on the place, discovered the garage door open and what appeared to be the victims of a home invasion. Cycling to the nearest phone box, he called for an ambulance and then contacted his sergeant who was already asleep in bed.

Marianne's father was dead. There was nothing they could do for him. The shot had penetrated his heart and killed him instantly. Was she sorry? She should have been, she supposed, but she wasn't. He had tried to kill the man who meant more to her than life itself, just as he had murdered Vincent's father. If she was faced with the same situation again, Marianne wouldn't hesitate to act as she had done in the clock tower at Paradise House.

She was still in the hospital when Christmas came around and Clare came to visit with Preston and the children. They arrived in the afternoon, bringing gifts and goodies and bursting with good news.

"Annie, the doctor says you'll be able to come home soon. Isn't that wonderful? Preston and I want you to come and stay with us while you're convalescing."

This news, far from buoying her spirits, alarmed Marianne. "But…really, I don't think I need—"

Clare held up her hand. "Let me finish. Getting you back on your feet is going to take time, they've told us, months of therapy, and you'll need help."

"It's very kind of you, Clare, but Vincent can manage."

"Oh, for heaven's sake! You know very well…"

Preston cut her off abruptly. "Vincent agrees with us that it would be for the best if you came to stay with us," he said patiently.

"But what will he do?" Marianne was suddenly filled with anxiety. They looked at each other and once again Preston answered. "I imagine he'll probably go back to Swannington. I'm sure they're waiting for him to return to the university. They won't be able to hold his position open indefinitely."

"But he wouldn't go back without me." Marianne was becoming agitated, and Clare, sensing that trouble was brewing, sent the children to go in search of a coffee machine.

"Annie, be reasonable. Everyone thinks it would be best if you came to stay with us. We all want to help. And the sooner you get back on your feet, the sooner you'll be able to go back to Swannington. Right?"

"Well. Give me a chance to talk to Vincent about it. He'll be here tonight."

"Of course," Preston agreed, but Clare merely gave an imperceptible shake of her head and the visit drew to a close.

That night, the dreams began again. Arthur Hemmings, cold and malevolent, and her father looking at her accusingly. She cried out in terror. Almost immediately, the night nurse came running into the room and the figures vanished.

In the ensuing days, Marianne saw a steady stream of doctors and specialists. The dreams continued and she sank into a deep depression. When Clare next visited her, she was accompanied unexpectedly by Emily Foxworth.

"Hello, my dear," the old lady greeted Marianne as she took the chair that Clare had drawn up to the bedside.

Marianne smiled weakly. "It's so good to see you, Emily, but you shouldn't have come all this way to visit."

"I had something very important that I wanted to discuss with you, and I thought it better if I came here in person rather than calling you on the phone."

"Does Vincent know you're here? He'll be delighted to see you. He visits me every night."

"Yes, he knows I'm here," Emily Foxworth said with a catch in her voice. Clare has told me that she's spoken to the doctors, and they say that physically you are ready to go home, but they think a period of rest and recuperation would be beneficial, not only for your body, but also from a psychological standpoint."

She held up her hand to forestall Marianne's objections. "Vincent agrees with me that the best thing for you now would be to spend some time at the sanitorium in Beckham. The sea air will do you good and we'll be there to make sure you have everything that you need."

"But the cost! I could never repay you."

"Don't worry about that. Vincent and I will take care of everything. All you need to do now is concentrate on getting better."

"Well, if Vincent thinks I should."

"Yes, he's in full agreement. It's for the best, you'll see." The old lady stood and bent to kiss Marianne's cheek. "I'll come to see you as soon as you're settled at Bartlett Hall. God bless you, my dear."

Emily Foxworth touched Clare's arm, and the two went out, leaving Marianne to ponder the proposed move to Beckham.

One week after Marianne arrived at Bartlett Hall, she received the promised visit from Emily Foxworth, who was shown into the lounge. Marianne was seated by the window and did not, at first, respond to Emily's greeting.

"How are you, Annie?" The old lady repeated. "I would have come before my dear, but they told me it would be better to wait for a while."

Marianne turned slowly and smiled. "I'm doing well, Emily, but I won't be sorry to go home. Vincent says it won't be long. He comes here every night, bless him, but I know it's a strain. "

"I don't think you need to worry about him, my dear." She patted Marianne's hand reassuringly as they sat together, looking out towards the fields that ran down to the cliffs overlooking the sea.

"How is Judith?"

"She decided against coming with me. Her health has not been too good of late, and she didn't want to pass on any kind of bug."

"I'm sorry to hear that. That was thoughtful of her. Will you tell her from me that I hope she'll soon feel better?" The old lady nodded, and they sat quietly for a few minutes, Emily Foxworth giving the younger woman time to gather her thoughts.

"Emily … about Vincent's father. I'm sorry about everything that happened."

"That's alright, my dear. Don't think about it anymore."

"But I must, Emily. If you can bear to hear it, I must talk about what happened. I've tried to explain to them here, but I must know that you understand. My mother and Vincent's father, I had no idea. You do believe that, don't you?"

"Of course, Annie. Don't distress yourself. It all belongs in the past."

"I don't think Matthew ever knew that Lewis was his father," she said after they had sat silently for a while. "Perhaps it would have been better for everyone if the truth had come out much sooner. My mother went to the grave with her secret." Marianne gave a deep sigh. "My father let it eat into his heart until it drove him mad. Matthew suffered a lifetime of vindictiveness and recrimination, and Lewis Foxworth paid the ultimate price. I feel so guilty, that in some way my family robbed the Foxworths. We took the man who was your husband and Vincent and Judith's father and destroyed so many lives in the process. I feel responsible, now that the others are gone. I'll never be able to fully atone for the death of Vincent's father," she said in despair.

But Emily Foxworth was shaking her head. "No, no, my dear. You mustn't think that, for one moment." She hesitated, and then said, "It breaks my heart to see you blame yourself for what's happened. I must tell you something, my dear, that I never thought I would ever repeat to anyone, not even Judith. I think you deserve to know, and it may help you to accept what happened in the past. Lewis Foxworth was not Vincent's father."

"But that can't be. They looked so much alike, Vincent, his father and his…" Marianne stopped, aghast at the implication.

"Yes, Desmond Foxworth. Not his grandfather as he believed, but his father."

"Does he know?"

"No." She hesitated, then continued. "But I hoped you would tell him, Annie. Would you do that for me? I know it's a lot to ask, but I think you are the only one who can tell him now."

"I'll tell him, of course, if you want me to. But, forgive me, it's so hard to take in. I still find it difficult to understand."

"It's quite simple really, my dear. I was lonely. Lewis and I should never have married. We didn't love each other and we knew almost immediately that we'd made the most colossal mistake, but at that time, divorce was out of the question. Lewis lived his own life. I didn't interfere. In those days a woman accepted her lot, whatever it might be. He was free to go and do as he pleased while I was left at the house in Whitehaven to keep up appearances, as they say. His father used to call on us every once in a while. I think he guessed that things were not as they should have been.

"Until then, I must tell you truthfully, Annie, Desmond had never expressed his feelings for me, although," she added with a ghost of a smile, "when Lewis first took me to Foxworth Manor to introduce me as his intended bride, I couldn't help falling for his father's undeniable charm. I did, after a while, get the feeling that it wasn't just because I was destined to be his future daughter-in-law that he took such a liking to me. But in time, when he saw how things were between Lewis and me, he no longer felt the need for restraint, and we became lovers."

"But Daphne, was she still alive then?"

"Yes, poor woman. She loved him in her way, but I didn't care."

"Do you think she knew about the two of you?"

"I'm sure she had her suspicions, although we were very discreet. I think a woman knows these things instinctively, but as I said, I didn't care. Derek loved me, and that was all that mattered. I know, it must seem shocking to you, but these things happen, Annie. When you fall in love with someone as much as I loved Derek Foxworth, you brush aside any and all obstacles. That kind of love can overcome the most insurmountable of barriers, as I believe you know, my dear." She looked at Marianne and smiled.

"Yes, I do know, Emily."

"Well, you can probably guess the rest of the story. I found that I was expecting a baby."

"But didn't your husband find out about you and his father? Forgive me for being so inquisitive, but he must have known it wasn't his child."

"No. You see, until then, despite the fact that the marriage was a failure, he always demanded his marital rights. And when Vincent bore such a striking resemblance to the Foxworth side of the family, there was no question. Of course, I knew who the father really was, dates and everything, but I managed to persuade Lewis that the birth had been premature. And then, of course, there was Judith. She was his child."

"And so was Matthew."

"Yes. Poor boy," Emily said sadly. "Of course, your father knew he was someone else's child."

"Yes, he must have guessed." Marianne pictured her brother as a young child. "That would explain why he treated him so badly for all those years. But why take it out on the boy? It wasn't his fault."

"True, but he was a constant reminder of your mother's infidelity, and that he couldn't tolerate. In the end, it drove him to discover who the man was, and he took the ultimate revenge. To kill his wife's lover and have her live the rest of her life believing that he had deserted her was poetic justice. How he must have gloated when he watched her day after day, wondering what had happened to Lewis."

"And Monica found out about Vincent, didn't she?"

"Yes, when she was working at the Hall. She discovered the truth when she came across a piece of paper that I thought had been destroyed a long time ago; a document that Derek had hidden among the books in the library.

I don't think she realized the implications at first, but then came the fiasco with Vincent, when Judith walked in on them, and I had to get rid of her.

"She must have racked her brains to figure out how to get even, and she finally put two and two together. She came back the following week and said that if I didn't pay her off, she would tell everyone that Derek Foxworth was Vincent's father. I had kept the secret for so long, I didn't want Vincent to think any less of my dear old boy. He loved him so much as a grandfather. I couldn't risk destroying that, so I paid up, and paid and paid.

"Then when the girl got pregnant, her demands became insufferable. She wanted money to set this boyfriend of hers up in a business of his own. I think it was the only way she could get him to marry her. When she came back for the last time, I told her it was too much. I wasn't going to be blackmailed anymore. I'd almost decided by then, to tell Vincent and Judith the truth. Of course, she was furious, and I'm guessing when she told her boyfriend that the plan to get him his business had fallen through, he left her. She was on the point of blurting out the whole story when we bumped into her at the vicarage that afternoon, but luckily the Reverend put a stop to it."

"Do you think he knew? Did she tell him?"

"She may have done, but if she did, he kept it to himself."

"And what happened after we left? Did she still try to get money from you?"

"No. After what happened at Diffingham, I never heard from her again. She had the baby and went away somewhere. I don't think we'll ever be bothered by her again."

They sat there, each thinking about their own family secrets and intrigues until Emily said, "We must put all that in the past now, my dear, and learn to accept what has happened. Believe me, it's the only way. Life goes on, you'll find. I know what happened at Paradise House was absolutely devastating, for us both, but time, even if it doesn't completely heal all wounds, does help to make the pain bearable."

"I just thank God that I have Vincent. I couldn't get through all this without him, Emily. He means the world to me."

"Yes, I know my dear. But you must be strong. He wouldn't want you to grieve over the past," Emily Foxworth said with tears in her eyes.

Father Raymond, Marianne's second visitor, arrived two weeks later, in the middle of a violent thunderstorm. The atmosphere that day had been oppressive, the sky dark with cloud upon cloud building up into a massive black mountain until finally the heavens opened and the rain came down in torrents. Lightening flashed across the heavens as Marianne watched from her window, and the thunder, at first a mere rumble, quickly reached a deafening crescendo as it shook the panes. The wind tore in from the sea, bending the trees and catching at anything that was not anchored to the ground by root or nail, sending leaves and debris blowing about. Just as the storm had reached its height, there was a knock on her door, and one of the nurses came into the room.

"You have a visitor, Ms. Clay. Marianne was curious to know who could have come to see her amid such turbulent weather.

Father Raymond entered the room, his hands outstretched to grasp her own.

"Annie, how are you, my child?"

"Father Raymond. How good of you to come all this way, and in such weather."

"Would you believe it was sunny when I left St. Simeon's? The storm only started when I got off the train at Whitehaven. Luckily, I was able to get a taxi, but even then, I got quite a soaking."

"Perhaps God's trying to tell you something."

"And what would he be trying to tell me, Annie?"

"To stay away from me, possibly."

"Is that what you want?"

"No! No, I'm sorry Father Raymond. I didn't mean to sound ungrateful for your visit. But I can't help wondering, having tried every kind of drug known to man and countless hours of therapy, have they now finally had to resort to bringing in the church?"

"No. They didn't call on me, but when I heard that you were here, I remembered our conversation the day after Matthew's funeral, and I felt that I must come and see you."

Father Raymond was looking about him, at the room that Marianne now essentially called home. He noticed a painting hanging on the wall behind the bed. A knight doing battle with a fire-breathing dragon. There was a red leather-bound copy of The Rubaiyat on the bedside table and a journal lying open on the desk by the window. He seemed lost in thought.

"And do you think you can help me?" Marianne's voice recalled him to his purpose.

"I would like to try, if you'll let me."

"And just what do you expect me to do? Get down on my knees and pray to God to deliver me from the demons that are my constant companions." She laughed derisively.

"No, I don't think it's as simple as that. But it probably wouldn't hurt."

"I'm sorry, Father, but I don't think even God can help me now."

"I'm grieved to hear you give in to despair, Annie."

"What else can I do? I've begged Vincent to take me out of here, but he says he can't. If I could just go home."

"But won't the demons, as you call them, follow you there?"

"I don't know, but I want to go home, back to Vincent, back to the life that we had."

"And what does Vincent say?"

"He says the doctors think I should stay. He wants to take me home, but they won't let me go."

"And do you not think that they know what's best for you?"

"What's best for me? Do you think it's best for me to be shut up in this place? I feel like a sacrificial goat, tethered to a stake. When the demons come, there is no escape. I'm trapped in this room. I've been lucky so far, but Vincent can't always be here to protect me." Marianne passed a hand over her eyes. "Oh, the nurses come when I call out for help, of course, but I can see they think I'm crying wolf. It takes them longer and longer every time, to get to my room. One of these days they'll ignore my call altogether. Eventually, he'll get to me, and then, will your God stand between me and my fate."

"I'm sure he would, if you had faith in him, Annie."

"There's only one person I have faith in, Father Raymond, and that's Vincent."

"I told you once, not to put so big a burden on that man's shoulders. But now... I'm beginning to believe that he is the only one who can save you."

Father Raymond did not stay long after that. He promised to come back and see Marianne in the near future, and she watched him as he made his way outside to the taxi that was waiting in the rain for him.

That night, Marianne had a much less welcome visitor. She was sitting by the window watching the driveway, waiting for Vincent to arrive. The fog coming in from the sea made for poor visibility, and there was a chill in the air. She sensed that she was not alone. She turned, expecting to see Vincent already standing there, but she found to her horror instead, emerging from the swirling mist that seemed to have infiltrated the room, Arthur Hemmings. He just stood, with the long carving knife in his hand, looking at her, smiling, knowing she had nowhere to run, no place that she could hide, no one there to protect her.

She cried out, "Stay away from me!" and reached down to pick up the chair that she had overturned, holding it in front of her in an effort to ward of any attack.

"But we have some unfinished business." Hemmings took a step forward.

"Leave me alone! What did I ever do to you?"

"You couldn't leave well alone. She should have stayed buried, but you had to come looking for her." Hemmings advanced another step, brandishing the knife.

There was only one person who could save her now. Marianne screamed loud and long, "Vincent! Vincent! Help me!" And in the next moment, he was there beside her, and Arthur Hemmings, thwarted once more, had vanished.

The nurse on night duty came hurrying into the room and found Marianne crouched beside the bed, sobbing.

She saw Matthew only once. He came one dreary afternoon as she sat watching the rain falling. At first, she attributed the chill that she had suddenly felt to the changing of the seasons; the leaves were beginning to fall. But she knew as the chill turned to an icy grip that it was something else and, fearing that Arthur Hemmings had returned once more, prepared to defend herself. Instead, it was Matthew who stood there. Dear Matthew, smiling.

"Hello Annie. What a mess we made of life. Still, everything's alright now. How are you dear?"

Marianne couldn't speak. The tears were running down her face unchecked. Dear Matthew!

"All forgiven. All forgotten, dear. Don't cry," he said. "It was a tangled web, wasn't it, after all? Mum and Dad, Vincent and his father, who would have guessed? Never mind, it's all been put right now."

She just stood there and nodded, and before she could say what was in her heart, he had gone.

Her father put in a brief appearance, very contrite. The madness that had seized him and led to the disastrous encounters at Paradise House had evaporated, and he begged Marianne to forgive him. It wasn't easy, but Vincent had persuaded her that he wasn't really responsible for his actions, and so against her better judgement, Marianne told her father that she forgave him.

Her mother and Adele came too. Just a fleeting glimpse of Adele, for she arrived just before they came to bring Marianne her evening meal. She only had time to utter two words, "Thank you," before the door opened, and she was gone.

Her mother's visit lasted longer, and they talked for hours about so many things. They seemed to understand each other so much better now, after all that had happened. They spoke at length about the Foxworths and how strange it was that they had both fallen so madly in love with the Foxworth men. They talked about Clare and Matthew and Marianne's father, and when it came time for her to leave, Marianne knew instinctively that she would never see her mother again.

Another visit from Arthur Hemmings at the end of last month served to warn Marianne that danger was never very far away. It was there lurking in the mist waiting its chance to finally settle old scores. But, as always, Vincent had been there to rescue her.

30

MURDER AT THE HALL

IT WAS LATE IN OCTOBER WHEN AN ARTICLE APPEARED on the front page of the Penhampton Gazette:

MURDER AT BARTLETT HALL.

Early yesterday morning a body was discovered by staff at Bartlett Hall, an exclusive sanatorium located five miles outside the village of Penhampton.
The victim, a woman, believed to be a resident of the Hall, was found in her room, stabbed several times. The police are said to be studying video tapes provided by the Hall in the hopes that they may reveal the identity of the assailant.

Asked to comment on the murder, Dr. Eugene Phillips, who had been the head of Bartlett Hall sanatorium for the past fifteen years, would only say that everything was being done to ensure the safety of the other residents and that there was no cause for alarm.

Beckham police were making no comment other than to say that enquiries were well in hand and they would be issuing a statement later that day. Naturally, relatives of those living at the Hall were wondering just how safe their loved ones were, following this brutal and mysterious attack.

The surrounding area was rife with speculation as to whether a killer from Bartlett Hall was on the loose. The incident at the Hall served to enforce the opinion of many in the immediate vicinity that it did not belong in an area that was populated by so many young families. Dr. Philips assured the local authorities that all the people who belonged at Barlett Hall were still there. No one was missing. The police had questioned all the residents as well as the people who worked at the Hall, including a young woman, Monica Jenkins, who had recently been hired to work in the kitchens.

When questioned by the police, Dr Philips, with some reluctance, gave them full particulars of Marianne Clay's admittance to Bartlett Hall. His written notes regarding the case read as follows:

"She had been discovered one night in late November, two years previously, at Paradise House in Diffingham in Kent, by a constable who had gone to check on the property. The owners of the house were away and he was surprised to see the garage door open. Looking inside, he found Marianne Clay lying unconscious in the room above the garage and immediately went to summon help."

"Shortly after, paramedics arrived on the scene and discovered not only the woman but two men in the tower that housed the workings of a clock, both shot, one fatally, the other barely alive. He was, however, able to tell police that he had been shot by the other man who was in fact, Ms. Clay's father. Subsequently, Clay and his daughter had tussled for the gun, and she had fallen down the stairway. He gave his name as Vincent Foxworth, and he died shortly after being taken to Beckham Hospital."

"It wasn't until she had regained consciousness and was considered well enough to speak to the police that they realized the case was much more involved than they had at first supposed. Nevertheless, her explanation had them puzzled, and it became obvious that Ms. Clay had been deeply disturbed by the events that had taken place at Paradise House. After recovering sufficiently from her physical injuries, it was decided to move her to Bartlett Hall.

During one of my sessions with Annie, I shall refer to her as such, as that is how she asked me to address her, she told me that her father had admitted to killing Vincent Foxworth's father and that the body could be found in the grounds at Paradise House. I notified the authorities, and a search was conducted. The remains of a man, buried many years ago, were discovered. The identity of this victim proved to be that of Mr. Foxworth's father, Lewis Foxworth, who had been missing for many years, supposed by his wife and family to have run away with another woman.

"Annie's insistence that she could see and talk to people who had been dead for many years was, in itself, not uncommon. The two incidents that had occurred in the house on Wellington Street were indeed of great interest to me, and I made every effort to obtain information regarding those events. No one in Swannington, however, seems to have been aware of this supposed ability of Annie's. At least she never discussed it with any of her acquaintances there, or the police who were involved in the investigation of the stabbing, and subsequent fire resulting in the death of Annie's brother, Matthew.

It was no wonder that all these tragic events, following so closely upon one another, should give rise to such an agitated state of mind, and one would naturally expect some such abnormal psychological tendencies as a result. But I must say that despite the bizarre nature of Annie's claims and my professional predisposition to find a logical explanation for such phenomenon, I became more inclined to give credence to her story.

Her inability to accept the fact that Vincent Foxworth had been killed was understandable in the circumstances, she was absolutely devoted to him, but her insistence that he visited her every evening seemed like the imaginings of a deeply disturbed person.

What troubled me most was her belief that there was someone who was trying to kill her; the man who she claimed had stabbed her at the house on Wellington Street. She said that he came to her frequently, but that Vincent had always been there to save her. Her 'knight in shining armor,' as she called him

When Annie was found dead in her room, it was, of course, a tremendous shock. On the face of it, there appeared to be no logical explanation for what happened. It clearly wasn't a case of suicide, as no weapon was found. And upon investigation, the police appeared to be baffled as to how anyone could have entered her room unseen.

I don't think we'll ever know for sure, but personally I am certain that on that fateful night, Vincent Foxworth did not appear in time to save Marianne, and she became the second victim of Arthur Hemmings, a murderer who has been beyond the reach of earthly justice for more than eighty years.

271

AUTHOR BIO

Sue Farwick combines her lifelong fascination with the murder mystery and supernatural genres in her novels. Born and raised in England and now residing in the USA, she is an avid genealogist and gardener. In addition to her fiction writing, she writes about her experiences as an amateur photographer and regularly writes for her blog *The Nature of Things* under the name 'Mac's Girl.'

Visit Tribuspress.com/Sue-Farwick or scan the QR code below for more about Sue Farwick and her publications, and to connect with her.

Scan for More About Sue Farwick

More from Tribus Press

From Sue Farwick

The Eternal Song: Book I in *The Connections Series* (2024)

> Lucy Welbourne's seemingly ordinary English life takes a dramatic turn when a series of strange events leads her to seek answers from an enigmatic figure. But will his unconventional and paranormal methods help her untangle the mysterious happenings in her life? Join Lucy, a woman caught between two eras and two lives, as she uncovers the mystery of her existence and relives a past life of passion and self-discovery.

From Christopher and Simone Carroll in Children's Books

Seahorse Protectors: The Mystery of Trash Island (2024)

> In the magical Kingdom of Seabrook, five young seahorses have one mission: protect their vibrant underwater home. Led by Coral, the brave and determined leader, the Seahorse Protectors patrol the ocean, ensuring safety and harmony. But when the mysterious Trash King begins building a plastic island, the Seahorse Protectors face their greatest challenge yet. Coral and her friends must navigate danger, uncover secrets, and rally their courage to confront a foe who threatens the entire ocean. Will they restore peace to Seabrook, or will the Trash King's toxic kingdom consume them all?

A tale of friendship, bravery, and the power of teamwork, *Seahorse Protectors: The Mystery of Trash Island* inspires young readers to care for their community and believe in the power of standing up for what's right.

WINNIE-THE-POOH AND THE HONEY JAR MISHAP (2023)

Join Winnie-the-Pooh and his friends on an enchanting adventure through the Hundred Acre Wood. This whimsical tale, written and illustrated by a father and his 5-year-old daughter, pays homage to the 1926 classic by A. A. Milne and E. H. Shepard. It marks the opening book in *The A. A. Milne and E. H. Shepard Legacy Series*, proudly presented by Tribus Press.

As Pooh and Christopher Robin set off for a picnic with their dear friends, Pooh's tummy begins to rumble. They decide to make what should have been a quick stop at Pooh's house for a yummy snack. However, Pooh's curiosity and independence lead him into a very sticky and comical misadventure. Along the way, Pooh learns valuable lessons about friendship, listening, and asking for help.

NINA THE SLOTH GOES TO PARIS (2025) & NINA THE SLOTH GETS LOST (2025)

The father-daughter duo is back with the first two books in their new series, *Nina the Sloth*. Meet Nina and her Hoatzin bird friend, Squawk, as they go on epic adventures.

WINNIE-THE-POOH LOSES HIS HEAD (Coming Soon)

Pooh seems to have "lost his head" when he becomes obsessed with his new phone. Join Pooh and his friends as they try and solve this very modern dilemma. Join the father-daughter duo for their second book in the *A. A. Milne and E. H. Shepard Legacy Series*.

Scan to Connect with Tribus Press
or visit Tribuspress.com for More Books

www.ingramcontent.com/pod-product-compliance
Lightning Source LLC
Chambersburg PA
CBHW022149170626
46807CB00005B/2135